D1561557

Strike the Wok

An Anthology of Contemporary Chinese Canadian Fiction

edited by Lien Chao and Jim Wong-Chu

We acknowledge the support of the Canada Council for the Arts for our publishing program. We also acknowledge support from the Government of Ontario through the Ontario Arts Council.

Cover designed by David Drummond

Permissions acknowledgements for previously published work can be found on page 250.

National Library of Canada Cataloguing in Publication

Strike the wok : an anthology of contemporary Chinese Canadian fiction / edited by Lien Chao and Jim Wong-Chu.

ISBN 1-894770-09-9

1. Canadian literature (English)--Chinese-Canadian authors.
2. Canadian literature (English)--21st century. 3. Chinese Canadians--Literary collections. I. Chao, Lien, 1950- II. Wong-Chu, Jim, 1949-

PS8235.C5S77 2003 C810.8'08951 C2003-906472-7

Printed in Canada by Coach House Printing

TSAR Publications
P. O. Box 6996, Station A
Toronto, Ontario M5W 1X7
Canada

www.tsarbooks.com

To All Those Who Came with Their Dreams

Acknowledgement

On behalf of the anthologized writers, we want to thank TSAR Publications, Nurjehan Aziz, and M G Vassanji for initiating this project and for their continuous commitment to publishing minority writers in Canada. We are grateful to Vassanji, whose insight and editorial critique helped us shape the anthology. Our heartfelt gratitude also goes to Virginia Rock, who has helped us with the final proofreading. We also want to thank Avianna Chao, who never says no whenever there is computer work to be done.

We want to thank all the writers who responded to the call for submission to this anthology. Without their enthusiasm and support, it would have been impossible to us to bring out this anthology in such a short time.

Lien Chao and Jim Wong-Chu
November, 2003

Contents

Introduction

In the late 1970s, when Jim Wong-Chu, Paul Yee, SKY Lee, and several others were researching Asian Canadian history and compiling the first Asian Canadian literary anthology, *Inalienable Rice: A Chinese and Japanese Canadian Anthology* (1979), theirs was a political action that gave birth to a literary movement. The emerging writers launched "epic struggles" (viii) to break through the historical silence of the community and to reclaim collective history and identity for Asian Canadians.

The publication of *Inalienable Rice* signaled the birth of Chinese Canadian literature. A decade later, in the late 1980s, Jim Wong-Chu traveled across Canada with a mission to locate emerging Chinese Canadian writers for a second literary anthology, *Many-Mouthed Birds: Contemporary Writing by Chinese Canadians* (1991). Its publication came at a critical time to reinforce the growth of Chinese Canadian literature. Many first-generation Chinese Canadian writers, such as SKY Lee, Denise Chong, and Paul Yee had just published their first major works and were receiving critical attention from "mainstream" readers and critics. Since then, the Asian Canadian Writers' Workshop has nurtured many writers, among them, Paul Yee, Wayson Choy, Madeline Thien, and Larissa Lai, who went on to win major Canadian literary awards.

In the early 1990s, when I was researching material for a comprehensive study entitled *Beyond Silence: Chinese Canadian Literature in English* (1997), I was also passionately engaged in a mission—to launch Chinese Canadian literature systematically into the mainstream of the academic world. The fact that both *Inalienable Rice* and *Many-Mouthed Birds* employed a mixed-genre configuration had helped to map writers into a new literary landscape to be known as "Chinese Canadian." I noted then that "the anthology is one of the literary forms most capable of embracing writings in different genres and of introducing an emerging literature into the mainstream" (33-34).

In this new century, Chinese Canadian writers play an important role in Canadian literature. While first-generation writers are at their prime productive age, talented young writers have emerged. When *Swallowing Clouds: An Anthology of Chinese Canadian Poetry* (1999) was compiled, its editor Andy Quan and the veteran editor Jim Wong-Chu had no doubt that it was time to make an important strategic shift and produce this time a single-genre anthology. The reason is simple: Chinese Canadian literature has grown into an acknowledged force in Canadian literature today, and there are many more Chinese Canadian writers. Obviously a single-genre anthology would be appropriate to give a more concentrated and fuller presentation of Chinese Canadian literature.

Readers who have followed the development of Chinese Canadian literature in the last two decades will not be surprised to learn that we will continue to publish literary anthologies. Our bicultural and, many times, multicultural and multilingual background and our century-long community history make an ever-fertile ground for storytelling. The continuous influx of new Chinese immigrants from all over the world and the active interaction between Chinese Canadians and other cultural groups in Canada provide the most intriguing material for diaspora writing in the age of globalization and in the broader sense of world literature. The desire to share our stories with other Canadians has given birth to this anthology.

The call for submission to the new anthology was sent out during Asian Heritage Month in May, 2003. Two weeks later, digital submissions started to flood in via the internet from across the country as well as from Asia and Europe. By mid-August, we were overwhelmed with the response. In our invitation we were careful not to set any limit to the subject matter or the style of the fiction to be submitted; as a result, we were rewarded with an interesting and diverse collection of stories. From this rich pool, we have chosen twenty-five new stories for this anthology; in addition, we have chosen four previously published works; together, the twenty-nine stories illustrate a wide range of Chinese Canadian experiences, fictional themes, and narrative voices.

We present this anthology to continue the tradition set by the previous anthologies and thus as a new chapter in the field of Chinese

Canadian literature. Our approach links sociohistorical milieus with aesthetic merits, in other words, culture with literature, emphasizing an important element in reading minority literature. We were alert to discover emerging writers and those who were willing to risk exploring new territories. We hope this anthology gives Chinese Canadian writers a proud place in which to belong, a place not only in the area of Chinese Canadian literature, but also in the national literature of Canada.

We open *Strike the Wok* with Larissa Lai's new story, "Two Houses and an Airplane," to provide a framework for the anthology. Lai's story quietly weaves some complicated "double visions" into one intriguing narrative. The doubles include two houses, two provinces, two worlds, two countries, two cultures, two generations, two women, two men, two languages, two dialects, two identities, among others—-everything seems part of the other, or a mockery of the other, and complicated, as distant and shifting as memories can be, and yet at the same time as unified and localized as life appears to be. Lai's story embodies various subject matters and embraces the literary tropes of diaspora and hybridity, which appear widely in this anthology. Following Lai's story is an excerpt, "The Mark of a Stray Female Survivor" from SKY Lee's new novel-in-progress. What is in progress is probably an old ghost story regarding the scattering of the Chinese diaspora, or perhaps it is a new genesis about women.

Community history and family saga are in the foreground of many stories. Some address race, ethnicity, and culture, others reveal family secrets. For example, Paul Yee's story, "The Friends," depicts a group of Chinese bachelors meeting in a Chinatown teahouse to eat and to talk about their lives of smoking, gambling, prostitution, their families in China, and the lack of opportunities for the Chinese in Canada. The large number of bachelors talking simultaneously at the beginning of the story is a stark depiction of the bachelor society that had resulted from the discriminatory immigration policies that had barred Chinese from entering Canada for half a century, even for the sake of family reunion. This background explains in some respects why the quasi father-son relationship exists between young and old bachelors. In

Wayson Choy's story, "Nanking," the life of a Vancouver bachelor bears the consequences of the Japanese invasion of China in the mid-1940s. Concealed in another quasi father-son relationship is the story of two men in an ambiguous sexual relationship, a taboo in traditional Chinese society. Some stories deal with dirty linen or skeletons locked away in the family closet. Among them, Kam-Sein Yee's story, "Family Secrets," reveals the guilty conscience of a dying old Malay who collaborated with the Japanese when they invaded his native Malaysia in the 1940s. In "Eczema" by Lydia Kwa and "Just Dandruff" by Jessica Gin-Jade, written from the perspectives of female characters, the writers have aired some dirty linen—-sexual violation of daughters by fathers.

Also written from the perspectives of young female characters, a number of stories depict conflicts fueled by family and social expectations. The excerpt from Edward Lee's novel-in-progress, "Into a Far Country," describes a Chinese immigrant family settling in Yarmouth, Nova Scotia, a cold and racist environment in the 1950s. The episode challenges a frequent Chinese immigrant norm, when the daughter decides she wants to become an artist instead of working in the family restaurant. "Locks" by Alexis Kienlen epitomizes generation conflict, specifically the tension between a father and his teenage daughter. The daughter, who resents helping out in the family restaurant, decides she doesn't want to repeat her mother's life. By cutting her braids and dashing out into the rain, she seeks, symbolically, her own freedom and self-expression.

Several stories in the anthology deal with interracial and intercultural issues. Some focus directly on skin colour and ethnic identity. In "Versus" by Loretta Seto, Opal, a Eurasian girl, struggles to balance her life between the expectations of her divorced white mother and her Chinese father who has recently married a Chinese woman from China. In "A Hole in the Wall," Gein Wong depicts how Chinese immigrants may be patronized by their fellow Canadians. "Seeking Special Chinese Lady" by Fiona Tinwei Lam portrays seekers of interracial romance and how stereotypes function as cultural definers. Ritz Chow's story, "A Porous Life," shows a different kind of skin obsession, one related to the southern-versus-northern prejudice originating in

China. Sherwin Tjia's "Shoplifting Tiger, Bomb-making Dragon" draws attention to identity crises in young Chinese Canadians who speak the language of denial. My own story, "Neighbours," suggests that intercultural exchange is a two-way process.

Various narrative forms are present here. Winston C Kam's "The Re-education of Ah Mow and His Subsequent Demise Thereof" reads like an ironic fable. The story is about survival and tragedy in the current economic climate of China. Terry Woo's "Cheap Razor Blades" reads like a dramatic monologue of a Generation-X man's self-pity over no real pain or suffering. David M Hsu's "Prodigies: A History Lesson" juxtaposes factual information with personal experience to make history more accessible, and personal life more meaningful. In a pungent short piece, "Snaps—-A Satire," Iris Li debunks some widely-known Chinese stereotypes.

Other well-crafted stories in the anthology include Goh Poh Seng's "Tall Tales & Misadventures of a Young WOG (Westernized Oriental Gentleman)" set in the romantic countryside of Ireland. Andy Quan's open-ended story, "Ants," describes the relationship between two gay men: "ants," as a metaphor, shifts from being a negative to a positive signifier. In "Antiques," ben soo presents elegant experimental prose by eliminating quotation marks and the capital "I." "The style is the story" summarizes what fiction means to him.

The four previously published stories included here are by Fred Wah, Wayson Choy, Judy Fong Bates, and Madeleine Thien. They are placed at the end of the anthology, with Thien's "Bullet Train" as the last story of the book. The content of Thien's story has little or nothing to do with the writer's racial identity.

Why "Strike the Wok?" The title of this anthology derives from the desire we have always had—-to make our voices heard, and to make noise to celebrate the talents in the community. "Wok" here partly functions as "gong," a traditional Chinese musical instrument. This anthology has gathered two generations of Chinese Canadian writers, including winners of the Governor General's Literary Award, the Trillium Book Award, and other literary awards, as well as new writers; it includes writers who were born in Canada and those born abroad, writers currently living in Canada and those residing elsewhere. Jim Wong-Chu and I are proud to present this collection to readers. We hope that you will enjoy these stories and find in them whatever inspiration you are looking for, and that they will help to banish the stereotypes of the past.

Lien Chao
November, 2003

Bibliography

Chao, Lien. *Beyond Silence: Chinese Canadian Literature in English.* Toronto: TSAR Publications, 1997.

Chu, Garrick, et al., eds. *Inalienable Rice: A Chinese & Japanese Canadian Anthology*. Vancouver: Intermedia Press, 1979.

Lee, Bennett and Jim Wong-Chu, eds. *Many-Mouthed Birds: Contemporary Writing by Chinese Canadians.* Vancouver and Toronto: Douglas & McIntyre; Seattle: U of Washington Press, 1991.

Quan, Andy and Jim Wong-Chu, eds. *Swallowing Clouds: An Anthology of Chinese-Canadian Poetry.* Vancouver: Arsenal Pulp Press, 1999.

Larissa Lai

Two Houses and an Airplane

I moved into this apartment because the house it is in reminded me of a house on another coast, one that my parents and I had lived in briefly in one of our many attempts to make a permanent home. I have only the basement, but it comforts me to know I am living in this house. It looks so much like the other one. The original house, at St Joseph's in St Mary's Bay, Newfoundland, was tall and white; it had a green roof, and windows with a ghostly stare that faced right out into the grey blue water where its first owner had drowned at the height of a sudden gale hungry for boats full of working men and boys. I don't entirely understand the reason for my nostalgia. We didn't stay there for long, and the house was freezing cold.

The Vancouver house has that same tall whiteness, that same bleak but stoic sort of front, a green roof, and a cheerful sunshine-yellow door that seems oddly incongruous with its cool exterior. I can't explain what makes it homey. The front yard is overgrown with fireweed and foxglove. In the back, an unwieldy crab apple tree has littered its bitter fruit over the uncut grass. I can't understand why someone would plant a crab apple tree in Vancouver, a climate where much more luscious fruit would easily take, unless it was an accident or the doing of some terribly homesick Maritimer preferring the fruits of home to those of Eden.

The fact that it is Lynda's house helps. Helps me at any rate. I'm not sure she cares one way or the other. I always get the distinct feeling that Lynda doesn't like me much, or that she resents me. But maybe that has more to do with Lynda than me, I don't know.

The basement has been recently refinished, and I am the first one to live here since then. I splurged on a real Persian rug for the living room floor and painted the walls an earthy terracotta.

I can't explain the nostalgia, although I am willing to chalk it up to the influence of the media, especially all those house and garden magazines, which I still sometimes pore over, guiltily, revelling in the glossy images of sunlit living rooms framed with white curtains and filled with burnished wood furniture and cushions covered in bright Indian cottons, or those innocent yet voluptuous neo-Victorian bedrooms with their antique vanities and beds piled high with downy quilts and lace-edged sheets. A big white washbasin with a chinoiserie design of birds and a pagoda at the bottom, like the one in my parents' bedroom at St Joseph's, would be lovely.

I can't deny the longing I feel, especially on damp evenings such as this, when I first step into the warmth of the apartment. What compelled my parents to buy the original? True, it had been relatively inexpensive. It had looked out onto the water. It had also been seventy miles from town. But one couldn't deny there was a romance to it in spite of all the suffering that had taken place inside.

I remember the stories and my own childish chill at the thought of them. My parents had bought the house from the grandchildren of an old Mrs Peddle who had died in the house, years after her fisherman husband. Her children had all set up homes of their own in the two-surname, one-street town where all the houses faced the sea. Dora Peddle, the little girl who lived next door, told me that Old Mrs Peddle had died choking on her own lungs and if I listened carefully late at night I could still hear the choking noises from the other side. Dora's eyes grew banshee-wide and I thought I could see the flicker of Mrs Peddle's lingering intelligence behind them. The idea that my new friend was the descendant of a ghost was decidedly thrilling.

I cannot explain my terror of the oil lamps except that I associated them with Dora's wide eyes and Old Mrs Peddle's choking noises. The best of what Mrs Peddle left behind in the house had of course been taken away by her younger relatives, but many things still remained—a washbasin in the bedroom, quite useless since the advent of indoor running water, a few blue and white chinoiserie plates with the bird and pagoda design on them, a white porcelain chamber pot, and four oil lamps each containing a half-burnt wick and a measure of dark yellow kerosene.

I was terrified of those lamps, imagined a lamp beside an open window sweeping off a table and setting the lacy tablecloth on fire—the flames spreading to the curtains, sweeping up to the ceiling and engulfing me and my parents in their beds, helpless, groggy and near-paralysed by sleep. Had I seen a movie where something like this had happened? Late at night in my dark room I would lie awake, unable to escape these images of flames rushing up curtains quick as startled birds.

My mother has just been there, courtesy of Bruce. For her next trip, she has decided to go to China— with or without me. "Your choice," she says. "I'm buying my ticket next week. That will be your last chance."

Lewis picked my mother up from the airport. My mother thinks Lewis is a bright young man. Lewis thinks my mother is a wise granny of the Revolution. Which is strange, because Mom is dating this white guy. If I or Lynda or any of our friends tried a trick like that, Lewis would excommunicate us toot sweet, lesbian, bi or straight.

When he dropped Mom off, the car was already packed with camping gear. He was in a hurry about something. I didn't ask.

The first thing my mother did was make a pot of Red Rose tea, which we now drink, with tinned milk and sugar, one of the few habits we picked up in Newfoundland. She puts out a cheese board with a big generous wedge of old Gouda and a square of pale yellow Edam bought by the loaf from Mrs van der Leeuw, the Dutch lady who orders them in from Holland every six months. Mom brought them in her carry-on, thinking I must have missed them. "I got you a lobster too," she says. "They're not in season yet, but FP always keeps a few in the tank."

I think briefly of the crayfish in one of the tanks and the aquarium, but if the truth must be told, I do miss lobster, and am perfectly willing to have the guilt of their boiling deaths on my head in exchange for that rich deep-sea flavour.

When I was a child, lobster season was a big deal. We went down to the wharf at Portugal Cove, or sometimes down to St John's Harbour and bought them greenish black and deadly looking, with little pegs of wood inserted into the joints of their claws so that they couldn't open and snap at us. We took them home and let them have a good run around on the kitchen floor before we dunked them into a huge pot of boiling water on top of the green General Electric stove that had come with the house when my parents bought it. My mother missed the wood stove we had out in St

Mary's Bay. It provided a slow steady heat and a kind of romance we desperately longed for.

Mom puts out careful slices of perfectly rectangular bread to go with Mrs van der Leeuw's cheese. "Bruce bought a breadmaker," she says.

I have been hard on my mother. Quiet and cooperative as a child, I grew into a rebellious beast just when she thought the danger had passed. I met Lewis Low in my first year at university, which, having been a bright child, I entered at the tender age of sixteen. Lewis was two years older. We took the same sociology course together and read Marx together for the first time. I laugh now, when I think about our earnest, angry discussions about false consciousness. We talked like old, bearded men. Both the children of hard-working immigrants, we had had relatively comfortable childhoods, but we spent a whole summer competing to prove who was more working class. We never talked about race. When my mother complains that I don't seem to be growing up, I tell her I'm *immaturing* as fast as I can. She breathes an exasperated, long-suffering sigh.

We dropped out in second year, shaved our heads, and took jobs pushing coffee like true proletarians. Lewis got a tattoo of a giant cobra swirling up his arm. I'm afraid of needles. All the anger went inside instead. My mother said we looked like a Buddhist monk and nun gone bad.

"I just want you to be happy," she said, but I knew it wasn't as simple as that. Especially when Cousin Amy had just been hired by a prestigious accounting firm, and funky Cousin Myron was climbing the corporate ladder at Spike Records. Even delinquent Cousin Jonas was working as an adjuster for ICBC, carefully tallying the dollar value of lost arms and whiplashed necks.

She wanted me to go into business, hoping that I could avoid the boondocks, find a job in a big city. *Boondogs*, I used to call it as a child, mishearing my mother's pronunciation. *Watch it like a hog*, that was another one, as though pigs could have the piercing eyes of a bird of prey. I escaped them, though not in the way she had hoped.

She didn't blame me or try to deter me from my newly chosen path. This past year, while Lewis and I nearly killed one another, Cousin Amy married a Hong Kong shipping magnate, but I didn't care. My mother told me I was invited to the wedding, but she herself wouldn't go, as she wasn't sure that she believed in the institution of marriage.

She makes me pickled loh-bak the way she learned from her Korean neighbour. "Never had this when I was growing up," she says. Most of the things we ate when I was a child were my mother's inventions, since not much was available by way of Chinese groceries in St John's. We had pork roasts with potatoes and garlic-fried broccoli. Somewhere along the line, we learned to eat boiled cabbage with white vineagar and salt, which was one of my favourites, though I haven't eaten it since I left. We ate veggie sticks— carrot, celery and turnip— the kind that are purple on top and yellow on the bottom. Lo-bak was unheard of anywhere. We ate pineapple beef with green peppers— tinned pineapple being readily available at any supermarket. We got our soy sauce from Mary Jane's, the only health food store in town. At Mary Jane's, I liked to run my fingers through the open burlap bags of lentils, brown rice, and split peas until the tall guy with the ponytail, beard, and Lennon glasses put a stop to it. I never tasted tofu until one of the local hippie types started making it and selling it out of Mary Jane's dairy cooler. My mother bought a square every time they had it, steamed it whole and served it with a dollop of oyster sauce (imported from Toronto) and a sprinkle of chopped green onions. Ginger came from Toronto too. She ordered it by the pound and stored it in the deep freeze down in the basement.

Recess time at Our Lady of Lourdes. I remember eating raw peanuts and organic sultanas out of a small brown paper bag. "Give us some," said Jackie Murphy, eyeing the promising-looking bag.

I poured some into her hands. "Eewww. What is it?"

Got a similar reaction to my three-bean salad consisting of garbanzos (or "chicken beans," as my grandmother calls them), kidney beans, and French-cut greens beans from the supermarket deep freeze, in a vinaigrette dressing. "Chink food," said Sandy Hilliard.

In another memory, I am at Sobey's with my mother. As she heads for the dairy case in search of a nice piece of non-dyed sharp cheddar, she asks me to go to the produce section and choose some fruit. (My mother has read that the orange colouring they use to dye regular cheddar cheese is carcinogenic.) I can't be more than eight years old. I feel proud that she trusts me to choose fruit on my own. I eye the pyramid of crisp mackintosh apples from Nova Scotia. I ignore the large bright oranges from Florida. I know that if oranges are too orange it means they have been dyed, and therefore aren't really all that good for you. There is a mound of pears in the cooler along the wall that looks promising. My mother has taught me how to choose pears. You must eye the bin carefully and then pick up one that looks like you'd like to eat it. You cradle it in the palm of your hand and then gently press your thumbnail into the skin. If it sinks easily into the flesh then the pear is ripe. I try this with one, and then another. My thumbnail goes in relatively easily, but I can't really tell whether it goes in easily enough, having no basis for comparison. I try with another pear, and then another. I don't notice the footsteps behind me, until the produce man is upon me. He grabs my arm. "Enough of that, little girl," he says. "The pears aren't there for you to ruin." I feel humiliated and disappointed.

The one place safe from all these small affronts and indeterminate let downs is the woods. My mother has been reading Ray Guy's "Stalking the Wild Asparagus." Miriam Hamish, an Englishwoman who lives up the road, says his section on mushrooms is really good. She and her husband Roger, who also works on the Hibernia, have been having great success with chanterelles and russulas.

In no time flat, my mother and I have mastered the art. We walk down the woody path behind the house, cross the bog, and a little further through the woods 'til we reach the abandoned airport arterial road. The municipal government had once begun constructing a road there for a new airport, then given up the project before the road was even paved. Vicki Bonnell says there are bakeapples growing in the bog, but I have never figured out what a bakeapple looks like. Chanterelles, though, are easy to find in the early fall, about three days after a good rain. We walk down the arterial road for a ways. The ravine beside it grows deeper as we go along. Half an hour or so down, they begin to appear, bright orange against the dark humuslike earth on the other side of the ravine. We walk down one side and up the other.

I squat among the clusters. My mother has taught me how to do this. Carefully, you insert your fingers into the earth at the base of the mushroom and then lift it out whole. That way nothing is wasted. We find more mushrooms nestled under the sweeping lower branches of spruce trees at the top of the ravine.

At home, my mother fries them in butter and we slurp them down. What we can't eat we string with needle and thread and hang them on the mug hooks below the spice rack to dry. Later, my mother realizes that it's possible to better preserve the flavour and the juices by freezing them in baggies after frying. We eat them in stir fries and on pizza for the rest of the winter.

Wild mushrooms on pizza? That wasn't our only special addition not available in a million years at Mr Jim's, the local pizza chain. The other one was anchovies.

When she was twenty-four, my mother travelled to Venice following the footsteps of Marco Polo in reverse order. Blasphemy, you say? Inverting the proper order of things? She had no thoughts of turning back the clock, or of reversing history, but it is strange the way her journey reads now, like the backwards reading of a holy text, a Satanic incantation, if only such journeys, such recitations of the foot, could undo all the violence the Church has done. But forget God for now. I'm telling you a story about anchovies.

There is a lot of salt fish in South China, where my roots are, and a lot of salt fish where I ended up, but my first memory of it is in the form of anchovies, sparingly adorning a homemade pizza in a careful circle so that each slice contains just one salty pungent surprise that you might or might not notice, nestled among the chanterelles and hiding under a bland layer of Kraft mozzarella.

The use of anchovies was one of the most worthwhile mysteries my mother brought back from an otherwise inscrutable Europe.

So there were those first childish anchovies, perhaps too sharp and biting for my millions of undamaged taste buds, but I remember them with clarity and a rush of saliva. We made them on whole wheat crusts, it being the early seventies.

My grandfather's favourite dish was haam daan tsing jue yook— salted ducks' egg and minced pork. He eats it almost every night. But on occasion, my grandmother will use salt fish instead of egg. The fish is drier and firmer than those oily anchovies we used on pizza, richer, more redolent of the fermentation process, and less fishy. Within walking distance of my grandmother's apartment in Hong Kong's mid-levels was a street lined with salt fish shops. As many varieties as there are stars in the sky were displayed in bins temptingly positioned on the sidewalk and raised to hip level, where a swinging hand could easily reach out to touch. Others were tied in bundles and hung along a wire just above eye level, so that shop keepers could tell when you were looking and know that a few friendly words or more likely a few modest price quotes might reel you in as surely as the goods themselves once were, baited by an appealing bit of fly or worm. There were round ones, as wide from fin to fin as they were long. There were long narrow ones that my childish self would cheerfully poise at shoulder level as if to receive a well-pitched baseball. All of them were an appealing tan brown and covered in a light dusting of salt.

In my grandmother's day, children were fed plenty of the stuff in their morning *jook*, as it was a well-known wisdom that lots of salt in childhood made you a strong, healthy adult.

In Newfoundland, it took me a while to get around to sampling fish 'n' brewis, dried salt cod stewed together with softened hard tack. This, I suppose, was the winter food of those long-ago English and Irish fishermen who settled along the coast in the 1600s. The fish was less salty and more flakey than the salt fish in Hong Kong and without the interesting bite of fermentation. It was not particularly appealing to me or to any of my local-born acquaintances. They liked steak and bologna. Fish, said my Newfoundland Studies teacher in Grade Ten, reminds people of being poor.

Shortly after I first met Lynda, she invited me to her place for dinner. Front row centre on the evening's menu: curry laksa. It consisted of a big bowl of noodles with shrimp and pork and slices of fish cake in a rich soup redolent of the scent of coconut, spices and, you guessed it, salt fish. I drank it down and breathed it in, feeling giddy and sexy. Afterwards, she touched my face. Her fingers smelled of salt fish and coconut.

"You smell," I said.

"So do you," said she.

Lewis hated her at first, until he realized she had all these ideas about racism and history that had never occurred to him. Then they became fast friends in the most annoying way. I'd talk politics with them until the competition about who was more oppressed started, and then I'd go to the study and sleep on the couch. Until I moved into Lynda's basement. Then I'd just go home.

My mother and I have been talking about Newfoundland a lot. "I imagined it would be like Ireland," my mother says. "Romantic, you know, and sad.

Like an Oscar Wilde story."

An image of the little mermaid flashes through my mind, her grave and irreversible decision to give up her lovely irridescent tail in favour of legs.

"And of course, it is beautiful. All those stark cliffs and all that dark tumultuous water. And all that fog."

"But so far away from anything else."

"Yes, well, you make do with the options you have." She pauses. "Have you decided?"

"I would go in a second if it wasn't Bruce's money."

"But it is. That's the option you have."

"I know."

"I don't understand why the fact that Bruce is white is such a big deal. I didn't raise you to be so conservative."

I glare at her. We sit together silently ranting at each other in our heads, until the tension is unbearable.

She gets up abruptly. "Think about it," she says. "I'm going to the supermarket."

I am relieved when she is gone. I wish Lewis were here so he could process the offer with me. Upstairs the screen door slams and I can hear Lynda plod down the back steps. She got pregnant about six months ago, by artificial insemination. She is starting to show in a serious kind of way. Through the kitchen window I see her amble across the garden with a watering can in her hand. She is heading for the tap. Her squashes in their brown troughs are already swelling full and round. I feel uncomfortable looking, though I can't say why. She turns on the tap and water rushes out. She puts the can under it and stares dreamily into space. The can fills and then begins to overflow. Water gushes over the brim. Startled back to reality, she tries to turn the tap off, but the pressure has mounted and she cannot fight it down with her puffy swollen hands. As she struggles, she slips and falls flat on her bum. I rush outside to help her.

"Thanks Ilene," she says. Her relief is palpable.

"What are you gonna do when you're even bigger?" I ask.

"I'm strong, I'll manage," she says.

"I heard about Meg."

"What can I say? Clearly I misjudged her in a big way. At least Lewis still comes around sometimes."

"Lewis, what a winner."

"I thought you two were getting along."

"Guess again. I think he's seeing someone else."

"He does go out of town a lot."

"Why does he do it, Lynda? Doesn't he know it will hurt me?"

"Of course. That's why he does it."

"You're so cynical."

"Yeah, well."

"Sometimes it isn't healthy. I mean we both know Lewis isn't evil. There is logic to his choices. He doesn't do anything out of active malice."

"Not active, no."

"Jeez, Lynda. Well, what about Meg? She's not actively malicious. You're not doing yourself a favour by thinking so. Don't squirrel yourself into a corner."

"Well what happened with her then?"

"I did hear something. I don't know if you want to hear it."

"Try me."

"I heard she's in therapy. She came into the bathroom once while you were bathing, only she didn't see you. She saw this huge white snake as thick around as a bucket. It flipped her right out."

Lynda has disappeared back into her part of the house when my mother returns. My mother has discovered the Bo Jik, the Buddhist vegetarian restaurant on the corner. She comes back with a vegetarian mock duck and goose cold plate, some fried tofu skins wrapped around slivered vegetables, lotus root in coconut sauce, stir fried gai-lan, and some smooth red and green bean jellies for dessert. "I thought we could just make the rice here," she says.

"There's something I've been wanting to tell you," my mother says when the food has been reduced by half. She always buys too much food. She also always saves important discussions for the last minute.

"What?" I say.

"Bruce and I have been making investments."

Lewis would scowl, but I don't. I'm a practical-minded woman. "That's great, Mom. What kind?"

"Bonds, mostly," she says. "They're the safest, you know. And then Bruce said, Well, isn't it awfully selfish of us to take care of our own interests only? So we decided to invest in China. There are some wonderful things happening over there, things Chinese people everywhere should be proud of."

I am a little taken aback. My mother has never been the patriotic type. I wonder what kind of mind-set I might revert to when I am older. "So what did you do?" I say.

"We invested in a factory there. One of my cousins, you never met him, is a part owner. We thought, why not? My family is helping with China's economic recovery. We should help too. You never know. We might make a lot of money." She laughs, a touch cynically, and I am relieved because it reminds me of the mother I know.

"What kind of factory is it?"

"A toy factory. Nice, don't you think?"

I remember her telling me how she had few toys as a child. Just one doll, with yellow hair, which a rich aunt had given. My grandfather took it away from her when she was ten. "He said I was too old for it. I was heartbroken, but I didn't want to give him the satisfaction of knowing. Besides it was during the American sanctions. Hong Kong was poor. No kids had toys."

"I don't know," I say. Lewis has been doing research on the exploitation of child labour in Asia. I don't think he would approve of my mother's investments. I get up to do the dishes, but then the phone rings. Speak of the devil. It's Lewis.

"I heard Lynda fell today."

"How did you know?"

"I just called her. I'm worried about her."

"I'm surprised that you worry about anything."

"Give it a rest, Ilene. Just do me a favour, will you? Check on her from time to time."

"Frankly, you're in no position to be asking me favours. And besides, Lynda doesn't want my help. I don't think she likes me."

"It's because you're so freakin' childish. This is serious business, okay. Just check on her from time to time. Consider it community work if you want."

"I don't. It's you that needs to make every waking breath a political one."

"I'm calling long distance. I'm gonna go now."

"So go."

I hate the way our phone conversations go, but I can't help myself.

Sometimes I think I would just like to put my arms out and hug him, and then we won't need to have these vicious little conversations that don't do anyone any good.

I add some more rice into one of the styrofoam boxes and plop on a little of the other stuff as well.

"I'm going to take some food upstairs to the landlord, Mom," I say. I feel funny calling Lynda the landlord, but my mother has a terrible head for names. And besides, she is my landlord.

I go upstairs and bang on the screen door.

"What do you want?"

"I thought you might not have had dinner yet."

"Lewis sent you, didn't he?"

"Not exactly. He just said maybe I should look in on you from time to time."

"I wonder if he'll continue to try to control our lives from beyond the grave," says Lynda. "I guess you may as well come in."

Lynda has been watching TV and makes no move to turn it off just because I'm here. We watch five minutes of a home improvement show where a woman with fake blonde hair shows the studio audience how to press leaves between sheets of wax paper. Lynda switches the channel. A woman is running through a dark forest in her nightdress, face pale and hair streaming. I figure it must be another of those serial-killer shows or something. Lynda watches intently. The commercials come on. There is an ad for Singapore Airlines. A cheong-sammed air hostess stands beside an elephant holding a parasol above her head and smiling sweetly.

"Charming," says Lynda wryly. "I wonder if I could convince them to put me in that ad." She sticks out her belly. "Maybe as the elephant. Have you decided about China?"

"Do you think I should go?"

She turns the volume down a little. "Do you want to?"

"Yes, but, well, it just seems kinda...shoddy. Because of Bruce."

"Why does he want to put up the money?"

"I dunno. Maybe he wants to replace Dad. Maybe he thinks he can buy people's love. Who cares?"

"You can't stand this guy."

"Not really, no."

"But money is money."

"Yup. And dignity is dignity."

"I can see what you mean."

"Lewis can't. He thinks I'm spoiled."

"Then you don't want to go."

"I think I'm afraid to go. I'm afraid I won't fit in. I mean, I don't speak the language. I don't have the demeanour. And I don't...well, I don't want to feel like an outsider there. You know? It's like, as long as I don't go, I can imagine I belong somewhere. But if I do go, and I feel like a freak there, then there won't be anything left to dream about. I guess you think that's silly."

"It's a bit strange."

"Thanks."

But you know what I mean, don't you? Besides, I think what I want to put my time into, what I think is worth fighting for, is an identity here, you know? I don't want to be white..."

"Clearly.

"I want history of my own. In this place."

"We have one."

"Yes, but it's largely unwritten and unacknowledged."

"I don't see how a little travelling is going to keep you from your record-making or whatever you want to call it."

I was outraged the first night my mother spent away from home. I was fourteen years old and had enough stress with the first appearance of pus-filled zits on my face and the first episode of hot smelly blood gushing between my legs. We had only been in Vancouver for a year. My father, Edison Lam, at work by night and asleep by day, had become a ghost in our lives, except for supper and the few brief minutes afterwards, which he used to get ready for work. My mother could not have picked a worse time for the blossoming of her second adolescence.

"He's so cultured!" Veronica sighed, moony-faced as any Juliet. "He recites Shakespeare and Byron."

"He's a schmuck," I said. "I can't stand it."

The more pussy pimples that appeared on my face, the creamier my mother's skin became. Her body grew longer, more elegant, her hair lustrous and thick. She coiled it into a loose bun and poked a long wooden chopstick-like stick through it and replaced her track pants and Whistler sweatshirt with formfitting dresses, often slit just a tad higher than was really modest. She disappeared many nights at a time, resurfacing in the day early enough to serve me omelettes at breakfast, pack tuna-fish sandwiches for lunch, and encourage the completion of homework before dinner.

She took meticulous care of my dad too—which was odd behaviour for such a liberated woman. She washed his uniforms and undershirts, made his favourite foods for dinner—pork chops with peas and mashed potatoes, lasagna without the cottage cheese, chicken pot pies with Campell's cream of mushroom undiluted for the gravy. All the things he had wanted to eat through the seventies when their diet consisted mostly of brown rice and legumes of one sort or the other.

Dad took it all without a word, although he bought QuickPicks everyday now, sometimes as much as ten dollars' worth, as though a big bonanza might turn his life around and bring his wife back to him. Maybe he thought it would stop my shoplifting. He never confronted me about it, but I know he knew. I'd purposely lay hairs across the edge of a barely opened drawer like they did on *Dragnet.* I often found them shifted or gone. It was a kind of game, a terrible one, malicious on my part and invasive and curious on his. I think if he had said something, even once, I would have stopped, would have plunged forever into the depths of guilt. But he loved me too much and he never said anything.

Late one afternoon, perhaps three hours after classes were over, I came back from a particularly daring heist, fat girl T-shirt bulging with booty. I removed my coat too carelessly and an edge of shirt came untucked. Lipsticks, compacts, gum, and scotch tape clattered to the floor, though not loudly enough to drown out the sound of my father's slippers slapping against the worn carpet tacked to the battered staircase. I scrambled to tuck my shirt back in and cram the stuff back down the neck, but I'm sure he turned the bend near the landing soon enough to have seen me. I pushed past him without a word and ran up to my room. Though I remember it as an accident, lately I've been wondering if there was a touch of intention behind my carelessness. At any rate, my father never blamed me. He blamed my mother.

Flash forward seven years later to the Vermilion Pavilion, a restaurant of pan-Asian cuisine, where the cooks are all Chinese, except the owner and the head chef, who are the aging hippie children of two well-heeled families from the British Properties. However one thinks of the situation politically or morally, the fact remains that the cooking is fabulous. Fish in black bean sauce steamed to perfection, curry laksa, Dungeness crab in light pepper batter, oyster omelettes, hand rolls in which the seaweed maintains a perfect balance of crunch and tenderness, chicken with peanuts, rare beef in noodle soup. The owner and head chef have backpacked across Asia collecting recipes as they went.

Into the tastefully lit, quietly romantic atmosphere they've provided, Bruce Kowalsky leads his wife of four months and his stepdaughter, yours truly.

"So much less crowded and noisy than a regular Chinese restaurant," says Veronica.

"What do you mean 'regular'?" I demand, surly as can be.

"Let's order some wine, shall we?" says Bruce.

"Yes, how civilized," says Veronica.

"You do drink, don't you Ilene? Of course you do, all you university types drink."

I glare at him. "I'm not *in* university."

"Well, why not? If it's a matter of money, sweetheart, I am your stepfather, you know. You don't have to feel shy about asking."

I look at my mother and roll my eyes. She glances at me nervously and then looks away. "Let's just see what's on the menu, okay honey?" she says to Bruce.

"All right, pet," says Bruce, not looking at her. He flags a waiter down and rattles off a mouthful of Mandarin.

The waiter shakes his head, embarassed. "I speak English and Cantonese only, sir."

Bruce pulls his face into a teasing scowl. "You should learn Mandarin," he says. "1997's coming up fast."

(I make quiet puking noises.)

"Something to drink, sir?"

Bruce orders a bottle of Chateau somethingorother, faking a French accent. I stick my finger up my nostril.

"You should really try the smoked duck," says Bruce without missing a beat. "It's excellent."

"Whatever you order is fine with me," my mother says demurely.

"Mom," I groan. Where did my feisty feminist mother go?

"Mom what?" says Veronica under her breath. "Just be nice, okay? We can talk about it later."

Just then, the doors burst open, and a gush of cold air fills the room. Seven young Asian women with ragtag clothes and streaks of blue and purple and orange in their hair stride into the restaurant and push their way past the freckled hostess with her pretty kimono and blonde hair up in a bun. They make little noise but rapidly disperse through the dining room and begin handing out leaflets to the irritated diners. It takes the manager and two burly waiters fifteen minutes to remove them one by one, a difficult task, because as each is apprehended she makes her body go limp and heavy and almost impossible to drag out. It gives the others time to complete their work. I take a pamphlet from a girl with blue bangs and thick glasses with funky-in-a-nerdy-sort-of-way black rims. The pamphlet says: *Down with Neo-Colonialism. Appropriation Is Racism.* "Right on," I say. But the girl scowls at me. "If you believe what we believe, then why are you eating here?"

"I could come with you," I say, making to rise, but then my mother grabs my arm fiercely. The removal squad arrives at our table, and the blue-haired girl goes limp.

"You really embarrassed me just now," says Veronica, when Bruce goes off to pay the bill.

"I embarrassed you?"

"Just make an effort, sweetie, please. Bruce is not the bad guy you think he is. He's suffered a lot in his life too, you know. And he really wants you to like him. He's still hoping you'll go with me to China."

A pause. "I don't want him to give me anything."

"I don't know when you got like this. I never taught you to be so ungrateful, I'm sure."

In the end I go. Lynda says, "You may as well play out your karma, since you've already done all the processing for it."

"Karma chameleon," I say. "You sound like Lewis."

Bruce has thought of everything. As he sees us through the gate, he presses a hundred dollar bill into my hand. "Buy a few cartons of Marlboros at the Duty Free," he says. "The Chinese love American cigarettes.

For Veronica's sake, I squeeze out a monotone "Thanks, Bruce."

"Oh honey," says my mother as we approach the security gate. "Bruce just wants you to like him. Please try."

"I am trying, Mother," I say coldly.

My mother bites her lip and looks hurt.

I don't know what I expect of this trip. Mostly I just want to get away from the bad scene with Lewis. I have rehashed old arguments over and over again in my head, like lost chess games, trying to discover how I might have won. If pressed, I might say I wished for a transformation, or at least, I wished I might just grow out of a way of being that leads nowhere.

The transformation begins on the plane. It's not the kind I might have said I wanted, and since it isn't, I don't notice it, but that doesn't stop it from happening.

"Take the window seat," says my mother. "I've seen this view before."

"It's alright, Mom. You take it."

"I'll just sit in the aisle seat here. I doubt anyone's booked it. These flights are never full."

But at the last minute, four well-dressed Japanese businessmen come down the aisle. Three of them take seats in front of us. The fourth is the legitimate occupant of the aisle seat. He isn't rude to my mother, merely puzzled that a small Chinese woman occupies the seat with the number he holds in his hand. Veronica moves into the middle seat. He smiles graciously, takes off his overcoat, folds it, and carefully places it along with a slim black briefcase into the overhead bin and sits down.

A flight attendant comes down the aisle, checking seat backs and tables in preparation for take-off. She glances at us briefly. I think to myself, "She sees a family here." A mental comparison of my father Edison against the Japanese businessman makes me grin at the absurdity.

I can't say what it is exactly— both men would be about the same age and both have a gentleness about them. If Lewis were here, I would have said, "He seems so Asian." And Lewis would have said, "That's so essentialist." I would have felt defeated by that and kept quiet. But since he isn't here, I keep glancing at the businessman until he becomes noticeably uncomfortable.

The aroma of coffee presses into my lungs as the plane slants into the sky. A few rows back, a baby starts to cry.

"You were like that once," my mother muses.

"A long time ago, Mom."

"So small and helpless. How things change."

"That Bruce is turning you into a complete mushball."

"Oh honey, just try to be a bit nicer about Bruce, okay? I know a lot of people have a hard time with mixed marriages, but I raised you to be open minded, didn't I? And besides, you've hardly chosen a conventional lifestyle yourself."

The plane is still ascending. Behind us, the baby howls.

"What's so unconventional about me and Lewis? We even bicker the way you're supposed to."

"You know I never liked that Low boy. Not just because of his funny hair. Didn't you say he was part Japanese?"

"Mom," I say. If Lewis were sitting beside me, I might have ventured a few words about imperialism and the colonized mentality, and my mother might have snapped back something about the Japanese occupation of Hong Kong during the war. But the businessman glances sideways at us and I lose my nerve. I just say, "How about if we talk about it later?"

My mother smiles to herself as though she has won the argument.

The Cantonese woman sitting with her family across the aisle from us takes an orange out of her bag and begins to peel it. She calls loudly to her husband behind her to ask if he wants some.

As the plane moves closer to China, the Chinese voices on the plane seem to grow increasingly louder. I feel myself ease into the clamour as though into warm water. The sounds are familiar—the sounds of Dad and Mom and their extended families years ago, before I was born, gathering for barbeques or launch boat picnics or drives to Clearwater Bay when the water there was still transparent and you could float on your back for hours staring at the hot blue sky. Of course, I cannot understand a word. The voices engulf me like a hungry if vaguely benevolent beast.

SKY Lee

The Mark of a Stray Female Survivor

At the unsettled dawning of the worlding, there was not meaning with which to anchor myself. I couldn't complain about my hollow aching emptiness. Or explain away my dark fluidal enormity. But forbore in mute loneliness. But one day, after a very long, solitary time, I looked down to see a pale puny man point his small if offensive god at me. He seemed ridiculous and of course, I brushed him off. Except he insisted that I be slave to his peevish concepts of creation and destiny. I supposed I should have offered up more resistance. I surely could have swallowed him whole if I wanted. to Except I was by nature, a feckless sort. And I didn't want to get sick from a meal of his toxic flesh. besides

In retaliation for my indifference, to him (for he demanded a great deal of attention), he named me monstrous, as indeed, I was. As indeed, it was monstrous that his Godhead should be at the mercy of his flesh. I myself was quite comfortable in my own native skin, thank you very much. Nevertheless, contact had been made. The contagion passed on And wouldn't you know it, I did get somewhat intrigued by his persistence.

What on earth did he so deliriously lack? Perhaps, for a deluded, distracted moment, I thought I needed some of his terror. In order to kick against the suspension which dangled us both. But no, quite decidedly, I'd have rathered not! But then again, I was already contradicting myself. Ho hum, we only know ourselves—indeed, we can only know anything at all in flawed relationship to one another. Never mind! If that's as good as it gets, then I'd just as soon go home, and retain my option to pass the night in some confusion.

I mean I may be nothing but impossible, but at least, this nothingness I know something about. My sentience may be spread indescribeably thin, and my soul, nothing more than unbearable dark matter, and my suicide, as indistinct and inconsequential as any anonymous slave disappearing in the crushing jungle, but I'm not so terribly alone in the rushing crowds around me, all stubbornly trying to both see and avoid what we can, of the freak accidents which happen in traffic in front of us. As long as I tell myself that I am what I am, though raped and battered, and murdered. From time to time, I surge to play out my buoyant desires, like the rapids of a free flowing river, snaking through night and day, flooding light and dark, widening sorrow and joy, with oceans to love.

PART I: THE MARK OF A STRAY FEMALE SURVIVOR.

In my taunting, smart alecky way, I told my lady Eve my story. I wasn't born, you know. I was lost and found instead, a crotchety, old soul already, hollering by the side of a well-travelled road to and from antiquity, called the Sacred Way of the Southern Seas. How picturesque was the effect of my description! I said that this was the route of Marco Polo, on his sacred way to discovering spaghetti, ice cream and bomb terrorism for whities.

Whities! Eve screeched back with as much drunken hilarity as a peeled cocktail onion. She didn't know a Marco Polo from a Robinson Crusoe. Both were foreigners whereas she was proud to be American. And I, the delighted native, grinning from ear to ear, seventeen years old, was quite the party girl myself, hoping to be seen as a bit more exoticized American than exiled Chinese, but hey, I knew my place! I readily understood that, with my close proximity to Eve and her Hollywood face, the very same one which won over the West, I retained my important Orientalist role as well.

So, what of it, if I told a story or two with an extra bit of instinctive flair? (I couldn't have let Eve have all the fun now, could I?) And what difference did it make, with all the straining and craning for conquest and spectacle that I had seen by then, if I squeezed bit of glamour out of an used tube, onto my small face? Let me tell you, it wasn't anything to write home about!

But we Chinese, do so love our sacred ways in every which direction, if the truth be unknown. This one at least suggested a meandering path through Burma, Vietnam and into Sinca pura, such sea swiped places, being the penile ends of massive continents, would have just as likely flicked me off into the vast ocean as not. And I, with no place left to go except impossibly far-flung ones, in turmoil, swimming, with wave after endless wave crashing down upon my beaten head!

The Chinese pedlar who found me, found me stark naked. Ma called him Ol' Seedy, because that described him well enough. And apparently, he described me well enough, as a female infant with a sweet dumb smile, eating pebbles and crawling about on my bare belly on the dusty shoulders of a road, beneath some one-eyed memorial stone arches, just outside of the ol' town of Singapore on the island of Singapore. About five months old, no weeping sores or social deformities—yet! A brilliant cyan bruise on my scrawny bastardized butt from a well-aimed kick out of heaven, by the almighty Jade Emperor himself, straight into dirty human hands! A few minor scratches, a bit underfed naturally, for those hard times, but it was more or less clear that some poor, hapless fool had done her best by me.

Lucky for me, that wild dogs didn't get to me first! So claimed Ol' Seedy, who wondered if someone else, always luckier and harder of heart, had not happened by before him, and stripped me of my raiment. This stray remark handed down to me by word of mouth, has always led me to wonder if my worldly belongings were of some worth. But who can say for sure! In those days, even a two-by-two inch square of pissed-upon cotton was worth something to somebody, where a bawling female baby was not. Forgive me for even mentioning this! Delusions of grandeur are better left unexpressed. Mine look especially pitiful on paper.

So, next, the ol' fart took me to town and tried to sell me. He either had too big a heart, or too big a bite. Maybe, he figured a few strings of cash, was worth the maddening baby wails of hunger and distress, which he would have had to philosophically forbear. But ever mind, soon enough, my puerile cries turned into cowering silence as I weakened.

It would, after all, be a few more hungry days before my virgin-whore-of-an-earth-mother, Lee Lily happened along. Just as it would be another lean decade, before the next big love of my life, Eve Bronwen Friend, happened along, in her turn. Needless to say, how happy I was to have at least two women pick me up, dust me off and show me the way—even if it was the wrong way, to love, pleasure and joy. Behemoth, by myself, I wouldn't have known how to even begin, never mind, reverse the existentialist damage done to me, by such a haphazard dawning of life!

A motherless orphan mothered by a mother-fucked mother! Never mind, I was one of the chosen after all. So join me in the singing of the praises for all the virgin-whores-mothers of this earth! It's just always good to begin with a prayer as well!

I was three years old, when I cleverly figured out that babies pop out of the globular mommy belly. Naturally, I asked my precious Lo Mo, if I came out of hers. I had been told the story of my foundling origins, of course I had. Nonetheless, I still hoped against hope that she would say so. I simply needed myself to have sprung out of her belly so bad!

Aiiee, Ma should have lied, because at the same time that a mother's womb suggests a whole universe in itself, it also speaks of physical, mental, emotional and spiritual continence, as opposed to lost continents. A mother, you see, is a body of knowledge. And a real mother of confinement results in a real progeny of conformity. All faith in the corporeal system absolutely intact, spirit quite unbroken (if a bit taken for granted). She should have lied, I tell you, because then I never would have felt the need to become the writer of my confounded orphan's story—this silly, long script filled with baby wails from the dark side of the moon.

Instead, Ma replied honestly. And suddenly, there it was. A big, bloody, black hole in the otherwise untrammelled, early evening sky of my early being. From which no utterances was possible! A nothingness so infinitely troubling, in fact terrifying because it threatened to engulf and collapse me, like a great, cosmic flush toilet, crushing every last pituitary trace of me right out of planetary existence (otherwise known as writer's block)!

Mind you, at three years of age, I didn't exactly explain it like that. One can't complain about it at any age, if the truth be known! Ma, with the best motherly intentions and an absurdly incomplete map of the human heart in mind, bought me a new tin bucket and shovel instead, since we were picnicking on the beach at the time. She told me, if that nasty ol' hole bothered me so much, I should fill it up.

With what, mother dear? asked I, the little brown waif, with the big brown eyes. With very wonderful stories, she glibly suggested as she waved me off. She was so enjoying herself. Just make them up as I go!

Well, so, being both young and impressionable, I tried to do as her cups suggested. Yes, in the beginning, the art of storytelling was all fun and games. Everything appears simple enough, as long as one stays within the norms of perception. But I must have taken a wrong turn or something. Even worse, maybe, just maybe, I never had any norms of perception ever to begin with. At any rate, I promptly lost my ending. And fell into the holes in my stories. And what glory holes of mythic proportion they turned out to be. I soon spent all my time, trying to get out by dumping futile meaning into them, with nothing but a little, provisional, bent toy shovel, thank you very much, talk about haunted innocence.

So, what am I trying to say here? I'm getting ahead of myself. Well, perhaps, as I haven't yet said, the year was1903 and Ma wasn't anymore than seventeen, herself, and her suggestion, if you think about it, was rather extraordinary for her day and age. But it caused me a lot of distress in my lifetime, because I lived to a pretty ripe old age, myself. And am still living, obviously to this damnable day, tripping right along with this god-awful, twentieth century! That is if some 100 years' worth of self-pitying, self-indicting, massively self-absorbed chasing of my own pathetically self-conscious tale constitutes a life?

I am old now, and morbidly tired, with profound doubts about myself, on top of everything else. But before I die, I should at least identify myself, if only to myself. So, who am I but a wannabe writer, who harbors profound doubts about herself? And what doubts might these be? Well, for instance, I have always wondered, (in fact, worried that) if one wasn't exactly born, then how can one die precisely? Excuse me! In my spirit world, I need a death. Without death to quell my restive bones, I shall be forced to go on and on forever. But perhaps, more to the point, if I don't have an honest beginning to the story of my life, is it even possible to find something that will ever make it right in the end.

Those of you who are not as old and tired and famous as I, are probably wondering, with good reason, what is the matter with living forever? Doesn't being immortal, as monsters and goddesses are immortal, sound great! Well, all I can say to you, is that I've known a few goddesses and monsters in my day. They're not at all what they're hyped up to be. They wander through our culture of death, without the solace of death, just like you or me or any other hungry ghost, more present after dead than in life.

Aah, but don't listen to me! What do I know? As a writer with writer's block, I am always at a loss when I try to explain myself in relation to ... ahem, in flawed relation to my word ... I mean, world. Perhaps, I really mean my larger social reality. And then, there is a desperate message on my new fangled message machine to please, please, please not decease before fully unravelling the mystery of my story of my life—there being some editorial doubts about me, and the validity of my stories apparently. I press a cute little button and it plays over and over again.

Admittedly, earlier today, I was a little upset at the caller, and I did threaten to kill myself, but just for dramatic effect. But I have since, realized that I should cease and desist from my distraction of myself, and get on with the task at hand! I've barely begun my lifestory, and already, I yearn for a quick and easy death ... ah, fix to it. Not that I blame myself! Who doesn't crave salvation from their quest for exiled meaning, as deeply disturbed as it was, in my case, right from the very start?

Alright then, let's get real here! I remember that there was already a book, a fawn book which my mother had started for me, innocently enough. See me at three then, too dark and serious to be utterly adorable, but I was ever so much less ambiguous back then. I would have just completed my baby-slave chores, and achieved the herculean task of sitting cleanly at, with eyes level to, my mother's table in her study. Stretched before me, a magical landscape of fragrant ink pools, sculptured soapstone palettes, pillarlike inksticks and stout ceramic jars of solid pigment. Elegant brushes of every elongated shape and size, all of which never stood on their own, but had to be delicately propped up, or laid down, or suspended, with bated breath, over great snowy plains of white rice paper.

And Lo Mo, slow as a turtle's egg, did things step by stately step. There was no reason in the worlding back then for her to hurry. She applied comical, wired spectacles to ears and bridge of nose, opened the appropriate drawer in her private escritoire, in order to draw the book out. She smoothed out the chosen page of it, and just studied it for the longest time. And then studied it some more.

Ah so, that was my mother. She did this writerly thing to me. She infatuated me with this arcane process of signification, and illuminated it too, with pen and ink illustrations. An amazing likeness of Ol' Seedy, the baby dealer with his woven basket, its dirty handles unraveling. A lively depiction of Flood Boy, lugging the basketcase that was me, home. A lovely one of Ma, young, gorgeous, with me. I was so cute. I was so found—all fattened up for market, ecstatically drooling, an embroidered cap upon my beloved head. And finally, an awfully abrasive, and in my opinion, disproportionately large portrait of my See Nye or nanny, with her chipped, chapped hands about to slap and pinch, for goodness—particularly my goodness's sake! Such a dead-on dislikeness of her, right down to the gold stops on her decaying teeth!

Mind you, nowadays, I can only vouch for the existence of such a book, tussore silk bound, handstitched, and beribboned. It along with everything else, got lost in my overseas flight. It was just a ragged, fawn colored, old thing after all. And I was just an orphan, starved for knowledge, and trying to tell what I believe I know, of fact and myth.

Of fact and myth, I say! There was a dim photographic exposure, badly done, as I recall, of my Ma's house in interrupted progress. Her house was never finished, as a matter of fact. I feared that foreign-made photograph immediately, conducting as it did, my memories and hence my imagination, along starker paths to my own past. As fascinating as it was, with its grainy, eerie, ghostlike textures, the result of an one-all-consuming-eyed wooden box on monstrous spider legs, it was its destructive gaze that I rejected absolutely. Intruding as it did, upon the prettier picture that I have, of my mother, in a house of her own making, with foxy-haired inkbrushes at clever hand, adding little flourishes to her sketches, here and there to my fawn book, wrinkles to the truth carefully touched up or smoothed over!

But I was never in that photograph. Although I remember quite distinctly, facing the startling puff of smoke. By the time the framed thing came home, I had already been rendered invisible. Except for the mark of a lone female survivor!

GREAT GOON YUMMY

And so, I write on the wall, in the voice of my mother, Lee Lily who resided in Singapore on September 10, 1900, the One Hundred Ninety-Second Year of the Reign of the British East India Company (est. 1709).

"I have just bought a baby—female, off course! Yes, yes, I know it was a dumb thing to do Risking what pitiful little I myself had in life, and for what? I didn't care, I just had to do it, by Goon Yummy! Perhaps now, I too shall have a stake in the heart of life. By the time I got home, I was rapturous with excitement.

"Calm down, I told myself! Still thyself! A castaway infant bought for cheap, is ordinary enough, isn't it? This is the time-honored thing which women like me do when they need an extra pair of hands to stir the toil and trouble.

"Should I have asked permission? But from whom? The Master, of course! Surely, he isn't to be bothered with such paltry details. Sometimes, I don't see him for months on end. Then, from See Nye, my crabby old niangyi servant? But I'm supposed to be the lady of the house. This set me giggling. I don't know why.

"I tore off my infant's dirty rags and wiped away as much filth as I could with my scarf. I saw again, that she was indeed beautiful, with the most remarkably long body and limbs! I laid her in a soft layer of my own underclothes, still warm from my body and soul, and hid her in the private parts of my garden, on two rattan armchairs, placed face to face against each other, to form a loving cradle for her, beneath the perfumed shade of the ilang ilang, softly singing a lovely refrain to her,

> *Baby waits, baby wails. May the Good Goddess of Mercy, who loves all the lone stray female survivors of this world, find her in this lost world!*

"Oh, but sadly, I had to leave her then. Oops, I almost forgot to do my hair and put on my toupee—for I must return to that venal world I inhabit as a woman. I have guests—guests who bind and gag me. And I must, I really, really must do what is expected of me.

"The two biddies from the Master's big house drop in whenever they feel like it, at the rudest times possible, if at all possible! They have found me out of place. They will plot to use this against me, but to whom, I wondered? Who can be bothered to listen to their endless grievances anymore.

"I dutifully lugged the hot and heavy tea thing up the stairs, and straight onto the unsuspecting laps of my most unwelcome guests, lazing about like stiffs on the lounge chairs. The immobilized mother with the bloodied betel nut mouth and hideous, cracked-earth wrinkles on her powdered face! The inert daughter in a particularly unstinting western dress and scarf of apple green silk, mechanically plying her gorgeous fan back and forth, beneath her incredibly sad and angry face! Oh but baby waits, baby wails! Their amah forever blithering and fiddling with incidentals on their tray.

"It is the daughter who is most curious about me, actually. She has overheard the most intriguing things about her father's newest and most inconsequential whore.

"Oh, but the beings we inhabit! I keep reminding myself that they are not my enemies, but lowly slaves just like me, if only they realized it.

"Last night, Mah See Hung, second in rank to none other than the Grand Marshall himself, in the Heishe Society, was rumored to have paid me a visit. And he's the closest thing to a discerning connoisseur that they have in this backwash place.

"'And Mother,' hissed the daughter, 'they say he was ever so impressed with her.'

"'That's unbelievable,' retorted the mother, 'I don't believe it, he would never dirty the hem of his gown in a place such as this.'

"'Lo Mo, they say she can really sing in the old way,' persisted the daughter.

"'Squawk is more like it.'

"'Yeah, but Mother, they say that he will come again. And next time, he wants to make a huge party of it.'

"'Where in the hell is her bloody tea?' exclaimed the mother, getting annoyed, 'We've been waiting here for more than half a day.'

"'Yeah but Lo Mo, I wonder what they say about her is true, that she is the daughter of ...'

"'Shut up! Here she comes ...'

"It is my job to curl over like a timid little animal trying to protect its underbelly, and to hang my head in an acceptable posture of shame. Which is, of course, I did to perfection under their steely gaze. Because I always do whatever it takes to get rid of these two pig-bitches as quickly as possible. They only come to my humble abode to lacerate me for a bit of sport and entertainment. As if that can possibly erase some of the pain and terror in their empty lives?

"And so, I entered. My mask had its own clever little peepholes. And I was already thinking of ways to get rid of them so that I could devote myself to my baby dying a thousand deaths for the want of a mother.

"'Ah, Second Mistress Man, you look well. And Little Miss Man, you look as well as can be, as well,' I smiled as I entered. A warm smile followed by a perfect smile. With my many smiles (never baring teeth), I imagined them turning to stone for all achingly dull eternity! With every flawless greeting, I damned their puniest female efforts on earth all to hell!

"They rolled their lethargic eyes at me. They see nothing. They understand nothing. They rolled their eyes far back, into the back of their heads.

"'Ah, Big Lily,' Second Mistress Man heaved a sigh. 'You finally make an appearance. Where on earth have you been? You're all sweaty again, dripping like a coolie. Surely, we didn't catch you out and sneaking about again. Aye, the liberties you sluts take!'

"'Last time we spoke, I thought that you understood that parading yourself up and down in public is not de rigueur,' added Miss Man.

"'Aiiee, yes, but I'm sorry. But I didn't go so far, really I didn't. That shop by the temple on Balestier Road, really, my worse frivolity was some aimlessly haggling back and forth, over the silliest thing ... oh, but it was most exquisite veil. I hadn't ever seen anything like it. But the insolent fellow wouldn't back down on his price. Neither did I know what I was trying to prove. I shouldn't have opened my mouth to begin with. The old pedlar wouldn't shut up after that. Hah, everyone's down on their luck these days, aren't they?'

I chipper, chirping in the cold hard face of their cruelty.

"The Little Miss's smug smirk then, 'Lily, why didn't we see you "take a sedan chair" home?'

"Oh how clever! And I am not supposed to understand the not so funny pun for 'kicked out tramp?'

"Second Mistress Man started up with her splendiferous daughter-of-a-rich-farmer drawl, 'A Lily ah, we just dropped in to warn you. Lo Yeh came very close to throwing you out again the other day, you know. He complained that this neighbourhood is just two streets away from the street of our Man clan association temple. It rather offends him to think that the stink of his son's whoring wafts so close to home and ancestor.'

'Yes, it took Father a good, long time to talk the old man back down, didn't it, Mother?'

"Second Wife cast her cold indifferent stare past me, into what I hope, is the bleakest future possible, and sighed, 'Poor Wing Him. At his age, he makes a pathetic sight as a lover boy. I must say though that this Big Lily (a.k.a. My Unbound Feet) has clawed a lot further and clung on a lot longer than the last "wild chicken" that he kept, in that hovel close to the foreigners' sector, in that alley off Boat Quay. Oh my, how did that harridan try to put on airs!'

"I smiled. Aiyee, the effort to appear perfectly composed in front of these two! Hives popping forth all over my anguished body! It takes much fortitude to ignore their stinging itch, like miserable beggar children, trapped beneath the polished surface of reality. Beneath my dress, unruly red welts rise like great lost continents, their integumentary contours, mapping out the inroads of alien invasion upon my embattled, interior landscape. On the suave surface, I simply smiled at my body's tendency to betray me.

"'Surely, Auntie,' suggested I, drawing out my embroidery panel, with its razor sharp needlepoint and colorful thread. For now, I only sought to enliven the conversation, because it was high time for their visit to end. 'You didn't bother your esteemed Lo Yeh about me? How could I, a little nobody, be the cause of such furor in the Man household? Perhaps, you, as first concubine, as *neiren,* as owned territory, privy to the Master's heart and soul, and with his family's interests in mind, may haggle a bit, here and there, that is if circumstances are not too far below your dignity. But surely, the Great Patriarch was not troubled with such trivialities, was he?'

"I got her. Right in the kisser. Cool as a cucumber, I stole an elegant sidelong glance at Second Wife's thunderous face, and caught the last flicker of venomous misery before she stuffed it back down her constricted throat. Still, she with the long stick in her sleek chignon, parried well. It was young Miss who could bear no more, no howl!

"'How dare you, shameless, stinky cunt bitch, cross words with my esteemed mother,' she yelped.

"Ahh so, the by-now familiar tirade begins again. I need say no more.

Now is the sensible time to dummy down and wait, in order that they might finish exercising their shrieking vocal chords all the faster. So pressing is their insane need to slaughter the last scraps of my humanity! Not that I take any of their bullying personally! Believe me, I can even take their side.

"Yes, in order to pass the time, let me do so! How dare I get away with all that I get away with? Vile aberration of a lone female survivor that I am, assaulting their assiduous sense of patriarchal order. Uh oh, I hear them calling nefarious multiples of my name. A new one rings out, 'Demon fiend!'

"Oh please, I don't deserve such supernatural acclaim. Oh, but dig it in, why doesn't she? Oh, alrighty then, my head self depreciatingly bowed, long face feigning defeat, solemnly passing the requisite amount of captive audience time. Oh but I see myself more a common rat, seeking a paltry meal wherever I can eke it out, hanging onto the rafters over the hookah bed whenever the opium pipe is lit.

"As far as my eyes can see, there is as always, an appalling number of us, scurrying along the squalid fringes of human existence. Never, no matter how famished, fight over food with especially the female ones of them! We are sure to be exterminated. It's the far better part of rodential valour not to bare teeth at them, for there is no creature on earth more spiteful than humans ...

"... waiting, still waiting for the malevolent pair to 'tijiao' into their sedan chair, and fly back from whence they come, my mind drifts in and out. I hum a little tune,

"'*Baby waits, baby wails! ...*'

"I tell myself a little tale then.

"I am a hungry rat. A sleek, fatuous cat creeps into the room. It behooves me to keep a beady rat's eye on it. If only to jealously watch it finish its dish of minced meat, and lick its chops afterward, as it coyly turns its head. Out of the corner of its eye, it glimpses its own tail swishing, and pounces with marvelous speed. But the tail is impossibly gone. Instincts still dictate though; the feline claws furiously after it. Strangely, nothing again! Empty-pawed. Wounded pride. And yet, with tail twitching, the cat coyly turns its head again ...

"Whether the cat realizes the elusive tail is a part of itself, I can not say but as a rat, I am fascinated. At first, I think the cat unbelieveably stupid. I also hate cats because they contradict rats. But then again, I realize that cats are small miracles. They have magic and allure following them all the days of their lives. As a pasttime, this has to be, without a doubt, extremely fulfilling. And the reason cats have a mythic quality about them, that is forever young and surprisingly vulnerable. What do I have, but my begrudgement and contempt? Where is my pretty dish of meat? Who is the real idiot here?"

I named you, "Yummy," after "The Goon," if only for now. See Nye put the word out on the streets, for a wetnurse. Within the dusky hour, a filthy young rag of a woman, Jun Tou, was discovered skulking inside our gate with two little ones of her own—a piteous nurseling that looked worse off than you, and Dead Boy, then two years old, with his ghastly split-lip deformity. They looked so thin and beaten. See Nye told her no, she wasn't right for the job. But she refused to leave, not without a good, hard whipping. What could See Nye and I do when she flattened herself into the passionate likes of a dead bed bug before us, on our clean, newly tiled floor yet?

The first food we gave to Jun Tou, she guiltily passed onto the boy. See Nye and I could have said no, but instead, we both watched, in rapt fascination, as her rice disappeared into his spongy little mouth. So this is what it is like to be a mother.

Later, while See Nye scowled, I tucked them all into a bed of straw outside, under the stairs to the Master's quarters.

"Wow," I remarked, I just didn't think, that the care and feeding of my little foundling would be so complicated. See Nye rolled her eyes.

"Don't forget, tomorrow morning," She wrathfully reminded me, who had indeed forgotten, "the male louts who would rent this woman's weeping teats, will come early to negotiate her price."

To the stone bench, in the middle of the courtyard, I shall go then, with a large bowl of sweet, steamy rice wine. There, I sup and wait for its first, exhilarating flush through my world weary body. Tiny coconut oil wicks on either side of me; their flickering flame doing nothing to dispel the darkness around me.

The wind's hot and humid tonight. Its sighs rustle the tough vegetation around me. I feel the heaviness of stone gathering dead weight in my chest, overtaking my heart. It terrifies me because I cannot breathe;

I soon gasp for air. I have no choice then. I have to get the wine down quickly. Stone, paper, scissors—wine melts stone. I slurp like a mad woman then, spilt liquor drenching my lap.

This is way I quicken myself. This is the way I flee, by flinging myself into the bird flightness of lightness of being. Even as See Nye and I both willingly lock ourselves into the kitchen and storeroom at night. Paradox slay us, titter, titter, titter, for if I am to be the oil vat and she, the rice bin, Yummy, you be the little pickle jar! Just not the leftover crabmeat, kay? Not in this putrid heat! Altogether now, press our buttocks firmly, widely against the hard mud floor! And shut our vat-rat-cat-twats! It is imperative that we keep ourselves under wraps, out of reach, cleanly screened and bonded from all manner of flies and undeserving food snatchers. Here, in the chicken coop of our imagination, we must all remain untouched, unstirred and uneatened by the vixen. No, not even the Master's quarters, with its fancy, wraparound verandah and impressive porticos, is as safe for groceries like us.

My master, Merchant Man Wing Him, bought me, Lee Lily, a virgin courtesan from my brothel owner. And See Nye's bid for the job of wiping a whore's ass was the highest by far. Six months of garnished wages to a middleman wasn't so bad a price to pay, all things considered, See Nye said so, herself.

She was thirty eight; I was fifteen. She was as ruddy and ugly as a cooked crab and I, as fresh and tender as a white leek stalk. We didn't have much in common, but as a dish, in aroma, taste, texture and color, we complimented each other to delectatious perfection.

She was a rival Hokkien whereas I was the Cantonese foe. In the daily dogfights between us fragmented Chinese, she and I really shouldn't have become the close allies, which we did become. But, by tiny sparks of longstanding feuds and and great flames of xenophobia, See Nye and I, both being lone female survivors in a traumatized world, as aforementioned, were already cooked!

Lydia Kwa

Eczema

In the hallway outside the doctor's office, there were two rickety rattan chairs. I sat in one while Papa was inside with Dr Hu. A dead cockroach was under the other chair. Mommy would not approve if she were here.

"Natalie, come in," intoned the doctor from behind the frosted glass door.

My fingers were itchy, all ten of them red from scratching. The skin was peeling off, like the bark of the jambu tree in the garden. I shuffled in slowly, rubbing my hands against my dark burgundy shorts. Both Papa and Dr Hu rose up from their seats. The doctor's fingers curled tightly around a long object on his desk. He picked it up, and I saw its thin, golden blade flash in front of the desk lamp. He pointed it at me.

"If you don't stop peeling your fingers, I'll have to chop them off!" His mouth was a fiery gaping hole in his face.

I blinked at the glint of the letter opener. Everything else in the room fell away into a blur. The chairs, the pictures on the wall.

Papa's voice boomed, "Natalie, you better listen to the doctor." He came towards me and tugged at my arm, dragging me closer to the doctor. He said to the doctor, "Look at how ugly it is."

Papa grabbed my wrists to expose my hands, palms up. Dr Hu peered down at them, the sides of his mouth turned down in disapproval. I tried to count the beads of sweat that lined the high forehead. He made a short grunting sound and turned back towards his desk. He put down the letter opener, grabbed a pen, and started to scribble on a piece of paper. When he had finished, he hesitated for a moment, then reached into one of the drawers, rummaged around, and produced a small tube half the length of a tube of toothpaste.

"Take this and follow the instructions," he stated to Papa.

When we got home, Papa handed me the tube of cream, then he locked up the scooter. He fished around in his shirt pocket for the piece of paper, stared at it for a few seconds, and turned his gaze down at me. "Doctor said to put this on your fingers three times a day."

"What is it, Papa?"

"For your eczema."

"Eck-see-mah. What's that?"

"Your fingers! They have eczema."

We walked up the path that cut through the front yard to the house. A lot more jambus had fallen from the tree, their red and white bodies eaten through by worms. I could see where they'd been eaten, the brown holes. My hands throbbed. Eczema was eating my fingers away. Or would the doctor have to chop them off?

There was a sudden gust of wind. I looked up at the sky. Dark, fast-moving clouds. Maybe a storm tonight. I'd overheard my parents talking about last week's accident, a young girl killed by lightning under a large frangipani tree in Upper Serangoon. I imagined myself under the jambu tree, bolts of lightning seeking me out because of my ugly hands. I shivered and ran into the house.

Upstairs on the second floor of the house, behind Kong Kong and Mah Mah's bedroom, Mommy was in the kitchen ironing. I went into our bedroom and placed the tube of cream on the dressing table, slipping it behind the makeup set. The room was a mess because we were moving out next week. Some of our things were already in boxes, but we hadn't finished packing yet. Papa was tired of having fights with Uncle downstairs and Simon two houses away. I was happy we were moving. A new home on Tanjong Katong Road.

I sat down on the edge of our bed and thought about this worm called "eczema." I remembered the stump at the end of a beggar's arm. That young boy who sat in front of the big Catholic church on Aljunied Road Saturday afternoons, with his tin cup and a crumbled photo of himself even younger in a nice sailor suit. I stopped to look at the photo one day when my parents and I were on our way to a restaurant near the church. In that photo he was about the same age as me.

Six or seven. I couldn't tell if he still had his hand under that suit, because the sleeves fell well past where his hands were supposed to be. Was his hand gone because his doctor had to take it off? Or maybe something like eczema had eaten it away. I curled up my body and pretended I was on the street with a tin cup, begging for food and sympathy. I squished up my face in expressions of pain and despair.

Papa came up the long flight of stairs, his steps slow and heavy. I tiptoed to the door and looked down the corridor to the kitchen.

"What is it, Gordon?"

He groaned and sighed, his bad mood showing. "Dr Hu warned Natalie. Shame on me, to have a daughter like this." I could see the right side of his face. His upper lip was drawn back, revealing his yellow front teeth.

"What do you mean, 'warn'?"

"The doctor told her he's going to cut off her fingers if she doesn't stop peeling the skin." He laughed, his belly heaving.

"Gordon, that's not funny!" She stopped her ironing, placed the iron upright, and glared at him.

"Oh come on. Just a little scare. He's joking," he whispered to her, as he planted the scooter helmets on the side table next to the food cupboard. He smiled, looking more relaxed all of a sudden.

I drew away from the door. My right pinky began to twitch. I looked at it. There were tiny circles inside, eyes trapped under the skin. The more I stared at them, the bigger those eyes grew and the more there were of them. They were on all ten fingers, up to the first or second joint. They stared back at me, trying to tell me something, but I didn't know what. It always felt good to scratch and break the little eyes, but this made the skin very red and then eventually I had to peel it off. I sat down on the bed. I didn't understand why Dr Hu would joke about my fingers. Why did Papa think it was funny? More itching. I extended my fingers out. Sometimes this helped with the itching. I began to think about the girl who was struck by lightning. A horrible feeling crept into my belly. I saw myself burnt to a crisp, like a piece of blackened toast, but my fingers stood out, swollen and red with the eczema. I jumped out of bed and grabbed the tube. There was some writing on the label which I couldn't read. The tube was shiny with a silvery sheen, like a rocket out of a comic book. It must be expensive. I twisted off the cap and squeezed the tube. I kept squeezing yet nothing came out. Why wasn't it easy like toothpaste? Then I noticed there was no hole where it was supposed to come out.

"Natalie, what are you doing?" Mommy came into the room and squatted down next to me. "Come, I do it." She turned the tube around to look at the label, then she took one end of the cap and pushed it hard into the top of the tube. There was a popping sound. A thick white substance oozed out. It looked like a deliciously fat worm. I sniffed it. Smelled nice. Mommy rubbed the cream all over my fingers. It covered up the redness and made my fingers look very pale. Funny, I thought, one worm to cover up another.

Papa entered the room. He glared at Mommy. "You spoil our girl. That's why her fingers are like that."

"Spoil? If I don't take care of her, who will?"

My fingers flared up with itchiness. I hid them behind my back, one hand grasping the other, and scratched frantically. Papa jerked his head towards me. His eyes widened.

"What are you doing?"

He took a few big strides towards me. His body arched over mine, as I crouched on the bed. He reached behind me to grab my right hand and twisted the arm up into the air, then did the same with the other.

"Not so rough!" Mommy pleaded.

Papa's voice sank to a low whisper. "She needs to be taught a lesson. Spare the rod and spoil the child."

He gripped both my wrists together with his left hand and dragged me across the room. The rough edges of the packing boxes scraped at my legs. I tried to twist my arms free but Papa was much too strong. He stretched his right hand up to the top of the armoire and brought down the rattan cane. He began with my legs, exposed between shorts and sandals. Then my arms and hands. The peeling skin on my fingers was opened up further by the lashes. I gasped from the sharp, stinging pain. Tears fell from my eyes as I listened to the swishing of the cane. Something strange happened next. I began to watch my body being caned, as if I was somewhere else, hidden in a safe corner. Long welts appeared on my arms and legs. Was that Mommy pleading and crying? I couldn't see where she was. She was very far away, calling out to me from the other end of a long tunnel. I heard her sobs rise and fall away. I caught glimpses of Papa's face. It was covered with sweat and his eyes were large with anger. He kept chanting, "You shamed me, you shamed me."

After Papa finished, he flung the rattan cane down and walked out of the room. I heard him in the bathroom, the tap water running. It seemed to go on forever, that gurgling water sound, while I lay on the floor looking down at my hands. I sat up slowly and stared down at my T-shirt. Tiny spots of blood splattered over its whiteness. I pulled my hands in towards my chest. I shivered. My body was like a stone, cold and hard. A stone wanting to belong in some river, where the water would rush in a continuous torrent over me and take away the blood and the stinging pain.

Mommy lifted me up and carried me to bed. The room had grown much darker. She switched on the light. The glare was too much, so I closed my eyes. I felt her cool hands gingerly touch my wrists. She helped me out of the shirt, and put a clean one on me. Next came the sensation of something very light and soft covering my fingers. I opened my eyes and looked down. She had covered up my fingers with Purol medicated powder. Pus was slowly seeping through, mixing with the powder until my fingers looked like mushy dough. I thought of the beggar boy. Maybe he would collect enough money someday to get a new hand. My fingers throbbed, as if they were going to burst open again.

I sat in the back seat of Esther's black Volkswagen holding up my fingers against the crimson vinyl upholstery. My fingers were still covered in powder, but pus kept leaking out. Mommy was next to me. She leaned over and whispered, "Never mind, no one will know." She must have guessed that I was worried.

We were going to Telok Ayer Quay. Pastor's eldest daughter, Esther, was going to Australia to study. Her brother Simon was driving us to the Quay, with Esther in the front passenger seat, and I wedged in between Papa and Mommy in the back. Everyone from the church would be at the Quay to send Esther off. Everyone would see my fingers and know. It was going to be worse than being struck by lightning. At least if I was dead, I wouldn't have to see people's looks of disgust when they saw how ugly my hands were.

Eczema. Why did it spare other people's hands? Was it something that came out of the air, or maybe the water, and sneaked into my hands when I wasn't looking? One thing for sure, it drew my father's anger the way that girl drew lightning so rapidly to her waiting body.

The street lamps on Nicoll Highway were just coming on. As the car drew closer to Telok Ayer Quay, I could make out the lit silhouettes of ships in the distant harbour. I brought my fingers up close to my nose and sniffed. The way great-grandma's dog Lucy always sniffed at me. The smell was like raw, wet earth. It made me think of the time I sneaked out into the front garden in the pouring rain, when Papa and Mommy were out, and Mah Mah had fallen asleep thinking I was still lying beside her under the mosquito net.

When we got to the Quay there was no crowd there. The Pastor and his wife had already arrived and were smiling at everyone. There was only one other family from church, the Hos, with their children Cherry and Linus. I didn't want to play with them, especially Linus. He was bigger than me and a bully. Once, when Mommy brought me over to their place, Linus said something nasty to me when we were alone in his room. He said I wasn't really my parents' daughter, and they'd paid very little money to get me. I was angry so I pushed him onto the bed and tried to pull his hair out. His stupid hair with the fake curl in front.

I sneaked a look at everyone then kept my eyes down. I could see the dark water between the boards on the wharf. I hid my hands in my pockets. They were burning hot instead of itchy. I wanted to slap Linus so badly. I ran up the gangplank behind Papa and Mommy and was lifted up onto the ship by a tall man with curly red hair.

What a nice place the ship was! We gasped as we followed Esther and the porter to her cabin. Lamps looking like full moons shone out from the walls instead of the ceiling, and red cushions made out of some very soft cloth were stuck to the long seats. We wandered around a while through the hallway, then a loud horn sounded. Papa and Mommy shook hands with Esther. Mr. and Mrs. Ho, Cherry and Linus did that too. No one asked me to shake hands with them, so I was glad. I hid behind Mommy. Pastor and his wife patted Esther awkwardly on the back and shoulders and said, "May the good Lord bless you!"

"Natalie, go say goodbye to Esther." My father smiled down at me. He gripped my shoulder firmly, nudging me to walk towards Esther. I forced a grin and wondered what to say. Then I remembered that TV show with the men on the ship, *McHale's Navy*. So I mumbled, "Goodbye, Esther. Anchors away."

Esther laughed, her lovely white teeth showing through her red lips.

"Oh, very good. Never mind, don't force her, Mr. Ng. Natalie's just shy."

After we got off the ship, we waited until it finally pulled away from the wharf. I watched the large shape slip away into the far darkness. If I had hidden away on the ship, I would be on my way to Australia with Esther now. Everyone walked back to the parking lot. Simon was leaning against his sister's car, a cigarette in his hand. He scowled when he saw us and threw down his cigarette.

I was walking along the street late at night. Which was the right way home? It was so quiet. There was no one else around to ask. Then I saw the gorilla lumbering towards me. It looked like my toy, except it was very much bigger than me. I turned and ran. It wasn't long before I could feel its hot breath against the back of my neck. My legs gave way just as I neared a fork in the road. I fell to the ground. My heart pounded louder and harder until it began to sound like a hammer. I couldn't get up. I turned my head and saw a huge paw swing towards me. It was covered with fur but its joints were spurting large drops of blood down at my face.

I screamed. I went on screaming until the images melted away, and I woke up in the bed, my body soaked in sweat. I was next to Mommy, who was sandwiched between me and Papa. She woke up with a start, and began to shake me. "Stop, Natalie, stop!" I sat up. My father stirred slightly and muttered something. He turned onto his side and continued snoring.

After Mommy went back to sleep, I stayed awake a long time. I listened to my parents slip back into their separate worlds of sleep. In the dark, I could still make out the fuzzy shapes of half-packed boxes. My clothes and toys were in some of those boxes. How far could I carry one box? Quite far, if I balanced it carefully on my head. Just like that picture of a milkmaid that was on all the cans of condensed milk. I would keep on walking until someone found me somewhere in Katong, maybe even Changi, the box on my head balanced perfectly like a milk can. Then that nice person would take me out for a nice meal, and put me in a soft bed after. A bed with red cushions like the ones on the ship. I looked at Papa and Mommy again.

If only eczema could go away. Maybe then Papa would stop being angry at me. I couldn't remember when it was that Papa changed. The

Papa of the early photos, the one who let me take my first baby steps on his chest, the one who smiled as he held me gently in his arms. He'd become another person, the one who loomed over me, as dark as the room, as dark as the shadow of Mommy's sleeping body. He always loomed. Why did Mommy have to sleep through the worse things, except if there was a loud noise?

Maybe photos were lies. Like that crumpled photo of the beggar boy. Everyone smiles when their pictures are taken. Wasn't it Papa who sneaked around to my side of the bed late at night, whose hairy arm woke me up with its touching? Weren't those his hands which held mine over his wet and sticky thing? No photo of that. Maybe he will be happier after we have moved to our own flat. Out of Kong Kong and Mah Mah's big house. Away from Uncle. It was all eczema's fault.

I didn't want to fall asleep. That gorilla was waiting to chase me. What could I do? I got out of bed and quietly made my way to the dressing table. My hands carefully felt the surface until they found the tube. This time it was easier to squeeze the white cream out. I covered my fingers with the good worm. I sat in the corner, leaning against the armoire, my knees drawn up to my body. I waited. As long as I stayed awake, I would be alright. As long as I kept putting on the cream, there was a chance the eczema would go away.

Andy Quan

Ants

Jerry is washing the dishes in his particular noiseless way: the soft sounds of water and soap, the dull thud of a rinsed plate touching the rubber-coated dish rack or the washcloth laid over the porcelain counter. His hands, sheathed in bright pink gloves, never allow a piece of cutlery to hit another, two pots to clang. It's a buzz of activity without sound.

From his vantage point, Jerry can see outside to the narrow space that runs up alongside his modest house to the fence dividing his yard from the neighbour's—the lazy ones next door whom he can't quite figure out, as opposed to the nice, elderly couple on the other side whom he asks to collect his mail if he goes out of town. The fence is painted a dull red—fire engine, he supposes, when it was new, but now that it is peeling and worn, he's not sure what to call it. He remembers being singularly unimpressed with his last visit to the hardware store to find paint for the bathroom. How many names did they have for off-white? It was the colours, not the names that were important.

He looks at the fence with disgust. He's been observing it for weeks. Any time that's light enough, he can see ants crawling along the scored surface of the fence posts. What are they after? Where did they come from? While he's rather partial to nature documentaries, nothing he's watched has given him insight into this.

He'd really been disgusted when he first saw a trail of ants crossing from a tiny gap in the window to a row of canisters filled with flour, sugar, and pasta. They'd reached the sugar, which he threw out, disliking the wastage. Good. Jerry had swept them efficiently into the sink and, as an afterthought, turned the water to scalding hot to wash them down the drain. He wiped the rest of the area with a bit of vinegar and bleach, but didn't know what else to use to stop their invasion. He wet a paper towel, folded it, opened the window, put the towel where he thought they were getting in, and shut the window tight.

That was the start of it really: the war against the ants, but more so, the deterioration of this living-together arrangement with Mick. He had foreseen it not working out in any case, but really, if Mick didn't do something soon, this was the end.

It was never really a good idea. Jerry had been living on his own in the house since the breakup with Joe three years ago, a house which still half belonged to Joe—they hadn't quite worked out what to do with it. It wasn't that Jerry liked living on his own, but he had certainly gotten used to it. Mick was unexpected. Jerry wasn't interested at all in dating and relationships. How could you ever replace something that was twelve years long? Why would you even bother?

So they hadn't really talked much the first few times they met. Sure, the restaurant Mick had suggested after a meeting or two in the bar was more formal than Jerry had expected, but still they hadn't really *talked* there. The conversation that was now happening was mostly in bed: lively, not one-sided, a little challenging even, but in a good way.

Jerry felt as though someone were watching them speak. It wasn't *exactly* as if Joe, Jerry's ex, was in the room, but his presence was certainly there: a photo of the two of them on the bedside table; the mirror in which Jerry admired the shape of Mick's arse—a gift from Joe's sister; the condoms which were Joe's favourite brand and then favoured by them both.

Mick hadn't seemed to notice.

There didn't seem to be similar evidence in Mick's small apartment in what Jerry thought was an extremely ugly utilitarian building. But maybe Mick didn't have time to leave his mark on the space. From what Jerry had gathered, he'd had a much nicer apartment before, until his business partner had ripped him off and left him in debt, his apartment mortgaged, legal proceedings underway, an outstanding bill which the lawyer was letting him pay in installments. Mick had borrowed money from his brother, reopened a smaller shop, and moved into the apartment, which he hadn't spent much time thinking about whether he liked; he just needed somewhere to stay.

"So, how's lighting?"

"Bright. How's mobiles?"

"Mobile."

That was their routine in their second month of dating—in their first month, they seldom talked about their jobs. But as the details were exchanged, Jerry was impressed by the entrepreneurship of the small businessman, in Mick's case, someone running a shop that sold lamps and lighting. Mick in turn was impressed by Jerry's ability to deal with the machinations of a customer-service branch of a large mobile-phone company.

At the same time, Jerry was impatient with Mick's long hours, and his involvement in details that Jerry was sure someone more junior could take care of. And Mick, proud to be his own boss, was unsure how Jerry managed to take orders from a young hotshot, or from all the other layers of management that seemed to exist.

Still, they respected each other in an adult way, a distant way, when they talked of each other's professions or personal lives. It was a different relationship than what Jerry was used to. He and Joe had been like best friends and brothers and lovers and every other category all rolled into one. Mick didn't seem to be used to anything: he was one of those gay men who had been married for years—eight, in his case; two children, grown up, whom he saw regularly; one or two relationships of a few years' duration in his thirties. Almost the reverse of Jerry, who had a few longish but not long relationships before meeting Joe at thirty-five and guessing that they'd spend the rest of their lives together.

Jerry is still wiping the counters of the kitchen when Mick emerges from the shower, his towel wrapped around his waist, but his hair and torso still wet. He looks up in surprise.

"Phone call. I promised Maire that I'd call her at exactly seven and it's seven now." He grabs the telephone off the wall from its holder.

"Finish your shower. You're dripping on the floor."

"No, she doesn't have a mobile, she has to leave soon and . . . Never mind, I'll explain later." Mick dials the number and turns his back to Jerry as he listens to the ring tone.

Jerry looks at Mick's back, lean and long. There is a perfect twin crevasse on either side of his spine and beads of water from the shower cling there like a string of pearls. Jerry presses himself gently against Mick's back, feeling the moisture come off onto his dress shirt. Mick continues talking with Maire but reaches back absently with his left hand to touch Jerry's thigh. Jerry, holding Mick lightly around the waist, leans away with his upper body to watch his lover's back dry completely in the air.

Mick finishes the call and goes to put his clothes on. He has surprisingly few possessions, or so it seems to Jerry, though Mick has explained that there are various boxes and pieces of furniture with his brother. When he left his wife, Jerry had explained, he'd felt so guilty that he'd taken nothing with him. It was a pattern that he still carried with him. How much does one need to live with anyway?

Still, Jerry wonders whether he wouldn't be more comfortable with a few more things of Mick around. He doesn't want to feel as though Mick were a boarder. They sleep in the same bed, but so far Mick's clothes are in the spare room, some of them hung up, and some of them lying across the bed. Should he invite him into his closet too, as well as his home?

Jerry was the one who'd made the suggestion: a combination of utility (typical of Jerry) and spontaneity (very unusual).

"How are you going to find time to find an apartment?" he'd asked. It was meant in earnest since Mick's new shop was taking long hours to get everything running smoothly.

"I'll find time," replied Mick, detecting something in Jerry's voice.

"But I've not seen you a lot the last two weeks."

"Your work hasn't been much less busy."

"I know."

"And I don't have much of a choice, you know it was a short-term lease. Maire's got a friend who finds good rental units, and I'm hoping I can promote the new boy at the shop to assistant manager."

"Maybe you should try to find somewhere close to me."

"Uh, OK."

"How about really close?"

"How close do you mean?"

"I've got that extra room, and there's more than enough space in the house. It doesn't have to be permanent." Jerry taps his chin with his finger twice. "But I think it would be sensible."

"Are you asking me to move in with you?"

"No. Not really. I guess, technically yes, but it's just to make things easier for you, and probably for us..."

"Only lesbians move in together so quickly," remarked Mick, and Jerry relaxed into laughter. He wondered, What have I done?

"Mick," he now asks, "did you get something for the ants? I thought you said you'd get it this week."

"Oh. Sorry." Mick hits his head with his palm in a comic gesture. "I keep forgetting."

"This week?"

"You know how forgetful I am."

Not really, thinks Jerry. Mick notices the expression on Jerry's face and matches it with one of equal incomprehension.

While this incident stays with Jerry, it doesn't seem to with Mick, who offers a different excuse the next week. "A delivery was late and..." What is wrong with him? It doesn't make sense for Jerry to get whatever that needs getting—Mick has the head for hardware sorts of things and there are no hardware stores or supermarkets around where Jerry works in the city. And really, it's one of the few things that Jerry has specifically asked Mick to do, and he's going to stick with it. They are living together after all.

"Is everything OK?" asks Mick after a session of love making which, while satisfactory, was missing something.

"Yes. Fine." Jerry answers a little too quickly.

"If you want me to pay more rent, I've already offered."

"Don't be silly."

"I know I've been busy. Let's go to a movie this week."

"I'd prefer going out to dinner."

Jerry doesn't know why he's so snappy lately. He doesn't think it's like him, though his coworkers would say he's been like that some weeks. This has been going on for a while though. It's not as if he's invested a lot in this relationship. He'd basically given up on finding someone. He hardly met anyone his own age, and younger men were fine for sex but not relationships. He'd been living long enough in Sydney and he seemed to know most of the men in the bars, if not by name, at least by face. Mick showing up at the backyard BBQ of someone Jerry didn't even know that well; the fact that they seemed to hit it off both on a mental and physical level; and that they'd successfully arranged a date for afterwards, seemed really, looking back at it, a bit improbable.

"You didn't have to do that." Mick points to the bedside table.

Jerry asks absentmindedly, "Do what?"

"You've put away the photo of you and Joe." The absent space on the table. "If you want to do that, that's great, but you don't have to do that for me."

"I just thought it would be..." Jerry's not quite sure what the end of the sentence is. He'd never put away the photo before. Even when he'd planned for someone to spend the evening, he'd considered it a point of pride to keep the photo there and explain later if asked. "That's my ex. We were together twelve years." Come to think of it, he'd perhaps said this to Mick the first time they'd had sex. Maybe this was why Mick was pointing it out.

"You were together for a long time, Jerry. It's natural to have reminders."

As if the bed, mirror, house weren't reminders enough. As if Mick was the type of person to carry around reminders, Jerry thinks with sarcasm. "Okay," he answers out loud. A flush of blood hits the lower parts of his body and he awkwardly tackles Mick back into bed.

"Hey, hey... Mmmmm..." replies Mick.

Things go smoothly and then not so smoothly, according to Jerry. They're coming up to three months of living together, which makes it nearly nine months since they met. Gestation. How did older men like themselves manage to do something that younger and inexperienced men do, like move in together so quickly? Mick doesn't even seem to be fussed by it all. Is he just like this all the time, natural when alone, natural when together? He glides in and out of the house. They make time for each other, sometimes successfully, other times not. He sees his own friends but they've met some, if not all, of each other's inner circles. Jerry's seems to quite like Mick, and Mick's is happy that Mick seems happy and content with Jerry.

"He's a bit uptight sometimes," Mick tells his oldest friend Maire, "but I like that. He reminds me of my mother."

"Eww. You're dating your mother?" is Maire's response, though she quite likes Jerry herself.

"You did move in together a bit suddenly," counsels Brett, Jerry's oldest friend. "He's nice." He lets that hang in the air. "And sexy."

Jerry says nothing. He's trying to decide whether he really minds that Mick put his toenail clippings into the potted plants in the back garden. And he seems to leave water to pool around the edges of the bathroom sink without wiping it up. And couldn't he do the dishes just a bit more often instead of just the drying? Maybe what it really comes down to is the toothpaste tube being squeezed from the middle. Surely he must notice that Jerry squeezes it from the end each time, so that the tube is full and unblemished, no matter how much paste is left. And what about those ants?

"I don't remember you having problems living together with Joe," Brett comments.

On the anniversary of the breakup of Jerry and Joe, Jerry is preparing steak, something thick and formerly bloody, something to cook through until it's well done, though he'll leave Mick's a bit rarer, the way he likes it. Jerry's managed to leave work unusually early. He shut down his computer, swept his briefcase up into his left arm, and walked out before anyone could notice. He'd been avoiding talking to people all day anyway. On the way home, he used his mobile phone to call Mick, to tell him he'll cook tonight, can he be home by seven p.m.?

"Where's the wine?" He looks up at Mick from the plum tomatoes he's slicing up for a salad.

"Sorry, I didn't bring any. You didn't ask," answers Mick, a bit defensively.

"Well, we don't have any. Can you run back out to the bottle shop?" Jerry asks, in an efficient tone.

"Sure." Mick throws his jacket on a chair and reverses direction. He senses that it's not a good time for discussion but knows that there is wine in the house and is perplexed at the flawlessly spoken lie. He often brings a bottle home when they'll be dining in, but tonight he didn't.

When Mick returns a few minutes later, the steaks are laid out on plates, the salad in a bowl between them, wine glasses and cutlery in place. "Thanks. Looks great," he says grimly.

Jerry blurts out then that this was the day three years ago when Joe had moved out of the house, to a friend's "to think," and that the relationship from then on had ceased. "I told you about the breakup, didn't I?" asks Jerry with doleful eyes.

"Yes, you did," replies Mick, returns the glance, then looks down at his plate. "The salad looks good. What dressing did you put on it?"

Jerry sees the evening ahead of him with perfect prescience. He will talk about Joe some more, because he needs to talk about Joe. Mick will listen, change the topic, and listen again before he suggests that they both talk about something else.

"Oh, just a little olive oil. And some balsamic vinegar. Nothing much."

This is it. He's told Mick a dozen times to do something about this, and he's sure that Mick's gotten the picture. Their local supermarket is sure to have something, and there's a hardware store not far away either. Jerry even left a curt note on the counter as he'd left for a swim. "PLEASE DO SOMETHING ABOUT THE ANTS TODAY!!" The paper was gone by the time he returned, as was Mick. Had he forgotten that Jerry had an out-of-hours meeting with his colleague Mona today? Jerry had come home and then had to leave for the meeting before Mick returned—from shopping Jerry hoped, though he might have snuck in a workout at the gym.

Days like these are funny. How can you live with someone and not see them the whole day? It is like tag-team wrestling and neither one of the pair can be with the other inside the ring at the same time. Jerry stops at a traffic light, the last one before reaching home. If Mick hasn't done anything about the ants, Jerry will sit him down for a talk this week. He won't mention the ants, oh no, but he will talk about a number of other things that aren't working, and ask if they have really thought this through for Mick to move in. Maybe they are moving too fast. Maybe this just isn't working.

Before Jerry enters his home, he takes a quick deep breath and perks himself up to walk inside with determination and energy. He knows, right away, though, that Mick isn't in, there's an absence of his sound and smell. He drops his shoulders and changes his step to a lazy stride. He rounds the corner to the kitchen and sees a note on the table. "Had to return a videotape to Maire. Back at 7:30." How long does it take to return a videotape? Maire lives just ten minutes away. Jerry thinks, I'm too old for this.

There are grocery bags still on the kitchen counter. He doesn't see one that looks like it's from the hardware store. The perishables are all put away, and Jerry opens the refrigerator door, just to check. Eggs. Milk. Margarine. He steals a glance at the window, though he knows he'll need to stand right in front of the sink to see properly.

Would he have gotten some sort of ant poison? A spray or a powder? He must have done it. How would he have the gall not to, after being asked so many times? *This is it. I'm looking.* He steps across the kitchen. One-two-three. His arms on the counter, braced, as if expecting an earthquake.

There isn't one; but a strange shock goes through him as Jerry's vision focuses and sees the ants. More ants than before but not in their usual lines, instead a horizontal slightly tilted mass. *What did he . . . How did he . . .* Jerry scans the countertop and knows that the new shape has been left out there on purpose. It's even got a smile on it, this grinning plastic bear-shaped container with a yellow twist nozzle on top. Honey.

Jerry looks in amazement. Written in sweet, liquid lines on the fence in surprisingly neat block letters, connected to each other with the tiniest lines is:

I LOVE YO

That's all it says at the moment, though there seems to be an "I" in the making which might just transform into the proper letter, a pulsating many-legged symbol made of bee's labour and the spent fertility of wildflowers.

Jerry will look back later to see if the rest of the word has filled in.

David M Hsu

Prodigies: A History Lesson

At the age of four, I made one of the worst mistakes of my life and for it I had nobody to blame but myself and the Public Broadcasting Service. PBS preempted *Sesame Street* late one evening to cover an important piano recital direct from Vienna. If I had known better, I would have closed my eyes and run out of the room, but instead, young and foolish, I drew closer to the fire. Interest piqued, I stayed and watched a series of black tuxedos dazzle the audience with tantalizing displays of piano virtuosity. When the performance ended, I announced to my parents that I wanted to play the piano.

*

The company Steinway and Sons was founded in 1853 by Henry Engelhard Steinway in New York City. Steinway was a master carpenter in Sessen, Germany, but potato famines had ravaged the German economy into such a depression that in 1849, along with millions of other Europeans who moved across the Atlantic, Steinway and his sons arrived in New York City seeking a new fortune building pianos. The first piano they built, no. 483, original retail price of five hundred dollars, now sits in the Metropolitan Museum of Art's Instrument room.

*

When I was six years old, I went to a professional hockey game for the first time. My father had gotten a pair of tickets from a colleague at work and together, the two of us made the pilgrimage to Maple Leaf Gardens in downtown Toronto. The Leafs were playing the Capitals that night in a wholly insignificant and unremarkable regular season game. The arena left us chilled beneath our jackets and the players appeared miniscule from my vantage point high above in the grays. The urinals in the building resembled sinks and we left the building with five minutes still to go in the third period so as to avoid a traffic jam. None of that mattered though, for I was hooked. The next day, I announced to my parents that I wanted to play ice hockey. Nothing happened.

*

Wolfgang Amadeus Mozart never had the fortune to play on a Steinway, nor did he play ice hockey, but by age six, he had showed his first musical compositions to his father who, observing the child's obvious genius, became overcome with emotion. That year, his family took him and his sister on a musical tour that included Munich, where he played in the court of Empress Maria Theresa and Joseph II, the future Emperor of Rome both of whom took much delight in his visit. After I started learning the piano, my father, a history buff, started telling me stories such as this one about Mozart.

*

My piano teacher, Mrs Lee, had the sort of tragic Chinese life story that Amy Tan writes books about. Back in China, she'd been a high level concert pianist and her husband a highly respected neurosurgeon. The cultural revolution, though, saw to it that people of their kind had no place in China, and they fled to Canada as a result. Here, not only did her husband lose his license to practice medicine and end up having to set up shop as just another Chinese herbalist, but she was forced to become a lowly piano teacher, giving weekly hour-long lessons to tone-deaf brats like myself.

*

On the weekends, my father took my sister and me to the public library near our house. There, he'd sit and read the few Chinese news magazines the library stocked, while we busied ourselves with the children's section. Now, with hockey on the brain, I began to make a beeline for the sports section. Dewey decimal number 796.06. Ice hockey. I devoured all books on the subject, first in the children's section, and then through to the adults' section in the other part of the library. I read the same books as grown men two, three times my age.

It was through these readings that I encountered Wayne Gretzky.

Universally recognized as the best hockey player in the world, he played in Edmonton for the Oilers and I didn't get to see much of him here in Toronto. Still, there existed an overabundance of books with the Dewey number 796.962 G at the library to keep me satisfied. G for Great. I read these books studiously, memorized his accomplishments with the rigor normally reserved for times tables and stocked up on colourful anecdotes about the man's life. For instance, when Wayne was barely a year old, his father had laid out a thin sheet of ice in the backyard of their Brantford, Ontario, home for the son to learn to skate. The men at the hardware store had looked on incredulously as his father purchased a lawn sprinkler in the dead of winter, but it was essential if you wanted the ice to be sufficiently smooth. From these humble beginnings, a Canadian legend was born. I told my father this story, but ever pragmatic, he only laughed. "A sprinkler in the winter? That would make the pipes explode!"

*

Every day, after Ninja Turtles but before dinner, I practised the piano. I sat there on the hard, wooden, rectangular piano bench in front of our piano and did my best not to squirm and fidget while running through the pieces my teacher had selected for me that week. One, two, three times through each piece. Then on to scales. Again, one, two, three times each, through C major, D major, E major and so on. I learned quickly that the faster I whipped through the scales and pieces, the sooner practice would end and so I stormed through my practices imbued with the ferocious intensity of a young Beethoven. The whole time, my mind was elsewhere, perhaps the street hockey game going on out on the street or the Leafs game on television later that night. Somewhere else, anywhere else. Then, as soon as I'd passed the minimum practice requirements, the keyboard lid shut and I left to conquer new worlds.

*

Sometimes my dad would take note of my practices and point out to me that as a child, Mozart had practiced the piano eight, ten hours a day. He also told me that as a thirteen-year-old, Mozart had sat down to listen to *Miserere*, a choral work of which copying of the transcript had long been forbidden, and having listened to the piece only twice he had been able to write out the nine-part work perfectly on a piece of paper hidden in his hat. I grimaced but I appreciated the story. Truly, the man was not of my world.

*

Today, though it accounts for fewer than three percent of the pianos sold in the United States, and one percent of the worldwide market, Steinway represents the pinnacle in piano-building achievement. Over ninety percent of concert pianists play exclusively on Steinways (in its heyday, this figure was up over ninety-eight percent). To put this in perspective, Louisville Slugger baseball bats are used by only sixty percent of Major League players. Furthermore, a concert-level grand piano costs in the neighbourhood of 125 to 150 thousand dollars, and the most expensive piano ever sold was of course a Steinway, an Alma Tadema Steinway from the 1880s that fetched 1.2 million dollars at Christy's in London.

In just over a hundred years of existence, the Steinway company has entrenched itself not only in the concert world, but also in the popular imagination as the maker of the best pianos. The main piano in the White House is a Steinway, and celebrities like Martha Cook and Eleanor Roosevelt have all owned Steinways. Furthermore, thanks to the efforts of the Steinway company, the first company to advertise pianos regularly in the United States, pianos became a symbol of social standing and fostered the early twentieth-century image of the dainty, sweet woman as well versed in housekeeping as in Beethoven and Brahms.

*

Every day after school, when I wasn't on the piano, I was downstairs in the basement, whirling around the smooth cement floor on roller skates strapped to my sneakers, hockey stick in hand and a tennis ball at my feet. In these circumstances, the dark and danky basement transformed into the Montreal Forum, Maple Leaf Gardens, Chicago Stadium, Boston Garden, Madison Square Garden, even the Hartford Civic Centre if the schedule called for it. All of these places and more. I whizzed up and down the rink, sending pin point passes to my line mates, firing shots into the top corner of the net with deadly accuracy. I broke all the league's scoring records, setting marks even Wayne might never approach.

*

At the age of ten, I had become so dominant in my basement and in the street hockey games outside my house that I thirsted for more competition. I tried again, attempting to impress upon my parents the merits of taking up minor league hockey. Again, they steadfastly refused, "Absolutely not. Chinese people are too small to play such a rough sport. You'll get hurt out there. Remember the Lins? Their son Craig signed up to play ice hockey and ended up with half his teeth knocked out. Why don't you play soccer instead?" And so I spent a year unhappily as a fullback for a house league soccer team. It wasn't the same. The game moved too slowly, the ball was too big, the nets too wide and the goals too far and few between.

*

My father told me that by the age of thirteen, Mozart was famous. He'd already written sonatas, concertos, symphonies, religious works, and even some operas. He went about doing his best trying to collect said works so that our house would be filled with the great composer's presence. To that end, he accumulated an impressive set of Mozart LPs that sat next to a record of songs from the Cultural Revolution on our downstairs music rack. I never heard him listen to an individual record more than two or three times.

*

At the age of fourteen, Wayne Gretzky was a national celebrity. He'd already appeared on *This Country in the Morning* on CBC Radio with Peter Gzowski, on account of having scored an unprecedented 378 goals in a single sixty-eight game season as a junior against children several years older than him. From then on, the wait began. When would the boy go pro and when he did, how good would he become?

*

As part of the Royal Conservatory of Music's piano syllabus, I had to take other music classes that supplemented my piano lessons. These included rudimentary music theory, and later, harmony, history and counterpoint. Rudimentary music theory was easy, drawing notes and clef signs, learning how to write out scales and time signatures. Harmony, however, proved to a little more difficult. Chord progressions. Dominant cords, subdominant, diminished cords. What went where and why? To this day, I still don't know, but I managed to squeeze past the exam with a 60, just good enough to pass, mediocrity at its finest.

*

It wasn't long before my sister started playing the piano, following my footsteps. I found her playing maddeningly infuriating. The reason for this lay in the fact that in our old house, the piano and the television both sat in the family room, across from each other. One couldn't watch television while someone was on the piano. I had to sit through her practices with the television turned to mute, satisfied only to be watching the games that were taking place, if not to hear their sounds. My sister of course, was unaffected. She didn't like hockey.

*

In 1981-82, Wayne Gretzky, now fully grown and a superstar for the Edmonton Oilers, obliterated nearly every major National Hockey League scoring record. In his memoir, he attributes his tremendous season to the simple fact that, "I decided to try shooting more." He scored 50 goals in the season's first 39 games, eleven games faster than it had ever been done, and finished the season with 92, 16 more than had ever been scored in the sixty-seven year history of the league. He also became the first player to record 200 points (goals plus assists) in a season, with 212, and four years later he'd break even that record and finish with 215.

*

Having survived the rigors of musical harmony, I next had to take music history class. The text for this class was entitled *The Enjoyment of Music,* as if one needed to be taught pleasure. These classes covered music history, from the renaissance to the baroque, or was it the other way around? In any case, I had to sit down and memorize the names and life stories of a long list of composers as well as their notable accomplishments.

For Mozart, I learned that he composed the following: Orchestral music, including some 40 symphonies; concertos, including 5 for violin and 27 for piano; operas, of which *Don Giovanni*, *The Magic Flute*, and *The Marriage of Figaro* were the most significant; and an assortment of choral and chamber music.

Fortunately, my music history teacher, a classical music buff, taught me some things that weren't in the textbook. Apparently, Mozart spent a great deal of his life in bordellos and probably caught several sexually transmitted diseases. He went so far as to suggest that Mozart's delusions, portrayed so glaringly in the movie *Amadeus*, could easily have been the delusions of grandeur associated with syphilis. Needless to say, I didn't include such unsubstantiated claims when answering the exam question about Mozart.

*

In 1987, Wayne Gretzky was sold from the four-time Stanley Cup champions the Oilers to the Los Angeles Kings, a misfit club with a long history of futility that disturbingly didn't even play in Canada. Now, no longer surrounded by his great team mates, Wayne was asked to carry the Kings by himself. That spring, in the playoffs, he met his old friends from Edmonton in the first round and beat them in a thrilling, seven-game series in which he scored two goals in the final game. Five years later, Wayne would single-handedly carry the Kings to the Stanley Cup finals.

*

As I grew older, my piano accomplishments reached a plateau. Good enough now so that my parents could no longer follow what I played, I learned to hide not only my mistakes, but to cheat and employ trickery to shorten my practice times. Days would pass and pieces would be left untouched and sometimes even my piano teacher couldn't tell if I'd done my homework or not, lavishing praise on me for pieces I hadn't practised all week.

*

In his later years, Mozart struggled increasingly to regain the success that had come so easily as a child. The same people who had lavished praise on him as a child, now resented him for his past successes. He feuded openly with his patron, the archbishop of Salzburg, and split from him in 1781, thereby abandoning the traditional patronage system, chafing at the restrictions it had imposed upon him. Now he sought to establish a career on his own in the eighteenth-century music world, but this proved impossible even for a man of his talents. His music, though played to occasional acclaim, was for the most part too sophisticated for the Viennese public he wanted so badly to please, and it didn't help matters that he proved to be inept at managing money, spending his final years frail and languishing on the fringes of poverty.

Mozart died tragically at 35, his death consistent with rheumatic fever. He was virtually penniless. There were no mourners at his funeral as per Viennese tradition and it is said that it snowed and stormed on the day of the funeral. This last bit, in fact, was false. It was a calm and mild day the day they buried him. Evidently, even the gods didn't see fit to mourn his passing.

*

All the euphoria and prestige surrounding the Steinway Company have not come without controversy. By the 1960s, time-honoured production techniques had fallen on hard times, with many long-time craftsmen slowly replaced by new recruits off the street with no knowledge of pianos. Inevitably, the quality of the pianos suffered. As well, the painstaking craftsmanship by hand that had long been the company's hallmark was starting to show its age. It was amidst this uncertainty that the company was sold to media conglomerate CBS in 1972, and since then it has changed ownership two more times. As a result, for over thirty years, the world's pre-eminent piano company was taken over by people with no experience in the piano making industry. With these changes came further mechanization of the piano building process, which according to experts has further reduced the quality of the product.

In 1995, in what would have been an unheard of move, pianist Andre Watts, then of the New York Philharmonic, was so unhappy with his piano's sound that he went so far as to abandon the Steinway line and switch to a Yamaha concert piano, only to return to the fold a few years later, albeit not as a recognized "Steinway artist."

Now Steinway faces an uncertain future. The music world is notoriously fickle, and though Steinway still towers over its peers, its share of the concert world has been slowly dropping. Where it will go from here is anybody's guess.

*

I played ice hockey for the first time in university one winter when the city froze some parks and let kids roam free on the ice surfaces. There, with my ice skates and hockey stick in hand, I watched helplessly as ten- and twelve-year-olds whipped around me on the wing like I was a lead post. I spent half the time just trying not to fall face first into the ice, and by the end of the night I had sore muscles in places I hadn't even realized musculature existed. It didn't matter though; the exhilaration of being on the ice, legs churning and snow falling softly while I flew, albeit slowly, from one end to the other, was enough.

*

In 1999, now a member of the New York Rangers, Wayne Gretzky retired. He was almost forty years old and had played in nearly fifteen hundred games. In those games, he'd scored 894 goals and added 1,963 assists for a total of 2,857 points. All of these were records. To put that in perspective, the next highest point total belonged to Gordie Howe, whose 1,850 points were not only over a thousand points less than Wayne's, but were also less than Wayne's *assist* total. Needless to say, none of these records will be easily broken.

*

The same year Wayne retired from the NHL, I retired from the piano. I was eighteen years old and going into my last year of high school, when it was decided I'd be better off devoting my attention to my studies and trying to get into the university program of my choice than to spend another year languishing on the piano. By my rough estimate, over fourteen years, I must have spent roughly 175,000 minutes practising the piano at home and another 32,000 minutes at my piano teacher's house. None of these were records and for all my efforts, I was only able to complete Grade Ten of the Royal Conservatory of Music's Piano program with second degree honours.

Sometimes, I still open up the piano keyboard and play a few tunes, but my fingers usually feel like mush, and it takes too long to re-teach my fingers the fine movements that I flippantly disregarded as a child. There's not much point anyway; it would take me years to learn to play something truly impressive and if I have a hankering for good music, it's simply easier just to listen to a CD if I so choose.

I still have the piano though. I'm saving it because some day my kids will need something to learn to play on, and after all, it is a Steinway.

Edward Y C Lee

Into a Far Country

On the night Fei Jen fled the village, Grandfather gave her his finest brushes, made from the hair of goat, rabbit, weasel, and mountain pony. He told her to dry her tears; she would find many wondrous marvels to paint and draw in her new home across the sea. In the Gold Mountain, the rain glittered like shards of diamond, and the trees were so tall you could climb a week without reaching the top. The *lofan* were all giants, and they were the colour of corpses, buried in a winter grave.

Fei Jen heaved a sigh, shivering in the cold air. It was Sunday morning in late October, and the wind stank of fish and seaweed. She was high up, perched on the fourth branch of the red maple that grew beside the New Lotus Cafe on the corner of Main and Lovitt Streets.

Six weeks before, when she and the rest of the family arrived in Yarmouth to join Bah and Elder Brother Kai, the tree had been dense with fiery leaves of red and gold, each twice the span of her palm. Now the maple was bare, its bark coarse and dead beneath her thighs. The days were growing shorter; and the sun, on those rare occasions when it pierced the clouds, was a pale reflection of the one she remembered in her Chinese sky back home. Last night she had asked Mah to lay another blanket on the bed she shared with Elder Sister Sui Jen, but Elder Brother only laughed when she asked if this was the famous Gold Mountain winter, arrived prematurely.

Fei Jen chewed her pigtail and scanned the uneasy sky. From the tree, she could see deserted Main Street and its storefronts that hawked Coca-Cola (*"seven cents a bottle—easy on your purse!"*), halibut-and-chips dinners for fifty-five cents, and girls' dirndl skirts for one dollar forty-nine. A car, shaped like a giant tortoise, squatted by the curb. At the western end of Lovitt Street, where the town melted into the harbour, fishing boats rose and fell with the surf, their wooden hulls thumping in a mournful rhythm. Where were the diamonds? What giants? How could Grandfather have been so wrong? Dismayed, she shook her head. With all of Gold Mountain available, what demon had possessed Bah when he chose *Yah-moun*?

In Yarmouth every morning was the same! It rained, or it had just rained, or it was about to rain. It was always cold, and getting colder, and the dank Atlantic air seeped through everything she wore, even the shiny yellow slicker Elder Brother had given her three days after her arrival. "Here, try this on." There had been a wry smile on his face. "You're going to need it."

Thunder rumbled in the distance, and clouds scudded across the sky like an army of panicked crabs. Elder Brother had been right again. The rain was on its way. Soon she would have to go inside and do her chores. Fei Jen tucked her sketch pad and pencils into the pockets of her slicker.

Although Bah had forbidden their climbing the tree, she had resolved to reach the sixth branch up—one higher than Little Brother Ming had ever climbed—before the rains came down. A sudden gust of wind shook the treetops, and she grabbed for the trunk as cold dew splashed her face. Releasing one hand, she tugged her hood over her head. Under her slicker she wore her finest Sunday dress and her smooth-soled patent-leather shoes. Bah wanted her at her "most presentable" best that morning for her first visit to the *lofan* worship hall.

Two weeks before, Bah's friend, the *lofan* minister, had spoken to them in the New Lotus and invited the entire family to his church. Welcoming Fei Jen and Little Brother, the Reverend Weaver held out two leather-bound volumes with gold-leaf pages. "Children, I have gifts for you. These are Bibles."

Little Brother shrank behind Fei Jen as the man beckoned. The Reverend was tall, with elbows and knees like doorknobs, and his hands were as wide as dinner plates. His face was fearsomely pale with eyes like ice on water, and eyebrows so fair they faded against his forehead. Squeezing Little Brother's hand, Fei Jen swallowed her fear and stepped forward.

"In these books," said the Reverend Weaver, "you will meet Jesus, the best friend you'll ever have." Bah stood behind them watching. The Reverend's wife, a woman with hair as bright as papaya and cantaloupe, chatted at the lunch counter with Elder Brother.

"Yes," Bah said. "They should both meet Jesus. Especially you," he shook his finger at Fei Jen.

Pulling herself upward, she swung her leg over the fifth branch. In China, Grandfather had brandished his cane at the black-robed missionaries and shooed them away with a curse. He warned her of terrible *Yeah-thloo,* the *lofan* Jesus ghost who commanded his followers to drink his blood, eat his body, and nail themselves to wooden crosses. Now Bah wanted her to meet this Jesus. Whom was she to believe?

On the fifth branch, Fei Jen rested for a moment. Overhead, the sky had darkened to tarnished silver, and seagulls wheeled in lazy spirals, retreating from the coming storm. Glancing at the house beside the tree, she saw that the second-floor bedroom where her two brothers slept was empty. The whole family was downstairs, working in Bah's restaurant.

Slowly, Fei Jen drew herself to her feet, keeping one hand on the raspy trunk. Until now she had been lucky. Although in full view of the restaurant's side windows, no one had noticed her. Last week, Little Brother had tumbled from the second branch as they explored a deserted squirrel's nest and ripped a gash on his left calf. Bah had threatened to chop off their heads if he caught either of them in the tree again.

Climbing was forbidden. As was shouting in the restaurant, playing tag in the kitchen, or bringing frogs into the dining room. Still, Fei Jen wanted to sketch the seagulls and the lobster boats clumped along the wharves of Yarmouth Harbour. She wanted to draw the fog-shrouded lighthouse on distant Cape Forchu that thrust into the ocean like a bony finger. Grandfather had taught her that an artist must always paint whatever she felt was important, no matter what anyone said, and Fei Jen believed that the sixth branch of the red maple was the best place from which to do it.

Straightening, she realized why Little Brother had failed to get any higher. He was half a head shorter than she was, and even on her toes, the sixth branch was well beyond her grasp. Biting her lip, Fei Jen released her grip on the tree trunk and took three careful steps forward, her arms out wide like a tightrope walker. She stretched upward until the muscles of her back felt like they might tear, but the sixth branch remained tantalizingly out of reach.

The wind whistled through the tree, swaying the branches beneath the soles of her shoes. Lightning flashed in the clouds, and a seagull called out a shrill warning. Fei Jen glanced down; the ground was very far away. She wished she was wearing her canvas runners with the rubber tread, but she reminded herself that she could run as fast as any boy in the fourth grade and she could throw a ball farther than many of them.

Hesitating for only a second, she gathered her strength and bent at the knees. Then she threw herself upward—and caught the branch with both hands! Suspended in the air, she hung free. As she kicked, her shoe tumbled to the ground. Her heart racing, Fei Jen flung her leg over the tree limb and pulled herself up. She gave a small whoop of triumph as she planted herself securely onto the sixth branch. If only Little Brother could see her now!

For a moment, she imagined herself as a phoenix with wings of red and silver, like those in Grandfather's stories, rising and falling on the wind, singing with the thunder and drinking in the wild air of the storm. She soared past the Boston Steamships warehouses and over the lobster traps stacked in rows on Yarmouth Bar. She looked out across the white-tipped waves, and scanned the very curve of the earth, the ocean spilling away on either side. Fei Jen was so very high up, she could spy into the restaurant without being seen.

Through the big windows, she saw Mah polishing the soda fountain and the chrome ice cream box. At the lunch counter, Elder Sister used a spatula to scrape the hard bubblegum from beneath the mushroom shaped stools. Little Brother stood on tiptoes behind the cash register, reaching up to drop slivers of dried shrimp to his goldfish, Ning and Ping, who circled indolently in their bowl beside the cartons of Players' Cigarettes.

As she watched, handsome Elder Brother emerged from the kitchen dragging the bucket-on-wheels and a mop. With smooth, languid strokes, he swept the mop between the rows of high-backed walnut booths, moving gracefully, as if in a dance.

Craning her neck, Fei Jen could just see Bah. He was seated, his back stiff and straight, at his favorite table in the restaurant's front window. A copy of the *Yarmouth Herald* was open before him, as well as his worn *Webster's Dictionary of the English Language.* He sipped slowly from a cup of coffee on a saucer at his right hand and nibbled at a sugar-glazed butter roll on a plate.

She edged closer for a better look as the first drop of rain landed on her hand. From this angle, Bah bore little resemblance to the man in the photograph Mah had kept on her dresser back home in the village. The picture had come from Gold Mountain where he had gone years before to make his fortune. In it, Bah was a young man, his hair thick and dark, and the skin of his cheek as smooth and lustrous as the surface of a pearl. He was dressed western style, in a tweed jacket and a vest that stretched tightly across his broad shoulders. A hat shaped like an overturned rice bowl sat on his left thigh. His eyes were glancing upward to the right at some object out of view, but Fei Jen had always believed they reflected a courageous, self-assured light. Sometimes she would sneak into Mah's bedroom late in the evening and gaze at the picture, dreaming of Bah and his fabulous adventures overseas.

It was hard to recognize the confident youth of the faded photograph in the bald-headed Bah she had come to know in the new land. "Walk, don't run!" "Help Mah clear table four!" "Stop teasing Little Brother!" Nothing she did pleased Bah.

As for his fabulous adventures, just what had he accomplished in Gold Mountain? Last week, Billy Hugh Williams and Matthew Wallace, two naughty *lofan* boys from her school, had hurled a barrage of rocks against the garbage cans in the yard behind the restaurant. Bah had rushed out, splattered apron encircling his waist, his face red and hot. "Get out there, you bad boys!" Then he had switched to his more expressive Chinese. *"You dead-naughty* lofan *ghost-boys! I'm going to slice off your heads!"* Fei Jen had watched from the window as the boys scampered off, laughing and sneering. Even some of Bah's customers in the dining room had chuckled into their coffee cups.

A flash of lightning lit up the harbour. Thunder followed and rain sprinkled her face. Pouting, Fei Jen knew she would do no sketching this morning. The storm was almost upon her. As she edged back toward the bole of the tree, her eyebrows tilted mischievously. Inspiration seized her. There was something she had always wanted to try from this height.

Twisting about, she hooked her legs through the fork in the branch. She checked that her pencils and sketchpad were secure. Taking a deep breath, she shut her eyes and counted slowly. One, two, three, four, five. Then she released her hands and let herself fall backward into the open air.

Fei Jen hung from the branch, suspended by the crooks of her knees. Opening her eyes, the sky and sea had traded places; the ocean threatened to spill down into the heavens. Blood rushed to her head, and she stretched her hands toward the ground. The world spun in a dizzying twirl; and the wind whipped dust and dead leaves into her face. Upside down, ankle anchored, Fei Jen laughed delightedly. If only Little Brother could see her now!

She was still laughing as she noticed Bah get up from his table and cross the dining room, his coffee in one hand and his newspaper in another. Her laughter was choked short as he approached the side window. She held her breath as he gazed out into the street.

Fei Jen froze, her heart in her throat. Upside down, she hung just above the range of his vision. Through the window she could see the pink crown of his head beneath his hair, the tortoiseshell frames of his glasses, and the starched whiteness of his shirt. He stood there, glancing down at his paper, sipping his coffee. Fei Jen tried not to breathe. Don't look up. Don't look up.

Time seemed to stretch. The wind rattled the big window pane and the rain began to fall in earnest. Wet, her head throbbing, she couldn't hang on much longer. Just when she thought she would have to move, Bah stepped away. Fei Jen gasped in relief; but something on the ground caught his attention. Returning, Bah pressed his face against the glass. It was her shoe!

Bah looked up. Father and daughter locked eyes. Through the rain-streaked window, his mouth dropped open. He jerked backward as if his brain refused to believe the image from his eyes. With a choked cry, Bah stumbled against a booth, spilling his coffee over his shirt and newspaper.

"Fei Jen!" His bellow pierced the thickness of the glass. "Fei Jen! Get down! Now! Get down now!"

The world spun to right-side-up as Fei Jen pulled herself up. She slid to the bole of the tree, tearing her dress. Clawing at the trunk, she felt for footholds with her feet, her heart pounding as she fell to the fifth branch. Dead leaves whipped across her face and her fingernail tore against the bark. Bah continued to shout. She dropped to the fourth branch, fell to the third; she skipped the second altogether.

The sky burst open as Fei Jen leapt from the maple. A sheet of cold, dark rain fell upon Yarmouth. She hit the ground running and scrambled toward the back of the house as Bah opened the side door. She wanted to run—down the street—to the wharf—across the water—anywhere!

"You *dead-naughty* girl!" Bah shook his fist. "Stop running! You come back here right now!"

Fei Jen bolted past him into the narrow street. Thunder shattered the sky, as the storm, driven by the west wind, struck with full force.

"Fei Jen! Come back!" Bah's voice was torn from his lips by the wind. He swung his hand through the air as if he were slicing with a meat cleaver. "When I catch you, I'm going to chop off your head!"

The rain blinded her, and the wind ripped the pencils from her pockets. An empty trashcan lid bounced across the street. Fei Jen's breath came in ragged gasps. Behind her, Bah yelled and waved his hand. She ran on and on, heading toward the wharf.

Iris Li

Snaps—A Satire

"Do you have problems with your mother? No, no, let's say an authority figure. A person of a backward, archaic time who effectively subsumes your already confused identity under the blanket statements and power traps of...aha...leftover patriarchal authority."

"Sir, my novel is about resisting recognized and general statements of cultural identity. It's about *not* writing in clichés such as the domineering Chinese parent—the big, bad Chinese mama. It's about finding new ways to express identity. The common representation of a young Chinese slash North American girl as a victim of two conflicting cultures has been done dead."

"Hmm...I see where you're coming from, that is to say, there are as many stories of Chinese women as there are stories of women!"

"Umm...right—what I am saying is that there can be a balance of cultural identity within a person. Not everything is spelt in rifts or binary oppositions. My main character, Marina, isn't some Chinese maiden debating whether or not she should tell her Caucasian boyfriend to not spill soy sauce all over his food. She's a lonely bugger with an obsession with online personals, tea nomenclature, and chronic nose picking."

"Right, a bizarre darling. Look, let's set things straight— "

"She's bisexual."

"Funny, funny. Look, I'll be blunt. Your writing is good, solid, stylistically subversive. But the main character is Chinese and there's nothing in the book that makes her distinctively Chinese. No conflict, no anguish over being a cultural mutt. She's not torn between being a product of Western and Chinese values."

"Cultural hybrid."

"No musings over the idiosyncrasies of the culture—like having superstitions about the number eight. No cringing when her mainland relatives slurp their noodles in an Italian restaurant. No delicious tingling when she receives a real *cheongsam* in the mail."

"You're quite knowledgeable about these things."

"My girlfriend is from Taiwan. Taught me a lot about these things. Her parents even gave me a name in Chinese—well, they just say my name with a Chinese accent but it's rather endearing hearing your name mangled that way. Even understand quite a bit of the language."

"*Gai-dan.*"*

"Hmm?"

"Okay, so my writing is basically shit that doesn't sell. Readers want a waif, someone closely connected enough to her culture to be suffocated by it."

"Exactly. The writers we represent are like nerds who scout out obscurity. We want the bone truth, the little quirky details about life. But we need them to write stories that sell. We had an Asian Canadian writer who wrote a collection of short stories about—get this—drug addicts in Vancouver's East Hastings district. We thought we were being daring and onto a genre of writing that would explode into a renaissance of CanLit. Did a shitload of publicity and promotion. Book sales—sobbingly dismal. That's when we took you on. That's when we realised you were just right for us. All those pieces you wrote about the white boyfriend oddity, connecting modern Chinese Canadian life to mythic China, preparing great Chinese feasts. And then you changed, you submit in this epic about a loser with few cultural definers."

"But what you don't see is that culture is a given in my novel. Marina's culture is already effectively part of her character, it imbues all her actions, it makes her think twice about all her decisions. So yes, she is in some ways indecisive, but her hybridity of culture gives her an additional vantage point. She's able to decipher between the nonsense from both cultures, distil what she likes into her personality, and live her life rather harmoniously if not somewhat blandly. For example, she speaks Mandarin but not as well as she would like. So what? She accepts it, moves on."

"To me, she's conflicted about her, as you say, hybridity."

"Existential."

"Inhibited due to internalized racial tension."

"Self-possessed."

"A social miscreant who lacks consistency."

"Delightfully individualistic."

"You don't see what I'm saying here. She's so fucking general! What makes her Chinese?"

"Because she knows she is."

"Bollocks. Our readers buy books from writers like you to escape. To read about characters unlike themselves and yet still be able to grasp the struggles they face. They don't want to read about characters from books you don't have to go into a specialty bookstore for."

"Fuck you. What you want from me are caricatures. You want me to write in the ilk of recognized Chinese stereotypes—just slot different names in each time, right? The good, obedient daughter who fights to be her own person but never succeeds. The trampy whore of a cousin who rebels against her upright upbringing and subsequently got into a car crash because she drove while hitching up her skirt to make it shorter, lost control of the wheel, crashed into a parked car, which burst into a crescendo of flame and rendered her ugly and deformed, thus serving as a profound lesson to the good, obedient daughter never to stray from her parents' teachings."

"Brilliant. Make that into a story."

"And Jonathan Swift thinks eating plump babies is an excellent source of protein?"

"Hmm?"

"Fuck you. You want me to write about Chinese characters but you're not ready for Chinese characters. You have in your head characters, characters of difference but they must exist in the Chinese culture *you* are familiar with. The culture that has been packaged, sold, and prostituted to you through centuries of invasion, objectification, rejection, revulsion, and generalization. You're ready for individual Chinese characters so long as they fit a recognized mouldy mould of what a Chinese character should be. They always have to be agonizing about something—*everything's* a bitch in the life of a Chinese. Or exotic. All Chinese writing must be filtered through this filthy sieve of exoticism.

Sex becomes magic, dragon-lady sex. Dogs become food. A grandmother becomes a sagacious fortune cookie. You don't understand the notion that some people can balance their so-called conflicting cultural identities and it becomes boring, becomes normal, becomes something like...yourself. Sometimes, we're just not as different as you would like us to be. I tolerate the fact that you might not understand the notion yet but try to look beyond the boundaries, eh?"

[Silence]

"Let's talk about your author photograph. You're quite big for an Asian girl. Can you slim down a bit for the retakes?"

*Egg, a derogatory term for Caucasian males who are "white on the outside and yellow inside."

Lien Chao

Neighbours

Bathed in the bright early summer sunshine, Sally stands at the north-eastern side of Yonge Street and Eglinton Avenue, waiting for the traffic lights to change. She has recently moved to the area because it's one of Toronto's more vibrant neighbourhoods. The two streets at the intersection are not wide; when the traffic lights switch to red for either of the streets, for a moment the entire block is put on hold, as it were. Drivers rest their feet on the brakes; pedestrians at the four corners have an opportunity to exchange looks. Sally knows this happens at all the intersections of the city, and standing elbow to elbow among strangers reminds her of Beijing, the city where she lived for thirty years before coming to Canada. Sally likes the big city, where she can be close to excitement and at the same time not be involved if she doesn't want to. She can be an onlooker, like right now at the street corner, waiting for the traffic lights to switch.

Sally holds a Styrofoam coffee cup in her hand as she listens to the rhythm of morning traffic. Calculating the time she has before the lights change, she tips over the cup carefully to her lips, so that it doesn't spill over her new silk jacket. Walking toward a garbage stand, and using the empty coffee cup to pop open the flapping device, she tries to drop the cup in without getting her fingers dirty. But for some bizarre reason, the white cup falls onto the sidewalk and rolls away like a wheel. Sally is annoyed. Now her traffic light has turned green, opening a floodgate, and pedestrians rush into the street. Intuitively, Sally follows. Half way across, she turns around. Did she forget something?

Sally sees a thin old man bending down on the sidewalks near the garbage stand. His head is below her eye level, so she can't see his face, but the top of his head has thin brown hair. His bony shoulders stretching forward and one hand resting on his knee for support, with his other hand he picks up the Styrofoam cup from the sidewalk. Sally's face turns red. Why didn't she take care of her own responsibility? But now in the middle of the crossing, she doesn't have time to ponder over her guilt. The traffic lights in front of her are turning amber, she hurries over to the south side of Eglinton and then into the subway.

Sometimes when she stands at the intersection of Yonge and Eglinton, waiting for the traffic lights to change, Sally wonders why there are more newspaper boxes than trees in the area. Does this mean people in this neighbourhood read more? It seems that way. She has just discovered a Toronto Public Library branch north of Eglinton. She remembers public libraries in China, readers were not allowed inside the book stacks area, the librarians would go in to fetch the books. To her surprise, here readers of all ages and from all walks of life go through the bookshelves themselves. Sally can find up-to-date academic magazines and various government documents for her research projects. The library has ample space too. When she gets tired, she can browse through fashion and art magazines or go upstairs to view an art exhibition. She watches kids flipping through books with such intense interest that they remind her of her own daughter left temporarily behind in China. If only she could bring her here now! How much the six-year-old would enjoy the books!

Through the loudspeakers comes an announcement that the library is closing in ten minutes. Sally gathers her notes from the table. Stretching her back with a silent yawn she feels her left foot touch something rolling on the floor. She looks down, it's an empty coke can. Two teenage boys shared the table with her this evening. It must have been left by them, though drinking is not allowed inside the library. Teenagers all over the world are the same! The overhead lights start to blink as a reminder. From the nearby tables several readers get up to leave. Sally puts her notes inside her folder. People walk by her table on both sides. Suddenly, from the corner of an eye she sees a man bend down to pick up something near her feet. Oh, the empty Coke can! She feels embarrassed as if she were the guilty party. "It's not me, I didn't drink here," she stammers to explain.

"I didn't say it's you, Miss," answers the man politely. "I just don't like to see people litter, that's all." The man didn't blame her; she feels relieved. But why didn't she pick it up earlier when she touched it with her foot?

Heading towards the red exit sign, Sally recalls the incident of the old man picking up her coffee cup from the sidewalk a few weeks before. Is it the same man? No, it can't be. Today the guy is in his forties and he has full black hair. It's not the same man. Then there is something about Canadians, she mumbles to herself, they care about their environment. At the exit, she watches the man drop the empty coke can and a clear water bottle into a plastic blue box.

Down Yonge Street the scent of fresh lilacs brushes her face like a soft breeze. An old couple sits on a bench in Eglinton Square, a cane leaning beside the woman. What are old people doing here at night? Watching the traffic lights? Sally recalls a similar scene in Beijing. One afternoon, she was at the Xidan Book City, one of Beijing's most popular stores. There were a lot of people outside on the square, some sat around the base of its outdoor sculpture, which depicted a pile of huge books. Sally decided to rest her feet, so she sat down next to an old couple who had several shopping bags. Suddenly, the old man stood up, passing his plastic bags to the woman, and ran towards the sidewalk. He shoved one arm inside a public garbage stand, from which he pulled out an empty water bottle. Sally was bewildered. The old man walked back to the woman, looking triumphant as if he had a trophy in his hand. "Are you—collecting bottles?" Sally saw that inside the bags on the old woman's lap were empty soft drink cans and water bottles. "What for?"

"Sell them," said the old woman, as her husband put the empty water bottle inside the shopping bag.

"How much can you get?" Sally asked, curiously.

"Ten cents each," he answered humbly, "not much, but it helps. We're old, factory closed down, no pension." He sighed.

The old woman passed a wet towel to her husband. "Clean your hands." She turned around to Sally and said, "You see, young lady, if we can each pick up a hundred bottles or cans every day, we make 20 *yuan* a day. That's 600 *yuan* a month, and we can live on that."

"Good for the environment," Sally murmured, knowing that the old couple didn't need her moral analysis. At the time, she didn't know the word "recycling."

But now she knows the word and appreciates the concept. But going out of the way to pick up other people's litter as these Canadians do is beyond her. Passing the old couple sitting in Eglinton Square, Sally has a naughty thought: if she dares to drop an empty Coke can on the sidewalk, she can bet on getting a public flogging by the old woman with her cane!

Warm summer breeze soon changes young lemon-green leaves to dark foliage. Flowers of many kinds and colours bloom in front of restaurants and stores. Then comes Canada Day! Sally is not a Canadian, but she hopes one day she will be, because she has begun to like this country and its people. A notice on the library's bulletin board says that on Canada Day there will be an outdoor concert in Eglinton Square. So here comes Sally, wearing a cool white cotton dress with red birds flying, their wings spread out wide. The colours of Canada Day. In front of the Grand and Toy store there is a crowd. Rows of chairs in the sun, some seats still waiting occupancy. Three wheelchairs are parked in the back. Sitting down, Sally smiles at the old couple next to her.

"I'm Elizabeth, and this is my husband, Joe," smiles the old woman. "Go get yourself a free drink, Miss." Elizabeth motions towards the front.

"Don't be shy," adds Joe encouragingly.

Sally feels inadequate; but after watching others drinking from identical plastic cups, she goes up to the front and picks up a cup of ginger ale on the table. The Salvation Army Band is here: middle-aged and senior men and women dressed in out-of-date uniforms, looking both funny and serious. They play a good selection of music that seems to resonate around the entire neighbourhood. "Do you want to come to our building tonight? We can watch fireworks on the roof," Elizabeth says to Sally at the end of the concert.

After dinner Sally rings the buzzer to the old couple's apartment. She doesn't know exactly why she has come to visit them, strangers she has met only today. Perhaps they remind her of her own parents in China, or the old couple she met in Beijing who collected empty bottles and tin cans for a living, or perhaps it's because she wants to buy a vacuum cleaner and she needs advice. The buzzer rings like the hoarse voice of an old man. Then from the speaker comes out a woman's soft voice. "Is that Sally?"

"Yes, Elizabeth, it's me," she answers delightedly.

"Come up, 903." The door hisses, opens slowly.

Inside the one-bedroom apartment, Sally feels disoriented, thinks perhaps she's having an illusion that she is inside a country farmhouse. The furniture is old and heavy with carvings on the back of the chairs and on the legs of the table. It reminds her of the furniture her family owned before the Cultural Revolution. Later the Red Guards threw it into a bonfire. On the walls, there are framed photos in light brown or dark gray. There is a large balcony outside the sitting room, but from where she stands, Sally thinks it looks like a workshop.

Joe tells Sally to make herself at home, Elizabeth offers a choice of tea or coffee. "Because I was born on April 21 and have the same birthday as Queen Elizabeth II, my parents gave me my name," she smiles, "but my husband is not Philip, Duke of Edinburgh, you know, what's his last name?" She laughs. "So, would you like to have a cup of English tea?"

"I'd love to have a cup of English tea, Madam," Sally puts on a mock British accent. They all laugh.

Over a cup of Red Rose tea, Sally takes out the latest flyer from Future Shop, the store a few blocks north. She asks the couple what kind of vacuum cleaner is more effective and less expensive.

Putting on his reading glasses, Joe starts reading the advertisement. He mumbles and grumbles to himself, shaking his head. "Too expensive, too much money," he continues to shake his head as he speaks.

"That's what I think," echoes Sally, "but we can do nothing about their prices."

"Yes, of course you can." Joe puts down the ad on the coffee table.

"Like what?" Sally asks suspiciously.

"If you don't mind a refurbished model, I have one for you," says Joe.

Sally doesn't understand the word "refurbished," but she understands the second part of the sentence. Joe has a vacuum cleaner for her. Is he a salesperson? Her eyes quickly sweep over his face. She cautions herself that she shouldn't buy anything before first doing her own research. Meanwhile Joe has stepped out onto the balcony. Shortly he brings in a red vacuum cleaner. "Here it is, refurbished, this baby is like new," he beams at Sally and Elizabeth, patting the body of the vacuum cleaner affectionately. Plugging it into a power outlet, Joe rolls the roaring machine on the floor like a dancer.

Sally doesn't know what to say. After Joe has turned the appliance on and off and returned to the sofa to finish his tea, she asks him timidly, "So, how much is it?" She had no idea that this old man, a neighbour she met this morning, sells secondhand vacuum cleaners in his apartment.

"$200, no taxes," Joe says seriously. Then he bursts out laughing. "A real deal, young lady."

"No, Joe, please don't joke with her," his wife interrupts.

"OK." Joe stops laughing. "Sally, didn't I make myself understood? You can *have* it, I mean, have it, take it home, if you don't mind a refurbished model."

"It's yours if you need it," Elizabeth repeats.

"Really, free for me?" Sally asks, not quite believing. "Thank you very much, I would be delighted to take it home. But what are you going to use?"

"Oh, don't worry, we have our own. You see, Joe picks up stuff from the dump behind the building," Elizabeth says, "you know, residents throw things away, when they are not working."

"But a lot of the times, there is nothing seriously wrong with the machines," Joe says, raising his voice to emphasize. "It's just dust, dirt, you know. People dispose of just about anything nowadays." He starts to shake his head again. His wife nods.

"So you repair them?" Sally can figure out what happens next.

"Yes, he spends time cleaning them up and making them work again," Elizabeth says. "Then he gives them away to people who need them. Over there, on the balcony, go have a look."

Getting up from the sofa, Joe motions to her. "Come, come with me, I'll show you."

Sally follows him.

This is not exactly what a balcony is supposed to be, Sally thinks. It's a workshop. A large toolbox, a working bench, and a tabletop. On the shelves, built against one of the walls, Sally recognizes various objects: a manual sewing machine, a coffee grinder, a food processor, an electrical wok, a few bicycle wheels and inner tires.

"All the appliances here are refurbished and in good working condition," says Joe proudly. Sally smiles, her vocabulary has been enriched today with a new word, "refurbished"; she doesn't even have to look it up in a dictionary.

When they hear the noise of fireworks, Joe, Elizabeth, and Sally rush to the elevator and up onto the rooftop. Under the starry summer night sky, a cool breeze clarifies Sally's mind. Young children and teenagers have brought their music, drinks, laughter, and noise to the rooftop. Young mothers scream at their kids every now and then. Suddenly, fireworks shoot up in the distant sky; everybody exclaims.

Sally asks Joe and Elizabeth why they chose to live in a mixed building instead of one for seniors. "Wouldn't that be quieter?"

"Oh yes, it would be," Elizabeth answers, "but Joe and I like to live where things are happening, we like excitement."

"So do I," says Sally, feeling closer to the old couple than before.

"However, having said that," Joe inserts, "there are problems. In the last few years, some single mothers have moved into the building with their kids. What do kids do, eh? So, now you see graffiti inside the elevator and laundry room, you see empty pop cans in the common areas."

"We pick them up, wherever we see them," Elizabeth says.

"But what about their mothers?" Joe adds. "Do they know it's their responsibility to educate their kids? Especially, some of them don't even go to work, they live on welfare. On taxpayers' money." Joe hasn't stopped shaking his head. Sally regrets having started the topic. Now their conversation is heading towards a dead end.

Another splash of fireworks in the sky. Another interval. Sally decides to take a chance. "So, I guess you won't like me either," she looks at Joe and Elizabeth anxiously.

They don't understand. "Why? What makes you say that?" They look puzzled.

"Because, because I'm divorced and I'm a single mother," Sally says quietly. "But I'm not on welfare. Back at home, I had wished that the state had some welfare schemes to help single mothers with kids. And there weren't any. I went through a very difficult period after my divorce. Sometimes, in order to save money for food, I walked three hours to get home instead of taking a bus." Sally doesn't know why she tells this to the old couple. It's not relevant. This is Canada. People here don't understand it. But for some reason she wants to share her experiences with them, wants them to understand. So she continues, "Perhaps the single mothers in your building have circumstances you don't know about. Perhaps they are struggling against their personal crises. Perhaps they need advice, just as I did with the vacuum cleaner."

In the open sky there goes the loudest explosion of the night. Hundreds of rockets shooting up and exploding, tens and thousands of colourful flowers flashing and glittering in the sky. Sally, Joe and Elizabeth clap their hands like kids.

It's around midnight when Sally bids good night. Joe and Elizabeth give her big hugs and kisses on the cheeks. They would like to have her over for dinner soon.

Sally walks down Yonge Street carrying the refurbished red vacuum cleaner in her hands. At the intersection, waiting for the traffic lights to change, she recognizes familiar faces from the neighbourhood. Tall Kelly is at the northwest corner, selling *Outreach,* a newspaper sold by the unemployed and the homeless. At the southeast corner, disabled George, a self-proclaimed Hollywood agent, sits on the granite steps outside the CIBC branch. George usually asks people who pass by if they want to go to Hollywood. On the southwest corner, Dave's hotdog cart is still surrounded by a large crowd. Sally smiles broadly at her neighbours.

Harry J Huang

Card Order

I bought a quilt, a set of bed sheets, a pillow, and many other things at Wal-Mart the day after my student visa was approved. It was a huge pile, hardly possible to carry out of the store.

"Do you want to have a card order?" The salesgirl asked me after I made my payment.

"A card order?" I repeated.

"Yes."

"A card order?" I had learned shopping conversations, but I had never come across anything like a "card order." "According to grammar rules, 'card order' must be a thing, because it comes after 'have'," I said to myself.

I never hesitated to ask if I did not know something. I had even earned a reputation as a "thick-skinned learner." She looked into my blank eyes, waiting for me to say yes or no. The queue behind me was long and a middle-aged man was frowning at me.

"A card order, eh?" I repeated once more.

"Yes?" she was still waiting.

"But what does a 'card order' do?"

"Well," the friendly girl answered patiently, "if you have a car ordered, a driver will take your things to your home. So you don't have to carry your shopping yourself."

"Oh. No, no, no! Thanks!" I flushed, and I don't know why I did, even today. I never blushed when I asked an English teacher or a stranger on the street about anything I did not know. I collected all my things, hiding my face behind my quilt. I dragged the bags to the exit of the store, stopped at the sidewalk and got a taxi myself. Inside the taxi I stopped sweating and subsequently my wet shirt cooled me down.

"Such good service in this store," I said to myself. "A card order?" I laughed at myself. "I knew it was grammatically wrong. Think of the logic too! A card order!" I tried to calm down.

"The way to learn is to ask," I reminded myself of my own mottoes. "The more mistakes one makes, the more one learns. What's the big deal about the 'card order?' No one there knows me anyway." Soon the taxi pulled up at my destination, the Glengarry Residence. My friends were waiting for me. I paid the driver and moved everything from his trunk, but when the taxi was leaving, I felt extremely distressed that I had forgotten something.

"I think I forgot to give him a tip," I shouted to my university friends.

"Run and stop him. He's still there."

I ran. I called. I waved. But he was gone. What I saw was another taxi quickly making a U-turn and pulling up beside me. I did not move, wondering what to do. He lowered his window and said, "The door is open."

"Oh, thanks. I—" I did not know what to say.

He was all ears, leaning against the passenger seat on the right-hand side.

"I don't need a taxi. I forgot to give my taxi driver a tip. Could you pass it onto him, please?" I handed him two dollars through the window.

He hesitated for a second, then raised his hand to take it, "Okay. Thanks." Then he stared at me and asked, "You arrived at the international airport last night, didn't you?"

"Yes, but how did you know?" I became quite uneasy.

"Remember? I drove you to your friend's home on Jarvis. You had a brown travelling bag, right?"

"That's right! Oh, sir, I am so sorry. Will you please keep the tip for yourself then?"

Ritz Chow

A Porous Life

Life falls through me because I have large pores. It is an inherited trait, this bulbous nose with deep pores opening flesh to air. My aunt tells me that pores benefit the circulatory system: toxins escape through skin much more easily and heat is tunnelled away in hot weather. Somehow, my skin makes me a better person.

"We are people born into the sun, into the sweat of rice fields. Remember Yolly, we are solid like stalks of sugar cane," she thumps the table and then wipes her nose, which has beaded with sweat. To her, my pores represent fluidity, or transparency. She looks into my face as if it were a pool, as if the past were lucid in what my dermatologist calls "obvious sebaceous openings." I try toner. I swab on the latest cucumber and milk mixture. My hands juggle sleek colourful bottles of astringents. My favourite girlfriend says I look fine. I look at her perfect complexion and reconsider the word "fine." I glisten and glow with open skin, until my openings close.

Blackheads. Sebaceous plugs pigmented by air. Some foundation should even me up, give me a uniform colour that is not my own. Maybe "natural beige," but not "skin colour." My skin is never its own colour. I wish I were an astronaut. In space, my blackheads would eject and be sucked into black holes, and then my pores would close from the pressure of the galaxies. I like physics and punching numbers into elaborate formulae. I can scrawl onto a page the distance from the moon to my nose. Numbers reach from one porous surface to another.

Learning has never been a problem with me. I'm good with

numbers. Aunt Oi-Mei thinks that's the only thing Chinese about me. "Everything else is just too Canadian," she laments with a begrudging note of pride. When she feels affectionate, she calls me "juk sing" and ruffles my short, buzzed black hair with burgundy streaks. I call her "village maid" when she gets too provincial and clucks at the foreign lifestyles in Canada. We are each other's keepers. She balances my uneven blend of Chinese and Canadian cultures with her adamant refusal to lose sight of tradition. Our meals reflect this. We have fried rice with Spam, along with steamed bok choy, drizzled with sesame oil and oyster sauce.

The cosmetician sighs and yawns with a small twitch at the corners of her mouth. I have never seen anyone enjoy her boredom more. She cups her chin with her right hand and dangles her left hand off the counter's edge. The long blue nails on her left hand tap the silver-edged glass case. My face becomes a surface of intense scrutiny.

"You know...," she begins, her eyebrows arching with serious consideration. She pauses, and then stands in silence, shifting her gaze from my nose to her stock of various creams and lotions.

I fidget with my necklace of square wooden blocks that spell out "yeah, so?" But there is no comma and the question mark doesn't curve well—instead, the interrogation point loses its point, and looks like a whacked out *l*. Besides, everyone squeezes it together when they read it, so they look at me and say, "Yeahsol. Cool name. What's it mean in Chinese?"

Blue-nails has worked herself beyond my nose and her counter. She is bent over, rustling through boxes and pushing aside sheaves of paper. It is Friday afternoon and the office ladies slowly fill the aisles with their moulded hair and reapplied rouge. I shift from one sneakered foot to the other. Blue-nails clucks and shakes her head, mumbling under her breath. I catch fragments of "it's here, I'm sure" and "blackheads, hmmm." Finally she reappears with a red cardboard package. She looks triumphantly bored.

"Here," she stretches her mouth as if in a yawn, or as if she were stretching a wad of gum from one cheek to the other. "The last black-head remover. Ya want it?" There are five office ladies lined up behind me with their bulk purchases of lip liners and eye shadow. They look expectantly at me. I feel my pores expanding with embarrassment. My hand goes to my beaded change purse where I fumble with folded bills. Blue-nails stretches her mouth and her arm reappears with a blue bottle. "Toner. For after." She's so fluid, her voice could be oozing from the entire surface of her body. She's so elastic, her body could be covered with those bored, endlessly stretching lips. She hands me the bag and I crinkle it out of there.

Lately I have taken to plucking my eyebrows. When I first began, I had almost no hair left. I was getting the angle wrong and had to keep plucking. Never pluck when you're sleepy or hungry. My girlfriends thought I looked perpetually startled without eyebrows. They said it had something to do with all that whiteness above my eyes. Newly plucked eyebrows are so obvious. The skin is so white when hair is removed. Hair must be a good filter of ultraviolet rays. No wonder I can still think after all these years in the summer sun without a hat. It's my thick, black hair. Or rather, was. Plum is a nice dark colour too. I pluck my brows in such a way that my left brow arcs up into an inquisitive angle. Beth likes my thinned brows so much that, when we go dancing she moves up against me and licks them with her pointed tongue. I like Beth. She's my favourite girlfriend.

The blackhead remover is a slim instrument ending in a flat disk of metal with a tiny hole at its centre. The cardboard box in which it was packaged has been ripped. If I read carefully, I can make out the directions: "To remove blackheads: place...press against the skin...hole over the blackhead...press." When I press the metal disk down onto my nose, nothing emerges through the small hole. I lift the metal and the blackhead is still there but now it's ringed by a red impression left by the blackhead remover. There's a knock on my door. I look up and Beth walks in with her olive green cracked-leather jacket.

"Hey," she wiggles her fingers in a wave and plops down onto my bed, displacing the binders and wet towel. "Come here," she gestures to the space she's clearing on my bed. She tosses the damp towel onto the orange shag carpet and pushes my notebooks and binders off to the side.

"I can't," I mumble with my palm over my nose. I hold my nose like a sore wound. I lift the slim metallic instrument in the air for Beth to see. "Node surgery."

What I like most about Beth is her exasperation. She does the best sighs. They are a perfect mix of resignation, indignation, and affection. I close the bedroom door then dive into her. I kiss her perfect nose. She emits a wondrous sigh, which causes her nostrils to flare slightly. "Yol," she admonishes me and wraps an arm around me as I lean in to her, "you really have to get over your nose."

"That's easy for you to say." I turn to eye her sleek nose. "With your northern royal nose, it's easy not to consider the trials of what a southern peasant nose like mine must endure." I'm sure Beth's ancestors came from northern China. Her skin is so white and flawless that blood vessels appear at the surface of her translucent face. I imagine her great-grandmother wrapped in yak fur with wind-burnt red cheeks while my ancestors toiled in the hot fields in southern China, their skin opening again and again to release the body's water and salt in rivers of sweat. The Yellow River is said to be the sweat of peasant labourers overflowing from the many flooded rice paddies. It is as golden as the skins of farmers, as cloudy as eyes that have hardened from the constant sting of the sun.

Beth sighs and kisses my porous nose. "Not! The Yellow River has a northern tributary in the mountains and flows north to south. How can the river's origin be the sweat of southern peasants?"

Beth is one of those rare symmetrical people who look beautiful from every conceivable angle. I tilt my head until she is perpendicular to my line of vision. "Once," I whisper as I hover close to her skin, which smells of apples and mint, "the world was upside down and sweat flowed south to north." I run my finger under her chin, along her jaw and to her ear. Her eyelids close and I lean close. "Or perhaps the river began with the northern people who had shed tears for the many deaths caused by the harsh climate of the mountains." The tip of my tongue travels lightly along her ear to the edge of her closed eye, brushing thin, papery skin—such a fragile covering for our sharp visions. I lift my tongue and kiss her forehead.

She opens her eyes and surveys my face to see if I am serious or, at best, sincere. "Mm, you sure make history tactile," she murmurs. Between Beth and me, truth is a fast game. We are its players. Mostly, it plays us. She pushes me aside and pins me to the bed. "Let's see that nose of yours." She leans down, squints, then turns on the desk lamp and positions it over me. She sits on my chest with my arms pinned under her thighs. I can't escape her scrutiny. I let her in through every pore.

*

My parents spend their time between Hong Kong, San Francisco, and Vancouver. I guess I'm what you call an Asian baggage kid, who's plopped down on foreign soil and left in large houses full of furniture and devoid of people. But I am a variation of this phenomenon. My parents didn't send me over from Hong Kong. We lived in Toronto until two years ago when we moved to Vancouver. They bought a house for me to live in and then they moved to Hong Kong. My first year alone in the house was calming in a gothic kind of way. The rooms were empty. The air was empty. My head became empty. I couldn't walk through the long halls without blanking out on where I was or who I had become. I did well in school, especially in physics, where I could roll silver ball bearings down banisters and buy electronic kits to test the static in silence. Then Aunt Oi-Mei moved to the city. Living with Aunt Oi-Mei was my idea and my way out of emptiness.

For many years, Aunt Oi-Mei lived in San Francisco with Jason. He was a publisher and specialized in translations of popular Chinese fiction. He would rummage through the backs of bookstores in Chinatown and say "doh jai" to the merchants. He's six feet tall, Irish American with a red bushy beard, and more Chinese than any member of my family. Sometimes, being Chinese is like that—the unlikeliest people are more Chinese than you. I think that's why Aunt Oi-Mei left him. She couldn't compete.

"Besides," she explained, "I left Hong Kong to be North American not retro-Asian. Humpf. You have to move forward in this world, not backward." I shrugged. My parents move in circles. I never know which way they're going, just that I am the one standing still.

Beth met my parents once. They were passing by on their way to San Francisco. When my parents—the Foo Frenzy, she now calls them—dropped into Vancouver last summer, they ploughed through the house and closets, buying furniture and clothes for me. They had to keep their only child up on the latest fashions since both their businesses rely on trends.

My father is an executive in an electronics firm. He's fast-talking, has a shiny forehead, and carries a slim cellular phone. "Beth. Like Eee-liz-abeth," he said, tapping his fingers against the cell phone clipped to his belt like a cowboy with his colt 45. "Like Queen Eee-liz-abeth, eh." His eyes ran around the room when he spoke to her. "Veeery classy."

Wondering whether he was admiring the new paint on the walls or commenting on her name, Beth smiled politely, following his gaze.

"Beth," my mother growled at her through a cigarette-worn throat. "Nice face. Slim body. Never gain weight." Short, clipped comments, as if she were cutting sentences to fit the person with whom she was speaking. Mother inherited two clothing factories in Hong Kong from her polygamous father, who left everything to the children of the second wife when he died. She's as precise and determined in her speech as her pinning of fabric on the models before a runway show.

Beth said she could see my parents' continuous energy in me, except my parents' energy is rampant while mine is reined in and sharpened into a small point. "Focused," Beth announced to me after their visit, "that's what you are, Yolly. Wildly focused."

I have been focused on my body for this past year. So has Beth. We are focused on bodies. Wildly focused. She's my first; I'm her second. Touching her leaves me distracted with sensation. I lose track of where her skin meets mine. Her breath opens against my neck and my lungs squeeze shut with her exhalation. She kisses my lips and my toes tingle. It's like a mixed-up version of the medical mystery of phantom limbs. In my body, new nerves invade existing limbs and burn fresh memories into old patterns of flesh. I guess we're something like what love is except without the children, without the mortgage and new car. It's something about the way my pores open and hers don't. We are two different kinds of being Chinese. Where I open, she closes.

In the university physics class of that first year in Vancouver, we all had our own group. Beth was in the "New Asians" group. English-savvy, she spoke to the other kids more than those in her social crowd. I arrived in the middle of the first term. I moved beyond the peripheries of all the groups. Beth couldn't understand why I didn't just choose one. Although she moved between groups, she liked to have a home base. "It's easier to hang out by myself," I said to her when we first bumped into each other outside school on Broadway. "That way, I never forget anyone, especially myself." Beth smiled and we went for coffee.

If you were to ask Beth, she would say she's open and I'm closed. She thinks I spend too much time in my room typing away at my latest story and punching numbers into my scientific calculator. For her, being open amounts to being receptive to people, being outside and doing things in the fresh ocean breeze. I tell her she sounds British with all her talk about social graces, fresh air, and walks. I can't believe she just moved from Hong Kong two years ago. Maybe being Chinese in Hong Kong means being British.

If you were to ask me, I would say Beth is open in a closed way. She is unrelentingly honest and direct to a certain level; beyond that, she remains silent and evasive. I, on the other hand, am closed in an open way. My parents taught me that in business you give nothing away. Your secrets become your advantage. But in personal matters, you must give all. Like in families, you can't hold back, or resentment builds.

With Beth, I am as open as my pores. Emotions roll out of me while hers trickle out. But when we kiss, when her body slides over mine, there is nothing closed about her. We are trying to be ourselves together. Some say we're trying too hard because we're the new Canadians, caught between countries, living in one and knowing neither. Aunt Oi-Mei says it is all in the pores.

Loretta Seto

Versus

A smooth oval face. Thin eyebrows that have been carefully plucked, brushed, darkened. A small blunt nose with a weak bridge, too-high cheekbones beneath liquid black eyes that watch, unafraid. A resolute rosebud mouth which, when relaxed, settles into a natural pout. The tilt of the head is lifted, just so, held in a way that some would call prideful, others arrogant.

This is her stepmother's face. A Chinese face. This is the face of the woman her father has married.

Her mother wants to know all about this new woman.

"Is she really from China? Right off the boat, I guess, eh? What's she like? How did Ted meet her?"

Opal, who is thirteen, is eager to tell her mother everything, everything about the stranger who now lives in her father's house. "She's from some small province in China, and she can hardly speak English. Dad met her last year when he went to teach at that Beijing university. She's *thirty*."

Her mother, who is ten years older at forty, rears back her head, as if personally offended by such a fact. She lights a cigarette, unmindful of how Opal shifts away from the stream of her exhaled smoke. "That's typical of Ted. He always had to be in the power position, you know. He couldn't stand it when we were together because I wouldn't let him bully me."

Opal does not protest. Although her parents have been divorced for over three years, her mother's acrimony over the breakup is unlikely to end any time soon. Opal knows her mother feels cheated out of many things—their old house sold and the money divided, the alimony payments that her mother says barely cover the cost of rent, and, most of all, not winning sole custody of Opal, which her mother maintains is the bitterest pill she's had to swallow.

"She only knows how to cook Chinese food," Opal continues, warming up to the subject, "and she never even tried a hamburger before she came here. She didn't even have a TV in China." This is important for Opal to mention; she carefully watches her mother's face to gauge her reaction to such a bizarre fact.

But her mother is contemplative, only half listening. "You know what it is. She must have married him to get out of the country. You know how it is in China, what with the communists running things. What sane person wouldn't want to get out of that?"

Opal only vaguely knows what communists are and what they mean. She looks around at the tiny kitchen in which they sit, in her mother's small apartment. Comparing it to her father's house, she wonders not for the first time how such different people could fall in love and get married. She remembers how, when she was five or six, her father and mother held hands, kissed, looked tenderly at each other. How different now—the cold phone conversations and icy looks given when her father drops her off at her mother's apartment for the weekend. She wonders if her father loves Liang—that is her stepmother's name—when he never holds her hand or kisses her or speaks softly in her ear. In front of Opal, he treats Liang as though she were only a friend, with whom to joke and talk about inconsequential things.

"I guess you live in a Chinese house now," her mother says, interrupting Opal's thoughts. "Just remember, you're half white. You can come here any time."

She does not like being told this, reminded of her halfness. She does not look much like her mother, but resembles her father, with his lean Asian face and slanted eyes. She sometimes thinks her life would be much easier if she had inherited her mother's white features, the wide blue eyes, the light hair, the fair complexion. But this is not the case.

"So do you like her?" Her mother's voice is guarded, her face closed. Opal recognizes the look—her mother is waiting for an answer she does not want to hear.

"No, not really," Opal answers slowly. She sees her mother relax, and she feels good that she has made this small bit of happiness.

"Oh. Well. That's too bad." Her mother's voice is nonchalant, casual. Relieved.

It is not entirely true. Opal finds her stepmother intriguing; she often watches Liang busily preparing dinner while she pretends to do homework at the kitchen table. Liang's movements are always quick, efficient, full of tightly coiled energy. Her slim compact body maneuvers around counters to get at cupboards, drawers. Stir frying, she yields the spatula with military precision, tossing, flipping, quick, quick, quick. The dishes which emerge from the wok are always tasty, always fill the house with unfamiliar but pleasant aromas.

Opal wonders if this is why her father married Liang. Her mother does not cook much, she prefers to make sandwiches, soups, meals that are born from tin cans or plastic jars.

Three nights a week her father is at the university teaching a Mandarin class. On these nights, Opal and Liang are left to eat alone, quietly, in the kitchen. When her father is not there, there is not much to say.

On such a night, Opal sits at the table, her math book open before her, but she furtively studies Liang who stands at the stove, her back towards her. Liang is scaling a recently dead fish under running water, handling the slippery body with ease. It is from Chinatown, one of the few places where Liang will shop, yet Opal imagines that even there she must feel displaced, when everyone mostly speaks Cantonese and will stare at anyone who speaks Mandarin as if they were a foreigner. Opal herself has only been to Chinatown a few times in her life; she does not like it—the loudness, the dirt, the chaos. People who push without saying excuse me.

As they eat, Opal wonders what Liang thinks of her. They rarely talk, and only to communicate a need or desire, or ask a question. Where is my mug? Pass the napkins please. After the meal, Opal will wash the dishes. This is a silent agreement they have come to—Liang will cook, Opal will wash.

Do her father and Liang talk about her when she is not there? What do they say? Maybe her father talks about when he was married to

Opal's mother, and how bad the last years of the marriage were, the endless bickering, the furious silences. Or maybe he tells Liang all about Opal, her likes and dislikes, her habits, her embarrassing secrets.

"You like fish?" Liang suddenly asks.

Opal is so taken by surprise she nearly loses hold of her fork. "Yes. It's good. Very good." She speaks slowly and clearly. She feels flustered, offguard.

"Mnnm," Liang says, making an unreproducible sound. She continues to eat.

Opal feels disturbed, as if she has been lifted and shaken, before being set down in her chair again. She watches Liang through the cover of her eyelashes, waiting for another overture, but there is none.

Later that evening, when Opal is in her room, she remembers that she has left her math book in the kitchen. She returns there to find Liang, sitting at the table, the math book in her hands. Liang is studying it, reading it as though it were a novel, her eyes travelling down one side of the book to the next, before turning the page. From the shadow of the doorway, Opal watches, unseen.

The next evening, Opal's father is home for dinner. Liang is almost gregarious, a smile stretching her lips. The two speak together in Mandarin, a language of which Opal only knows the simplest phrases. Her father inquires in English how Opal's visit to her mother's was, a question he is always careful to ask after every weekend, because he believes in presenting a rational front to her, to prove that he is above the pettiness and recrimination that he senses her mother indulges in. She answers the same as she does always, saying she had a good time and describing the food she ate. The part about the food always gives her father a look of self-satisfaction, as though he is thinking that at least at *his* house Opal is served healthy, generous meals. This is in part why she does it, to give him a chance to put another mark on his Good Parenting score card.

As usual, when Opal and her father speak, Liang looks on silently, intently, trying to see into their words, penetrate their full meaning. She never asks for translations from Opal's father, although he will sometimes offer them, and she will listen with the same serious concentration.

Near the end of the meal, Liang leaves the kitchen and returns with a brochure in her hand that Opal recognizes—she has seen them at her school, pamphlets advertising night classes for adults. Liang hands the brochure to Opals's father and asks him a question, Opal assumes, though it sounds more like a statement. It is the mild surprise on her father's face that makes Opal pay attention—she gazes from one face to the other, her father's strangely equivocal tone answered swiftly, immediately, by Liang's insistent one.

"What did she say?" Opal asks, unable to contain her curiosity any longer.

Her father ignores her for a moment. Then, still looking at Liang, he answers, "She says she wants to take some ESL courses."

Opal does not understand it, but she senses her father's reluctance to agree to Liang's proposal. "I think it's a good idea," she risks.

"Do you?" her father replies.

"Yes." Opal's voice takes on a stronger note. "She lives in Canada now. She should learn English."

Liang is quiet, her eyes on Opal's father, unwavering. She does not look angry, but merely patient, watchful, determined. Opal's eyes are on Liang's face, trying to interpret her expression, how she manages to remain so calm, when she must want it badly enough to ask her father for it. If it was Opal's mother, there would be shouting by now, accusations of chauvinism, red faces of anger and hate. Instead, there is only quietness, underlaid by the tension of waiting.

"I guess you're right," Opal's father relents. Opal sees Liang's eyes lower immediately, knowing she has won. There is no open smile of triumph or gladness. The meal continues.

Opal thinks she sees Liang cast her a look of thanks, but she is not sure. Only after dinner, when Liang offers to wash the dishes, does Opal know for certain.

Her father protests. "Opal, you ought to do your share of the chores around here."

"School test tomorrow," Liang interjects. "Math."

She is already practising her English. Opal nods, feeling playfully devious as she shares in this deception with Liang. "That's right, Dad. I need to study."

"Okay, get going then."

Leaving the kitchen, she turns to see her father and Liang standing side by side at the sink, hips and shoulders touching—Liang washing and her father rinsing, nothing standing between them but air.

*

Liang's ESL classes are every Tuesday and Thursday evening at the local high school, the same one Opal attends during the day. Coincidentally, these two days are the same days on which Opal's father is home for dinner. Liang cooks early and leaves the food covered in the oven so that Opal and her father can heat it up with ease.

Opal and her father eat alone those days, much like they did before her father married Liang, except that they have better food now. Sometimes Opal is tempted, although she does not yet dare, to ask her father why he married Liang, a poor China girl with only a high school education and no TV. Why, when he was born in Canada and had been married to Opal's mother, a modern western woman?

During one of these meals, Opal looks across the table to her father as they quietly eat. Without thinking, she asks, "Why didn't you want Liang to take ESL?"

The moment the question leaves her mouth, Opal realizes it is a mistake. She keeps her eyes on her plate, almost hoping that he will ignore the question. He will not yell at her, she knows, but when truly angered, his face will harden with an implacable silence that can linger for days—a characteristic that Opal has heard her mother pinpoint as one of the main reasons for the divorce, proclaiming it completely maddening and unbreakable.

Her father surprises her, however, by replying. "What makes you think that?" His voice is carefully controlled, neutral.

Opal meets her father's gaze, which is neither annoyed nor condemnatory. Encouraged, Opal lifts her shoulders and shakes her head. "I don't know. It just felt like it."

When he does not answer immediately, Opal assumes the subject is closed. But she is surprised once again when he puts down his knife and fork and says, "Of course she should learn English, if only so that you two can talk to each other more." He raises an eyebrow at Opal, before the corner of his mouth twists into a half smile. "Maybe I was feeling selfish. I guess I just like it when she's around."

It is the closest he has come to expressing how he feels about Liang, and Opal cannot hide her grin, feeling a rush of warmth for Liang, who has made her father happy again. Then, abruptly, Opal thinks of her mother's enduring bitterness and a vague guilt settles over her, subduing the warmth until it is nothing but a stone that sits in her stomach.

At night, she studies her own face in the mirror, searching for some feature of her mother's. The ears, perhaps, the pointed chin. The slight uplift of the nose. Still, she cannot be sure if these are real or imagined. Not even when she holds up a portrait photo of her mother next to her face.

"Of course, honey. You've got my nose for sure. And around the eyes too."

Opal feels this last part to be a lie. They are sitting on the patio of a café near her mother's apartment building having fresh fruit smoothies, weak sun filtering down on them through the ragged awning above.

"But why do you ask? Did Ted say something?"

"No." Opal shakes her head. "I just wanted to know."

"It doesn't matter who you look like"—her mother reaches for her cigarettes and lighter—"you're my beautiful Opal baby." After she has taken a deep drag, she looks absently past Opal and out to the sidewalk where people saunter by walking dogs, pushing strollers. Her voice takes on an introspective quality as she continues, "I knew I had to name you Opal the second they put you in my arms. You were glowing, in my eyes you were glowing just like your name—it was a sign or something. Ted wanted to call you Jessica, but I wouldn't let him."

Opal sips her drink, her eyes on her mother's face. She has heard this story more than a dozen times, but it never fails to intrigue her. Each time, she tries to imagine herself as her mother describes—pale and delicate, iridescent and multicoloured—but the image that always comes to mind is the photo taken a few days after she was born, where she is wrinkled, brown, and squalling.

"What did you say to him?"

"I just told him flat out that your name was going to be Opal, and as far as I was concerned you couldn't be named anything else." Her mother continues to smoke, looking almost dreamy. "He didn't like it, of course. He was used to having things his own way. Still is. But I put my foot down and he couldn't do one damn thing about it. Who knows, maybe that's what started this whole thing."

Understanding is slow to seep into Opal's mind, but when it does, it hits with the force of a knife, cutting her inside, swift and deep. This is one side of the story she has not heard before—she has considered the notion that she herself may have been part of the reason for her parents' divorce, but it has always been a vague and shadowy idea, harboured beneath layers and layers in her mind. Now she feels as though it has been dragged from the mud, placed in the light, harsh, glaring, and inescapable.

Suddenly, her mother's eyes flash back to awareness, and she looks at Opal, chagrined. "Oh my God, what am I saying? I didn't mean that at all, honey, I'm just babbling." Her expression is suddenly pleading. "You know that, don't you?"

"It's okay," Opal says. But it's not.

Her mother looks upset as she stubs out her cigarette in the plastic ashtray on the table. Even after the butt is clearly extinguished, she continues to grind it down until it has fallen apart and stained her fingers with nicotine and ash. "Are you finished?"

It takes a moment for Opal to realize her mother is referring to her drink. There is still half of it left, but Opal does not think she can swallow anymore today. She nods.

"Let's get out of here." Her mother scrapes her chair against the pavement as she stands.

"Okay."

As they leave, Opal feels her mother's hand rest lightly, briefly, on her shoulder. Then it is gone.

The following evening, when Opal is back at her father's house, in her bedroom studying, she hears a faint knock on her door. "Come in."

It is Liang, a book tucked beneath her arm, her expression hesitant, almost shy. "Sorry, no bother you?"

Opal shakes her head, feeling awkward. "No, you're not bothering me. I'm just studying." It is strange seeing Liang in her room—this is the first time Liang has ever come to seek her out. Usually, after supper when the dishes are washed, they will withdraw to separate rooms, Liang only occasionally joining Opal in the den to watch TV. Opal points to the book Liang holds. "Do you have a question about English?"

"Yes. You please help me?" Liang asks with raised eyebrows.

"Sure." Opal motions for Liang to sit down on the bed.

Liang struggles to make clear her questions by pointing out passages in the book while Opal tries to explain the differences between "the," "a," and "some," and between concrete and abstract nouns. This last concept is harder for Liang to grasp; she studies Opals face intently as though the answers lie there, but shakes her head in confusion when Opal asks her to give examples.

Opal tries a different tactic. "'Concrete' means something you can touch. Like this book"—she uses her knuckles to tap the cover of the book—"or this desk." She knocks on her desk top, willing Liang to understand. In the back of her mind, she wonders how Liang can persist, be so diligent about learning when it must be more difficult for her than Opal can imagine.

"Book," Liang repeats. "Desk."

"Yes," Opal nods encouragingly. "And 'abstract' means something you can't really touch, but it's still real, like—" Opal thinks for a moment. "Like love." She uses her pencil to draw a small heart on a piece of paper. Then she draws an X over it. "Or hate."

Liang nods. "Hate. Love."

Opal is not certain Liang understands. "Maybe you should ask Dad when he gets home. He can probably explain it better."

Liang stands up to leave. "Thank you help me."

"You're welcome."

As Liang starts towards the door, she passes by the dresser where the photo portrait of Opal's mother sits, the silver chrome frame glinting in the light. Liang pauses to look at the photo, and Opal realizes that it is probably the first glimpse that Liang has ever had of the woman who came before her, the first wife. It has never occurred to Opal what Liang might think of her mother, whether there is resentment, jealousy. Liang looks at the photo for a long moment before she turns around to face Opal. "You mother?"

Opal does not realize she has been holding her breath until she has to let it out to reply. "Yes."

"She very beautiful."

Searching for the slightest hint of insincerity or scorn in Liang's voice, Opal finds none. "Thank you," she says, unsure of what else to offer. Strangely, she feels the urge to share something more with Liang, perhaps make a connection, however fragile. Instinctively, she knows Liang asking for help is a step she has taken towards a precarious friendship that Opal realizes she wants to reciprocate. "If you need any more help, you can ask me. If you want to," Opal adds. She hopes it is enough that Liang will understand.

After Liang has left, Opal thinks how extraordinary it is that gratitude can be shown without a word, without the slightest change in expression, be simply felt, in silence.

That Saturday Opal is at her mother's apartment for dinner; they eat mini frozen pizzas baked too long in the oven so that the bottoms are dark brown. Her mother has rented videos and they will stay up late eating microwave popcorn and painting each other's nails—girls' night in, her mother has said.

As Opal bites into another overly crisp pizza, she cannot help but wonder what her father and Liang are doing at this moment, without her there. The thought of sex crosses her mind, but it is such a repelling image she immediately stamps it out. She prefers to imagine them sitting in the kitchen or in the living room, talking the way they do whenever they are together, and when they think she is not looking.

"So how's the young new wife working out?" her mother asks. "Ted must be enjoying himself."

Opal does not like the sarcastic tone of her mother's voice. She is unwilling to go along with her mother's disparagement today, which is as inevitable as the cigarette her mother taps out of the pack and lights. She puts down her pizza and moves to the refrigerator to pour herself a glass of milk. "Do you have to smoke?"

"Do I have to smoke?" her mother repeats, incredulously. "What's that supposed to mean? I've only been doing it since before you were born."

"Dad's quit. He quit a long time ago."

Opal does not know where this is coming from, why she is trying to aggravate, to wound her mother. She feels poison forming, ready and waiting on her tongue. She drinks her milk.

"What's wrong with you? You never cared about me smoking before." Her mother gets up from the table, running her fingers through her light brown hair, her cigarette still in her hand. "Did Ted say something about this?"

"Dad never says anything about you." To Opal's ears, her voice sounds taunting, and she is suddenly ashamed. She looks away.

Her mother has stopped, is standing still, staring at Opal with eyes that are stricken. Then she turns her face, picking up the ashtray. "I don't want to talk to you right now," she says, her voice wavering. She leaves the kitchen; a moment later the bedroom door is closed.

Opal cleans up the remains of dinner, washing the pans and dishes and tidying up the counter. When it is time to sleep, she folds out the sofa bed herself, turns out all the lights in the apartment and lies down underneath the sheets. Her mother's bedroom door remains closed, a thin line of light spreading out from beneath it, shining, keeping Opal awake in the darkness.

On Sunday evening, as Opal is getting ready to leave, she wants to say sorry to her mother for what she said. They have been awkward with each other all day, verbally tiptoeing, both afraid of a repeat of the incident last night. She knows that if she does not do it now, she will not be able to do it at all. Just like her parents, who rarely apologized to each other, even after the most vicious of fights, when they would pretend it had not happened, even though it still sat between them, boiling and building with each added insult.

A car horn honks from outside; it is her father. Opal turns to say it, say the words, but her mother is already giving her a perfunctory hug and kiss on the cheek. "I'll see you next Saturday, darling. Have a good week."

It has not happened, they will pretend. She does not apologize. No one has taught her how.

On Tuesday, Opal goes back to school in the evening to watch a basketball game. After it is over, Opal waits. Her father will be here at ten to pick her up along with Liang who is still in her ESL class.

She wanders the halls of the school, looking at photos of graduating classes of the past, science posters with hand-drawn pictures of eyeballs, lungs, hearts. She passes classrooms that are filled with adults, all wanting to learn new things, cooking, sewing, bookkeeping, pottery, French. By chance, she comes upon the ESL class; the door is open and Opal can partially see in, see the teacher who is surprisingly her own English teacher, Mrs Whitton. She does not see Liang, who must be sitting at the back.

She wonders if she should stay here, if Liang will be happily surprised to see her waiting for her instead of outside the front doors as they previously planned. She does not know if this is what she wants, to have Liang think she has been waiting, so that they may walk out together, like she does with her friends after school.

There is no time to decide because the class is over, men and women, most of them Asian, exit the classroom. When Liang emerges, she sees Opal immediately, approaches her, smiling.

"Game finish?" Liang asks, her pencilled eyebrows raised inquiringly. "Over?"

"It finished early," Opal replies. She cannot help smiling back. "Do you want to go now? Dad might be waiting."

They are about to leave, when Mrs Whitton comes out, locking the classroom door behind her. "Opal!" she exclaims. "What are you doing here so late?"

Opal begins to answer, but Mrs Whitton does not wait, before continuing, "I didn't know you were Liang's daughter. You ought to be very proud of your mother, she's one of the best students in the class."

Opal feels redness seep into her cheeks. Liang. Her mother. Her eyes feel hot, she is inexplicably furious. Her lips tremble with rage. "She's not my mother," she hears herself spitting out. "She's just married to my dad."

She cannot bear to look at either Liang or Mrs Whitton as she turns and hurries down the hall alone, seething with fury and embarrassed humiliation. She thinks of her mother and she wants to scream and cry all at once. She feels so hot, she thinks she might explode. Bursting through the doors to the outside, she draws cold air into her lungs, wanting to be at home, wanting to be at her mother's, wanting to be alone, wanting, wanting things that can't possibly be. She does not understand herself.

She skulks around the darkness for a while, around the school, not knowing what to do. Her father might be looking for her, she thinks. Or maybe he and Liang have driven home themselves, so that she will have to walk, or take the bus. Crouching against the trunk of a fir tree, she shivers against the chill that has set in through her thin jacket. She has no watch and cannot tell what time it is.

Eventually she finds her father's car. Liang is already there, sitting up front, her head resting against Opal's father's shoulder. When Opal appears, Liang sits up and turns to look out the window. Neither of them asks where she has been.

She doesn't care, she thinks decidedly, defensively, as her father starts the car. But she does, she already feels sorry. She shrinks back into her seat, her eyes on the back of Liang's head, which is tilted at a proud angle. She does not know what to say.

When they get home, it is past midnight. Everything feels weary, the house, the people, the air. Her father goes upstairs immediately to his bedroom without looking at Opal or saying a word. He has a class to teach the next morning and she has kept him up, behaved like a child. He is probably thinking that she is just like her mother.

Opal follows Liang into the kitchen, waiting until Liang has faced her, before she tries.

"Liang—I..."

Liang looks at her, her eyes flat black, as she shrugs out of her coat. "Time for bed." She speaks without anger, her accent pronounced, but the words clear. Her mouth is held firm. "Go on."

In her room, Opal does not look at herself in the mirror, or at her mother's photo. Instead, sitting in darkness, she closes her eyes and wonders how such wounds can stem from the intangible, the smallest of all divides.

Kagan Goh

Life After Love

I'm sitting in the backseat of my parents' car, being driven to Saint Paul's Hospital. Again. This is the fifth time in four years. I have committed no crime, but I feel like a repeat offender.

"Mum, Dad. I'm fine. I'm not sick. I don't want to go to hospital."

For a second I think of flinging the door open and running away, beating the tarmac, retreating to the streets where so many of my mentally ill brothers and sisters live in poverty. Become another street kid living on the skids. But I stay, resisting the itch to run, for that would break my parents' hearts.

At Saint Paul's emergency ward I go through the routine of checking myself in as a patient. Reluctantly my parents leave, hiding their grief as best as they can, until the exit door swings shut. I retreat to my room, bury myself under a blanket to sleep my reality away.

"Wake up!" I am shaken awake. "If you sleep you'll never get out of here. They're watching us all the time. My name is Kevin."

Kevin is short and wears thick black spectacles. He looks like the stereotypical nerd. He's a chess whiz.

"Wanna play?"

"No thanks. I don't play competitive games."

"It's not competitive. It's only competitive if you play eight rounds. Challenge someone to eight rounds, that's personal."

He tries to explain the rules of the game. I remain silent, afraid to reveal my stupidity.

"Everyone picks on me coz I'm small."

It's true, everyone in the ward picks on Kevin except me. I guess I am the closest thing he has to a friend.

I can't control these dark thoughts of rape, incest, murder, violence, suicide. All my notions of goodness are stripped away revealing the dark sewer of shit and blood coursing through my brain. I'd renounce everything to be released from this torment.

Kevin advises me: "You must learn to discharge the Dark Side safely through art, exercise, or sports. You ever play computer games at the arcade?"

"No."

"You should try it. It's a great way of getting rid of your aggression safely. The number one rule is: Don't hurt anybody, including yourself."

The dull day is punctuated by a bland breakfast, a bland lunch, and a bland dinner. Collecting trays labeled with our names, we sit at the dining table and remove the covers. Surprise, surprise. The same meal we had the day before and the day before that, thinly disguised as something different.

Poking it with a fork, we attempt to analyze it.

I confess to Kevin: "I may be perverse, but I kinda like this food. Call me crazy, but I've always liked airplane food."

"You are crazy. No wonder they put you in here."

In my boredom I ride the stationary exercise bike going nowhere. I pace with the rest of the walking wounded, going round and round like a scratched record in the psych ward, trying to regain my sanity.

I ask a tall ginger-bearded fellow why he's here. He looks me in the eye and says:

"Because I'm a madman!"

"Whathappened?"

"I am an artist. I was working on this wire frame paper mache sculpture. I was spreading plaster of Paris with my hands and all of a sudden…wooooooooooosh!"

He spreads his arms to the sky like a pterodactyl taking flight.

"The sirens—woooooooo!—the blue and red, blue and red lights came and took me away."

The staff treat us with condescension as if our every request is absurd. Being treated crazy makes one crazy. The doctors and nurses joke at our expense, their laughter insulated behind plate-glass windows.

Anorexic teenagers, thin as skeletons, bones poking through taut flesh, push stands with saline bags drip-dripping into tubes stuck in their arms. Their only food. Why would such beautiful girls starve themselves? So weak, death just a whisper away. They pace round the ward frail as ghosts, Death's handmaidens, condemned to dereliction row.

A native girl called Doreen asks to see my journal. She leafs through my poems, drawings, doodles, and collages page by delicate page. She shows me her journal. Doreen must be sixteen but she draws like a child. Wild clashing colours across the page.

"Write me something," she says.

I pick up a felt pen and write:

Fortitude and pride
as the tide subsides
washing away
our fears of the day.
Usher in the stillness
that permeates this prayer.
Let us live in peace
and find strength within
when none seems there.

"That's beautiful." She makes a friendship bracelet for me. It's made of dayglow plastic. She slips it on my wrist next to my hospital tag. She hugs me and won't let go.

Later Kevin tells me she's a mother.

"She's sixteen and pregnant again."

A woman with Cruella de Ville hair named Veronica scolds herself, stuttering, "Damn it! Get away from me you blood-sucking vermin!" And she grapples with an invisible enemy, hands flailing in a manic panic, fists raining down upon her head.

I must be hallucinating. I see a purple green black nebula veiling her head like a dark storm cloud. I don't believe in auras but some things are true whether we want to believe them or not. I see every black eye, purple swollen bruise, bloodied stitched up cut she's ever had on her weatherbeaten face.

Kevin says: "She used to be a great beauty. Now she's a used-up crack whore. I bet you she was sexually abused as a child. All the men in her life have been assholes. Men who could not control their sexual impulses."

I feel a stab of guilt. Men who could not control their sexual urges. Men like me. I realize in my manic state that my uninhibited sexual urges are so profuse that if I'm not careful I too could commit sexual abuse. The DSM calls this "loss of insight." I don't want to become a pervert. This thought scares me into sobriety.

The ward is a human junkyard filled with the wreckage of discarded lives. Kevin and I enter the TV room where smoking is allowed. I can barely breathe. Doreen beams at me, puffing a cigarette. The rest tease us:

"Hey, Doreen, is he your new boyfriend?"

"Shut up!"

She turns to me: "Hey look at this." She stubs the burning cigarette on her arm. Still smiling, she shows me the brand mark.

"Don't do that."

"Why? It doesn't hurt."

"It hurts me to see you hurt yourself."

A nurse pokes her head in to check on us. Doreen quickly hides her arm and the stubbed-out cigarette.

The TV is spilling forth the same old prime-time deluge of sex and violence. Don't the hospital staff realize that this toxic, violent sewage is harmful to our fragile impressionable psyches?

I turn the TV off despite the protests. Kevin turns the dial on the radio, looking for something worth listening to. He tunes into an upbeat song by Cher.

"Turn it up!" demands Veronica.

"Do you believe in life after love?
I can feel something inside me say
I really don't think you're strong enough..."

Heads bop. Toes tap. The infectious melody of the song spreads like a sexually transmitted disease. Veronica, Doreen and the anorexic girls are dancing with reckless abandon, shouting the lyrics at the top of their cigarette-blackened lungs.

"I know that I'll get through this
coz I know that I am strong..."

The inmates have taken over the asylum.
We all let loose, going crazy and for a moment,
a brief moment...
we feel normal
(whatever that means).
No, not normal.
Human.
Human again.
Do you believe in life after love?
Yes.
Why?
Coz we're living proof.

Jessica Gin-Jade

Just Dandruff

"I was lying in labor for thirty-six hours with your father gone missing and all when you came," Madam Tan said to Hwee Lin. "He wanted to have you real bad, but when the time came he just wasn't there. We had been married just that long when it didn't matter where he was anymore except to remind him where to put the garbage. Seven years, it was... that fall...let me see, you were born in 1979...You weren't even alive when the Lau's first baby girl was born—she's graduated with a Master's in sociology now and going on to a PhD in physics—physics! Those subjects are as different as fish and flies, I never did understand that girl, but she's always been smart. And there's you now, going off to university—the little baby that your father wanted and I took care of, all grown up."

Hwee Lin had nothing to say to this as her mother paused for breath. She lay across the sofa, her back facing Madam Tan, her legs swinging in the air. Her elbows propped her at an angle. She was smoothing out the tangles in her unruly black hair, occasionally reaching back for the bubblegum-pink comb clutched expertly between the first and second toes of her right foot. She wore shorts and a pink bra. Her rose-tinted toes were bare.

Madam Tan sighed in her loud waspy voice as she sprawled on the floor, hunting out hidden mosquitoes with a wet mop. They were in the room Madam Tan shared with her husband, a large room with matching twin beds. A white ceiling fan tirelessly rotated and an old air-conditioner spluttered gusts of icy air into the room, making the floor-length curtains billow periodically through the open windows. It was the Singaporean monsoon again, hand in hand with vampish mosquitoes, starving flies, and the occasional bout of dengue fever. Yesterday, the neighbour's daughter had died of malaria.

On the other two floors of the house, Madam Tan ran a boarding house for foreign students from South East Asia. She tutored them in English and Chinese, charging cheaply for lodgings but always complaining about being undervalued. Her face was an odd shade of yellowed pink; once a peony in bloom, she now had the appearance of an aged Oriental Cabbage-Patch doll. Her one pride were her tiny feet, no bigger than a child's size eight. On these she wore special four-hundred-dollar Bailey shoes, low heeled and designed to ease arthritis. She walked fast, but was quicker in professing that her feet had never been bound nor had those of any women in her family—they were a modern-minded clan, and small beautiful feet were hereditary. She had studied nursing in Canada, being one of Singapore's pioneer females to be educated in a western country. This past she wore like an invisible medal, pulling her skirts in as she passed fish sellers in the wet markets. She taught by day and cleaned the marble toilets by night while the hired maid slept. Her husband did research at the local national university. It was this university that Hwee Lin did not want to go to.

The dark leather of the sofa was littered with coarse hairs that had succumbed to Hwee Lin's incessant tugging. She didn't care; at least, she wouldn't show that she did. Her father had picked out the upholstery, a difficult suede that collected hair and Madam Tan's loud rantings. The latter now noted her husband's good taste in selecting black leather: the hair didn't show up except under light…only dandruff did. Noticing a speck of white on the sofa, she instinctively said, "Scotch tape."

Hwee Lin tossed her head, scattering a trail of stray hair on the clean marble tiles, as she tested her head of well-combed hair. Her mother was mad; she picked up dust and hair with sticky tape as a hobby. Hwee Lin had once seen old flypaper in an antique shop and thought of buying some as a present for Mother's Day. But age had worn out the sticky glue on the strips, and Hwee Lin had picked a bunch of carnations instead. Her mother scorned flowers. Looking at Madam Tan happily crouched on her knees, picking at hair with Scotch tape, Hwee Lin regretted her choice.

"You have lovely black hair, like the keys of that piano you play," her mother chattered. " Too bad there's all this dandruff to ruin your texture, but you never would use the Head and Shoulders I got you."

"Canada has Head and Shoulders," said Hwee Lin softly. "You said you used to buy that when you were there. It was the cheapest, and you were a poor student."

"I wasn't poor until I married him, your father," snapped Madam Tan, sitting up on her heels. "There we were, two poor Chinese puppies struggling in a white country, with no kin, no friends."

"So you choose to create some by marrying each other," Hwee Lin's voice was soft, almost understanding.

"I married him out of pity," her mother spurted. "His father had just passed away, poor fellow, and he had run out of funds for school. Your father was a bright young man, and I couldn't see that go to waste. So I married him, a bright young man."

"That's what he said too," said Hwee Lin.

"Is that so. That he was a bright young man?" Madam Tan huffed.

"Oh no, just that you worked night shifts as a staff nurse to put him through graduate school," said Hwee Lin. "Father is very grateful for that. He speaks of you at the library every other week and..." Hwee Lin paused, drawing her tongue over her lips in contemplation. "...And he wishes his research allowed him more time to be home. Yes, that's what he always says."

"You know what, Hwee Lin?" said Madam Tan. "You could have stayed and attended the local Uni here, all your friends did. You could have continued to help your poor father at the library with his research. You wouldn't have to be all alone there in Canada, a seventeen-year-old—"

"I turned eighteen last week."

"That's right, you aren't jail bait anymore, at least there won't be any of *those* old men to worry about..."

"Mama, the legal age in Canada is nineteen," said Hwee Lin.

"That's not the point. I *told* you, didn't I, to keep away from that man? I told you you were courting trouble, acting cute with that squatting down and underwear showing and all. I warned you he would sniff your panties like a stray cat would old fish bones! That man was twenty-nine years old!" Madam Tan sat upright, her Scotch tape dangling from a finger, stray hair collected at the end. She waited to see Hwee Lin cry. Her daughter didn't.

"Mama, David is twenty-eight."

"Twenty-eight?" cried Madam Tan. "And an income of seven hundred a month, five brothers to feed and a wife he forgets to mention."

"Oh, he told me,"said Hwee Lin.

"And you didn't mind?" Madam Tan swerved around to face her child. She said the next line carefully, waving her Scotch tape wildly in the air. "You aren't in love with him, are you?"

Dandruff landed on the black sofa.

"Good God, no!" Hwee Lin had started to play with her hair again. More dandruff landed on the dark leather. It was beginning to look like Christmas.

"That's well then. Let me tell you, he wouldn't have cared for you," Madam Tan continued. "Your father and I, we were rare ones for love. I put him through school. That man of yours wouldn't... couldn't! All our other friends had won fellowships and such, but your father wasn't that fortunate. I was the lucky one—my head nurse adored me. She had us over at Christmas and I got promoted to be her assistant. Soon, I was earning fifty more cents every hour," Madam Tan sighed pleasurably. She could see the old hospital in Ottawa, its stertile white walls with landscape pictures in twin bedrooms. The pictures were supposed to help patients recover. The hospital had black couches meant to rest anxious families in the waiting room. The windows were always open in the summer, allowing full curtains to flutter in the breeze. A tape deck played soft ancient songs about unrequited love, mermaids, and drowned children. Madam Tan still had one of those tapes. The first time she played it to Hwee Lin was also the last time, for the tape squealed like breaking tires. The tape gave way after that, but Madam Tan still kept it in its cracked plastic cover. Her daughter wondered how a mermaid could give birth.

Hwee Lin was happy their house had no landscape pictures. She had heard her mother describe the sterile building with its smells of distilled urine too often.

"They loved me at the hospital, everyone. I could dash eight flights of stairs for a Dr Purple call: *Calling Madam Tan, Calling Madam Tan to Dr Purple in Room 14...* they were always amazed that I was a fast runner for my size." She leaned against the sofa, her Scotch tape forgotten amidst a tide of reminiscing. "And a Japanese doctor proposed to me there."

"Dr Purple?"

"No! Dr Purple was the code the staff used for crisis calls when the patients had gone purple in the face...that was the happiest time in my life, being in that hospital. And in just two years, your father graduated, a Masters in Library Science." Madam Tan didn't look proud.

"And he couldn't find a job in Ottawa so he had to come back to Singapore," Hwee Lin continued, taking up bunches of her hair in her hands and examining the ends. Satisfied that there were no tangles left to occupy her fingers, she resumed her initial position, her back to Madam Tan.

"He found a job eventually. And hired a maid so I would be easy," Madam Tan picked absently at the sofa with her tape now, not noticing her failure to stick dandruff to the hairy surface of her tape. "He bought us this house, this sofa."

Hwee Lin looked uncomprehending, then tossed her head.

"Some people bloom late. Your father was one of them," her mother stated this defensively. "Not like you. Look at you." Madam Tan gazed at the firm brown breasts nestled in pink fabric with distaste. They reminded her of the chocolate eggs they used to give out every Easter at the hospital, resting in pink tissue. "You don't even wear a shirt."

"There's no one to see."

Hwee Lin swung her legs over the edge of the couch, bringing herself to sitting position. She sat, left leg dangling, right foot crossed over the left, still clutching the bright pink comb. She turned to stare at Madam Tan. Her face was peaceful.

"One day left," Hwee Lin announced. "Tomorrow makes zero."

"You have been counting the days, haven't you? Well, so have I," said her mother. "You fly tomorrow. To Ottawa. I don't think you remember what it looks like, you were only four when we left. You must tell me how my hospital looks now."

Hwee Lin dropped her stare and began collecting scattered dandruff in her palms. She muttered something Madam Tan did not care to understand.

"I will miss you," Madam Tan continued. "You may not think it, but I will. Why couldn't you stay and let your father pay for university here I don't know. There was that good job with him at the library too. You didn't have to take that burasry. But you never were one to listen to me anyway. Ever since you were a little girl, it was always *your way, your way*. Like that time you wanted to go to Disneyland. You wouldn't take no for an answer and we had to take you to Penang instead. We always had to listen to you…you never cared about *us*." Madam Tan waited to hear she was cared for. She tore off another piece of Scotch tape to resume her dandruff-picking when she saw what Hwee Lin was doing.

Her daughter had gathered all the bits of dandruff into a little ball and was rolling the small lump in her fingers.

"I could melt all this scalp wax and put a string through it," Hwee Lin said, fingering her frayed shorts as if to find a suitable stray cotton wick. "That would give me a candle."

"You never listen." Madam Tan dropped her piece of clean tape on the marble tiles. "You never will. I told you, when that David man appeared, to stay away from him, and you wouldn't. All that prancing around in that pink bra, it never did no good. You know what I heard David say to his fellow workers? He said to them, 'If she wasn't leaving, I'd ask her to have me,' and one of his workers said, 'You could always do her then let her leave.' And David said, 'That's what I'm thinking too, but her mother watches like a night cat,' and then he said, ' Did you see what she was wearing today—it made me want to—fuc…k…' She stopped at the dirty word, horrified to hear herself speak it. She hurried on. "And he said 'I want her and I love her,' and I was all horrified to hear that last bit because he couldn't possibly love you when he had a wife and all, but I didn't tell you because I thought you were smarter than that and wouldn't take him." Madam Tan struck at the sofa and cried, "I told you to stay away but you wouldn't! I tried my best as your mother but you never had regard for me anyway. And your father wouldn't tell you. You are lucky to still be a virgin."

Hwee Lin frowned absently, still rolling the ball of wax in her fingers. She added an imaginary speck of dandruff to the ball and said, "I am not one, Mama. It isn't exactly what you think, but after David tried to make love to me and all, I realized that I wasn't a virgin."

Madam Tan gasped to hear this word from her daughter. She said, "Did he leave any scars?"

"No, he was very gentle. He played with my hair and said he loved me."

Madam Tan contemplated this for a moment, and tried to turn the subject her way again. "Do you ever think about your father's poor name?"

"I hear his name in my head every night."

"A raped daughter! What will the marketplace say—"

"Nothing. They have never known and they never will."

"What will you think when you are forty? This is a terrible memory, it will haunt you for life."

"It has already haunted me for fourteen years," said Hwee Lin wisely. "Afterwards I started locking my door at night but you wouldn't hear of it, so I hid the key, but he got to me at the library instead. Sex on metal shelves is uncomfortable, I often thought I would fall off one day but he pinned me down tightly. I always came out smelling of musty books."

Madam Tan looked at her closely. The girl was not lying. She looked at her daughter hopefully.

"You didn't tell me so I wouldn't hurt?"

"There was nothing to tell but how my butt always froze on those air-conditioned shelves," Hwee Lin said this placidly.

"Are you all right?"

"Don't worry, Mama. That's how our association started out. At least he's not paying for my university."

"But—he..."

"He loves you. Father told me that many times."

Madam Tan's face remained rested in her palms.

"He bought you this house. This sofa," Hwee Lin continued. "It just has to be cleared of the dandruff. I will do that—I need more for my candle. Don't worry, it never hurt."

"What did?" Madam Tan's voice came muffled beneath thick flesh.

"When David told me he loved me. But that was just once."

She needs to cry, Madam Tan thought. She needs my shoulder to lean on, its been too long. She tore a fresh piece of Scotch tape slowly, thinking how she would hold her trembling daughter in her arms, wondering if she'd ever craved sex at eighteen.

Meanwhile, Hwee Lin scooped white flakes from the sofa with her palm and molded her dandruff candle as her mother started to cry.

ben soo

Antiques

A comfortable feeling, what you get, sometimes when for no reason understandable invisible little magic handkerchiefs flutter down in swarms out of a luminous sky and transform baseness to beauty all around, a gauzy blanket of reticular balm, and even the ugliest putrescent green mailbox, bubbling paint down the bottom and covered in clammy grit, will become, like the sea anemone, sightly to behold.

So it was i chanced upon one of my old haunts. In this case the noun's literal. That's a qualification i always apply reverently in reference to this piece of real estate. There i was, sauntering along thinking about the migrating flight of birds, the taste of dinner, my chances with my lottery tickets (o!), the territories of homeless cats, increasing urban congestion, et cetera, when i turned the corner and came upon, not my favourite run-down duplex in the whole city, but the burnt out wreckage of it.

O, rack and ruin! A big heap of crazy, gray and blackened timber, shingles jumbled in a mess like abandoned autumn leaves after rain; window frames gutted of both glass and those blowsy drapes that shield cosy interiors; pockmarked, cancer-yellow urea insulation exposed to the sun and still adhering to some diseased building code; all of it cordoned off with irregularly plunked-down barricades—no-parking signs, no less. You cross out the "P" in "Parking" and you have "arking." Makes sense to me. Walk by and gawk all you want, examine eighty-plus years of permanence and tenancy gone as easily as a milk carton gets squashed. After a while a couple of dumpsters stop by, leave a hole and some tinder behind. And then suddenly a steel-framed monster grows in the hole, and next thing you know there's a pink stone facade and a beautician with a neon sign in the window, and some video rental store upstairs. Or, maybe, a lovely lilac neon molar.

Whenever i go to buy groceries i always detour by this house, just beeline by on the sidewalk, because all holy places need their supplicants and if by chance it is a spot only vaguely sanctified inside a person's turnip of a head, why then, it only needs someone to once in a while walk by and give it a nod and a greeting, and a little mental note appended to say, i'm well and all my teeth remain attached, though with a slight increase in metallic content. Hope you are okay.

i was much younger when i lived here. i mean, if there was a localized Cartier-Bresson and he'd caught me in some rigorously conceived candid postures then and now, you wouldn't notice much difference except for the more conservative clothes on the newer me. Older hair too, yes, but more of it, and naturally coiffed. The style is the story!

Kids in school, kids not in school but in the atmosphere of school, older people mixing around with kids in or out of school. Anyway i was in school and it all seemed that way. In those undergrad days before computerized registration it was quite a war story to have survived the process and be thoroughly screwed into awful time slots. Perhaps to those not in the know it was all just a lot of low-rent music pounding through walls and keeping them awake nights, them halcyon nights before the advent of electronica.

i got the place with the usual shenanigans. Dressed in my best Sally Ann estate remnants, facing a suspicious-looking little landlord in his doorway, beatific grin on my face fooling nobody. Yes yes, i'm a worthy and studious type, i'll study all night, take out the trash, and i've speakers the size of peas hooked up to my absolutely insignificant stereo. The man says to me, You're a good boy, he says, this is a special place; you be careful with it. He was just one of those guys, short and rounding, probably hell to deal with about the diseased plumbing, and the doorway he stood in smelled of cigarettes and grilled onions.

Grinning some more i thought, Oho, so i'm a good boy, am i? And he, as if answering this thought, said, Sure, you'll be fine, you're a good kid. Apartment is next door, upstairs. Check it out.

So it's almost four months later with the end of semester tumbling over the horizon, i'm installed in the apartment with all my own coffee grounds in the sink to show for it, and the least of my worries were the class papers that had backed up every which way. i had a part-time job which wasn't going well, waitering in a chicken wing diner on busy nights. It billed for plastic pitchers of beer and chicken wings by the basket, but what really kept it hopping were the boys and girls picking each other up. The resto manager, an Iranian dude who spoke lovely Persian to his various visiting family members, constantly wanted more zip out of us than we had arms and legs for. And you know boys and girls in college: with pennies they tip.

i had linear algebra in the morning and in the afternoon some institutional fogey who wanted original but traditional thoughts on *Middlemarch.* Twice a week there were physics labs with lab exams on networked TRS80 terminals. Remember eight inch floppies? Probably not. At night i read piles of submissions for a campus lit. rag run by a grad student whose idea of poetry was free and sparse verse in the guise of an Amerigo Vespucci delphic internal monologue.

On weekends i saw an American girl from the moneyed classes who was in serious training for social entry into the liberal elite. She had a well-directed social life with the right mix of institutional and artistic elements. Much more worldly than i; i was just experiencing life whereas she was gearing up to use it. i'm afraid she hadn't much time for the chicken wing diner, and Amerigo Vespucci was fine with her if there was a credit on the masthead in it, accountable by the number of hours spent acquiring it compared to the gravity of the accreditation. Reading general submissions just didn't swing the scale.

Always the decisive one, she broke things off when my papers piled up. Get a grip, were her parting words. She put it better; you know, used pretzel logic. So i was left in my kitchen on my nights off, playing My Dog Popper, knowing i'd bitten off more than i could chew and it was chewing me. That was when i had the first of those dreams about the woman in the apartment. In the physical reality i slumped on the zinc-trimmed linoleum table top, my head unceremoniously interred in the middle of an unreadable library book, overdue, about the travails of George Eliot. In the dream i was in the narrow hallway walking towards the kitchen. Someone was in it humming a song. i stood at the doorway, looking in upon a woman at a fold-up ironing board. She moved the iron back and forth over a shirt with a vibrating orange pattern. The iron had no power cord. It was wordlessly peaceful. Her iron went back and forth, back and forth, as though all that was important in the world was centered in that simple motion. Then she snatched up the shirt and held it in the air to show me, and i woke up.

i thought nothing of it, just the kind of hyperreal dream a lot of stress would sometimes induce. A few days later i was scrounging around in the used-clothing store for winter workie gloves when out of the racks i pulled this extra loud shirt with an orange floral pattern. i bought it for my own Xmas present. Made me inordinately happy.

The next semester i wasn't a better organized and more thoughtful guy. i had differential equations in the afternoon this time, and some other fogey in the morning who really wanted to make something of F R Leavis. i did have more friends, and they got me into trouble. i got in with this crowd some of whom were in architecture school and had collaborated on pieces for the literary rag. You know that kind of prose, showcases of anointed space, reserved and vaulted hyperbole and the holy trinity of conceptuality, reflexivity, and in behind a ghost of something like orgonomy.

In real life they seemed to have a lot of ins with upscale clubs, played parts in deals within deals with friends who had friends who swung sweet shines to import this or remodel that. Like the man said: Wawa. It paid better than the chicken wing diner, and i got to see a couple of trendoid venues in their pristine plywood phase, before they were painted five shades of sparkly black and had their lights dimmed for the evening. One of these night spots was run by a guy who called himself Boron. He followed the way of the roadie and the big amps of life had dropped on his head. Often he could be seen hopping about the half-constructed nightclub as though his acupuncturist had used wasps on him for needles. No wonder. Word was, in order to start up the place he'd borrowed money from the kind of guy who didn't make out loan contracts on paper.

Watching the clubbing crowd from the outside there seemed distinct layers to it. None was your Manon des Sources type of person. There were the yappy kids with parentally funded autos and barely postpubescent quasidesigner getups, there were those spanning less deterministic age groups who looked like extras from Wim Wenders and Road Warrior movies, and there were languid dudes in suave suits with the Helmut Newton women. Into the brew a spritz of pixie dust and Peg it *will* come back to you. Probably the view was very different from the inside, what with paycheck discrepancies and philosophic disjoints slicing down past style and rigmarole. My architecture friends were in with the sharp suits, while Boron and i affected similar T-shirts and thus bracketed the grunge slot at opposite ends—topologically all T-shirts are similar. He was a different breed altogether though, the dark side of that line: "somewhere i have never travelled."

Boron was congealed from a frenzy of distemper and industrial noise. i think he lived on his own solitary plane of salt and bent steel cacti, where mangy dogs favoured him more than cats would and from whence tumultuous memory was kept from busting loose by the clotted impassivity of his brow. Had his own Volker Schlondorff movie going, one in which he had the power of the scream but could never get it out at all. He also probably wasn't doing that well with his repayment schedule as he had to open the club even though we weren't finished building the place. He started operations downstairs with the pub thing. Upstairs was meant for dancing and the clubby stuff; we were still hammering that together.

It opened over spring break. Early the following morning after i came home knackered from the half-priced booze, i had my second dream about the woman in the apartment. i dreamed i was in the tub and the water had turned cold. It was a sunny day. Someone was humming in the apartment. i grabbed a long yellow towel and wound it around my middle, then padded out to see. The woman was there sitting at a cramped little dining table. She was absorbed with some items that were laid out on it; a pocket watch, a little bottle, lacquered cigaret case, silver chain, a ring. i could tell it made her sad to look at these things. i've thought about it a lot and come to the conclusion that sometimes people just have the gift of being able to clearly broadcast their moods and emotions without seeming to do anything. She did that. It's like having glitter globes in pure colours inside oneself that one can spin up.

i reached out my hand, which was still dripping water, to take up the watch. The woman put her hand over it though—well-grown and sinewed digits; shook her head. She picked up the cigaret case. It was a blue lacquered box with a yellow and white gleaming calla inlaid in the centre. She reached it out to me and opened it so i could see inside, where there was an inscription. It said, *—Loza—*. She put the thing in my hand and i woke up.

This time i saw the cigarette case in the window of an antique store. It wasn't identical; this one had a somewhat cheesy lighter attached. As it was Sunday in that time before seven-day shopping, i had to go back the next day when the store was open. No memory of emptying out my wallet to pay which i must've done as i recall having a tough time meeting the rent that month. What i still feel is the act of picking the thing up and clicking it open to find inside it was plated silver, tarnished, and there in the middle, behind where the stylized flower was inlaid, it was blank.

So one day next week after class i was at Boron's club, finishing up the job, fitting the granite applique to the front of the bar—it was tricky work because the bar was shaped like a series of randomly modulated sine waves. These friends of mine in architecture school, they liked to legitimize the kind of thing you see when you have the DT s. For instance the smoked mirrors in the club were all etched from the back with those little floaty squiggles that fill up your eye. Entoptic phenomena.

The entirety of my talk with the old geezer was transacted while i was pretzelled together under the bar using both pasty forearms, some toes and the knee on the other leg to push in place a lopsided sheet of faux granite until the glue stuck. He'll always be the old geezer to me. Just being mean. It's the thing. Probably until the end of his inordinately proclamatory days i featured as that cheeky hoo-hah. Me, under the bar doing the Rubber Man with spasms in the shoulder and icy needles lining extra crispy socks. Funny how physical discomfort keeps memory green. Like ever-fresh gangrene; any major dude will tell you.

Hey young professor, where'd you get this? A joke of course; those days i looked like classic Weegee material. This hand appeared in front of me holding my new cigarette case which i left on the bar atop a stack of Leavis-y books. i spied well-shined, patent-leather shoes under grey slacks. i said You'll never believe it. i dreamed some woman showed it to me and hola! there it was in some shop.

Is that so, the guy said. The hand withdrew upwards, then i heard the case click open. What i really wanted to do was ask him to please press his soft and well groomed palm right here and hold this veneer so i could stretch back to drain some lactic acid from my limbs, but instead rejoined, Yeah, totally true. Put it back, okay? Happened just last week only the one i dreamed about had an inscription in it. Zola or Lola or something.

Wham! something smacked the bar top hard enough the sweat on my face vibrated, and a beaky flushed face under neat white hair suddenly shoved itself against my chin. Cloudy eyes glared behind specs, one of those stony looks that say; Me head priest of Quetzalcoatl, you virgin sacrifice. Professor, he demanded, You know who i am?

i had no idea, though suddenly a terrible suspicion. His voice was thin and unwell but i was still petrified. Erm, i said, Erm erm. He spat, Why do you make up such a stupid story? and whitened his glare.

There i was crammed under the bar, glue all over my arms, wound up like a contortionist unhinged in his act with both legs good as slung around my neck, being grilled by an immaculately dressed and doubled over little old guy whose maddened face was centimetres from mine.

It's true, i trilled. This lady showed it to me in a dream. Not the only time either. Look, i fall asleep and she's there singing a song. Piping like the Great Gonzo and probably purpley plushed like him, i squeaked out the tune i remembered her humming.

That pulled him short. He stared at me a long time, those exchequer eyes melting down behind sharpshooter specs. His blood pressure dropped to nothing too. After maybe sixty pins had missed their opportunities to drop he awoke and sighed, Mary Mother of God. He held up a totemic business card. All right boy, he said, finish up here and don't come around anymore. i'd tell you to leave now but a man should always finish his work. He waved the card a bit and slipped it on the floor next to me. Come by that address tomorrow afternoon. He straightened and left my field of view.

i kind of hurried the rest of it so the sheets of plastic granite didn't fit so well. My hand-eye coordination had vamoosed.

The address on the card resolved to a dingy coffee snack bar with biscotti in a jar. There was ancient satellite TV in the corner of the ceiling playing some game. The decor wasn't yuppie or new; built up, not conceived. Sort of greenish with the patina of fossilized nineteen sixties plastics following no known Swedish colour scheme. Ah Professor, the old man greeted me, spinning around his stool and folding up a thin newspaper, smile lacing his aged face in horizontal creases. Come sit up here.

He walked behind the counter and made a couple of espressos. The weighty guy working there said nothing, just moved a cigarette and passed the old man the little cups. He placed one of them before me, sat down holding the other and asked me to tell my dreams, which i did. He looked down at the floor and nodded his head while i spoke. At one point he tipped his empty espresso cup towards the counter guy.

First let me give you some advice, Professor, he said. i know these kids you run around with. They know my grandson. They're not careful, do you understand? They're not very careful what they do and who they do it with. Where you were yesterday for instance, that's about to become a very bad headache for my friends, and it was these kids who got them involved in it. The man behind the counter served up fresh cups of coffee and moved off. So let me speak bluntly, the old man resumed: i want you to stop whatever it is you're doing with those children. Leave the city, at least until school begins in the fall. You're in school, yes?

The espresso burnt my tongue but i didn't show it. The old man reached under the counter and carefully took out a framed photograph. This is my mother and her sister, he said. It was a black-and-white picture of two nuns with long headdresses, standing in a hospital ward. That's one of the oldest hospitals in the city, he said. It's where my mother met my father. In those days nurses were nuns or lay sisters.

i pointed at one of the nuns. Yes, he said, That is the one, my aunt. When my mother gave up the Church for my father, and at that time it was still a difficult thing, my aunt followed her. i think perhaps she was a little in love with my father. i remember her a little; i remember her singing me to sleep. She was very kind. My mother always said her kindness shone from her face like a light. She died in one of the epidemics. i don't ask where you live now, it is something i can well guess.

He looked closely at the photograph down the bottom of his specs. We were very poor then. My mother loved her. She always told me my aunt had the gift of finding the goodness in a man's heart. She told me it was my aunt who first saw my father wasn't just some foul-mouthed dock worker with a broken hand.

This, he said, taking out something from inside his jacket, This my father gave me. It was the cigaret case, well worn, with one opalescent petal of the calla cracked. He opened it and put it on the counter with the inscription facing us. i could see that it actually read L.O.S.A. My young Professor, i confide to you this family story because my aunt has cast her light on you and given me a sign, and i believe that she knows how to see into a man. i therefore give you a little advice and my thanks.

He patted me somewhat formally on the shoulder. You can tell he had no wish to be my uncle or anything. i did have my hair done up in three colours. O well: just a messenger very happy it wasn't bad news.

i still had a half a paycheck coming but if the old geezer didn't agonize over it then neither would i. Well okay. Made my peace with F R Leavis, enough to get done with him anyway. Those were the days when tree planting was a much-talked-about summer opportunity and that's what i did to get out of town. i had one more dream some days before i left.

There was a cup of water in my hand. i stood on the back stairs, which was in shade because of the angle of the sun. She was at the back door; i followed her inside. She walked through the kitchen, where i noticed a dingy stove with gently whispering kettle and a teapot, on into the front room, to a crib under the window that still had yellow sunlight on it. It spread over the crib and across her plain dress. i hadn't known until then how short she was. The crib was neat and empty, surrounded by stillness. i felt none of the domestic contentment that had been a part of the other dreams. i felt a stifling summer heat. There was in the crib a little blue blanket, and baby clothes next to it all neatly folded. A toy rocking horse perched atop the blanket. She looked down at those, and up at me. The complete darkness in her eyes was terrifying. Her fingers slipped over her mouth. i lifted my hand to her and woke up.

There is i guess more to her story than the old man told me, or perhaps knew of. Society was much narrower then and perhaps kept its secrets deeper, even as we both lived in the same century, at different ends of it. i never looked up my architecture friends again once i got back in town the following January. Can't say what became of them. Walking by Boron's club i discovered it'd become an ultraviolet deli. Don't try those sandwiches under the black light.

Didn't find any big news items about the club, just there one day and deli the next. Efficiency in the shadows there somewhere i guess. Didn't try to hunt in antique stores for old toys either. Would've been very morbid and in any case i'm sure that's not what she meant.

Landed a gig in a record store. Stereotyped: alternative music guy. i sucked up to guidance counselors and snuck back in school. They'd put in computerized registration finally and it printed me a much more humane schedule than i'd had, but did land me an extra-intense nontenured prof who gazed farther into Buddenbrooks than ever before conceived.

And so there i stood on a perfectly normal residential afternoon so much later, looking up at the smoky remains of that story, this chaos of gray timber still soggy from firehoses and smelling of burning. i imagined they were something like driftwood; heavy when waterlogged, otherwise pretty much weightless and totally incendiary. Wrong-o. With my foot i shifted a split piece of it and it was bulky, dense. Grey on top but still vibrantly wood-coloured inside the tear. Crooked nails crowned the ends. Driftwood would be bleached all the way through.

i stood remembering, somehow without getting astringent about it, and then a bleary-eyed family-type allophone man trudged up to and loitered companionably gazing up with me. i lived here, he said simply. No! i exclaimed, my eyes widening, That's terrible! Are you all right? — i once lived here too, long time ago.

Yes i see you walk by often, he said. We all got out, wife and children. Everything gone, but we're alive. We're staying down the street. They said it was a gas leak. Insurance guy's supposed to come by.

He shifted his weight around for a moment, peering up at the wreck but really looking me over, and in a quieter tone said, The lady of the house got us out.

By making no inquiries i conveyed to him i knew what he meant. i said, Yes, i hope she's moving on to a comfortable place. i'm sure you'll be okay too, you know; she's like that.

i was surprised at myself for coming out with that. Age and wisdom, ick, and so on, i suppose. i hoped it was becoming. We stood there, and he crossed himself.

i think about Boron too.

Khoo Gaik Cheng

Rituals

Somnambulistic Saturday in Vancouver. Ash-coloured skies and rain like the continuous weeping of sad widows. The wall refuses to answer the plish-plashing, just as he had kept silent when I told him on the phone that I was about to graduate soon. Such rainy days remind me of fried rice with leftovers and shrimp, the voice of my godmother yelling from the greasy kitchen to us children out in front watching TV, "Set the table now! Set the table! Rice is ready!"

There will be time for fried rice tomorrow, but today I shall have rice porridge with minced pork, just as they do during funerals back home. I lay out my mourning clothes; a black T-shirt, faded black tights, and soft-soled black shoes. Clothes I had worn to my grandmother's funeral four years ago. Down comes the old shoe box off the topmost shelf, spilling its contents on the bed; photographs of Neil and me in various formal poses, sitting next to each other without touching, with smiles that I used to think were shy and representative of our feelings for each other, but which, I think today, foreshadowed our doubts. Here are the black candles and napkins I bought for the failed last supper. I had thought black would be easy to match then. Wonder what Mama would say if she were to see them. I know how *pantang* she is. She'd mutter a quick prayer to ward off evil. Then she'd throw them out immediately. "Ooh wah, what bad luck. Very *sueh*, very *sueh* indeed! Whoever thought black is stylish? You're not a westerner, you know. You're Chinese!"

I guess she must be right after all. It was bad luck to have black candles because Neil and I broke up on that candlelight-dinner-for-two-in-cocktail-dress night. So much for cool western sophistication. The tailor-made deep purple velvet sheath dress with the sewn-in bone, the one I had saved to wear for some special occasion … well, I guess being dumped constitutes an occasion deserving of its own category. Especially when it's your first boyfriend who called it quits. And you, blind as a fool, didn't see it coming. There is essentially no one to blame except bad luck and plain old naiveté. It certainly wasn't cultural difference, it was not that he couldn't eat spicy food, or minded my periodic lapses into Hokkien or my somewhat *chinchai* taste in fashion. No, it was pure bad luck that the distance, the total concentration he claimed he needed in order to stay competitive at med ical school didn't merely keep us apart but merited a wholesale breakup. And that's why I have to do this. Go through this ritual as if it's some kind of compulsory home remedy but whose effects I'm not quite sure of.

I remove my gold dangling earrings and put on the black clothes. I wipe off any trace of lipstick there is and head towards the porch. Outside, it is still raining but that won't interfere with my plans. Removing the grill from the barbeque set, I stoke up the charred ashes, vestiges of last weekend's party. There won't be a corpse, but there will be burning of some sort, and purging. Maybe a phoenix will rise from the flames. A Chinese one.

I have never been good at lighting fires. I swear, if I were a paid arsonist, I'd probably be unemployed ninety-nine percent of my life! But today, things are different. Maybe it's the recklessly indulgent way I pour the liquid lighter over the charcoal, the daring proximity of my fingers to the jet-black stuff as I pause to ignite it with a short match. It responds, flames leaping up higher and higher. I get up from my crouching position and wipe my sweaty brow, already smelling like a Girl Guide in kerosene-scented clothes, trying to build a fire at camp. Yet, I have never felt more competent in my life. I go rummaging through my larder for junkfood, in the fridge for leftovers, and into the bedroom for the shoebox of memories.

Outside on the porch, I arrange a makeshift altar. Simple, all one needs to do is to centralize the two candles in front, leaving about one foot space in between. Next, lay out the food. There are Fritos in a saucer, a Mars bar (I'm sure my deceased grandfather would appreciate this because such chocolates are expensive back home), a cup of cold coffee, some leftover stir-fry and a tupperware of rice. Yes, oh yes, some fruits too. All these go in between the candles. Traditionally, this would be a feast to appease the hungry ghosts, so there would be a photograph of my deceased grandparents before the altar. But this is no ordinary Hungry Ghost Festival. I don't really know what it is yet and putting up a genuine photograph of my ancestors or Lord Buddha would probably be blasphemous, so I leave those out. Next, I light two scented incense sticks and prop them up against a dry brick.

Open the shoebox one last time and it's like opening Pandora's box. Only perhaps more painful. I haven't looked over these photos since our breakup. Not that it hurts me to do so now, but in them there is nothing like Neil at all. They're basically dead photographs, without anima, without personality. I don't even look beyond the second picture before tossing the whole pile into the fire. Maybe my ancestors would have more use for them now than I would. We used to burn paper money after the festival feast. The night before, Grandma (when she was still alive), Mama and Godma would stay up folding coarse paper with a silver or gold square stamp in the middle of the page. They folded it into the shape of what looked like a sampan.

We broke up on the premise that we would stay friends. After the breakup, I spaced out my phone calls, my long letters detailing my daily agenda of English literature classes, interspersed with witty comments about eccentric colleagues at my work place, to once a week; and then, once every two weeks. It was hard to resist calling him, particularly when his telephone number, together with other passwords and emergency numbers international students carry on them, were already burnt into my brain, and the risk of rejection (call me a masochist), was so high. During those times when I called him, all I would have to listen for would be the brusqueness, the monosyllabic answers, awkward long pauses and impatient silence as I waited for him to ask me how *I* was doing, how *I* was coping. "After all, life can be tough outside of med school too, you know," I would have ventured to tease and then imagined him rolling his eyes, with that crooked smile slowly spreading over his face.

On the rare occasion that I actually waited for the phone to ring after dialing him, I would count the number of times it rang, "One, two, three…" and quickly hang up if he didn't pick up by the fourth time, before the answering machine did. I refused to humiliate myself by leaving a voice message full of ahumms and a tentative "I just called to say hi," when what I really meant was, "I wanted to hear your voice. I need this friendship to be sincere, not just some patronizing reassurance couples breaking up make to each other." No matter how much he might have meant it at the moment of utterance, God, I wanted to taste that sincerity, to hear it over the phone, weeks later, months later, maybe even years afterwards. Perhaps in an accident, when he was on duty as they were rolling me into the Emergency ward, and he recognized me instantly despite the distance of time and separation. The lurch of guilt, the worried frown, his warm hand over mine, I savoured the thought.

The romantic in me believed what I wanted to believe. When asked how things were with him, he had initially responded willingly enough. School was tough, many late nights, several study groups, tests each week, not enough sleep. Somewhere along the way, Neil had become the centre of his world. Nobody else. Definitely no "us." I wondered then about his mother, his sister, his high school buddies who had also worked with us at the Thai restaurant on the Drive.

"Neil? The last time he came back for Christmas, he didn't even call us," Joe said when we bumped into each other on the street two months later. "Does he keep in touch with you?" he asked.

"Me? Are you kidding?"

Joe shook his head, smiling sadly. "Too bad, you guys made a nice pair. Guess medical school changes people, eh?"

I shrugged. "Yeah, well … maybe he was just brain tired and needed to rest after all that cramming for exams ..." Joe gave me a look that said I was making excuses for someone who didn't deserve undue loyalty, so I trailed off.

But enough about Neil. Let's see ... anything else I can put into the fire? I look around and remember I ought to have priests in saffron chanting. Prayers to calm the mourners and smoothen the celestial path for the dead. Orange robes. Oranges, anything orange? Dirty yellow? Yellow? Paddington and Garfield!

So, with the help of a small bruised bear and an equally grotesque-looking cat, I set up a prayer service. Paddington is stripped of his dusty galoshes (he doesn't get out into the rain often enough) and faded raincoat. I line him up against Garfield, who has lost a whisker or two in his nine-minus-seven lives. I want to wipe the smirk off his face but I don't, because he's a present from my best friend back home. Next, a prayer. Where from?

No mantras. I have a small picture of the Goddess of Mercy in laminated plastic that I keep in my wallet, but the quotation at the back is in Chinese characters. The Bible? Why not? Or maybe I'll read from the Book of Apocrypha. It's the only part of the old holy book I truly enjoy. Maybe I ought to cry. Or induce tears. I remember Auntie Fan Li at Grandma's funeral, trying to compose herself after a large bout of tears and then starting on a fresh round when she saw more visitors entering the gate. Crocodile tears, we younger ones thought, not knowing or understanding the type of background our mothers came from. It is only now that I remember reading somewhere that the more one cries at funerals, the better the dead look in the public's eyes. They have wonderful caring relatives who mourn the leaving, and who will no doubt fight viciously over the inheritance, pushing forward male heirs at the reading of the will. But there were no tears from me, and there are none now. I didn't really know my grandmother, and I'm having serious doubts about ever having known Neil at all.

The later stranger who had shut me out seemed such a contrast to the shy gentle Neil Fromme I knew, who bussed tables and complained about the brown-noser and lousy tipper of a waiter, Jack Chan, yet who did nothing in retaliation. "But you worked just as hard if not harder, you should tell Tip," I had urged over and over again.

"Nah, come end of summer, I'll be out of here. S'not worth it. Cheer up, it's not so bad," he smiled, rubbing my back affectionately.

Something's burning, something familiar. I rush outside and it's the rice. One of the candles has fallen into it and melted part of the tupperware away. I empty cold coffee into the mess. Smoke, toxic fumes, and suffocating blackness spread out in a sheepish grin. No phoenix here. "Burn the rice? How can you burn the rice? Other people are starving, you know, and you burn the rice? How disrespectful!" Not to mention irresponsible and *sueh.* I remember how in black-and-white Malay movies they used to show the old mother who would accidentally drop the rice pot. This was always a harbinger that the protagonist son would die in the following scene. Classic. Then there was Mahsuri who grew out of a magic pot of *kerak nasi* or burnt rice. She was wrongly accused of adultery by the villagers, who upon killing her realized their mistake when white blood oozed out of her wounds. As for me, I'm no Mahsuri; born of spirits, legendary heroine of the island of Langkawi. I'm not Auntie Fan Li. I'm not ... anything.

Perhaps the end of summer and Neil's going away to medical school were signs I had missed or misread due to sheer inexperience and the earnestness of first loves. I sigh, a year later and I feel older now. The storm has wreaked its little vengeance and the rain is pattering into anonymity. Like a disenchanted voodoo priestess, I sit, surrounded by trifles to which I attach magical significance. Goose pimples, and for what? I get off the floor and start clearing up, humming an old love song absentmindedly. The phone rings and I'm thinking, tomorrow ... I will wear bright red.

Fiona Tinwei Lam

Seeking Special Chinese Lady

Susan had been waiting at the cafe for nearly fifteen minutes. She had decided that after thirty minutes, she'd just leave. She'd been nursing her tea for too long—it was cold. She didn't want another. She hadn't been able to focus on her novel. Maybe he'd decided she wasn't worth meeting after all. She'd scrutinized every single man who'd come into the café, checking whether he had brown hair and was wearing jeans or a brown blazer. There'd been one false alarm. Thank goodness she'd stayed in her seat and kept her mouth shut.

She'd been glancing through the personal ads over the past year but hadn't had the guts until now. Before she'd turned thirty, the personals had amused her. People seemed desperate. Men pushing fifty writing of their youthful appearance and financial security, indicating a preference for slim women at least a decade younger, with no baggage—as if men were the only ones allowed to have any. Women looking for soulmates for fine dining and walks along the sea wall. But the years of being a spectator to her friends' lives—their marriages, pregnancies, new homes, children—had worn down her resolve.

There were always the ads seeking Asian women that she used to have such contempt for—"Oriental Woman for LTR", "Asian Lady Wanted"—always written by a white male. The ads never disclosed why being Asian was particularly desirable. It was as if they were requesting a particular ice cream flavour. Or make of car. This week's issue had contained a new ad:

Seeking Special Chinese Lady
DWM, 42, professional, financially secure, seeking an Oriental lady 20-35 for dining, theatre, and possible travel. Must be cultured, witty, attractive, fit and slim. #5628

Susan knew she wasn't slim, attractive, or fit. She was twenty pounds overweight with an aversion to all forms of exercise. Occasionally, if she had just washed her hair and had put on fresh makeup, she could pass for somewhat cute for almost an hour. Although she didn't want to risk operating under false pretenses, she figured being Asian might be sufficient for her to pass muster.

It had been the word "special" in the ad that had caught her eye. The word "Chinese" paired with it made her think of those dinners for four on takeout flyers for pseudo-Chinese food. What did "special" mean? Who was more "special"—a woman from mainland China, Taiwan, or Hong Kong? Did third-generation Chinese count, or was that more ordinary? How did being Chinese make one "special," given that there were over one billion on the planet? Susan wondered if she qualified as "special." Did being a daycare worker count? Being an enthusiastic reader of Dr Seuss? Or the speedy way she could calculate change after all those weekends she'd spent during high school at her family's corner store? The way she could imitate Preston Manning? But an Asianphile? She shook her head and started to pull on her sweater, readying herself to depart. What was she thinking? Better to be single forever than be with someone so pathetic that he'd choose a girlfriend by race. And it wouldn't work anyway—he'd find out she wasn't "authentic."

Another man entered the café. He went straight to the counter to place an order. It couldn't be him. But after he'd paid for his coffee, he glanced at the people at the tables. She saw him examine every Asian woman in the place. She'd already counted—there were two Japanese students sitting together gossiping and an elderly Taiwanese woman reading the paper beside what probably was her husband. She was the only one sitting by herself and wearing the promised black skirt.

He came over to her slowly, almost reluctantly it seemed to her. "Are you Susan?"

"Yes, and you must be number 5628?" she said in an attempt to be witty. Hadn't he asked for a witty woman? He started, furtively looked around the cafe to check if anyone had heard her. Whoops. "I mean, you're Frank McInnis, right?" He was wearing a tan plaid jacket with wide lapels. The few long strands of hair that were stretched across his oval head appeared to be brown. It had to be him. He seemed ill at ease, his pale grey eyes shifting under hardly visible eyebrows. He'd said he was 170 pounds—he looked thirty pounds less given the way his clothes hung so loosely on him. His hairlessness and lankiness together somehow reminded her of a crash test dummy. At least he was as ordinary-looking as she was. She smiled encouragingly at him.

"Yes." He sat down. "So we meet!"

They stared mutely at each other for a moment.

"Yes, it's good to finally meet you," she responded lamely.

They chatted about the weather and the traffic while his eyes closely scanned her face. She wondered if she should have put on more cover stick. She nervously tugged on her left earlobe and tried to change the subject to distract him from her face. She pointed to the book, tried to talk about that.

"I never read fiction." He saw her slightly crestfallen expression. "Well, that sort of writing is mostly for women. I read nonfiction. Better to spend that kind of time learning something new."

She tried talking about movies. But he'd been away and hadn't seen any of the recent films. He didn't seem interested either. Finally she returned to the subject that had seemed to predominate during their single telephone conversation a few days before. They'd ended up talking for an hour much to her surprise, although he'd dominated the conversation. "So from what you told me on the phone, your separation from Mei-Ling was pretty rough." She put on an understanding expression, the kind she used when parents rushed in an hour late to pick up their kids at the daycare centre where she worked, making her miss her bus connection home.

"Yes." He stared at his coffee, as if stirring his thoughts in with the spoon. "Anyway, now that she's found that professor, she's happy."

"Mine's happy with someone else too." He didn't ask her to elaborate so she asked him more about his ex-wife. It was clearly a favourite topic.

He looked up, eyes staring out at the distance as if Mei Ling were approaching them now. "God, Mei Ling is elegant. She has this long, silky hair down to her midback. Has this porcelain complexion. Great taste." Suddenly, he dropped his gaze again, laughed ruefully. "Maybe that's why she dropped me."

Susan smiled back sympathetically. She could imagine Mei Ling, lily-like, a modern Kuan Yin with long fingers, designer clothes, and a beatific smile. He told her how he'd met her when she was a visa student from Shanghai studying music here. She'd married him, only to run off three years later with one of the faculty after obtaining her doctorate. Susan watched him sag into his clothes as he continued describing his marriage. She exerted herself to make a few lighthearted remarks and change the subject. But nothing worked. It was as if Mei-Ling were sitting at the table between them right now, wearing a silk cheongsam, jade hanging from her ears, fingers gracefully interlaced, eyebrows raised over luminous eyes, plummy lips pursed in amusement. *You're nothing like me.*

"—and then there was Bali. Mei Ling found this wonderful place that sold gorgeous batik work. Almost every room in our condo had a wall hanging until she left . . ." He suddenly looked at his watch. "Hey, don't we have a reservation? I'm getting hungry." She thought about making an excuse but couldn't think of anything plausible. She'd never been good at lying. And she kept remembering being told by her mother that she was too critical. "So choosy means you'll never have a man," her mother always said.

They walked a few blocks to the restaurant she'd selected. She'd read about it in the paper—a hole in the wall that offered authentic, country-style cuisine. The place was full of Chinese families—kids, grandmothers with grey hair scraped back from their foreheads, famished parents all sitting at purely functional tables with plastic tablecloths. Almost everyone was focused intensely on eating. She liked seeing people enjoying themselves this way—whatever the world was like, at least there was food.

They stood at the entrance. Susan noticed Frank quietly appraising her body from behind. She hoped the long skirt had managed to hide most of it. She'd worn the highest heeled shoes she had, making her almost 5'5"—she remembered Frank saying that Mei Ling had been tall. Susan tried to stand straighter, holding in her stomach. She finally flagged down a waitress to seat them. The waitress looked at Frank—conspicuously the only white guy in the place—before showing them a table in the corner by the kitchen, right by a table with a kindergarten-aged boy squabbling with his slightly younger sister over a pair of chopsticks. The boy was wearing a worn-out sweatshirt with "Harvard" on the front that was a few sizes too large for him. The little girl had a "fountain-head" sprig of hair at the top of her head in a barrette, just like one of the girls in Susan's daycare. Susan sighed resignedly. It seemed to be her fate to be always in close proximity to young children.

Frank noticed Susan glancing at them. "Cute kids," he said as he sat down.

The waitress handed over two ancient-looking laminated menus and rushed away, clearly harried. She kept pushing back from her face the tendrils of hair that were escaping the elastic holding her ponytail. There was only one other waitress in sight and the restaurant was full. Susan turned to the back of her menu. There they were—the inescapable dinners for two, four and six, with wonton soup and honey garlic, sweet and sour something. She noticed that in the front there was a list of several dishes written up only in Chinese. After having glanced around him when they entered the place, Frank now seemed to be in a fugue state, looking right through her. When the waitress came back to plunk down two glasses of tea, Susan pointed to the page.

"Could you please tell me what this is?" she asked. The waitress looked up from her notepad and glared at her impatiently. Frank raised his eyebrows.

"Ni di hai mut yeh?" Susan tried again, trying her best to bring in the tones. It had been quite a while since she'd used any of her very limited Cantonese. She repeated her question to the waitress, but seeing the look of incomprehension on the woman's face, switched back to English. "What are these dishes?" She reached for the tea, gulped some down, scalding her throat.

The waitress pressed her lips together in disapproval. *"M' gong jung mun ah?"* A few people turned to look at Susan.

"*Sic teng, m' sic gong*," Susan mumbled. Actually this wasn't true. She understood only about ten percent of simple conversation. The waitress sped through a synopsis of the main ingredients in Cantonese. Susan struggled to remember her food vocabulary, the only words that were somewhat familiar. "Uh, that's pork, that's shrimp, that's hot pot with noodle, that's sea cucumber—she says you won't like it," Susan quickly translated. "What would you like to eat, Frank? Why don't you choose?"

"My favourite is kung pao chicken. Mei Ling used to make it for me at home."

Susan flipped through the menu anxiously. She didn't see it. Why wasn't he helping her out. He just sat there sipping his tea.

"Do you have kung pao chicken?" she asked the waitress. She already knew the answer.

The waitress stared at Susan as if she had just asked for *coq au vin.*

Susan whispered, "They don't have it. This is a Cantonese restaurant—kung pao chicken is Szechwan I think. Why don't you look in the menu to see what you'd like?"

He opened the menu with a sigh, flipping through it without much energy. He turned to the page that listed the chicken dishes a few times, as if kung pao chicken might suddenly appear and Susan and the waitress were lying to him. He closed the menu. "I'd like a beer, but otherwise why don't you just order. I'm sure you know what's good here."

Susan wasn't sure at all. She knew she'd be on tenterhooks for the entire meal, worried that he wouldn't like the food. She wondered if that faraway look in Frank's eyes meant Mei Ling was still hovering between them. Mei Ling probably had been able to speak Cantonese, Shanghaiese, *and* Mandarin. The waitress was waiting, getting impatient. Susan ordered one dish that sounded different, and one that sounded familiar and hoped he would eat. Afterward, she kept looking over at the two bickering children at the next table, wondering whether she should intervene. Their grandmother wasn't doing anything to stop the fighting except to utter the occasional mild rebuke without effect. Then the waitress came over with a plate of spring rolls—it appeared that the kids were hers—to hush them. Each child grabbed one and wrapped a paper napkin around the circumference, holding them up like hotdogs. The boy ate off the top of his before drenching the inside with soy sauce. Susan smiled, remembering how she used to do the same as a child.

Ten minutes later the dishes arrived at their table, steaming and sizzling furiously. Frank started his third beer, having finally recovered from the absence of his favourite dish. After wrinkling his nose and cautiously nibbling a small spoonful, he studiously avoided the salt fish, pork and tofu hotpot. *I will not eat it, Sam I am, I will not eat green eggs and ham,* I *will not eat it with a fox, I will not eat it in a box,* thought Susan. At least he didn't talk about Mei Ling as much this time, but described his travels in Thailand while cleaning up the chicken in black bean sauce.

"I really think it's an inherent characteristic of Thai women—the country just produces beautiful, really feminine ladies."

Susan said nothing. She was savouring the hotpot. When it arrived, the casserole had still been bubbling. The silky tofu slipped between her lips, slowly dissolving in her mouth amongst the chewy bits of pork and the pungent flecks of salt fish. It was the ultimate comfort food with a pearly mound of steaming rice. This was the kind of food she had longed for at home when growing up, but never had. They'd had frozen food and produce that was about to go bad at the store—nothing that took much time or effort to cook.

At the end of the meal, she nibbled on the orange slices brought by the waitress. The kids at the next table had long finished their spring rolls and were now playing tug of war with their chopsticks. Susan suddenly realized that Frank hadn't asked one thing about her during the entire meal. Maybe he knew all that he needed to know from their one phone call four days ago. Maybe he decided daycare workers' lives weren't very interesting.

Finally he asked her, "I hope you don't mind me asking why you don't speak Chinese?"

Susan hated it when people asked that question. She tried to sound cultured and witty. "Just grew up in an English-speaking environment I guess. Maybe too much Jane Austen."

"Don't you think it would help to learn your own language?" he said. "Especially in this city. It could help you with work or if you ever travel to Asia."

She reined in a retort about the state of his Gaelic. Didn't want to be rude. He sounded like her relatives lecturing her about Chinese school.

"What is it?" He could see the tension on her face. "Did I say something wrong? You aren't ashamed of your heritage, are you?"

Susan's stomach clenched, her throat tightening. She made her face as blank as possible. So much she could say, better to say nothing at all. What would a century's legacy of railroad workers, small town cafés, and laundries mean to those who saw Chinese culture and history only in terms of Ming vases and Great Walls? "No," she said quietly. "Of course not. I just think we probably have different ways of looking at things. Why don't we talk about something else."

"Okay." He seemed confused.

There was a sudden crash and the sound of water splattering. A glass of water had fallen off the kids' table during their tug-of-war. The waitress rushed over from the other side of the restaurant. She scolded her children in Chinese while she wiped up the mess and picked up the pieces of glass. The grandmother remained placid in her seat, having offered a mild admonishment, and continued to pick at her teeth with a toothpick. The little girl looked ready to cry, and the boy was entering a deep sulk. They'd clearly reached their limit—just like Susan had. She rose from her chair, snatched a few take-out menus from the front desk and came over to their table.

"Let me help," she offered, smiling to the waitress, who looked up at Susan mutely, clearly exhausted. Susan quickly folded the take-out menus into two boats and a plane. She put them on the table. She had done this so often at the daycare. The two children stared at her and then at the origami, fascinated.

"Go ahead—they're yours!" Susan moved one of the boats around a few plates while she held the plane up with another hand. She swooped the plane in the air before landing it front of the girl. The boy had already grabbed the boats, laughing and jumping up and down. The two kids started to play as if nothing had happened.

The waitress sighed and almost smiled. "Thank you. Very nice." She looked at her children. "Long day. Everyone tired."

"Yes, it's been a long one." Susan agreed. She went back to Frank, who had been watching.

"That was great." He nodded his head. "You work in a daycare, right? Mei-Ling never liked kids, even though I wanted them. Guess being a father isn't in the cards for me." Frank stared wistfully at the two kids playing with the paper toys. Susan suddenly felt Mei-Ling's apparition vanish.

"For men it's never too late. Think of Trudeau," she replied, almost feeling sorry for him. But it didn't matter now. She just wanted to go home.

"Do you want to grab dessert somewhere?" he asked finally after a long silence. There was now a faint spark of interest in his eye.

For a moment, she almost considered agreeing to go. Maybe she was being too critical, maybe he'd had a bad day, or maybe it was just too soon after his divorce. Then she thought of how relieved she'd be to be back home, alone. Maybe she'd finish reading her novel. "I have some errands to do early in the morning so I should probably get back," she said as graciously as she could.

Frank shrugged his shoulders, his indifference returning.

The waitress appeared abruptly in front of them to place a plate on their table. It held a hot crispy pancake filled with sweet red bean paste. "On the house." She laid two forks and two clean plates in front of them and stalked away.

"I don't like red bean," Frank said. "Especially that soup they serve at the end of banquets."

"But red bean symbolizes good luck," she grinned. "Sure you want to give that up?"

Frank shook his head. "Please go ahead."

Susan picked up her fork with relish. "You don't know what you're missing."

Gein Wong

Hole in the Wall

I don't speak Cantonese.

The blame for my linguistic deficiency falls solely on my parents. I was a malleable child, and they spoke to me solely in English. They never passed Cantonese on to me nor allowed that language to grow within me naturally. By the time I was cognizant of what was lost, Cantonese no longer felt like a language I could claim as mine. This loss does not sit well with me.

Most of the time there is an emptiness...

I feel empty when my parents are watching a Chinese movie with no English subtitles. I feel empty when I'm waiting for my parents to translate the menu in a Chinese restaurant. I feel empty when I hear my grandmother's voice on the telephone and I can't say a single word that she understands,

Every Chinese New Year my father would dial that long distance call. I would stand in the kitchen with the phone in my hand. I would hear the elation in my grandmother's voice, but that's all I could hear. My grandmother's words bounced off my ears, were deflected off into the atmosphere. I could never rationalize why my parents deprived me of my ancestral tongue, my oral lineage, and identity. Why would they voluntarily put me in this situation?

The clues were so subtle...

I'm six years old and sitting on the linoleum floor winding up my yo-yo. It's not really a special occasion or a memorable day. I can smell the fish my mom is making and I'm waiting for her to tell us to set the table for dinner. I didn't actually hear the knock on the door. I didn't actually notice that my father had put down the Chinese newspaper, gotten up from his armchair. and opened the door. What I do remember is my father screaming. I remember this because he rarely raised his voice in that exact manner. Sure, he yelled at us when we did something he didn't like...and he yelled at the TV when his favourite football team was losing...and he always yelled at my mom when she disagreed with him. But he was always polite in public...and there was a certain pain in his scream when he was at the door that day.

There were election signs on almost everyone's front lawn that fall. Some of them were small and orange, some were blue, but most of them were big and bright red. Some people even had all three signs hammered into their lawns. The orange signs had the name Olivia Ng on them with a picture of a smiling Asian women. The big red signs only had a name on them, Cedric Lee. I have no idea what was written on the blue signs, even back then I never paid much attention to them. The neighbourhood I grew up in had a large proportion of first-generation Asian immigrants. Cedric Lee won that election and I've always wondered if he got a lot of votes because of his last name and because he was a man. I've wondered this because even though his last name was Lee, he was Caucasian. And as far as I could remember, he never put his picture anywhere. I know he was Caucasian because I saw Cedric Lee. I saw him running over to our front door to see what was wrong.

The man at the door was holding a sign with Cedric Lee's name on it. "You vote?" he asked, "you know about election?"

I couldn't see the reaction on my father's face, but he responded by saying, "yes," politely, "what do you want?"

"I . . . a volunteer," the man said, pointing to himself, and then the sign, then to my father, pronoucing syllables slowly, saying, "Cedric Lee wants to...to talk to you."

That was the moment my father lost his composure. It was something I had never thought he was capable of doing. Cedric Lee must have heard my father from across the street, but by the time he got to our front door, my father was slamming it in his face. I am not sure which was louder, the door crashing or my father's pulsing scream: "I've been here fifteen years!"

He stared at the door for a few seconds, then he turned around and slammed the side of his fist into the wall. He then walked back into the living room, leaving a jagged hole by the doorway that would stay there until we decided to leave.

A decade later my parents decided to sell that house and my mother asked me to fix up that hole before buyers came to see the house. I bought dry wall paste and tried to patch up the wall, but it was still obvious that the dry wall had been punctured. Minutes before the first prospective buyers entered the house, I had hung one of my paintings by the doorway. I grabbed the first piece I could find. I was trying to paint a picture of myself, but it looked more like a cloaked figure in the mist.

A few days after the fist-in-the-wall incident, I was talking to my sister in her room. In between putting a John Lennon record on the record player and turning on the TV to watch a Green Hornet rerun, she scoffed at my father's reaction: "He shouldn't throw a temper tantrum, he should just learn to speak normally. Sometimes I don't even understand what he's saying." After that day, I started thinking of my father in the same light. I believed anything that my sister said. She was eight years older than me and I thought her words were born from the wisdom of the world.

Almost as ubiquitous as the front-yard election signs were the "for sale" signs stuck on the lawns. A lot of people were leaving the neighbourhood around that time. I only knew people were leaving because of the Sold signs and the moving trucks that would show up on the street. I never actually knew who was leaving—the people who lived in these houses never talked to us or knew my parents.

My parents never told me how they were treated when they first immigrated to Ottawa in the 1960s. They would only say things that were not directly painful, for example the Chinese food was really bad, and they had known all the Chinese people living in Ottawa (because there were so few at that time). Or they would tell stories, for example about the time when my father was sitting in a diner eating a hamburger and fries and he wanted ketchup; he didn't know the English word for ketchup, so he tried directly translating from Cantonese. The waitress gave him exactly what he asked for, a glass of tomato juice. He hated tomato juice, but drank it out of politeness and embarrassment.

When I think about it now, the intensity and frustration in my father's reaction at the door that day was compelling. I'd had never seen him react so strongly and so violently. At the time, I didn't really understand the condescending tone the volunteer was using. I didn't make the connection that his anger wasn't just a reaction to this one incident. I just remember wondering if it was worth punching a wall. After he put his hand into the wall of his house, he sat in the living room and didn't eat. Not because he was still mad, but because his hand hurt so much that he couldn't hold his chopsticks. For the next week, just before my bedtime I would help my dad rub some Chinese medicine into his hand. I loved that Chinese medicine, it was perfect for bruises, or muscle strains, or any bodily aches. You would mix a light brown powder with an odorous liquid the colour of soil. My father had brought a lot of this medicine over when he came to Canada, and he told me that some of my grandfather's friends used to climb the mountains in Hong Kong to gather the plants and roots needed to make it. He always told me not to worry, there would be enough medicine for my grandchildren. I found out later that we had one of the last stocks of this medicine and no one was making it any more.

Ever since I've moved out of my parents' house I've tried asking my mother what it was like for them when they first came. She would respond by saying something like, "Things are better now, you don't have to worry as much, why do you want to know about those times..." But yesterday when I was helping her peel potato skins in the kitchen, she finally started talking.

All my parents wanted was for me to fit in. She started telling me about how the Chinese were treated in the past. I needed to know what my parents went through, not just the airbrushed perfect pictures for memorabilia, but the actuality of their experiences. I wanted to hear about how my father had to go for hundreds of job interviews before someone finally hired him, and how he enrolled in accent adjustment classes. I needed to know that outside the supermarket, people threw eggs at my mother and told her to leave "our country" and get off "our land." I needed to have these stories with me to become the Chinese Canadian they wanted. She spoke continuously, pausing only to collect herself and hold back her tears. After the first few stories, she began including a few Cantonese words in her sentences. I didn't stop her, I just held her hand. Soon Cantonese words were filling her stories. I kept looking into her eyes, hoping to catch her gaze. Now her entire stories were in Cantonese. It didn't matter though. I heard every word.

Alexis Kienlen

Locks

The bottom of the blue bowl warms my palms as my father passes me the dish. His almond eyes, brown with greenish flecks of gold, stare into my own as he warns, "Be careful, Ling. I can't afford any more broken dishes."

I nod my head with a snap and scurry away, holding the bowl tight enough to break it. The soup inside splashes against the sides, threatening to spill out and burn me. I slow down and walk with small steps, like I'm walking on a tightrope. The customers look up as I set the bowl on their table. They smile and nod and I nod back. Their faces mean nothing to me.

I walk back to the kitchen, my steps quickening. The door swings open at my touch and shuts with a bang. I am in the comfort of the kitchen, eased by the boiling pots of water on the metal stove, the chopped vegetables placed on the counter in colorful rows and the meat sizzling in a huge, fire stained wok. The smell of the kitchen is my mother drawing me close to her. I look at the side of the pot on the stove. My face looks like my mother's.

The phone rings. I wait for my father to answer it, then realize that he is not in the kitchen and the cook is taking his break. The kitchen seems empty without my father's large hands and the sound of his knife against the cutting board.

My voice is squeaky and uncertain as I answer the phone. "Hello, Tang's Diner."

"Hey, Ling."

It's John, the boy with the thick brown hair who sits in front of me in chemistry. He's always swiveling around in his seat, squinting at my notes, trying to recopy my small, scrawly handwriting. Every Wednesday, Mr. Stroh asks me to be John's lab partner. I always feel like I have been sentenced to help him, although it's never really a punishment since I always seem to get caught up in his deep brown eyes. He leans forward to listen as I explain the long lists of numbers and letters.

"Hello?"

I feel flustered. "Oh, hi John."

"I was wondering if you could come over tomorrow to go over the lab. It's going to be on the test on Friday."

I glance at the tattered calendar on the wall. The dates under the picture of the smiling Chinese girl are covered with red Xs. Tomorrow is Thursday, one of the slower nights at the diner. My father won't mind if I don't help.

"Sure. Would you like to go to the library or come here?"

"You can come to my house if you want."

I accept and we agree to meet at three. I return the phone to its hook and go back to the main room of the restaurant. I am the perfect model of an obedient daughter.

That night, I braid my hair and tie it with a red ribbon, the same way my mother wore hers. I crawl into bed and slide the green blanket that my mother had brought from China with her, many years ago.

I hug the corner of the blanket close to my chest and fall asleep.

The alarm rings with a loud, irritating buzz. I jump from my bed and yank on a kilt and sweater from the floor. My shoes bang against the wooden stairs on the way to the kitchen. My father is already downstairs, sitting on a small stool facing the counter. He is drinking a steaming cup of fragrant jasmine. His eyebrows rise and fall above his glasses.

"Hello, Father," I say. My small hand brushes his as I reach for the sticky bun in front of him. My father grunts in my direction. He has never said much to me, especially since my mother died. I bite into the meaty sweetness of the bun and put a pot of water on the stove. I bring out the jar of instant coffee and my father scowls at it.

"You should drink tea. Good for you. Won't stunt and clog you."

I ignore him and spoon the brown crystals into one of the many red bowls sitting on the counter. I sip and the bitter taste fills my mouth.

I swallow and say, "I'm going to John's today after school. We're going to study for the Chem test tomorrow."

My father nods. Though he doesn't say it now, he approves. He likes it when I help others with schoolwork. I touch his hand and say goodbye and I am out the door and into the crisp, autumn morning, my feet crunching through the leaves that cover the sidewalk on the path to school.

The day passes and class blends into class, marks into marks, hours into hours. The final bell sounds and I am at my locker, cramming books into my backpack.

"Hey!"

I feel the hand on my shoulder and whip around to face him.

"Ready to go?" he asks and tries to blow the hair out of his eyes. It doesn't move, so he flicks it back with his fingers and finally tries to tuck it behind his ear. It doesn't stay.

I nod, then slam my locker shut. John turns and I follow him through the writhing mass of people in the loud, crowded hallway. Outside, the air is biting and I shrink into my jacket. He walks a few steps in front of me and I stare at the back of his neck. He crosses the grass and I follow, my feet crunching through the leaves. I'm still looking at the back of his neck when my foot hits something.

"Hey, watch it!" A girl is scowling at me, her skinny arms wrapped around the shoulders of some thick-necked jock. I blush and apologize, looking down at my shoes. John turns around and waits for me. I rush to catch up, my backpack banging against my back. He turns around again, reaching into his pocket.

"Want some gum?"

"Sure," I say and pop the stick into my mouth. It's peppermint.

He take two pieces, shoves them into his mouth and pushes his hair behind his ear. I fiddle with the end of my braid and ask how far we have to go to get to his house. He says it's only a few blocks more and soon we are talking and laughing about Mr. Stroh and his bright red face. At how he's always comparing chemistry to sexual attraction, especially while he's staring at Brittany, the girl with big breasts who sits right in front of his desk.

Soon wc arrive at a large wooden house that looks like a cabin. My feet bang in a staccato behind John's slower step. I notice the stairs are freshly painted and clean like they've just been swept. They're nothing like the well-worn stairs of our diner.

Inside the house, I am attacked by a Golden Retriever who puts his paws on my shoulders and starts licking my face with a large, pink tongue. I start laughing and shake my head pack and forth, trying to avoid wet, doggy kisses.

"Down, Scooter!" John has kicked off his shoes and is walking toward the kitchen. Scooter hops back down on all fours.

"It's okay," I say. "He wasn't bothering me."

I follow John into the kitchen.

"Want some hot chocolate?" He opens the cabinet and pulls out a tin.

"Okay," I say and perch on one of the kitchen chairs. I really don't want to mess up the cushion. John whistles as he bustles around the kitchen. Aside from his whistling, the grandfather clock in the hall and the dog, the house is still.

I watch John clasping his wide hands around the mug as he fills it. "Here you go," he says.

"Thank you," I mumble. It feels strange, being with John without my father's shadow hanging over us.

I sip the hot chocolate and it mixes with the gum in my mouth and turns into sludge. I don't want to look stupid by asking where the garbage can is, so I swallow the gum. John is getting our backpacks. We set up our books on the table in neat rows. He opens his binder and we start going over yesterday's lab. During our discussion, I continue to sip my hot chocolate and finally set the mug down, empty. While we're running through the periodic table, John leans close to me.

At last he says, "You've got hot chocolate on your mouth."

His fingers brush against my lips. I stop writing and sit up straight. Mama's hands used to wash my face when I was younger. I would always smile whenever she touched me, whenever I saw her smile. I look into John's brown eyes, inches away from me. He smiles a little. I look at his mouth and his lips and I also lean forward. I'm reminded of the old movies that I watch late at night in the diner, as his mouth comes closer to mine. I close my eyes. All the movie heroines do.

My first kiss feels nothing like I expected. It's squishy and wet and hot. I feel like I'm choking, but I don't want to look prudish so I keep on kissing him. I can taste hot chocolate and peppermint and after a while I get used to kissing and it feels pretty nice.

I feel good about myself. He probably can't tell that I've never kissed anybody before. I'm leaning sideways to face him and my side is digging into the table. I draw back.

I look down. "My side was starting to hurt."

"Oh," John says.

I can feel the heat of embarrassment in my face. Yet I have to ask the question. "Why did you kiss me?"

"I've wanted to for a long time." He looks down at his hands. "But I didn't think you liked me."

I grin down at my lap and suddenly a scrap of my mother's courage yanks me up by my hair. I raise my head and say, "I like you a lot." My fingers reach up to brush that lock of hair behind his ears. It stays.

John smiles back at me and only the chimes of the clock interrupt the moment. It's seven.

"I should get home and help." I stand up and begin to gather up my books.

"I'll walk you home." He grabs a coat from the closet and sits down to tie up his boots.

Outside it is raining and the earthworms are painting the pavement with their writhing bodies. The rain is cold and I pull my hands into my sweater.

John takes off his jacket and wraps it around my shoulders. It smells good, like flannel and soap.

When we reach the diner, the sky is a dark purple and the red light of the diner sign glistens off the wet strands of hair clinging to John's face. I hand him back his jacket and thank him. He thanks me for the Chem help and then leans over to kiss me. I lean forward and we kiss in the rain, under the flashing sign of the diner.

"Bye," he says and pulls back. He sticks his hands into his pockets.

"Bye," I say. "See you tomorrow."

"I'll call you later," he says, over his shoulder.

I smile at the Buddha sitting over the "T" in "Tang." Above the sign is my father's window. He is sitting in the chair in front of the window, staring down at me. His arms are crossed over his chest and his eyes are drawn to slits, even narrower than they usually are.

I walk into the front room of the diner. The old bearded man sitting at the counter does not even look up. I go into the kitchen, knowing my father will be down as soon as customers start arriving. I put the kettle on for tea and sit on a stool. My father's footsteps are slow, dangerous thuds on the stairs.

I go to the counter to get a teacup. I pick up a cup and begin pouring water over the tea when my father's voice startles me. "Ling!"

I whip around and the rope of my braid slaps me in the face. The tea springs from the cup and splashes across my hand in a hot, stinging path. I drop the cup and it falls as if in slow motion, shattering on the floor. I look at the broken pieces of china at my feet.

"I told you, no more broken dishes." He sounds almost calm. Then his voice rises again, like the thunder outside. "Why were you kissing that boy? How long has this been going on?"

My father is looking at me, arms over his chest. He wants answers; he wants me to speak a few words, but I'm not going to give him that satisfaction. I don't have to share my feelings.

"You haven't really talked to me since Mama died." My voice is full of scorn and truth. This is the first time I've ever talked back to him and it feels almost as good as wearing John's jacket.

"Don't speak of your mother. I don't want to hear." His voice is soft and he turns away.

I watch his retreating back, bent with age, and listen to the shuffle of his footsteps. I clean up the china pieces of the cup by putting them on the counter and look at the map of burn marks on my hand.

I sit, eyes closed and remember my mother. Her hands, her eyes, and the way she threw her head back when she laughed. When she found the lump in her breast, they took her to the hospital and she stayed there until she died. My mother was a brave woman; she didn't come home because she wanted me to remember her as she was. I have no idea how my father remembers her.

I throw the pieces of the cup in the garbage. They land with a hollow clank. My feet feel heavy and tired as I climb the stairs. I look at my face in the mirror, and suddenly seeing my mother's braid on my head, I know what to do.

The scissors are cold knives in my hands. I cut off the still wet ends of my braid. The hair falls like the pieces of the cup when it dashed to the ground. The click of the scissors is metallic and cold. I shake my head and the last bits of hair fall to the ground. My hair now curls around my face, like John's. I gather up the bits of cut hair and walk back downstairs.

The kitchen is empty when I return. I lay the hair on the counter like a bouquet of dead lotus blossoms and I walk out the back door and into the rain.

Kam-Sein Yee

Family Secrets

Saturday, August 9, 1997
Hospital Selayang,
Lebuh, Raya Selayang-Kepong
Selangor, Malaysia

08:0:08 A.M.

You've come. I've been waiting for you. It's been a long time…

…The year was 2601 on the Japanese Calendar. In 1941-42 the Japanese came on their bicycles.

…Of course, the Malays showed them the way… It was just after school. I sat for the Senior Cambridge exam and got the results three years after that in August 1945 when the Japanese surrendered…

They came along Ipoh Road…Ipoh Road… What?

My name is Lew Chi Tho, I am 82 years old… Sister, why are you asking this damn question over and over? I know where I am. I know who I am. I'm dying but I'm not daft. The time? It's noon. You should know it's noon.

I wish I could eat… Thank you Sister. Goodbye Sister.

You should have come sooner…

…Banaajees, Sikhs, Ghurkas, they were from India you know and what superb jungle fighters! The worst were the Malays—cowards really, "The Malay Regiment," they were the ones who kept retreating and running. They threw away their uniforms, I know. I threw my gun in the pond behind my house. If they had found the gun in my house, I would have been shot or beheaded. Why are you standing in the corner? You came all this way...sit down in a chair at least.

11:41:57 A.M.

Good breakfast? So late, lah. It's almost time for supper... No, no thank you. The needle in my neck, it pinches a bit. Yes, that's better.

They were all looting, but to tell you the truth, we were looting as well. My office was at the YWCA. We looted that as well: we took all the sugar, rice, milk, and flour. We used the ambulance to carry the loot. Very clever, we thought...

The last train to Singapore was at two in the afternoon. My fellow soldiers—I didn't know what happened to them. I think they made the train, but I didn't know who was on the train. I would have gone to Singapore, but they left without me, I made the mistake of going home to change my clothes...

Japanese soldiers pierced and bayoneted the looters... I saw them...

Before the Japanese came, KL was an "Open City." You could have taken everything. We hid in the brickfields next to the railway station... Everything that could be carried or loaded into the ambulance, we took. We took it to our Commandant's house on the other side of town...

Yes, I feel tired, I want to sleep. Come back tomorrow. You should have come sooner. Why don't the others come? They did? Oh, I don't remember.

14:47:26 P.M.

You still here?...Good afternoon Sister. How long have I been asleep? Yes, I want the hot water. Thank you. You have a very pleasant manner, Sister. How old are you? How many children? Oh, not yet married? You should get married soon. Goodbye Sister, see you tomorrow.

She's a looker, don't you think? Just like girls in my time, only they were properly chaperoned...

The Japanese started to come at two-thirty P.M. They came along Ipoh Road on their bicycles. Bicycle Troops we called them...several hundred of them came. We watched from the roundabout—we could see the heads of the looters on poles. They had done this to warn off the looters. Every roundabout, at every junction all the way to Selangor Club. What a display of heads! Then, they came past my house…

Once in a while, a Japanese sentry would get off his bicycle to put up more heads. They were smart, those Japanese. We were no match for them in the end.

They kept coming on their bicycles. It was not the right time for cars. No…no cars yet. They made us bow before the soldiers, like this…

If they didn't like you, they would detain you and you had to do labour. Carry stones for not bowing. Some chaps didn't bow. What's that? No, I didn't carry stones…

Where did you say you have been? I don't want your excuses, young man. You should have been here earlier. Yes, you say you're sorry…old excuses for an old man.

…but they were good at improvising anything. Bananas yes, plenty but no rice. No rice was available—we had to eat everything, even banana skins.

They posted me at the Toshiba factory. We used lime powder to preserve the rice in sacks. In the meantime, we ate tapioca and sweet potatoes. If you worked for the Japanese like I did, you got rice and a pack of cigarettes once in a while… Of course, you had to work like them but not everyone could.

You want to talk about that? I don't want to talk about that… Why do you keep looking at the clock? Oh yes, its time for my pain pill…needles now?

15:10:42 P.M.
15:15:14 P.M.
15:22:18 P.M.

15:49:27 P.M.

…To start our day, we had to put red ink on a white handkerchief. In a red circle. One red circle, to represent the Japanese flag. Everyday we did this. No, not like that, a bigger circle. Yes, that's it.

Every morning, we had to do physical training, one-two, one-two, three-four, one-two, three-four...Of course we counted that in Japanese, *Ee-chee, nee,san,she!* We counted up to ten very quickly. Oh, they were bad, the workshop people. But we all became *O Hi O!* Qualified...in the end... This was before I met your grandmother...

It was the drawing office all right, but we weren't drawing, we were making hand grenades in our factory... You know the hand grenades—all the parts were cast in the Ipoh branch...

We were "converting industry," hah, that's what they called it. We were making propeller shafts for the bombers. We took the two- and three-horse-power Benz engines and put them into war craft. We helped them take the engines from the tin mines and convert them to marine engines...

They were so good at it, those Japanese. They liked me because I learned fast and gave them no trouble. The engineers weren't soldiers really. They didn't have to teach me, but they did. That's where I learned all my engine stuff. They weren't bad chaps in the end...

Towards the end, I was asked to design a tan charger for them. I don't know if they used it... My boss, Yamata-San, nice chap really, he had a terrible time after surrender. I learnt a lot from him. Not like those Malays. They were the real coolies...

17:41:56 P.M.

Who's that? Oh, Dr Yeoh, yes, I know that. You don't have to tell me again. I've not got long, so why make me miserable? Do I really need all this? This hurts my hand. All these needles. Can't a chap get any rest around here?

Yes, of course I'm in pain. Morphine? No, yes, maybe later. I don't know. Where's Sister Ma? I forgot it's her day off. She works hard that one...

17:45:56 P.M.

You should know your roots, but young people are in too much of a hurry. Hurry up and go nowhere...

My family was from the Salim River in Tanjung. My grandfather was the best known chap. The "richest" man in Tokay then. An estate owner. The rubber plantations.

...We hid in the jungle on the estate for a while. There is always food in the jungle if you know where to look. My father wanted to cycle up to the estates to look for my mother but the Japanese soldiers made him carry stones to build bridges.

You see it was the British policy back then—a kind of a scorched-earth policy—to blow all the roads up. And they blew them all up. All the roads were lined with burnt-out cars. As if it mattered, no petrol was available anyway. Every bridge was damaged and broken by the British, our British friends...when they were our friends.

When you looked up in the sky, there were no British planes, the Spitfires, no American Hurricanes, no Hurons. They were just no match for the Japanese Zeros, hah! Once we saw a Spitfire going up. Going right up. And then it just disappeared. Poof! A Zero got it!

But they were mostly running away, lah—cowards too. KL, our beautiful city, it was open to anyone who could take it! Funny, I did pity the Brits and the Indians, they came just two or three months before and now they were retreating...but at least the Ghurkas, they put on a bloody good fight! At least, that's what villagers told us...

Yes, please, some water. Yes, fetch the Sister...something for pain. What time is your plane? You changed your plan? When will you leave, I see...not just yet. How are Susan and the baby? Ten years old already? Good, excellent. You should have more children, don't wait...

You are looking tired. You look old. You have more grey hair than me. I forget how long it has been since I saw you. Just a boy, fresh from your O levels. No, no blanket. No, I don't feel like talking about that right now but later...

18:30:36 P.M.
19:02:43 P.M.

That's it. How can I sleep with the racket from the AC? Turn it down. See you tomorrow. What? You are not leaving? Well, stay if you like, but I don't know why you bother.

09:30:36 A.M.

...When I cycled up north, it was over sixty miles to Tanjung Malin, Batung Kali, I could see from the bridge, all the heads of British soldiers, all slaughtered. It was hard to cycle because of the holes made by the bombs on the railway lines...

My family was safe, the Japanese passed by and Singapore was not yet occupied, my whole village was deserted. Everyone had gone into the jungle... the Japanese were still on their bicycles then... But they looted the house... and took all my photos but they did not touch the photo of Sun Yat Sen. I always wondered about that.

Nonstop they came, but there was nothing left to loot, all the eggs, chickens, anything..

Heads...all along the road, all the way to the Salim River, that's where the heaviest fighting was. They were all smelly...those headless bodies. On bicycle, you saw with your own eyes. You could see everything.

My family came out of the jungle after one month. They had eaten palm shoots, bamboo shells, small animals—what kind? Boar, mouse, deer, fish.

It was the estate workers who knew how to live. They even knew which trees could be eaten...it was all about survival. You didn't waste anything. Not like now. No dog food, old clothing, nothing. They were great improvisers, those Japanese. They used to make a funny kind of bread. You could throw it against the wall like a rubber ball. It used to bounce back. We always wondered what kind of wheat would do that...

They came to my house and took my photos and my stamp collection it was worth fifteen thousand dollars! But they didn't touch our photo of Sun Yat Sen. Did I say that already? Oh, never mind.

My neighbour, Tang, he didn't fare so well. He was a Chinese schoolteacher. So was his son. They were taken away and given the "water treatment" on High Street... It was at the Lee Rubber Building. Everyone knew...once you got in there, you didn't come out. The Ming Ping Bo! It was ninety-nine percent effective! They put the hose in your mouth and pumped the water until your stomach blew up. That's what they did if they caught you spying...

They are heroes now, but back then we thought them just fools. There were a lot of informers too, you had to be careful. You had to be very careful. You should always be careful.

I didn't know your grandmother then. She was in school in Pu Chong, the communist area. The Japanese didn't dare go there. Mary, she was a good dancer. We used to have grand parties at the Club and she would dance all night long...

Once I was held up by the guerillas. I was sent to survey the acreage of land in Cheras. We were planting sayur and tapioca because they were easy to go into the ground. I was scared. They had to let me go, the guerillas, because the workers vouched for me. It was a good thing that my father had let them keep their parangs. Now that's a big knife! Other estate owners took them away at night and locked them up but my father was a trusting man. You always carried a parang when you went into the jungle...

But it was too late for Fernandez, the Indian estate family—they got the husband, the wife the three children. They didn't kill the baby. I wonder what happened to him? I was questioned in a room, but I was not tortured like the others...

Be careful who you trust. Don't ever forget that. Chinese people never forget that. I never forgot. That's why I'm still here. When are the others coming?... It doesn't matter, I was waiting for you.

Yes, that's right, waiting for you...Yes, the Japanese...

The last time I saw them, they came to my house again for a few hours. And then we never saw them again. They took my bicycle and then they cycled on to Singapore. Just like that. That would be the year 2604 on the Japanese calendar... the year my results from Cambridge came...

19:31:01 P.M.

Is that the real reason you are here? Why do you even listen to them?

Then you have been a fool and wasted your time. I can't make the past go away, neither can you. I did the best I could, but I was a young man, what other choice did I have? I cannot I tell you...cannot...

Never mind, lah, what they said...You weren't there...you can't know. Don't listen to them...You can't even imagine it...

I'm going to sleep now. Ring Sister Ma and close the window... There's nothing more to say about it.

1200:00 A.M.
1200:00 A.M.

1200:00 A.M.

18:39:13 P.M.
21:39:02 P.M.

Sir, I'm sorry, My name is Sister Ma... Yes, in his sleep, peacefully. It happens sometimes, the morphine yes, it was strong, it would have been sooner, I think he was waiting for you... No, he didn't say anything...Yes, I'm quite sure. I'm terribly sorry for your loss...

Grace Chin

Ma's Kitchen

And then she said, "You know I'm upset."

Which was an understatement, and they both knew it.

Still, her voice seemed too loud in the space; what would the neighbours think? Leaned up against the fridge with hands jammed in his pockets, he must have understood this, since he didn't reply.

In the postdeath flurry, there had been no time. No time to talk, no time at all. The funeral was tomorrow. And here they were now, no time like the present, standing in their mother's kitchen.

"After all this, *Raymond,* what were you expecting, a party? Show some respect."

And he said, deliberately: "You. Don't. Let me."

Just like that.

His closed face and Sunkist-bright sweater screamed a thousand more disrespectful words, and she'd save that to bring up for later. But now, now old wounds were opened and anger was seeping through her skin, and she was too beat to care if she hurt him or not.

"*Let* you? Where were you when she was dying, Ray? When were you ever even *Chinese* except when it suited you? Does it ever suit you? I don't know."

"But we both know who looked after Ma. I went to see her every day until she fucking died, and every day she'd ask, 'Where is my son.' Do you have any idea what that's like?"

Ray still hadn't moved and wasn't going to, perhaps he couldn't; she could see that so clearly. Then he spoke again, and this time she barely heard him through the rushing blood in her head.

"I'm still your brother," he said, and when she understood the statement Melanie's anger did rise; quick as a lash, against her clenched teeth, her voice was a weapon.

"No. You left us. You're not my brother."

How simple things should be.

And now Ray was looking at her as if he was going to tell another lie.

"Just admit—" he began, his voice rising, and stopped. Looked at her, looked up, looked away.

"Admit what?" she said, but he was studying the floor now and so she turned her back on him, on his lie. A silence began—one-one thousand, two-one thousand, three-one thousand—and she felt her brother move at last, walk to her, stand next to her. He was way too close, already.

"It's not our responsibility, Mel." He tried again, as hard as she had ever known him to try. "Not dad, not mom. Mel. Listen."

He didn't say *please*, but his hand was on her shoulder and the word hung in the air between them. His fingers were cold. Or she was hot, it was too warm in this kitchen, with this closeness, with the blood beating in her chest. She forced a long breath and the blackness at the edge of her sight wavered, receded, although she could not look at him still, because she knew that lie too well. They had said it together many times, laughing, in the past, and she had never really believed it. But Ray had. And he was wrong, because they were responsible. She was responsible.

"Don't think you can just come in here," she said finally. "You haven't earned it.

"Did you help us? All this time. Not one thing. What the hell makes you think you have the *right*?"

There was that word, *please*, unsaid; and something else as well, familiar, unidentifiable. And she finally looked at him, for him, to see if he saw it.

But he no longer looked for her. It seemed he had just been waiting for her reply, to hear what she would say, waiting until just that moment. It seemed he knew, he was prepared; and not finding the thing he wanted, the thing he looked for, he released her and walked away.

"Sometimes it's not about you, Mel," he said. And laughed, just like that. But the laughter fell into the dead air and lay still, it did not soar, it had not freed him. The thing in her shifted, squirmed, shrank into itself again.

And nothing rose to meet it, to rush into the space. It was very quiet. Her brother wasn't there. Perhaps, perhaps he had never really been there.

So she spoke the thing aloud, to herself in the empty kitchen, into her mother's absence, her brother's many absences. "*I hate you,*" she whispered, or thought, or wished. Because there were no more words, the hour was past; there was no time, and maybe there never had been time at all.

Sherwin Tjia

Shoplifting Tiger, Bomb-making Dragon

Suzy Wong and I were walking down the street. She was in the sexy silky Chinese-style dress she had gotten from Le Château.

"It's cool," she said. "I was looking for a dress like this, but the ones in Chinatown were way too expensive." She was wearing wedge-shaped sandals and all the white boys we passed looked at her walking beside me. She looked back sometimes. "Those were the real deal," Suzy laughed. "They were made of real silk. Not this polyester crap."

I could see a small strand of red thread unraveling from her hem, but I didn't tell Suzy this. Her name's actually Susan, but everyone calls her Sue. Except me. I'm the only one who she lets call her Suzy. Like the dangerous Dragon Ladies from old Saturday-afternoon Chinese flicks.

We were on our way to get bubble tea. It's this cold sweetened tea served with dark pearl-like tapioca balls. You suck them up through an enormous straw so big you could fit your finger in it. The tea was expensive as hell, but it was one of the remotely few Chinese-style things Suzy and I did. Sometimes we liked to binge on that sort of thing. To compensate, kind of. We were both born in Toronto, and grew up in a part of Scarborough called Agincourt. Back in the eighties, when there were a lot of Chinese moving into the neighbourhood, people were calling it "Asiancourt."

Suzy swung her tiger-print purse from its faux gold-chain strap, shouldered the glass door of the smoky tea house open, and we went inside.

Canto-pop played from two kleenex-box-sized speakers hanging from opposite corners of the room. We sat down on freestanding benches at a small table next to the wall. Teen magazines imported from Hong Kong hung like towels on a rack beside us. I pulled one down and opened it.

"Look at all the Chinese people," I said. No matter how many times I saw them, I always marveled. I was used to no Chinese people in magazines. A girl came to our table with two menus. We perused them. I ordered a Honey Black tea with large pearls and Suzy ordered a Raspberry Green tea, also with pearls.

"Do you ever watch *South Park*?" Suzy asked.

"Sometimes," I responded. "Why?"

Suzy lit a cigarette.

"Well, you know how whenever Chef is talking to one of the *South Park* kids, he calls them 'Children'? Like, even if there's only one of them, he still calls them 'Children.'"

I looked at her. "Right, so?"

Suzy inhaled, then exhaled, blowing the smoke towards the wall of magazines.

"Well, you're like doing the same thing when you talk about Chinese people. It doesn't matter if there's one or one hundred, you always say 'Chinese people,' like they're all the same to you."

"Chinese people *are* all the same to me."

"But you're *one* of them," she pointed out.

"I *know* that," I said. "I've known that all my life. That's the messed-up thing."

"You're weird," Suzy told me, then laughed. "But I kind of know what you mean."

The waitress came back with our drinks and set them down in front of us. As she left I nodded at her back, "Look, Chinese people." Suzy laughed, "Exactly." She ground her cigarette out.

I took a sip of my tea and struggled with a pearl.

"Sometimes you have to suck really hard to get those suckers up the tube," I said. "But once they're in your mouth they're delicious."

Suzy sipped a bit of hers and said, "I'm not a big fan. I like the tea better. The pearls are fun and all, nice to look at, but they're kinda gummy."

I kept chewing away. "Well I love 'em," I said.

In the other room, behind a half-closed curtain, someone guffawed. I could see four boys playing cards and smoking. I'd have bet they were drinking something a lot stronger than tea.

"I wonder what they're drinking?" Suzy mused.

"I was wondering the exact same thing," I told her, and added, "wanna go for a beer?"

Suzy shrugged. "Sure. Now?"

"Maybe later." I lifted my drink. "First though," I grinned at her, "how's university? Everything you thought it would be?"

Suzy groaned. "My residence room is a little closet. And everyone else seems to know everyone else. They all probably went to the same private schools or something. When I'm walking down the street in the Ghetto, it's like I'm walking through a J. Crew catalogue."

"The Ghetto? What's that?"

She groaned again. "It's the *Student* Ghetto, and yeah, they actually call it that, like they were living in *poverty* or something. But for a lot of them, it kind of is. A lot of rich prep school kids slumming it. There's even this one house full of diplomat brats and they've got a big sign out front saying, 'The Embassy'. Another house calls itself 'The Mansion'. It's insane. For them, going to university is like—" she looked up at the ceiling, thinking for a second. "It's like an initiation rite. So of course there's going to be a *little* discomfort. But for Chrissakes, their rent's paid for, nobody's starving. They've got their cute little cars parked in front of their shitty houses, then they blow a coupla hundred on the weekend for a night on the town, plus they've got mommy and daddee back home to fall back on if they need extra cash for an on-a-whim skiing weekend."

That's exactly how Suzy said it: "daddee," with two e's.

"Do I sense a little bitterness?" I asked.

Suzy just shrugged and sucked back on her straw. Her frustration was obvious. Suzy had to work in her parents' convenience store growing up. And she loathed it. But even more than she hated working in the store, she hated how it fit the stereotype of what sorts of businesses Asian immigrant families started up. The store gave her plenty of time to read, though, and I loved it secretly because I got to hang out with her a lot in that cramped little place, talking, reading magazines, drinking pop, and snacking on candy. Ah, my misspent youth.

When we got outside, Suzy showed me the magazine she'd stolen. It was like the one I'd pulled down off the rack except it was called *CUTIE.* It had a picture of a cute-looking Japanese girl on the cover, with big doe eyes and wearing an equally cute cool outfit, complete with patterned leg-warmers.

"They've got the wildest taste," she proclaimed. "Lookit those scarves, those shoes. It's insane over there."

I flipped through page after page of adolescent Japanese girls putting on makeup, or standing deadpan in the latest styles. I'd seen my sister's *Seventeen* magazines, and everything was just subtly different here. I couldn't exactly put my finger on it, but there was a definite difference in aesthetics. They were both still pushing products, swaying their hips to Late Capitalist postures, but what was cool in *CUTIE* had a significantly off-kilter energy.

"I can't even articulate why this is weird to me," I said. "There's just something so odd about it."

At the bar we found a table and ordered a pitcher. Neither of us had huge tolerances, so a pitcher would do us fine. We'd see who got red the fastest.

On the wall were posters of Jimi Hendrix, Jim Morrison, James Dean, Audrey Hepburn, and Marilyn Monroe.

"Where's Elvis?" I asked.

Suzy scanned the room. "Maybe they forgot him. Couldn't forgive him for getting fat."

Laughing, I took a long tug on my beer. "That one's for the King," I toasted, and belched. There was an old Coke machine in the corner, one of the ones that looked like a small fridge.

"It looks like they took Bar Décor 101 or something before they tackled this place," I commented.

Suzy agreed. "Yeah, everything's so hackneyed. And it's weird to see so many televisions tuned to so many different channels." One screen had a sitcom on. I never kept up with them. They all started to look the same to me. Another screen had the Beatles on, and then the screen froze on a black and white still of them from their early days, before they went all mop-toppy. Suzy turned to me.

"I met this girl at Queen's. Elaine. She's in my res. She's actually on my floor. We started hanging out. She's Thai."

An old Offspring song blasted over the speakers and a group in the corner sang along to it for a second, then quieted down. On the TV was a clip showing, "A Hard Day's Night," the bit where they're on the Ed Sullivan show.

Suzy laughed. "So she met this guy during Frosh Week, and they've been dating for a while. You know what he said to her after they had sex for the first time?"

"What?"

"'I feel just like John Lennon.'"

I burst out laughing, almost spitting my beer all over the table.

"Oh my God. You're *not* fucking serious," I said.

"Dead." Suzy nodded. Then she shook her head from side to side, as if unable to understand what she just said to me.

Then we started drinking in earnest.

Soon Suzy and I were quite tipsy. We finished the pitcher and decided to order fries. She was red as hell and I knew I was too. Asians are supposed to lack the enzyme that promotes alcohol tolerance, or something like that, but I knew two Asian girls from university who could just drink and drink.

"Wanna get another pitcher?" Suzy dipped a fry into the ketchup, pulled it out, and put it in her mouth. Then she did it again. This time, however, she did it as if she were striking a match, and putting the lit stick onto her tongue. At this point, her bright cheeks matched her crimson dress.

"Um," I responded.

"C'mon," she coaxed. "Live dangerously!"

I smiled a sleepy smile at her. "I already do. I'm your friend, aren't I?"

"Hey," she said, adopting a baby-girl voice. "What are you saying? That *I'm* dangerous? Little ol' *me?*" She smiled and made her eyes huge, like Japanese animation girls. While I was laughing, she caught the eye of the waiter and motioned for another pitcher.

It was as if we were daring each other to drown ourselves in beer. I didn't know where it all went. All that alcohol. Somewhere in my belly you could have cauterized wounds.

Thinking about us, something occurred to me. I thought about a National Geographic magazine article I'd read a couple of months ago.

"Hey," I touched Suzy's knuckles.

"Hmm?" her eyebrows jolted up, then down, like a cat's back.

"Have you ever heard of Deep Playing?"

She squinted. "No, can't say I have. What is it?"

Through the fog I tried to recollect what it was all about. "Okay. I read about this a coupla months ago, so the details aren't too clear. There's like, these tribes in New Guinea, or somewhere, and what they do, they have cockfights."

"*Cock*fights?" Suzy's eyes got big.

"Birds," I hastened to clarify. "Cocks are *birds*."

"Oh." Her eyes returned their normal size.

"Anyway," I continued. "There'll be like, these two guys from different villages who are about to set their cocks at each other. And these birds are straining at their ropes, or whatever. Remember, one of them's going to *die,* right? And so people from the different villages gather round to watch. And before you know it, someone's betting his collection of tools that the cock from *his* village will win. Of course, that's a challenge that can't ride without someone from the *other* village betting *his* tools. And it's all downhill from there. Someone bets their cart, someone else their clothes, then their huts. Pretty soon, you have this unbelievable situation where the entire contents of *one* village are bet against the entire contents of the *other* village. And all based on the outcome of one small cockfight." Suzy's eyes were big again, and incredulous.

"So?" she asked, "What happens?"

"Well," I said, matter-of-factly. "One cock wins. And one village basically *owns* the other village after. And some anthropologists call this Deep Playing." My mind was decidedly faltering, though my voice stayed surprisingly smooth. "The cumulative risk of playing totally outweighs the potential reward. It's like betting your kid's life on a coin toss. There's something sick about it."

One side of Suzy's mouth curled up in a wry smile. "Then why the hell do they do it? If it's so stupid?"

I took another pull of my beer and shrugged. "It's like a dare, or a double dare, I guess. At some point it just gets silly, but you can't back out. There's more at stake than just stuff. You have your reputation to think about." There was a pause in the conversation as we both put more beer away. Finally Suzy gave me a puzzled look. Then she cracked a smile.

"That's so weird. Why in the world did you just mention that? I mean, as fascinating a concept as Deep Play is, what triggered you to tell me?"

I burped a little. "I dunno. I guess I was thinking about how we're drinking ourselves silly here, and how it's an example of Deep Playing. I mean, 'Let's live dangerously,' you said. So in a way, you threw down the gauntlet."

Suzy smiled.

"Yeah yeah. I remember what I said. But dangerous? You call this–" she gestured at the two empty pitchers, "*–dangerous?*" She half-smiled and raised one eyebrow. "Two people enter; one person leaves," Suzy paraphrased from *Mad Max Beyond Thunderdome.* Then she gave me this outrageously seductive look, which I enjoyed way too much, and said, "Show me what you're made of, cowboy."

Pretty soon we had another full pitcher on the table and I was wondering who was going to be the first one on the floor. I took a long look at Suzy's body. Purely strategic, you understand. We're both skinny kids, but I tried to guess her body weight. A number didn't quite form, but I was fairly certain I had a good twenty pounds over her.

Suzy poured us both another and suddenly I was mad and giddy and thinking, Hey, *I could do this all night,* and meaning it, and I tossed more down. I was stuffing the closet and closing the door and feeling really bloody good about it.

And after a while my Asian flush went away. I get really pale once I've drunk a significant quantity of liquor, as if the blood's needed elsewhere. And after another little while I get seduced by the illusion of clearheadedness, even though I'm totally smashed. I get very impulsive then. I get this sense of decidedness. Right then I thought about kissing Suzy right on the mouth. I thought about taking her dress off. Pulling her to me. She must've caught me staring at her, because she said, "Hey. What is it? Are you okay?" I let my eyes drift down to the orangey brown sticky table.

"God," I yawned. "I'm pretty wrecked. I'm fading fast." Suzy yawned too and I caught a flashing glimpse of the back of her throat. It was shiny. Shinier than her dress. It's her saliva, I thought, making everything wet. My own mouth was very dry.

"I got the feeling you were chickening out," Suzy said.

"*How* chickening out?"

"You know, when you mentioned Deep Playing. Nothing's worse

than someone who analyzes what they're doing as they're doing it. It's like a defense. Against living."

"I wasn't being defensive," I said, defensive. "I was drawing an *analogy.*" I used my hands to explain this, as if I were drawing a thin string taut between my pinched fingers. Suzy gave me a dubious look.

"Wanna settle up?" Suzy opened her purse, emptied its contents on the table. "Jesus Christ, this is a mess," she muttered. I could barely hear her over the music.

Spilled on the table were little tissue turds, silver change, a lipstick, a little blue barrette, masses of scrap paper with phone numbers on them, fake ID, real ID, some keys, some green Clorets gum, a pen, a little *Hello Kitty* change purse, and a coupla tens. I looked at the things she carried around with her in her purse and wondered how in the world it all fitted in there.

"You got a lotta crap," I pointed out. "How come you carry so much stuff around with you?"

Suzy laughed.

"I know, I know. But it all fits." She started to go through the papers, and pulled out a mangled business card.

"This is from some loser at Future Bakery who came up to me, all suave-like, you know, like he thinks he's James *Bond* or something. He stops by my table and hands it to me. Goes, 'What are you doing Saturday night?' and I'm like, 'Are you for real?'" I grinned and when we got up, Suzy left that card and others like it on the table after cramming everything else back into her tiny purse.

On the street we were supporting one another. I was halfway down to the sidewalk. We were laughing about something, I didn't know what, wondering when the hell the streetcar was supposed to come. I saw something in the distance but it might have been a truck. I said as much.

"Looks like something, but I might be wrong."

That was when Suzy kissed me on the mouth, and I was so startled, I sat down.

Terry Woo

Cheap Razor Blades

I wake up at one p.m. again, sprawled on the thin foam mattress I've called "temporary" for about six weeks now. The house is dead silent. Dad must have gone to work, of course, hours earlier; Mom has gone to painting or dancing classes or to *yum cha* with her friends. Or whatever. So I'm stuck at home. My parents' home. Alone. No plan. No life. No woman. No car.

I plod downstairs, only to be greeted by a grey, watery light, marginally reflected on the off-white, dull wall. The grayness seems just to hang there, accentuating the meaninglessness of existence with a mournful groan, as if someone has just died. *Shit.* That's southern Ontario in the wintertime. You know, if I'd woken up three hours earlier, I'd at least have been treated to a sliver of sunlight. It's a weird Canadian winter anomaly?often sunny at dawn until just before noon, and then clouding over...almost the exact opposite of San Francisco. And almost the exact opposite of Good.

But I usually wake up past noon, so I burn. Or freeze as the case may be. I read a number of United Nations reports on global warming a while back, claiming that Toronto would be the place to grow avocados and pineapples in the winter come the new millenium. And looking at the clouds now, the dirt-layered suburban snowdrifts outside, the unshoveled sidewalks and driveways...lordy, they couldn't've gotten it more wrong.

At the bottom of the stairs, I look around the scene that has greeted me for much of my youth...that is, when I actually belonged here. My house is a nice one, I suppose—a modest brick box in northeastern

Toronto, birthed by a large construction-company mother in the late eighties, when most land up here was farmland, golf courses, and had people with names like Burnett, McGill, and McGrath. Pretty clean and well kept, despite twelve-odd years of boisterous family living... well, as boisterous as Asian families can get. Classic Chinese Canadian décor: Mom's Chinese watercolour creations living side by side with modern art prints, statues of the Buddha next to Leon's furniture done in tasteful, slightly-out-of-date cream tones. The kitchen also filled with a weird mix of western and Chinese accoutrements—cans of tuna and Campbell's red-label soups stacked neatly beside large packages of sows' ears or pigs' collars...all sorts of quasimedicinal dried Chinese goodies my mom boils up into nutritious soups that stave off colds, scurvy, and errant silver bullets.

There were times long ago when my folks needed to travel all the way to downtown Toronto to buy that sort of stuff. We were living in London at the time, one of three Chinese families embedded in a neighbourhood of WASPs. We'd take these bimonthly two-hour drives into Toronto's teeming Chinatown to pick up anything and everything —canned this, chopped that, hung and dripping whatever, freshly scaled and beheaded albatross or aboleth or something or other. And after a *dim sum* session with the relatives, we'd go home and store the stuff in cupboards and freezers like survivalists, only without the fatigues and neo-Aryan hate literature.

The two-odd hours of traveling I remember quite well...aside from getting dizzy reading comics in the car, or squeezing my baby sister's fat cheeks, or listening to Mom babble about how boring London was and why we should all move to Toronto, the trips were mostly filled with music. The Olds we owned had a tape deck, and Dad, commander-in-chief of our music choices, would always play his oldies. But he didn't play the "cool" oldies so fashionable in Hollywood Baby Boomer nostalgia blockbusters these days. Just really, really square ones. Cheesy Johnny Horton historical sagas, old Bee Gees pre-disco ballads, jangly sixties beach guitar tunes, and (of course) various selections from the King (*maow wong)* himself.

It was freaking hellish. It's all been irrevocably cauterized into my memory and garnished with a strange, sickly nostalgia.

Today, as I float like molasses through the gray Canadian ether, only one of those songs echoes through my mind. A sad, sad song by Linda

Rondstadt? appropriate, since I have been stupefied by weeks of unemployment and twelve hours of sleep everyday.

They say that love's a gentle thing
But it's only brought me pain.
For the only man I ever loved
Has gone on the morning train.

I never will marry,
I'll be no man's wife.
I expect to live single (oh-whoa),
All the days of my life.

Merely recounting the lyrics does no justice to this mournful, lovely ballad...one that brings tears to my eyes because it seems like it's me, a twenty-seven-year old self-absorbed loser in a serious funk, a lousy Chinese Son, with no love, no income, motivation, or prospects. Living with his mommy and daddy.

Well, except for the "wife" part. Okay. A slight change then...

I never will marry,
I'm not husband material.
I expect to live single (oh-whoa),
In an existence that's pointless, as much as surreal...

A little too pseudointellectual, huh? How about this...?

I never will marry,
I'm not husband material.
I expect to live single (oh-whoa),
Eating instant noodles and Froot Loops cereal...

I am now cooking myself a bowl of instant noodles and looking at myself in the reflection on the microwave. Stiff Asian hair in punk-styled bedhead angles. Threadbare T-shirt rips at the seams, sporting the logo of some accounting company I used to work for in a former, more responsible life. Checkered Gap boxers, frayed at the thighs.

Unshaven, thick bristles obscuring nicks caused by cheap disposable razors and no-name shaving cream. I don't shave that much anymore, just to avoid those goddamn nicks. I suppose I should go to Shoppers to pick up that Mach 3 razor that's supposed to revolutionize shaving and cause cherubs to circle your chin every morning. But I won't. The nicks are just appropriate to my useless, forlorn existence right now. They are punishment and penance.

Okay, back to instant noodles. Add that little MSG packet—Chinese embalming fluid for the preservation of living corpses. A mug of one-percent milk. Open a can of some pickled and unidentified tentacled creature with unidentified Chinese characters on front. Halloween-sized Snickers for dessert. I plod into the family room with the payload, to slide the garbage down my throat whilst sliding garbage into my brain. Daytime television—the refuge of the damned.

Channel-surfing now. *Surf surf, surf surf.*

Surf surf... ooooh! An episode of *Blind Date.* Treat! In addition to Roger Lodge the regular weirdo attention-whoring whitebread couples they usually feature, they're also featuring an interracial couple—Asian chick, white guy, natch. A true "Hollywood Diversity Special"—*look at us, we are sooo diverse.* The other way around would be far too incomprehensible and ball shattering, I would imagine, to the typical *Blind Date* producer.

They didn't hook up, of course, because—*surprise*—how can a couple of different ethnicities *really* know each other? I mean really, *really* know? Especially if the only reasons for that coupling to occur were socialized, Anglocentric notions of exotic beauty that is the Asian Woman. I've got Jungle Fever. You've got Jungle Fever. We all have Jungle Fever.

I'm just jealous. I know that. The anger and bitterness I and many of my brethren feel may be mere jealousy. But I know in my green heart that it takes its roots much deeper, in a fundamental injustice in society that pervades a spectrum of issues. It has implications for our jumbled notions of Asian identity. Some are deemed of societal importance. Some are deemed trivial and stupid. Inquiring minds don't always want to know. But even that's a lame argument, because I have lost interest in all things sexual for...how long? Weeks now, I think.

I suppose there are ways to end this ordeal, many of them without the use of a twenty-two-gauge shotgun.

"GET A JOB!" shrieked my mom at one point, literally holding a wooden spoon to my throat. I'd woken up once again at around one pm. She comes from a family background that didn't much tolerate shiftless, unemployed bums.

Well, I could try. But why bother? Bubble or no bubble, I know I just hate accounting. I know I like music. If I did get another job figuring out tax breaks for a quarter-foot measure of pipe, I know I'd just hate it. I wouldn't be able to save any money—I'd just spend it all on alcohol and drugs to cope with the pain, with the same net result: not much. And if I wasn't laid off, I'd probably quit after a year, in disgust and despair, and end up back at home eating instant noodles and not shaving with cheap disposable razors. So really, in the long run, what's the blessed point? Why not just accept reality the way it is and, you know, that's it?

What I really want, I suppose, is to play the guitar full time. Be a successful jazz-blues session musician, tour across the continent, get rich and famous, marry Norah Jones, and buy a tropical island with my earnings and ride out the wave of Armageddon that Nostradamus says is coming real soon. But it's tough—there are plenty of people with similar aspirations, most of them more talented and passionate than I, some also with the ability to administer decent blowjobs to music executives and moneyed patrons. Better looking than me. Trust me. I'm in the know.

Eh, I know nothing. Because I haven't really tried. My guitar is lying in its cradle in the basement, under a stack of music, instead of in my hands. Maybe it's because a guitar in the hands of a true musician becomes an extension of him, putting forth what's deep in the heart. And I'm really not in the mood to sing a historical saga about a guy who's wasted his life in front of a pile of spreadsheets and a monitor crunching numbers, each figure sapping a bit more of his life and dignity, until he ends up... here. The eighth circle of Hell.

There've been a slew of articles in the recent past about Gen X "boomerangs"—adult children moving back in and living with their parents. They often earnestly cite factors such as lower real incomes, higher property values, higher rents, cyclical business cycles, "comfort and convenience" (in households that do not dispense wooden-spoon justice). I suppose I am one of these lucky sons-a-bitches, having this safety net I can fall into. A lot of Asians generally are. But it doesn't make me feel any better—I mean, why would it make me feel better? I've been socialized to accept a certain degree of progress in life… and being here and eating MSG-laced freeze-dried noodles isn't progress. It's just pathetic. And peculiarly Asian.

How about a bit of luck, then? A bit of good news, a small windfall, a winning lotto ticket? The pot o' gold under the rainbow. Looking out the window, at the gray supernimbus or cumulocirrus storm clouds, I don't see any rainbows. I don't see God, much less any luck—just a chaotic and pointless turmoil of particles, forming larger particles and systems of particles, all lost in a void. A lot like most people, in this life.

God—wherever he is, if he or she exists—won't give me that luck, because I don't deserve it, sitting here in a warm suburban home, spouting whiny Gen X-isms, devoid of any real suffering. *Luck*—wherever you can get it—will gravitate to those who need it, like that Georgia dude who was on parole who won $30 million in the state lottery. Good for him. I don't do *schadenfreude* or begrudge those who get it, the God or the luck, because I really do sympathize with the legions of people who are worse off than me.

After eating my slop and depositing the rest of my soul in the garbage, I plod into the bathroom to finally take a shower. Taking off my clothes, I look at my scrawny, twitchy form in the mirror. And I drop to my knees and let out a howl of despair.

Sweet mother of fuck. I am twenty-seven years old. I was once at a job I hated, and I got laid off, and I am now living with my parents. My room's been converted into a den. I'm stuck at home. Alone. No plan. No life. No woman. No car.

But isn't there, at the very least, hope? The box that Pandora foolishly opened still had Hope. At least I think so. Mom hopes that I will emerge from abject failure into the shining success I was always destined to become. Her linear Chinese mind cannot handle the fact that with my vaunted university degree and thousands of dollars in provincial debt somewhat paid off, I am not still slaving away at one of the big Five or Four or Three, saving money for a house, getting married, and giving her *mucho grande* face. She does not understand that you like what you like, and you hate what you hate. She does not understand that relationships are difficult these days. She does not understand that I have no spine, because I hate myself and I actually agree with her. She just does not understand.

I am weak. I have run home after my dreams ran out on me. And I hardly have enough energy to get up before noon, much less reach escape velocity and break free of this stupid orbit I've seemed to have locked myself into.

I look at the package of unused cheap disposable razors on the bathroom counter. I would like to plunge one of them into my wrists. But that would really hurt. And honestly? It's not the right type of razor. You can't do that sort of thing anymore, slash your wrists with movielike artistic elegance, because razors these days are not the kinds of blades that sick fucks plunge into apples and give to little kiddies dressed like Darth Vader on Halloween. It'd be like trying to slit your wrists with an electric shaver and coming up with only smooth, hairless wrists.

So I sit, cross-legged and naked in the middle of the bathroom floor, fluorescent lights flickering on my pale form, and once again ponder the pointless mundanity—mendacity—of life. My life.

I wonder if the Unabomber got his start this way...?
Eh, probably not.

Okay. Is there any redemption to this story?

Well... no. Not really. Just *"thinkin' about somethin' that don't have to add up to nothin'."*

But there's certainly no tragic ending to it—no slit wrists, no hung corpse, no body at the bottom of the Bloor Street Aqueduct, because realistically speaking, that's just plain stupid.

Buddy in this story eventually runs into a set of circumstances that gets him out of the house and into the world again. He gets another job. He discovers leasing and gets a nice conservative Honda Civic, no spoiler. He meets a girl, goes out with her, then breaks up with her. Or, he might get lucky, passionate, and actually start exploring the stuff his dreams of music are made of. Who knows? Some of these circumstances are good, some are bad, and some just cause him to be so busy that he can't think about instant noodles or cheap razor blades.

So…I guess it all comes out even. Life has a funny way of evening things out.

I guess it's not all bad.

Just keep the faith.

Winston C Kam

The Re-education of Ah Mow and His Subsequent Undoing Thereof

Ah Mow fancied himself the cleverest man in the village. How he despised his fellow villagers! What a mindless lot! And the village! What a miserable place! A man couldn't make a living there. And the village police officer! He kept harassing him! If only he could get to the city, he thought. It was easy there, easy to get rich. So people said. But he needed money.

One night, on his way home from a fair at a neighbouring village, he came across an ox limping along the narrow dirt path. Already in a bad mood after having lost all his money gambling, he struck the poor animal hard on the rump. "Out of my way, smelly old beast!" he shouted. But as he hurried past he came to a sudden stop. He had an idea! The beast must be lost, he thought, looking around. Seeing that the way was clear, he grabbed the beast and pulled and pushed it all the way home. When, after some days, there was still no hue and cry about a lost ox, he decided to raffle it off. Why shouldn't he profit from his labours? It was hard work dragging that smelly animal all the way home, not to mention feeding it. So Ah Mow spread the word that he had an ox to raffle. It was an unexpected inheritance from a distant relative, he told anyone who cared to ask. But he would only allow the villagers to view the prize from afar. He didn't want them to see how old and lame the beast was and, therefore, past its prime and useless as a beast of burden. Some of the villagers were not fooled, however. They laughed at Ah Mow and wanted nothing to do with his raffle. But enough were fooled that Ah Mow was able to pocket a nice sum of money. The day came when he drew the winning ticket and the winner came by to claim his prize. The man sputtered in rage when he saw the state of the beast. Ah Mow pretended to be shocked. "I don't understand. It must've fallen ill," he moaned. "Here I give your money back!" The man gratefully took back his money, glad that he wasn't cheated. But after he left, Ah Mow began jumping up and down in glee. He had fooled them all! Now he had both the ox and the remaining money from the raffle! That night he butchered the ox, and he sold the meat in the market the next day, increasing his profit even more. "Thanks to you I can now go to the big city!" Ah Mow sneered at the villagers. But the villagers jeered back, "You wait! There are many new things in the city! Things you do not understand! You'll be back!"

Waaah! The city was amazing! So many cars, wide streets, and buses and such beautiful buildings under construction everywhere! They looked like palaces! These must be the new things the villagers spoke about! Ah Mow laughed. They didn't frighten him. In fact he was excited and couldn't wait to start making a living.

As fate would have it, a tout hiring workers for a construction site approached him. But Ah Mow was not one to sell his labours, especially if the labour was hard and the pay cheap. He preferred the tout's job. All that man did was find people to work and he, in turn, was paid a small percentage of their wages at the end of the day. He could do that, Ah Mow thought. It suited him better. Could he find a job like that? He went to the tout for advice. "Speak to me at the end of the day," said the tout. "I'll tell you how. But you have to work…at least for today." Ah Mow agreed. It was for only one day. But at the day's end he was exhausted. He had never worked so hard before and he ached all over. Tired, he went in search of the tout only to discover that the man had fled with their money! The workers were incensed! The police were called and a search started. "He's fled the city!" someone howled. "The province, you mean!" another shouted. "The country!" screamed yet another. At first Ah Mow was shocked and angry. But then, gradually, he began to think that the man was quite clever, indeed! Right away he had another idea!

It so happened that there was another construction site nearby. Someone there had reported the owner to the police for using bad cement in the building. The owner blamed the foreman and promised to dismiss the man right away! Still, the police admonished the owner, telling him that he would be in jail now if there weren't such a pressing need for homes. They'll be keeping a close eye on him, they warned. Ah Mow went to the owner. "These police!" he spat. "They keep people from making a good living!" he added, thinking of the village policeman always spying on him, preventing him from making a living. He hated the police. He said to the owner, "If you want to save money...why not just fill the walls with garbage?" He pointed to the refuse, the bottles and cans lying on the street. The owner stared at Ah Mow and saw right away that they were of a like mind. He took him on as his tout.

Ah Mow's plan was that once he had won his boss's trust, he would abscond with the money. But on that fateful day, something quite unexpected happened. A worker, as honest as they come, discovered that garbage was being used to reinforce the walls. He reported it to the boss, who pretended to be shocked. He blamed Ah Mow. Right away he had Ah Mow beaten and kicked out. Poor Ah Mow! He didn't dare protest. The man was rich with many rough friends. He thought of going to the police but couldn't abide them. And it was his word against his boss's! He was furious! But what could he do?

Beaten, he retreated to a peach orchard to lick his wounds. These city people were cleverer than he was, he realized ruefully. Not so stupid like the villagers. Then suddenly he had yet another idea! He'll leave the country! He had heard people say how easy it was to make a living overseas. He'll go to Jianada (Canada)! It was easier there! But his money was running out...

He thought of picking peaches and selling them but there wasn't much money to be had in fruits. And it was too much hard work. Just then he heard a whimper nearby. Going to investigate, he discovered a civet caught in a trap. His eyes lit up! He had an idea! There was good money in meat, especially delicate meat like civet. He butchered the unfortunate animal and made for the market straightaway so as to have an early start the next morning. But on the way dogs, and even a fox, came by sniffing at the meat. He began to shoo them away when he had an even better idea! He laughed as he chased after the animals. How fortunate to have brought the civet skin with him! He would display it to show that *all* his meat was civet...

Early that morning, Ah Mow joined the row of meat sellers. He spread the meat atop the civet skin and waited. The true connoisseurs of meat turned up their noses at him and his meat. Only the truly ignorant and the poor bought from him.

Then an old crone, as toothless as on the day she was born, happened by and began examining the meat. She clearly didn't have any money and looked quite stupid, Ah Mow thought. He was about to chase her away when she said, "Civet! That's an endangered species."

Ah Mow was thunderstruck. "What? What's that you said?" he demanded.

"It's illegal to trap civet," the woman murmured, giving him a disapproving look.

Now Ah Mow had heard of such things, that it was wrong to trap certain animals. But that was so much foolishness!

"There're millions in the woods!" he shouted at the woman. He raised his chopper threateningly. "Shoo! Get away! Try to stop me from making a living, will you?"

Not long after, some men in smart uniforms began to slowly wend their way through the market.

"Meat Inspectors!" someone hissed.

A ripple of murmurs went among the meat sellers. A few abandoned their stalls and scurried away.

"Meat inspectors?" Ah Mow growled. "What's that?"

The seller stared at Ah Mow in astonishment. "Aiyaaa! You don't know? They check to see if your meat is good," he said. "It's a new thing. All over the country! All the cities! Even the villages! They're smart too. They can tell what a meat is just by looking at it."

"Bah!" Ah Mow spat. "Nonsense! They're useless!" he snarled. "They keep a man from making a living, is what!" He picked up his chopper. "They won't stop me," he muttered angrily.

"You better get out your licence..."

"Licence? What licence?" Ah Mow bellowed, now very angry indeed.

By then the inspectors were upon them. Suddenly, without warning, Ah Mow ran screaming through the small group of stunned men slashing right and left. One of the inspectors died instantly. Ah Mow fled, running as fast as he could in his panic. Why couldn't people leave him alone to make a living? He had no choice now but to flee the country.

He traveled to the coast and let it be known that he wanted to leave. Soon he was approached by a "snakehead," a man who smuggled human cargo. He had Ah Mow sign a contract to repay the cost of the journey with his labour. Ah Mow signed willingly. He was anxious to leave. Soon he was on a rust bucket of a steamer heading for Jianada. There were hundreds more like him on board, he discovered. They reminded him of the stupid villagers he had left behind, which soured his mood. But he brightened when he thought of Jianada, where they left you alone and you were free to make a good, easy living. So people said...

But as the ship neared Jianada, the captain warned them not to get caught. "Don't go marching in the streets like you're back home!" he snarled.

They grew worried and began whispering fearfully among themselves.

"What if we get caught?" asked one.

"Say you're a refugee," someone volunteered.

"Yes, yes! Say you're religious. You're being persecuted..."

"You ran away because they want you to become a spy..."

"Yes, yes, that's so!"

"You want freedom!"

"What about me? I can say that too...?"

"Ah! You're a woman! That's even better! Tell them they force you to have only one child. You're lucky. It's easy for a woman..."

Ah Mow snorted. He didn't know what to make of what he had just heard, or if any of it was true. But it didn't concern him. He had no intentions of getting caught, like these fools!

Ah Mow was not caught. Once ashore his instincts for survival led him right away to that part of the city where many like him worked and lived. Waaah! What an amazing city! Even better than what he had heard! So different from anything he had ever seen! Big, but frightening! But here he could do as he pleased! No one would bother him, and that excited him! Look at the people! They were all happy, making a living, making money! He had to start making a living too! He took the address he was given by the snakehead and studied it. He was supposed to go there and fulfill his end of the contract. But he couldn't bear the thought of his labours going for naught, for years, too! What kind of living was that? Immediately, he had an idea! He threw away the address.

That night he waited for the merchants to close their shops. He was hungry and tested their doors, only to discover that they were secured with heavy locks behind steel gates. Disappointed he turned his attention elsewhere. He went to the boxes of garbage piled up along the sidewalk and began rummaging through them. He found fruits and vegetables that were passably good. He had yet another idea! He ate his fill and kept the rest. Early the next morning he would canvass the neighbourhood in search of elderly folk who couldn't walk the distance to town and who, as a result, wouldn't mind buying fruits and vegetables brought to their doorsteps and sold at a cheap price. And so he made a few dollars. He did it for several more days until he grew tired. It was not a good way to make a living. He was much too smart for this and decided to chat up the merchants and become friendly with them. Who knows? Something might come his way. A few offered him work but it was too hard for a clever man like him. There must be an easier way.

Then one night, he saw several men unloading bags of crabs at the rear of a seafood merchant's. Crabs were expensive. If only he could catch and sell crabs he, too, would soon be in the money. Suddenly he had another idea! Why, the ocean was just over there! And it was free...!

The next night he followed the men to where they caught crabs and saw their lights winking on and off on the wharves that jutted out into the ocean. He watched as they pulled up their crab pots. "Waaah!" he thought, impressed. "So much crabs!" He was about to venture forward and introduce himself when, from out of nowhere, came policemen on the run. The crab men tried to flee but were rounded up and their pots confiscated. The crabs were thrown back into the sea.

Ah Mow was shocked and angry! These police! They were everywhere! Like cockroaches! But he was puzzled. He couldn't understand it. Weren't those poor crab men free to do as they pleased? It is a free land, yes? It is Jianada? He decided that it was a misunderstanding. And so after the police left, he went out to see what he could salvage. He found two pots that had somehow been missed and with these he embarked on a career as crab catcher.

For the next few nights all went well for Ah Mow. He caught many crabs and made much money. He was very open about it too. He flashed his lights about while he worked; he even sang. He was convinced that what had happened several nights ago was a misunderstanding. Then one night a policeman approached. Ah Mow was nervous but adopted a very friendly manner. He was positive that the police in this kingdom were different from those back home. He also understood a little English by then and was able to understand when the officer asked him what he was doing.

"Make living!" Ah Mow laughed, full of pride. He bowed three times as a mark of respect, something he would never do to the policemen back home.

The officer calmly explained that catching crabs was not permitted on the jetty, that only in certain areas was it permitted, that there was a season for it, that a license was required.

Ah Mow stared blankly at the officer. He wasn't at all sure he understood what the man was saying.

Then the officer did an astonishing thing. He began measuring the crabs!

"Waaah!" Ah Mow thought. "Crazy policeman! Why he do that?"

"Too small," the officer announced.

Ah Mow laughed. "Yes, they not grow yet! Small but gooood...!"

"No good," said the officer, shaking his head.

"Oh, yes, good. Sweet..."

"No good,' the officer repeated, promptly throwing the crabs back into the water. But because Ah Mow was friendly, he simply gave him a warning and told him not to do it again.

Ah Mow was dumbfounded. How could this be? This was a free country where a man had a right to make a living as he pleased. He became angry. That was all he was doing, making a living! Why was he being prevented from doing that? The officer didn't understand, he told himself. No, he didn't understand. Yes, that's it, he didn't understand! And so the next night Ah Mow returned to catching crabs convinced that the officer simply didn't understand.

But that night the same officer reappeared. This time he was not so friendly. This time he confiscated Ah Mow's crab pots. This time he charged Ah Mow with poaching. This time he demanded that Ah Mow appear in court the next day. This time Ah Mow became extremely angry indeed!

The following morning, still seething, Ah Mow appeared in court. Upon seeing the policeman in the hallway, he screamed at him, "You stop me make living!"

He pulled out a revolver and shot at the policeman. Now Ah Mow had never fired a revolver before. The kick of the weapon disturbed his aim and bullets went flying everywhere. The policeman did the only thing he could do...

Now Ah Mow had never been shot before, nor had he ever experienced such great pain. When the first bullet hit him in the shoulder, the jolt and shock of it brought on a moment of stunning clarity to him. Many questions flashed through his mind then and he began to wonder. But it was too late for wondering. For in that moment of exquisite clarity, Ah Mow was also able to see the next bullet speeding toward him, the one that would kill him. It pierced his forehead and came out the back, smashing his skull wide open.

And so it was that Ah Mow's brain finally tasted fresh air...

Paul Yee

The Friends

The food was the best to be had in Chinatown, but Chin was not eating. Across from him, Fong was feasting. Chopsticks prodded meat and greens, bones were cracked and spat out, and gulps of spice and whiskey shot to a warming belly. In between, Fong exclaimed slowly and deliberately, "Wah, this is good! Wah, this is tasty!"

Each time, Chin raised his glass in a toast, wanting to further honour his friend. Fong never indulged in fine dishes, claiming fears of a dependency on fussy cooks.

Eat 'til you're full, Chin thought. Who knows if we'll ever sit together again?

His eyes wandered over the teahouse. Tasseled Chinese lanterns dangled here and there but their filaments had severed long ago. Instead, bulbs on long twists of wire lit the hall. Among pillars of scrolls and mirrors pitted with splashes of grease, diners and drinkers crowded around wooden tables. Chairs were in short supply; some men were perched on crates. Rowdy shouts from a drinking game cut through the din of dishes and talk. It was Sunday night, and all those who worked the half-day came to Chinatown to join their own kind.

Chin steered his mind back to his friend. I know what needs saying; it's simple. I've bought a train ticket. Tomorrow I leave, for Winnipeg. I'll look up kinsmen; try a business. Your money? Of course you'll get it back.

"Ah, Pretty-boy!" A wallop to his back jolted him. All evening, strangers had been stopping. "Pretty-boy, you've had good luck! Got a little more for me?"

Chin saw a dark face leering at him. "Good luck? Fah! What good luck? Savvy, that's what it takes. I calculated it, every word. These past four years, that's all I've been following."

"You work so hard. The lottery is ruined. You going home?"

Chin ignored the sarcasm and replied, "Not going anywhere." He glanced at Fong. No reaction.

"You have lotsa time!" The stranger turned. "And you, Fong? Your old chum, is he treating you well?"

Unaccustomed to such attention, Fong nodded giddily. "Oh, one-and-the-same. One-and-the-same."

"Those two are funny!" The visitor moved on, shouting to the crowd. "Pretty-boy wins several hundred dollars, and they sit there eating as if nothing's changed."

Nothing? Chin flicked invisible daggers to his back. You think we eat like this every night? Screw your mother!

Fong flung down his chopsticks and drawled, "Enough. I'm full. This is fine food."

"So why wait?" Chin gestured at the dishes. "Don't waste it."

Fong drained his whiskey and chanted drunkenly, "Tonight there's wine, tonight we dine, tomorrow's affairs, that's tomorrow's time." He cupped hands over his belly while a contented smile settled on his face. "You won't work again, ever. Your life is good."

Chin looked away. Don't be so kind, he thought bitterly. I've never worked and my life stinks of shit. He tried to meet the eyes across the table. "It's as you say," he said. "Things are one-and-the-same."

"You're always lucky," Fong exclaimed. "Remember that shingle mill? I was pissing my pay like a leaky pipe. You walked in, not a cent on you, but you won the entire pot using my last nickel."

"Idiot, you don't know how to play."

"Can't play like you. You see through brass lids; you see numbers reflected in men's eyes."

Chin decided no one else was coming by. "Eaten full?" he asked. "Let's go."

"Where?"

"Wherever. Are they singing opera tonight?"

Fong shook his head. "Fat Old Shum says there's no audience these days. He's going to demolish the theatre and sell the costumes."

"Who would buy that trash?"

"His woman keeps nagging for China. But Fat Old Shum wants to stay here. Back home, they call his big wife 'Hammerhead.'"

Chin wanted to leave. "Want to watch some tables?"

"Stand all night on a full stomach?"

"How about Heavenly Nines? That's your game."

"And lose everything again?"

"What about the three-corner hotel? Maybe that soft-soft is waiting for you."

Fong frowned. "Don't bother me."

"Don't panic, you won't catch it again, idiot. Use the covers I gave you." He had forgotten about Fong getting sick. Good thing there had been money for a doctor. "Steam bath?"

"Want to die?" came the retort. "Full of food, full of whiskey, heat your blood, you'll explode."

"What then? Visit the book room and pretend to read?"

"Don't want anything. I'm going home."

Chin signaled for the bill. "Fine, go home," he said. "We'll talk another day."

He strode to the door, aware that eyes and ears throughout the room were following him. His toothpick flaunted nonchalance and dared a confrontation. Outside, rain had washed the city. Streetlamps glowing on the wet pavement cast extra light to the night air and addled him further. What did you do that for, idiot? You wanted to talk with him.

"Hey!" Short-boy Dick ran from the tea house, bringing the stench of stale tobacco and urine. "I was just telling the others, 'That Pretty-boy is different. I've known him for fifteen years. He's not like the others.' You, you respect your elders. I saw you invite Fong to a fine feast. I said, 'That Pretty-boy, he has a good heart.'"

"Fong is honest," Chin said flatly. "He's helped me."

"Oh, very honest," Short-boy echoed. "I see him and I say to myself, 'That Fong, he's a good man. He's not afraid of anything. He walks straight and true. He's like Gwan Gung, tall and strong. He'll fight any white punk. He's like—"

"What do you want?" Chin checked the door for his friend. "I have to go."

"That's so, that's so. You young people, you're always busy." Short-boy cleared his throat. "I wanted to ask you, if you could spare some tens."

"It's all in the bank," Chin declared. "I have nothing on me."

"What's a few tens to you?" Short-boy's nose went to Chin's chest. When there was no response, Short-boy jerked back and spat. "Bastard! No heart, no compassion. Damn you! You, you're best suited for ass-wiping. The God of Thunder will kick you, you'll see! Good begets good, evil avenges itself!"

He paused for air and Chin cut in, "Finished? I'm leaving."

"Go! Go die, bastard. Everyone's watching. You think people don't know? Fong treats you well, better than a son, and you steal his money. You don't know right from wrong. Now you run away." Short-boy screeched like a monkey. "Heaven knows, earth knows. One day, you'll be kneeling in front of me!" With that, he staggered off.

Chin stood stone still. Did all Chinatown know? He shuddered and fled across the street and turned the corner. The tea house and Shanghai Alley vanished behind him. Along Pender Street people sauntered by in purposeful groups. Chin exhaled and slowed down. In his head, he saw Fong in the tea house, carefully scraping every scrap and last drop from dinner into a tall tin can to take home. The diners would be muttering, "Good thing one of them knows how to save. One old, one young. One stupid, one smart. Same thing every time: one knows how to use the other."

Damn that Fong, thought Chin. Didn't he want to talk? Didn't he need to settle things? I can't repay him; the tally's long lost. I could give him something, but that would be stupid. What would he do? He's too scared to gamble, too stupid to invest.

Chin passed shops selling tobacco and jewelers' windows barred to the night. A fat tabby cat crouched behind one pane, wary eyes watching out. Did Fong really expect repayment, after all these years? He knows me, Chin thought, he knows my habits, he's heard my horse-track tales. He could have yelled, "Nothing to lend!" years ago.

"Hey, Pretty-boy! You hit it big!"

Chin saw the flash of black leather. Joe. "Just a few hundred. You, you touch that much in half an hour."

"Wish it were all mine!" Joe grinned. His father owned a big store and headed a family association, but Joe was a regular at the tables. "So, when do you leave?"

"Leave? For where?"

"Don't lie." Joe looked bemused. "I know you. You won't stay.

There's nothing here. Everyone has shut down. What did you plan to do? Open a department store?"

Chin shrugged. "You tell me. What should I do?"

"Go back to China, you've got capital. Head for the prairies. Open a café. People have to eat. Or go to Toronto. Just go!"

"Toronto?"

"Pretty-boy, don't think too much!" Joe reached over and lightly tapped his cheek. "Forget your buddy. You have your life."

"I know, I know. But I owe him."

"He owes you too. Didn't you help him find that job? Don't you sit with him whenever you come to town? Don't you take him to women?"

"But I—"

"He doesn't know people. He has no friends, so he gives you money. He thinks you're his son."

Chin pulled away. "I have to go." He plunged across the road, avoiding the sudden glare of passing headlights. I'm going, I'm going. Everyone wants me gone. All I have to do is tell Fong.

A boisterous clutch of nightclubbers swept by and left a cloud of sweet perfume in their wake. The women's legs gleamed long and slender like ivory tusks. They tottered and leaned against their escorts. Chin stopped. His eyes followed them into a gaily lit doorway, coloured lights twinkling like a Christmas tree. The smooth sounds of horns and piano sang out for a second.

I could have had any one of you tonight, Chin mused. And you would have clung to my body, night after night, once you saw what I had. You would have knelt before me, naked and obliging. He filled his mind with memories of womanly smells, dank and secretive. But nothing stirred between his legs.

Damn that Fong. He's ruining the whole evening.

Chin kicked the gate over the wooden planks. The communal house was an old frame building from the century's turn, deserted by waves of immigrants. The living room was lit, and Chin saw Fong dozing on a chair. He went through the never-locked door and shut it firmly.

Fong's head floated up. "Oh, it's you. Are you packed?"

Chin smiled grimly. "You've heard?"

His friend shrugged, and Chin breathed tightly. "And if I don't go?"

Fong's head lolled; his eyelids seemed about to drop.

Chin called out, "I came to say goodbye."

"Good."

"I came to talk about the money."

"Good."

Chin pulled up a wooden chair. Across from him stood a potbelly stove, un-stoked due to the early season. He leaned forward. "You know me well, don't you?"

Fong's eyes had closed. His long face was speckled with liver spots, some dark, some light, some shiny and others not.

"You know everything," Chin continued, "so will I make a fortune in Winnipeg?"

Fong cleared his throat but said nothing. The grandfather clock ticked on. Finally he said, "Don't ask me. I don't know the future. You're the gambler, not me."

"You gamble," Chin said. "Only you put your money on me."

"Wah, clever boy!" Fong smiled without opening his eyes. "You leaving tonight or tomorrow morning?"

Chin stood and took several long strides. "That money, does it matter?"

"Of course! Fifteen hundred, you think I'm playing?"

"When is it due?" Chin lit a cigarette. If he won't see me, he thought, he can smell me instead.

Fong's reply sounded distant. "When you have it."

"And if I don't?"

Fong shrugged. Chin squatted, smoke rising from his knee like incense. Fong's crown of bristly gray hair was close. "This money," Chin pressed, "doesn't it matter to you?"

"Of course it does. You think I work for fun? I have a wife. I have family."

"Then why throw it at me?"

"You needed it."

"You needed it too!" Chin wanted to shove Fong into the wall. "You idiot, you've thrown away fifteen hundred dollars!"

"Have not. You've thrown it away. You still owe me."

"But I can't repay you!" Chin dropped his cigarette and ground it under his shoe.

"No?" Fong's eyes sprang open.

"Think, you idiot!" Chin seized Fong's knee."I'm going to

Winnipeg. I'm taking all the money. I'm not giving you a cent." He felt like weeping. How could this man be so stupid? He's an ox; he's not human. I speak words and he sleeps. There must be a gaping hole in his skull.

Fong stared at him. "When you start something in Winnipeg, you'll make money. You'll send me some, won't you?"

"Yeah."

"Fine, then. I trust you."

Chin's head fell back. "Trust? Here? Everyone is busy feeding himself! Only you lend me money. Aren't you scared?"

"Scared? Of what?"

"Losing your money, idiot."

Fong blinked and then snorted. "If I were afraid, I wouldn't have come here. If I were afraid, I would have gone home long ago."

"Idiot," Chin hissed. "You're big, but your brain is a button. You—"

"Don't push me!" But Fong calmed immediately. "I'm no idiot. I gamble, just as you said. I take chances."

Chin's frustration went shrill as he shouted into Fong's ear. "Say I lose this money. I've never done well. Say I land in jail. Say a truck runs over me. Say I go crazy and can't recall a thing. What will you do then? What will you tell your woman?"

Fong paused before speaking ponderously. "What should I do then? Spank you like a baby?"

Chin bowed his head.

"Chase you like an ox-herder? Shout the Three Books at you?"

Chin backed off. "I want— I want to be released." He winced at the strange turn of words. "I want to come back."

Fong got to his feet. "Time to sleep. I work tomorrow." He padded across the room, his slippers slapping the linoleum floor. "You better go."

Chin's stomach lurched. "What should I do?" he cried out.

"Work diligently. Be charitable."

"You speak like my mother."

"Well, she has hopes for you too."

Goh Poh Seng

Tall Tales and Misadventures of a Young WOG (Westernized Oriental Gentleman)

I had not yet turned seventeen when my parents sent me abroad to study in Dublin. It was 1953, the year of the coronation of Queen Elizabeth II. The British Empire still held sway, although it was rapidly crumbling. Since Malaya was a British Protectorate, Kuala Lumpur, the capital city and my hometown, had joined in the celebrations.

But why Ireland? Perhaps it was because Dublin had a reputable university and medical school and was thought to be cheaper to live in than England or the United States. But what truly swayed my parents, however, was their presumption that holy Catholic Ireland was a safer place for their impressionable young son, less likely to lead him astray. Although they were not Christians, they believed every religion was good and ethical and who would cavil with that?

They were proved wrong. Dublin was not so cheap after all, and it certainly was not safe for the morals of a young foreign student. Within a year, I had been converted to Roman Catholicism, downed my first pint of Guinness, puffed my first cigarette, kissed my first girl, and written my first poem.

I had succumbed to Catholicism on account of acute loneliness and homesickness in my very first year at Black Rock College, a boarding school run by the Holy Ghost fathers. It was more my sensibility than sense, and my romantic nature, that made me respond to the religious rites and rituals of the church. I loved the dim, hallowed spaces, the light made soft filtering through panes of colourful stained glass, the odour of incense and the choral music. The atmosphere at these rituals moved me more than true spiritual conviction or doctrinal certainty. Often, the beauty of the church services brought tears to my eyes. I felt as if I was on the threshold of a nameless and indescribable holiness. I was eager to do good works, joined the Legion of Mary, and even contemplated becoming a monk. However, I was soon swamped by my studies at the medical school of University College, Dublin.

Leaving boarding school after a long year was like suddenly being freed from confinement. It was not surprising that I could not deal sensibly with this new freedom. I went after life with great avidity, like a famished piranha gobbling up indiscriminately every morsel of flesh, and even crunching the bones. I was an empty vessel eager to be filled.

In no time at all, I was in my element in the pubs of Dublin, drinking Guinness as well as the next man. I smoked a pipe, or actually fiddled with it, and read books till my brow furrowed. I became a sceptic and developed a general disposition to doubt everything, including my newly found Catholicism. I fell from grace as rapidly as I had gained it. In succession, I rebelled against colonialism, neocolonialism, capitalism, communism, the Irish Press, and Hollywood movies. I adopted a distaste for all manner of authority or orthodoxy and changed my opinions, beliefs, and values more often—it seemed—than I changed my clothes.

I was living through the tumultuous clashes between the cultures of the East and the West. At that age, it was an unequal match. I was overwhelmed by the Western World, swamped by its newspapers, radio, theatre, cinema, and books, books, books. So that after a while, I staggered about in a kind of shell shock, dancing merrily down the road towards deculturalization and cultural pariahdom, as though it was all fun and games. My mind was blown away when I encountered lines like Samuel Beckett's "The sun shone, having no other alternatives on the nothing new. Murphy sat out of it as though he were free."

Ever susceptible, if not gullible, I fell for the intellectual and philosophical fashions in vogue at that time in the west: namely, existentialism and the notion of the absurd. It was almost unavoidable if one frequented the pubs and the coffee houses. I became a person whose feet were no longer planted firmly on the ground. I inhabited the world of books while shunning the practical world, the real world.

Although I regarded myself as shy, nevertheless I made quite a lot of friends. Those days in Dublin, it was easy enough to meet people. All one had to do was to patronize certain pubs and coffee houses in the vicinity of Grafton Street. The Irish are legendary talkers, especially those who have kissed the Blarney Stone. They love to practise and display the art of repartee. A good conversationalist was highly appreciated, a true raconteur widely admired. They held court and drew loyal crowds about them.

In those early days, Joan and Garry Trimble counted as two of my best friends. They were both architects in their midthirties, with two young daughters and a gray-striped kitten. They were part of the miscellaneous crowd I mixed with, comprised of poets and novelists, journalists, students, artists, musicians, and some members of Telefis Eirrean and the theatre. Garry was a well-known sculptor specializing in bronze busts. As a sign of his distinction, he had been commissioned to execute a bust of Eamon de Valera, the Taoshack or President of Eire.

Garry was kind and gregarious, with big baby-blue eyes that stared wide at the world with wonder and disbelief. He sported a hair lick which flopped teasingly down over his forehead and which he constantly brushed aside with his hand. He looked like Bill Haley, the famous Rock 'n' Roll singer very popular in the fifties.

Garry was sweet and obliging, always willing to do favours for others, transporting them in his small yellow Volkswagen to and from the airport or parties. Dublin those days was very much a party town. Nightly, there was bound to be at least one party one could attend. No one was turned away provided he brought his "passport"—half a dozen bottles of porter or a bottle of cheap Spanish wine. In every pub, the buzz was "Where's the party? Where's the party?" At closing time, crowds of excited, drunken revellers would pile into cars and roar out to the party. That was a dangerous hour to be walking in the street, as the party goers, night-fevered and soused, made their reckless way out of Grafton Street and its environs. Once they were gone, an eerie silence descended on the town.

One time when I took ill, Garry came to check on me daily, made me hot soups and coffee, brought newspapers and magazines, related the latest gossip and scandals. He was affectionate as a puppy.

Joan was a bright, warm, and empathetic soul whom I trusted and to whom I confided my deepest secrets. We developed a special bond, Joan becoming my first, close, and platonic woman friend.

I spent a lot of time at the Trimbles' house, a small, converted, mews cottage in Ballsbridge, a desirable quarter of the town. I often dined with them, sometimes cooking curry or Chinese food, which they appreciated. Afterwards, we would loll on the hardwood floor, comfortably buttressed by big throw cushions and pillows. We loved drinking wine, talking till the proverbial cows came home. Sometimes I would sleep over, or babysit their daughters when they had an engagement.

They had built a small cottage near a village in Connemara which they loved. They spoke of the villagers with affection. The natives in that part of Ireland spoke Gaelic and a dialect of English few outsiders could understand. They had ingeniously and wonderfully corrupted the Queen's English, taking great liberties with it so that it became craggy like the mountains, rough like the coast, lyrical like the wind. This particularly interested and excited me, for by then, I had decided to write in English, an adopted tongue foisted upon me by the quirks of history.

I think it was Yeats who described Connemara as a land of terrible beauty. A desolate landscape with old, bare hills, stones and craggy shores, right on the Atlantic. I wanted to go there. I was ready to be enchanted.

The opportunity came in the long summer vacation of 1956. Summer vacation was one of those glorious boons given a university student. Although I did not have the wherewithal to do much, still, the largesse of some halcyon weeks of unstructured time, of escaping from the hectic schedule of the life of a medical student, with lectures and tutorials, demonstrations and clinical rounds, and long hours in the library, was nothing short of heaven-sent. It meant that I had more time to pursue other interests, especially reading.

Thus I jumped at the chance when Joan and Garry offered their cottage, telling me I could stay as long as I wished that summer. My bones sang for the green hills, the blue sea, the vast open sky.

After breakfast, I set out for Cloc Na Ron. It promised to be a fine day. No one was in sight and I had the road to myself. I had walked for about an hour when suddenly I heard a voice yell out.

"Heloo!"

I looked about and saw a man leaning on a staff down by the bog.

"Heloo, young fella!" he hailed again.

Lamely, I replied, "Hello."

"My son, could ya give an old man a hand, I wonder?"

Although he was some distance away, I could hear his every word distinctly.

"What can I do for you?"

"Could ya come down here a minute?" he beckoned with his hand.

I clambered down from the road to the flat field of peat. The man was in his sixties, tall and big boned, with a large head sitting precariously on a long body. His face bore detailed features, hinting of a tough physical life, and was as weatherbeaten as the rocks around the fields. But all was offset by his liquid blue eyes, reflecting merriment and mischief. A two-day stubble sprouted from his upper lip. He offered a wide smile from a mouth filled with tobacco-stained teeth. He had a cigarette in his hand.

"Hi ya, young fella!" he greeted cheerily.

"Hello, how can I be of help?"

"Ah ha! You see this pile of peat I've cut? You see that shed over yonder?" he pointed with a thick sausage of a finger. "Well then," he continued, "I've to haul them cut blocks over for storage to that shed. Can ya give an old man a helping hand? It will take only a short while with a strong, strapping lad like yourself helping out." He beamed at me and waited.

"Sure, be glad to."

The blocks of fresh-cut peat were each the size of a brick. We sat to work, each filling a brown burlap sack with the bricks, then tottering unsteadily with this burden towards the shed, which was about fifty yards away. It was heavy going. The old man had a limp. Despite this, he did as much work as I did, a grin hovering on his lips.. We did not speak, concentrating on our task. After a dozen trips, we paused to rest. It was hot. We took off our shirts. The summer sun rose to its zenith. Nothing stirred, no shady trees under which we might shelter, no sweet cordial wind to soothe our bodies.

"What's your name, young fella? Me, they call me Paddy."

"Tony," I offered him my Christian name.

"You from the big city.? From Galway?"

"Yes, I'm from the big city. But I'm from Dublin, not Galway."

"Dublin? Sure you come a long ways away. I meself have never been there, never set foot on it. Why, even Galway, I've been only a couple of times."

Yes, definitely tethered to his own place on earth. While I, I had become the footloose wanderer.

"Now, if you don't mind," Paddy said, "let's carry on with our work."

So again we began to load the sacks and carry them to the shed. We were soon bathed in sweat. We halted again for another breather. The heat and stillness were intolerable.

"No, I have never been to Dublin," he said, answering a question I had not asked. "Too far away, I am not drawn to places too far away. Also, I don't care much for towns and cities neither. Too many people, if you ask me. I hated Galway city. Big crowds, big noise. I never understand how people could live like that. I would go stark crazy if I linger more than a day there. No sir, I don't want to live in a city."

"You'd get used to it in time."

"I want none of it."

"Aren't you curious about the outside world?"

"Frankly speaking, no! I have no great interest in the outside world. They've nothing to do with me, and I've nothing to do with them."

"But we are all one big world!"

"No sir. Not one world. And I don't bother with what's nothin' to do with me. Too many busybodies bothering about everyone else's business, that's really what's wrong with the world today. I just mind me own business, that's all I want to do, leave others alone. All this here," he announced, sweeping grandly with his hand, "is my world! There's only one lifetime a man has, enough maybe for him to get to know his little bit of the world if he be lucky, if he be blessed, God willin'." And Paddy crossed himself.

He looked up at the sky, tilting his large head backwards. There, we saw crystallized in the bright light, a plane high up, skating gracefully across the white sky.

"That be the 12:05 flight out of Shannon, bound for Boston."

We watched it pass a moment, its drone reaching down to us from far away. Boston. Faraway places with strange-sounding names, but what have they to do with us, who stand here on this flat bog, earthbound and timebound? The sight made me marvel at the astonishing technology of man. Products of daydreams and fantasies, they seem improbable, farfetched, even absurd.

On that particular day, the two of us were stranded in time, and on that hot shadeless afternoon, there was no hiding place, and none at all for secrets. Under that transparency, we could only construct our speech with veracity and clarity. Paddy, the man who truly belonged, never ill at ease, was plain in his utterances.

"Are you married, young fella?" he asked directly, pushing out his square jaw.

"No, I am not!"

"Good for ye! Never get married, young fella, never get married," he admonished loudly to make sure I got his message.

"Are you married yourself, Paddy?"

"Me?" he pointed a finger at his own chest. "Married? Never! Never!" he barked.

"Why is that? There must be plenty of beautiful women in the village," I teased.

"Why? I'll tell you why! You see that hill over there?" He pointed. "There, on the leeside of it is me cottage. I have a field, a calf, and a milch cow, which is generous with the best of white milk in the world. I have most things I need. The rest is greed. Living alone, I need very little."

"Are you not lonely?"

"Never!" he asserted. Then, as if he had understood my overloaded question, laughed forthrightly and added, "And I can still get me a woman. There are a few who are always willin'. Now, to return to me tale. One terrible day last winter, with hailstones and a lashing wind, the hailstones large as marbles, a part of the thatch roof flew away. Oh, it went sailing in the wind like the Devil himself had willed it. The damaged roof began to leak, right over me bed. Rainwater poured down as from a hole in the sky itself. So, what did I do?"

"Well, what did you do, Paddy?"

"What did I do?" He paused for effect, before recounting, "What did I do, me son. What I did do was I shifted me bed from the leaking spot. That way, the rain no longer fell on me bed." He waited for my appreciative laughter, then continued. "Now if I was married, I could not have done that could I? You can expect me wife pushing me and nagging me to mend the roof. Why, a man would have no peace at all until he fixes the blooming roof. Am I right or not right, young fella?"

I nodded my agreement with a laugh.

"A man will have no peace with a woman in the house ruling the roost. Now, I admit, there are some men who would not have minded that, but yes, me son, I sure would mind that! I could not give away peace in me own home to a woman! Mark me words, if you want peace in your own home, young fella, never marry! Never, never!"

We returned to the task at hand. It soon transpired that I was fated to labour for Paddy that day. I put in some three hours of strenuous exertion, which was never my intention. I stayed until the whole blooming pile of peat had been transferred to the shed. I was sore all over but it was never dull with Paddy regaling me with tall tales and gossip, fleshing out the landscape with stories of the good souls who lived around Cloc Na Ron.

We finally parted company when our shadows had shrunken to the size of a football. Heading for the village, I dribbled the ball.

During the next few weeks, I encountered Paddy whenever I went to the village. Each time we would stop and talk. Conversations with Paddy were not discontinuous. Although there were gaps in time, his words fell into place like irregular pieces of a jigsaw.

Apart from cutting and selling peat, he took good care of his milch cow and calf. He was also an odd-job man and parttime postman for the village. I often saw him limping his way out of Cloc Na Ron with a canvas bag of mail slung across his shoulders.We became good friends.

Fred Wah

I Hardly Ever Go into King's Family Restaurant

because, when it comes to Chinese cafes and Chinatowns, I'd rather be transparent. Camouflaged enough so they know I'm there but can't see me, can't get to me. It's not safe. I need a clear coast for a getaway. Invisible. I don't know who I am in this territory and maybe don't want to. Yet I love to wander into Toronto's Chinatown and eat tofu and vegetables at my favourite barbecue joint and then meander indolently through the crowds listening to the tones and watching the dark eyes, the black hair. Sometimes in a store, say, I'm picking up a pair of new kung-fu sandals and the guy checks my Mastercard as I sign and he says Wah! You Chinese? heh heh heh! because he knows I'm not. Physically, I'm racially transpicuous and I've come to prefer that mode.

I want to be there but don't want to be seen being there. By the time I'm ten I'm only white. Until 1949 the only Chinese in my life are relatives and old men. Very few Chinese kids my age. After '49, when the Canadian government rescinds its Chinese Exclusion Act, a wave of young Chinese immigrate to Canada. Nelson's Chinese population visibly changes in the early fifties. In a few years there are enough teenage Chinese kids around to not only form an association, the Nelson Chinese Youth Association, but also a basketball team. And they're good, too. Fast, smart. I play on the junior high school team and when the NCYA team comes to play us, I know a lot of the Chinese guys. But my buddies at school call them Chinks and geeks and I feel a little embarrassed and don't talk much with the Chinese kids. I'm white enough to get away with it and that's what I do.

But downtown, working in the cafe, things are different. Some of the young guys start working at our cafe and my dad's very involved with helping them all settle into their new circumstances. He acts as an interpreter for a lot of the legal negotiations. Everyone's trying to reunite with long-lost relatives. Anyway, I work alongside some of these new Chinese and become friends.

Shu brings his son over around 1953 and Lawrence is in the cafe business for the rest of his working life. Lawrence and I work together in the Diamond until I leave small-town Nelson for university at the coast. We're good friends. Even today, as aging men, we always exchange greetings whenever we meet on the street. But I hardly ever go into his cafe.

So now, standing across the street from King's Family Restaurant, I know I'd love to go in there and have a dish of beef and greens, but he would know me, he would have me clear in his sights, not Chinese but stained enough by genealogy to make a difference. When Lawrence and I work together, him just over from China, he's a boss's son and I'm a boss's son. His pure Chineseness and my impure Chineseness don't make any difference to us in the cafe. But I've assumed a dull and ambiguous edge of difference in myself; the hyphen always seems to demand negotiation.

I decide, finally, to cross the street. I push myself through the door and his wife, Fay, catches me with the corner of her eye. She doesn't say anything and I wonder if she recognizes me. The white waitress takes my order and I ask if Lawrence is in the kitchen. He is, she says.

I go through Lawrence's kitchen door like I work there. I relish the little kick the door is built to take. He's happy to see me and stops slicing the chicken on the chopping block, wipes his hands on his apron and shakes my hand. How's your mother? Whatchyou doing here? How's Ernie and Donnie? Family, that's what it is. The politics of the family.

He says something to the cook, a young guy. Then he turns to me and says hey Freddy, did you know this is your cousin? He's from the same area near Canton. His name is Quong. Then in Chinese, he gives a quick explanation to Quong; no doubt my entire Chinese family history. Lawrence smiles at me like he used to when were kids: he knows something I don't. I suffer the negative capability of camouflage.

How many cousins do I have, I wonder. Thousands maybe. How could we recognize one another? Names.

The food, the names, the geography, the family history—the filiated dendrita of myself displayed before me. I can't escape, and don't want to, for a moment. Being there, in Lawrence's kitchen, seems one of the surest places I know. But then after we've exchanged our mutual family news and I've eaten a wonderful dish of tofu and vegetables, back outside, on the street, all my ambivalence gets covered over, camouflaged by a safety net of class and colourlessness—the racism within me that makes and consumes that neutral (white) version of myself, that allows me the sad privilege of being, in this white white world, not the target but the gun.

I'm not aware it's called Tofu until after

I leave home. It's one of those ingredients that are transparent to me in the multitude of Cantonese dishes I grow up eating. So, until my dad tells me what that white stuff is called, I'm unable to order it during my forays into Vancouver Chinatown. Even when I first try it out on a waitress, she looks puzzled and says something in Chinese to her father who's hanging out by the till. She comes back to my booth and says o.k., you mean dow-uw foo, bean curd!

But over the past forty years, tofu has come into its own in North America, taking a choice place among the burgeoning macrobiotic and cholesterol-conscious diet fads. Available at any supermarket. If I'd been smart in the sixties I would have invested in soybean futures. There's even a little hippie tofu industry that has sprung up to supply the organic craze marketed through local co-ops. I wear my Kootenay Tofu T-shirt with pride.

This is all to my delight because tofu is, after rice, basic to my culinary needs. I've rendered this custardlike cake from pureed soybeans; I've pressed it, frozen it, mashed it, and cubed it; I've boiled, steamed, fried and marinated it; I even use Tofunaise as a substitute for mayonnaise. One summer I planted soybeans with some improbable fantasy of building my own tofu from the ground up. My attraction to this food is more than belief, it's a deep need, obsessive.

My basic all-time favourite dish is braised bean curd with vegetables. Cut each cake of tofu into one-inch cubes and very gently stirfry along with some chopped green onion until the outer surface is lightly browned and the cake holds together without crumbling. Add some sliced vegetables: bok choy, carrots, green or red pepper, whatever you have around. Black Chinese mushrooms and water chestnuts are a nice option. As the dish is finishing, stir in a couple tablespoons of soy sauce and then some cornstarch mixed in water for thickening. This tasty and nutritious melange is spooned over steamed rice and washed down with oolong tea. There. That's a lunch.

Juk is a soup we always have after

New Year's because it's made with leftover turkey. I think of it as the bridge between our white Christmas (presents and turkey stuffing) and our Chinese New Year (firecrackers and juk). As far as I know, all of the Wah families have it and each is distinctive. Aunty Ethel's is pretty good but my mom still makes my dad's version once in awhile, though neither she nor Ethel add that little shot of rye whiskey he said was the secret to a really good juk. I couldn't taste liquor but boy his soup was the best, a real treat. But he also used the little red dates, which I'd pick aside; they're too much of a contrast, a little too sweet for the full-bodied ricey broth, and Ethel says you don't really need them.

But if you want to try them, get a package of small red pitted dates at the Chinese supermarket. Also, buy only the smallest package of chung toy (salted turnip) since you only need a couple of pieces. For the fu juk (dried bean curd) you'll have to decide between flat sheets or ropes; I prefer the ropes because they're chewier. Soak the whole package of juk overnight. Be sure to wash the chung toy, it's heavily salted. Peel and slice a few fresh water chestnuts. Optional is a bit of the dark seaweed and a few soaked Chinese mushrooms. Put all this with a couple of cups of rice into the turkey stock (you should have about 6-8 cups of liquid). and cook slowly for an hour or so, until the rice is overdone. If not very much of the turkey made it this far and you feel the need for some meat, you can add a bit of sliced pork steak. In the end you should have a thickish gruel, almost a congee.

Juk is even better than bird's-nest soup, though both soups share an intrinsic proprioceptive synapse: memory. While slurping a bowl of juk with the January snow still swirling outside, the memory of the bird itself, only a few weeks old, triangulates with a smoky starfilled night in China. Likewise, with the gelatinous bird's-nest soup, the taste carries images of men climbing the walls of dark caves in Yunan collecting the spaghettilike translucent strands of bird's nests, the frightened cries of the swallows themselves as piercing as a foreign language.

Wayson Choy

Nanking

That night of the ghosts, the self-appointed guardian of the elders, Mrs Lim, strolled three blocks east of Chinatown, along Pender, and looked across the street to see if her friend Old Yen were still alive.

The eighty-year-old man was alive, but things seemed very wrong. The big woman clutched her leather handbag tightly against herself. All of Chinatown knew that, in her oversized purse, Mrs Lim carried a thin legbone of a fox, silver-chained with jade amulets, to ward off demons. Twenty minutes later, she pounded on Larry and Lisa Yen's front door.

"Cannot stay," Mrs Lim said, stepping in. She leaned against the wall to catch her breath. Her white hair fell over her chubby face, a face as ashen as her grey winter coat. "Oh, must sit down."

Quickly Lisa Yen shut the door and led Mrs Lim into the parlour. Larry Yen offered to take her coat but she pushed him aside. Twice lately, Mrs Lim had burst in upon them. Her old village fears about seeing a ghost—or ghosts—standing about his father had exhausted Larry Yen. Each time, he had patiently tried to reason with her, to talk of shadows and light, not ghosts. But Mrs Lim would have none of his sensible talk. Twice, from a distance, she had seen *someone* standing beside Old Yen.

"You told Father?" Larry asked, worried that the old man would he dismayed.

"Never," Mrs Lim said, shaking white strands of hair from her face. "No need to tell."

The big woman eased herself onto the settee. It creaked, and Larry

Yen's back tightened.

"Three nights I go to play *mar jon* at Betty Lee's," Mrs Lim said, looking up at Lisa. "Three nights I look up and see him outside on the porch. Way past nine o'clock."

Wheezing, Mrs Lim turned, widened her coal-dark eyes to confront Lisa's husband.

"Tonight... I see him out there again, I see your father."

"Just getting sonic fresh air," Larry Yen said. Thank god, no mention of ghosts. Mrs Lim furrowed her brow. The way she tightened her grip on her purse made Larry Yen nervous. He had better say something to comfort her.

"Don't worry about my father, Mrs Lim."

The big woman pushed her worn gloved hands harder against her purse and it exuded a whiff of Tiger Balm. Larry waited.

"Old Yen *talk,"* Mrs Lim huffed, and glanced at Lisa. "He not talking to me."

Lisa saw the hurt and worry in the big broad face. Mrs Lim and Old Yen had been friends for forty years. Lisa reached out a hand. Mrs Lim gripped it. "No one there, Missy. No one. You go see."

"Larry, you better go," Lisa said, her part-Irish green eyes looking more sombre in the parlour light. "Your father's been so upset about the war news from China—"

"Aaanyaah, Nanking!" Mrs Lim cried, frantically patting her forehead. Unspeakable horrors crossed her mind. She shook her purse. Larry Yen pretended not to hear the skeletal rattling of jade talismans.

"They butcher women," Mrs Lim's voice pitched higher, "slay children, like olden days! Your poor papa understand."

She grasped Larry's hand, but he seemed unmoved. How could Larry Yen stand so composed before her when he knew about the brutal Japanese demons, and about her dear friend standing on that second-floor porch talking to the air?

"Your old father freeze to death," Mrs Lim half-shouted at this fool of a son. Her handbag swung up; she crossed her thick-sleeved arms over the leather straps, shivering. "Outside cold like mountain!"

Larry glanced at the black purse but said nothing. Surely the old woman was going to mention ghosts. He recalled how, a month ago, having tea at the B.C. Royal, Mrs Lim had almost bashed him with that same cauldron of a bag when he openly challenged her about her seeing demons, ghosts.

"He takes in nothing, sees nothing," she had huffily pronounced to the herbalist's elderly wife, Mrs Low "His teacup too full."

"He too smart," Mrs Low agreed. "He know too much about accounting."

"And not too much of account!" Mrs Lim broke into her sharp-tongued *Toi-san, "Mu kuang ju tou!* Eyesight like a pea!"

Mrs Lim's gold bracelets jingled as she laughed.

Later, Lisa made Larry promise her lie would not provoke Mrs Lim again.

"Old village nonsense," Larry afterwards declared to Lisa. "Mrs Lim sees demons and ghosts everywhere."

It was true. Mrs Lim had sworn she saw a ghost the same day her one-eyed husband was killed in the lumber camp. And for months she saw the ghost of that old dead Grandmother across the street from her, her old friend, the one who made those crazy wind chimes with the young Sekky. Then there was the time she and Mrs Wong, the tailor's wife, saw the opera house ghost .. .

"She thinks she's telling the truth," Lisa said. "Don't be so disrespectful."

But Larry Yen wasn't being disrespectful. He was being reasonable. Mrs Lim talked such nonsense. She may have frightened the old man. She had even gossiped with Mrs Jang, the butcher's wife, about ghosts standing about the front windows of his father's rooms. Larry mentioned this matter to his father, but Old Yen refused to discuss it.

And now Mrs Lim sat on the settee waiting him out, gloves off. The big woman pressed her pudgy hands together and shuddered with exasperation at his obstinacy.

"Not true Old Yen sit always by himself," she had pestered Larry in the tea room, the white hairs on the back of her neck bristling. She glanced at Larry's thin tight lips. What an idiot of a man not to understand.

"See right through ghost," Mrs Lim insisted, her hand pushing through the air. "Very tall man. He wear long blue coat like in Old China days."

Three weeks ago, despite her poor eyesight, Mrs Low had also seen a tall figure standing beside Old Yen.

"Mrs Low see same man, very tall," Mrs Lim stage-whispered. Lisa calmly took Mrs Lim's hand, as if to say, yes, yes, of course.

Now Larry kept silent, trying to be, as Lisa had urged him to be, respectful. Mrs Lim was not fooled.

Larry Yen had already, respectfully, discussed seeing spectres with her. She was seeing shadows, he explained, illusions. Mrs Lim listened with forbearance. After all, he was an educated man, an accountant, a rational, middle-aged Chinatown businessman... Perhaps, Mrs Lim thought, Larry Yen was afraid.

"It not demon ghost," Mrs Lim had emphasized, her goodwill glistening in her dark eyes.

Larry Yen still did not understand, but neither was he afraid. His father, explained Larry patiently to Mrs Lim, often lit sticks of incense and stout red memorial candles before the house gods. Before both the porcelain-white *Kwan Yin,* the Goddess of Mercy, and the warrior God of Fortune, *Kwang-Tai,* Old Yen often stuck slow-burning candles into shallow basins of sand.

Mrs Lim had nodded.

On her thrice-weekly afternoon visits, Mrs Lim was quite aware of the sandalwood incense inside Old Yen's rooms and often saw the candles aglow, and felt their heat. She and Old Yen drank their oolong and ate savory dumplings and talked of the old days. So much they told each other, and certain stories they told no one else.

"What you see beside my father," Larry had told her, "are only shadow phantoms."

"Yes," Mrs Lim nodded, solemnly. "Phantoms everywhere."

The larger front window especially reflected such shadows, repeated Larry. Shadow phantoms. Not ghosts. Shadows. Mrs Lim's eyes narrowed. She was almost betrayed into Larry Yen's foolishness.

"*These* not shadows I see," Mrs Lim hissed, "these move differently, as if ..." Mrs Lim's voice dropped an octave, her eyes darkened. She turned to Lisa. "There is this one ... very tall ... tall as your husband ..."

But this evening, after Mrs Lim's pounding on the door, after her barging in on Larry and Lisa Yen's quiet evening, Mrs Lim, gloves off, had not said a single word about seeing ghosts standing beside the old man. Instead, she had stuck to the plain and simple fact that Old Yen, outside on his porch, was going to freeze to death talking to himself.

"An old man of eighty should not be out there talking to himself," Mrs Lim said and shook her amulet-filled purse.

"You better go," Lisa again urged her husband. "Your father lives by his own rules."

"Go see," Mrs Lim said.

The edge of panic in Mrs Lim's voice made Larry Yen open the hall closet and reach in for his navy winter coat. Mrs Lim grabbed a pair of gloves off the closet shelf and unfolded a wool scarf.

"Cold like death," she said, waving them at him.

Larry Yen, snatching scarf and gloves from the big woman's hands, exchanged a quick look with Lisa and quickly closed the door behind him. He could hear Lisa offering Mrs Lim some tea, and the big woman saying, "Yes, oh yes, we talk ... I saw..."

Larry Yen didn't stop to hear what Mrs Lim saw.

Outside, Larry Yen buttoned up his coat. The damp, freezing air suddenly clung to him. He hurried from his house, half walking, half jogging to keep himself warm. In the windless night, his breath drifted from him like smoke.

Only five blocks, Larry thought. Climb those rickety stairs, talk sensibly, get the old man inside. Make sure his two rooms were warm enough, the two front windows well shut. The window frames were already stuffed with cloth and paper against draughts. Then, with the old man safe in bed, under three coverlets, he could run home, rub his hands above the kitchen stove and maybe toss back some scotch. He would be sure to complain to Lisa and Mrs Lim, if she were still there, about his father's stubbornness. No, the old man still doesn't want to move. And tomorrow, at the B.C. Royal, he'll declare for Mrs Lim's benefit, and Mrs Jang's and Mrs Low's, how he had insisted his father move in with him and Lisa. He, Larry Yen, the son of Old Yen, had decided. He'd explain to his father how they can't have people gossiping about the family, suggesting that he and Lisa were being neglectful. Larry Yen jogged with resolve.

If only his father would be less stubborn about living by himself.

"I trust to fortune," the old man threw back at him whenever lie asked his father to move from his rooming house.

Then Old Yen would insist that Larry light some incense to red-faced Kwang-Tai. This foot-high statuette with the fierce opera face, Old Yen had brought with him from China. It was a treasure given to him by a man named Sen-Dai, his opera company mentor and acrobatic trainer. His father had said this God of Fortune was at least three generations old and came originally from Sen-Dai's great-great-grandfather.

"Master Sen-Dai gave me this treasure," Old Yen would say.

"Sen-Dai is the past, Father," Larry would argue, even as he lit the sticks of incense and candles, watched the sweet smoke swirl around the fierce warrior face of Kwang-Tai. "Lisa and I are now your fortune. Come live with us."

Old Yen would listen, but Larry knew it was only halfheartedly. Hadn't Lisa and he always checked on him, made sure he had enough food and enough clean clothes, paid his bills? The old man had had such a hard life, why did he have to make the end so difficult?

"When I blind and deaf, I for sure live with you," the old man chuckled. "Give you and Lisa real trouble!"

Larry Yen's footsteps fell into cadence with his heartbeat.

Besides the problem of what to do with the old man, now there were other worries. All of Vancouver talked about the growing war in China. The West Coast was going to be vulnerable to Japanese attack. There would be curfews, blackouts. The whole world was darkening. Reasonable men like himself would have to hold the world together. The ghosts of Mrs Lim and the Old China gods of his eighty-year-old father seemed like small change.

As his feet hit the frost-silvered pavement, leaving melting shoeprints, Larry Yen resolved to defeat his father's stubbornness. In the last year, he had failed five times to convince his father to move in with him. Tonight he was determined to overrule the old man. Perhaps that was what Mrs Lim was trying to tell him with all her old-fashioned nonsense about ghosts. It was time.

"You're leaving this place, Father," Larry Yen said aloud. But between his heavy breathing, his voice sounded barely authoritative.

The old man would look away from him, thinking. Thinking about the old days, the old ways. Then his father would stare at Larry, his eyes dimming, watering with memory.

Old Yen would begin his story telling.

These stories—Larry Yen had heard his father tell them a hundred times before. In the last two weeks, since the desperate news about Nanking, the old man's stories more or less began with the same words

... *That month in Nanking when my fortune changed....*

"Be patient," Lisa had said. 'He always lives his life his own way. Listen to him. It can't do any harm."

Lisa and his father seldom spoke together much nowadays. When Larry had told his father thirty years ago that he was courting a mixed-blood girl, part Irish, his father was dismissive.

"She looks very Chinese," Larry persisted. 'Talks a dialect of Sam Yut."

As he jogged across Keefer, he remembered how pleased the old man had been that Lisa at least spoke Chinese.

"You wouldn't know she wasn't Chinese, except for her eyes."

Larry had fallen for Lisa's dark green eyes, her full breasts.

"Learn from her first," Old Yen said, "and marry real Chinese later."

And Mrs Lim and Mrs Low had together commented, as everyone commented in those days, "Mixed blood, mixed trouble."

But Lisa adored Larry's tall, Northern Chinese looks. She had not been discouraged by Mrs Lim's gossip nor by Old Yen's coolness. When Larry and Lisa married, against Chinatown advice, Old Yen remained courteous. He attempted to pay little attention to Lisa. But she always stepped in front of him and asked him about his Old China days. "Tell me in English, like you tell Larry," she insisted, refusing to be intimidated by him. "And don't talk *Toi* San or Cantonese," she warned, "or you'll be talking to yourself!"

And now, it seemed, Old Yen was doing just that.

The air, drifting off the North Shore mountains, smelled of crusted snow. The quiet evening, edged with the sound of his heartbeat and the flapping of his coat like wings, made him even more thoughtful. There was much feeling between himself and the old man.

Whenever he spent time with his father, Larry's duty was to listen to the old man's stories, to nod his head and pay attention and not let the old man catch him off guard. Old Yen recited the same stories, the same strands unravelling from the past. How fate had conspired against him. How, when he was a boy in the famous Canton company, the troupe had come to Nanking. How fortunate he had been until then.

When they were boys, Old Yen's two grandsons would shout, "Tell again! Tell again!"

And Old Yen would tell again how, at twelve, the only boy among the men of the opera troupe, he was slashed by the honed blade of a sword from elbow to wrist. Once he fell from a twenty-five foot high human pyramid (and here, the two boys and even Mrs Lim would look up and see in their mind's eye, a young boy tumbling down from the sky), and broke only the joint of his third finger. That same month, he was set ablaze by an oil-soaked baton flung by a demon magician. With self-mocking pride, his hands and body in the midst of miming each movement, Larry's father could flaunt the deep scar still visible along his right arm, chortle and wave his stunted finger with the still-discoloured fingernail, and if it were necessary, pull up his shirt to show the fist-sized angry patches of red tissue rippling like flames over half his back.

"A human torch," he laughed. "Everybody but Master Sen-Dai run away from me!" Old Yen's eyes would glisten. "The Master grabbed me. Wrapped his coat around me."

All these unlucky events had happened in one single month when the opera troupe performed in Nanking.

"That month my fortune changed," the old man repeated, looking up, as if talking to the sky.

Turning the corner to Pender, Larry felt uncomfortable. He had never taken his father too seriously, except to know he was there. After his mother died giving birth to him, the old man had farmed his infant son out to a Chinatown community of bachelor-men uncles and old widows like Mrs Lim. Some of them used to hit him when he was bad, but mostly they meant well. As he grew, Larry adapted himself to each situation, knowing his father would always come for him. And when his father did come, his lumberman's jacket smelling of cedar shingles and pine, Larry longed to hear his stories.

Somehow talk-stories became the way to learn. Mostly, they were nonsense—fables and fairy tales, and old myths about the early days in China or Chinatown. *When I was a boy...* Interesting the first few dozen times, those stories he heard from his father and the other elders when he was growing up, but they were only the tales of old men. North America was not Old China. The elders like his father could not ever accept that.

For months Larry had sensed his father's death was imminent. He stopped to catch his breath at the corner, his exhalations puffing white clouds into the cold clear night. He vowed to stay sensible, not panic, to see his father to a peaceful end.

So Mrs Lim had been seeing ghosts around his father, and according to Lisa, Mrs Lim only saw ghosts near those dying or dead. But, fact is, old people die. End of story. Crazy for anyone to believe that the dead could come back. Crazy. Of course he had allowed his boys to listen to ghost stories, but Larry Yen always told his sons the facts. "There's no such things as ghosts or hauntings," he told Danny and Colin. "Read your science books."

Old Yen did tell some classical tales, but not those romances about too perfect Princes and heartstruck Princesses, heroic warriors killing each other out of jealousy or love. Every evening, the Vancouver companies performed these tales unendingly.

"Cheap! Cheap!" Old Yen said of them to Mrs Lim. "Impossible foolishness!"

"Why?" she challenged.

"Life," he shouted back, "is more than any of those stories!"

And Mrs Lim kept her silence.

Old Yen's own stories centred on his growing up in that travelling opera company in Old China.

The stories of his being sold as a boy to be trained by the Canton Seven Flowers company were his father's single passion. As a small boy, the youngest in his family, Yen had fallen madly for the touring opera troupes. From the first time he heard their clashing cymbals in the village market square, saw the glitter of their costumes and the flashing dances and impossible acrobatics, he was captivated. Old Yen came from a beggar family, wily supplicants from dawn till nightfall in the dust of the market square.

At six, Yen had already been taught by his two older brothers and sister how to look forlorn and how to beg on his ragged knees for scraps of food or *a chin.* He soon discovered that a silver cent, worth five copper *chins,* would pay for a place for him to stand at the front of the makeshift precarious plankboard and bamboo stages upon which the wandering half-opera, half-circus troupes performed. Little Yen unabashedly danced and sang along with them, his hands flapping tattered sleeves to imitate the flow and grace of silk. Afterwards, left alone to play in the deserted market, he rubbed on his face mud makeup and strapped long waving willow stems about his head and about his thin body like the stage warriors with their peacock feathered headdresses and trailing silk banners. His brothers made him wooden swords and spears. His sister knotted together rags and torn dresses for his costumes. Palm leaves she wove into shields.

One day a tall man from a Canton company observed him at play before a small applauding crowd throwing *chin* at his dancing bare feet, and that afternoon spoke to his mother and father. His poor weeping parents bowed to the man, who handed them a small envelope, and that night he ate bowls of food with the troupe. There was even a bite of meat and fish that did not smell bad. He slept under a thick quilted blanket with a strange man who told him he belonged to him. "I am your father and mother now," the man called Sen-Dai told him. He was a beggar boy suddenly surrounded by crates of glittering costumes, silver swords and the hollow heads of monkey gods and clowns, beasts and dragons. And the smell of incense, which the troupe burned before a porcelain God of Fortune. It was all dazzling.

Old Yen always remembered how he did not even cry to leave his own family, though he remembered how his mother pulled his sister away from him, pulled her away as she screamed his childhood name, *Ming Yen! Ming Yen!* And then the smiling man called Sen-Dai picked him up and sat him on the bench of a painted wagon pulled by a horse. "And so began my life again," Old Yen would say of those years in the Seven Flowers company.

Larry Yen's breathing slowed down, his lungs burning. Over his racing heartbeat, he kept hearing his father's voice telling those old stories.

When he was a boy of seven, he had asked his father, "Are all these stories true?"

And his father always said, "As much as I'm telling you —that much is true for sure."

Larry Yen was satisfied, until he grew up and no longer wanted to listen to the stories of Old China, true or not, and, later, he watched with gentle amusement as his father enchanted Danny and Colin with the same stories. There was little variation. Always the Nanking stories dominated. *That month in Nanking my fortune changed ...* And always those tales concluded sadly.

Old Yen would tell how, when he returned six years later with the opera company to his home village, his twelve-year-old heart was full of happy expectations. He would find his family again, as Master Sen-

Dai his mentor and trainer had promised him. He would see his two brothers and sister again, all grown up now; he would bring them the small trunk of discarded clothing he had collected for them. Shirts that were not torn like rags. Gowns with metal buttons on them. He would embrace his mother and father and share with them his meagre savings, and watch their eyes widen as he poured handfuls and handfuls of *chin* into their palms. Sen-Dai had helped him save these coins, gathered all the clothing. Oh, his two brothers would greet him so happily, his mother and father embrace him so tightly, his sister weep for joy!

Instead—and here Old Yen always shut his eyes, turned his face upwards, shaking his head from side to side, like a prince torn by some immense tragedy—it was his own sobbing that everyone heard, his own boy's crying that caused even Sen-Dai to weep. As Old Yen recalled the sadness, real tears would come to his eyes.

In those days, bandits and war lords ruled China. Only a week after he, the youngest boy, the dreamer, the dancer, had been sold to the Seven Flowers company, his father had refused to pay begging fees to the demon war lord. And the Yens had been slaughtered. Their unwashed heads were hacked from their bodies, mounted on bamboo poles. A row of bloodless heads swayed in the air in the village square.

"Yes, that was so," confirmed Mrs Lim, when Larry asked about his father's stories. "Terrible, terrible ..." The Chinatown butcher and Mrs Low's grandfather remembered those days, too. They shook their heads. "Wicked, wicked time in China," they murmured, seeing in their minds those vacant-staring heads, telling again of the slaughter of the beggar Yens, the impalement of the tax-collector's family, the horrible death of others who defied the war lords.

"Now I had only the opera company for my family," Old Yen would say. "No more real family for me. Only Sen-Dai."

"But you managed to come to Gold Mountain," Larry Yen would interrupt.

In the Tong association halls, where Larry Yen did the accounts, the elders told many such tales to each other. There were also the secret tales, the whispered ones. When Larry told his wife about the whispering, Lisa felt she could not have lived in Gold Mountain burdened by such secrets. She would listen to a sad story only once.

Peering across Pender Street, he could see his father sitting on the bench just as Mrs Lim had reported, candlelight flickering behind him.

And when the old man finally dies, Larry Yen thought, all those stories will die with him, all those secrets will vanish.

Hearing stepscreaking on the staircase, Old Yen lifted his head and watched his son approach. Despite his eighty years and the thick bundle of clothes he wore, Old Yen sat straight up on a long plain bench, legs folded beneath him in the lotus position. The October night air tasted fresh on Old Yen's tongue and burnt cold in his nostrils. Since September, the war news from China had been growing darker. The Japanese were pouring down from North China. But the war news and the winter chill set him thinking of another time, when he was an opera boy.

"Cold like time in Nanking," Old Yen said aloud to the tall middle-aged son mounting the last flight of wooden steps onto the creaking porch. The old man's moist eyes reflected back the moonlight. Tonight he looked older than his eighty years, but his voice was firm, determined.

"I must tell you story."

"First, Father, let's go inside where it's warm."

Old Yen vigorously shook his head, shifted his thin legs. He looked even more frail this evening, but he meant to stay where he was. "I tell story," Old Yen repeated, his muffled voice barely escaping the layer of wool and silk scarves he had wreathed around his face and neck. His head was topped by the navy woollen cap Lisa had knitted for him three winters ago. Well, at least the old man was dressed warmly. A few more minutes outside wouldn't hurt.

"I tell you true story."

The night was bright with stars. Larry Yen sat down on the bench beside his father and pulled his jacket tighter around himself. His legs were still warm from the jogging. He could be patient.

Old Yen looked at him strangely.

"What are you saying, Father? What story are you going to tell me?"

"I never tell you all of true story," Old Yen said, speaking his best English, a language he knew his Canada-born son would understand a hundred times better than Cantonese. "Now I tell you."

"Yes, but could we talk inside?"

The old man ignored this. Larry Yen sighed. The cold was beginning to get to him. He remembered his gloves, slipped them on.

Patient. Be patient. Let him take this night for himself. The mountain peaks were silent.

"This best place to tell story," Old Yen said. "Important story."

The old man patted his own gloved hand on the bench for the son to sit closer. He was not going to step inside.

"I tell you true story," Old Yen was saying. "I tell you now love story."

There was no wind, only the crisp cold October air with its crystal clarity keeping both the old man and himself alert. Why not amuse the old man.

"Tell me your story, Father."

The bright moon shone between the mountain tops. There was a long silence between Old Yen and his son.

"You always tell the stories of Nanking, Father," Larry Yen commented. "All those terrible accidents happening at the same time."

"They have meaning," his father said. "I never tell you before. Love story."

Larry Yen looked puzzled. His father never told a love story before. He had condemned love stories as cheap romances.

"How—what do you mean?"

Old Yen looked at his son, his eyes glistening with remembrance.

"I never tell you before."

"Tell me what, Father?"

"Not all the Yens were killed, though people always say so."

"I don't understand."

Larry Yen shifted now.

"My only sister survived."

"Your sister?"

"Yes," Old Yen said, and closed his eyes. "The bandits made her see the death of our two brothers and our mother and father. She almost went mad. Then they took her away to sell her into a house of shame. She was young and pretty."

"But where?"

"In Nanking. Best prices. So many such places in those days."

"You were there on tour with the Seven Flowers company. You found her in Nanking?"

"No, no, she found me. I thought she was dead."

"But how, Father? How did she find you?"

"She remembered the name of the company that bought me when I was six years old. Seven Flowers. Famous company, but we played in the bad districts of Nanking. We were Canton opera company, more like a circus. Famous but not too much respect. Famous for all kind of thing."

Old Yen closed his eyes, remembering.

"Big Sister ran away from house of shame one morning, ran to the place where she heard I was. She buy a place to stand in front of the stage, like I used to stand. I was doing my acrobatics, flipping between the demon warrior's sword. You know we famous because we use real sword, real blades. And then I saw her. Oh, I could not believe it!"

The sword, slashing expertly between the boy's backward flips, narrowly missed young arms and limbs. The cymbals clashed, the drums thundered. Now the boy was to raise his arms, pitch twice his own height into the air and dive away from the flashing point of the sword, its gleaming edge gliding a hair's breadth from his upper torso. Between the third and fourth beat of the drum, as he readied to propel himself up, the boy saw his sister. A ghost. The drum beat fell into its sixth thunderous pounding. He remembered to push himself. He flung his arms up, a split second too late. The point of the blade pierced his arm, then its razored edge slid through the sleeve of the boy's arm like a knife through soy cake and sliced the right arm from elbow to wrist. A shower of blood sprayed into the air and he heard his sister scream his name, *Ming Yen! Ming Yen!*

"And so my sister and I met again," Old Yen said, "And so this scar on my arm forever."

"But I don't understand why you never told me this, Father."

"Shall I tell you how I fell from the pyramid? How I became a human torch?"

"No, no, Father, tell me about your sister first. Tell me why you have said nothing about her until tonight."

"All linked, my son." The old man took another deep breath and exhaled. His heart contracted, as if unseen old knots were tightening.

"Father, are you all right?"

Old Yen took another slow breath.

"In opera companies of Old China," his father began at last, "you must guess what happens to young boys."

Larry Yen began thinking of his father as a boy of six or ten or fourteen. "Boys are taught cruelly. They are beaten."

"Yes, yes, but I was not."

"I don't understand—what are you saying?"

"Sen-Dal protected me. When I was ten, he trained me *his* way. To sleep with him like a woman."

Larry Yen jolted hack. His father, a boy, huddled like *that* with a man. Larry Yen clenched his fists.

"Bastard!"

Old Yen smiled.

"Not at all. He was gentle enough. I came to like it."

This is my father speaking, Larry Yen thought. He felt angry, disgusted, amazed.

"I tell you everything, my son. Everything."

"But you came to Canada, you married, had a son."

"Yes, yes, so I tell you."

Larry Yen looked at the old man, his father. A rush of heat reddened his cheeks.

"The man who bought me, Sen Dai, he agreed to help me buy back my sister. He was a good man."

"How can you say that?"

"Old China ways are different." Old Yen grew impaticnt. "Now I tell you end of story."

"I don't think I want to hear more."

"Why not?"

"I don't want to hear."

"I tell you *love story,* my son. I tell you so you understand."

"Then tell me how you were scarred and broke your finger and turned into fire."

"My fault. All my fault. With my sister back, I thought constantly of her, of her bad years, her near-madness. I lost my concentration. Now in Nanking the crowds grew larger. Everyone came to see me kill myself"

Old Yen laughed.

"Yes, yes, my son, my fault!"

"Why are you telling me all this?"

"So you will know what you must know. Learn what you must learn."

"But you came to Canada!"

"Yes, but I came to Canada. My acrobatics were useless now. I was a danger to everyone in the Seven Flowers troupe. People came to see blood, to see me fail. To watch me die. Sen-Dai said I must leave. It would be unlucky for all of them if I stayed. SenDai was fair. He gave me money that rightly was my own. To save more money, I worked a few years in Hong Kong docks. I come to Gold Mountain. I worked in the lumber camps, on the railroad work camps, I worked and saved."

"And then you met Mother?"

Old Yen shifted again, ignored the question. He needed to tell his story his way, and not to be interrupted. The story was difficult to tell, so many memories were lifting from his heart.

"What happened? Tell me, father."

"Then I sent for my sister. It cost me three years' salary. She came, finally, but carried a baby inside her. Sen-Dai's baby." Old Yen closed his eyes.

"Six months later she gave birth to that baby and died ..."

"You said Mother died when I was born ..." Larry Yen bowed his head, his thoughts spinning wildly.

"My son, I tell you everything. Everything."

Old Yen slowly got up. He looked at the mountains, the moon, and paused to study the stars. He looked down at the bowed head of his son. "Cold like Nanking in the old days," he said. "That month in Nanking when my fortune changed."

Old Yen took his son's arm and motioned him to stand up.

"Mrs Lim right," he said, feeling suddenly lightheaded.

"About ghosts?"

"No." Old Yen sighed. "That I am not long here." The old man laughed. "Too, too long already."

The old man opened the porch door and waited for his son to take the first step inside. But Larry Yen found himself unable to move, his mind filled with moving shadows. When he spoke, his voice trembled.

"Sen Dal ... he was tall?"

Such a stillness descended upon that wooden porch, as if the Gods of Old China, of Nanking, had been high above the two unmoving figures, watching.

"Tall," the old man said at last, looking up. "Like you."

Judy Fong Bates

The Gold Mountain Coat

The small town that was my home was typical of many small towns in Ontario. It had one main street, one elementary school, one district high school, and five churches—Presbyterian, Anglican, United, Roman Catholic, and a Dutch Reform Church on the edge of town. Its distinctive architectural features were the funeral home and the post office. The funeral home was a beautiful whitewashed brick mansion with immaculately manicured lawns and tidy flowering shrubs. It was close to the centre of the town and infused it with a gentle serenity. The post office was neatly built of red bricks. It had a steep roof and a clock tower that rose up like a church spire. And the bell chimed every hour.

The main street of our small town had a dime store that sold everything from *Evening in Paris* perfume to stationery and hammers. It also had a clothing store, a jewellery shop, a hardware store, a drugstore, a barber shop, and a restaurant that served Canadian food. And, typical of all small towns, it also had a Chinese restaurant and a Chinese hand laundry.

My father operated the hand laundry and the other Chinese family managed the Chinese restaurant. I was the only Chinese child in the town. When my family first arrived, the restaurant was run by two brothers and their father, Sam Sing. The entrance of the restaurant was flanked by projecting glass windows. Just inside the windows on a shelf were several large dusty leafed sansevierias. The floors were covered with old-fashioned black and red lino tiles laid out in a diamond checkerboard pattern. There was a shiny speckled Formica counter with stools of circular seats upholstered in vinyl, and rimmed with a wide band of shiny chrome. Along one wall was a counter with built-in stainless steel sinks for washing glasses. Above was a shelf where the soft drink, soda, and sundae glasses were all neatly arranged in rows, according to size. Beside this was an ancient cooler with glass sliding doors that housed the milk, cream pies, and miniature china coffee creamers. But what I remembered most were the booths with the wooden seats and straight hard backs. Whenever I sat in one of these booths, I felt as if I had entered a little wooden room surrounded by brown grainy walls. There hung from the ceiling, a huge four-blade fan, that in the summer hovered and whirred—a huge humming dragonfly.

The proprietor, Sam Sing, stood behind the counter of his restaurant. He was a tall, straight-backed, grim-looking man with deep wrinkles cross-hatching his face. Sam rarely smiled, but when he did he showed a set of gold teeth that matched his gold-rimmed glasses. He rarely spoke, but when he did his voice had the raspy quality of sandpaper rubbing together.

There was nothing ingratiating about Sam. He glared at his customers from behind his glasses. In his presence, I was always struck speechless. I was afraid to return his gaze; I felt diminished and insignificant.

When I first met Sam Sing, he was already in his seventies; he had a head of thick, almost totally black hair parted at the side. He seemed robust and alert, and for a man his age he moved with amazing agility. My parents told me that Sam owed his exceptionally good health to drinking medicinal turtle soup made with Gilbey's gin. According to local legend, whenever Sam felt unwell, he asked a couple of local teenage boys to catch him a turtle from the nearby creek. The two boys arrived through the back door of the kitchen with a bulging burlap bag. Once, when I was in the dining room, I saw Sam give the boys a silver fifty-cent piece each from the cash register. The freckle-faced boys looked at each other and giggled, then left, clutching their coins. Sam stared after them, his eyes dark with contempt. I just barely heard the "hrump" he let out under his breath as he shut the money drawer. The older son walked into the dining room and as the wooden door swung away to and fro behind him, I caught a glimpse into the kitchen. The younger son held a cleaver over his head, poised to come crashing down on the squirming, unsuspecting, overturned turtle. The pieces of turtle meat were tossed into a large pot of water along with medicinal herbs, preserved roots, and dried gecko lizard. Then followed hours of simmering to produce a clear, brown, pungent, tonic soup.

Because of their work in the restaurant, Sam and his sons smelled faintly of cooking oil, in the same way, I suppose, that my father smelled of soap. Sam and his sons dressed alike. They wore white cotton shirts with the sleeves rolled up to their elbows and baggy black pants. And each wore a flat white half-apron tied around his waist.

Sam was proud of the fact that he had fathered two sons who would carry on his business and his family name. In contrast to Sam's stern, imposing demeanour, his sons were round faced, smooth skinned, and smiling. They reminded me of bookends; they looked almost identical, except that one was very fair skinned, while the other was very dark. Ken, the younger son looked after the kitchen, where he cooked French fries, hot beef and hot chicken sandwiches, fluorescent red sweet and sour chicken balls, and assorted chop sueys. John, the older son, spent his days rushing back and forth through the swinging wooden doors that separated the dining room from the kitchen, reporting customers' orders, and then cheerfully carrying out their dishes.

John always greeted the restaurant guests enthusiastically. He smiled and gushed in his broken English. Sam Sing spoke only when the customers lined up at the cash register, and then it was to blurt out the price of their meal. John often seemed embarrassed by his father's gruffness; there was an unspoken apology in his own exceptional friendliness.

The brothers were kind to me. I remember visiting the restaurant and frequently coming out with a double-scoop ice cream cone. Often the brothers came to visit my parents in the afternoon, during the quiet time between the lunch and supper hours in the restaurant. But Sam Sing never entered our house. His enterprise was prosperous, whereas ours was poor. Did he feel that we were beneath him? Or was it that we reminded him of earlier and more meagre times that were best forgotten?

I looked forward to the visits by John and Ken. They took a special older-brotherly interest in me. When one of them came to our laundry, he often brought me a special treat, such as an Oh Henry or Sweet Marie chocolate bar. These were always shyly, but enthusiastically welcomed, for my parents could not afford such luxuries.

What I remember most about Ken and John, though, was that in the winter they visited our house one at a time. Between them, they shared a single coat. It was a shapeless, black, wool garment. The pile was completely worn, the sleeves were permanently accordioned, the buttons were mismatched, and the corners of the collar curled upwards. Occasionally, when the weather was not too severe, one brother would arrive at the laundry dressed in the coat. A half hour or so later the other brother would dash over wearing just a thin sweater over his white shirt. This made my mother laugh and she teased them about their excessive thrift.

For many years, Sam Sing and his sons lived contentedly in this bachelor existence. The sons each had a clearly defined role in the running of the restaurant and Sam presided over everything. Ken had come to Canada unmarried, but John had left his wife, son, and daughter back in China. After working through government channels for several years, John was finally given permission to bring his family over.

My mother often helped John compose his letters back to China. Whenever he received mail from home, he rushed over to share it with my parents. One day he showed me a picture, taken in a studio, of his wife, son, and daughter. The wife and daughter had freshly permed hairstyles parted at the side, revealing high broad foreheads. The son was dressed in too-large overalls, the bib almost touching his chin. The mother was sitting down with her hand resting on her son's shoulder, while the daughter, who was a few years older, stood slightly but noticeably apart. I looked at this picture and felt the solemnity of their stares. It seemed strange to me that John was really the father. His youth and exuberance were in such contrast to the personality of my own father, who was over sixty when I was born. My mother was pleased that I would at last have Chinese playmates. Although both my parents were proud that I had learned English so quickly, I knew they were concerned that I was becoming "too Canadian." John told me that I would be in charge of teaching his children English and taking them to school. As he spoke, the brown in his eyes took on a liquid quality and his eyebrows were arched so that dark vertical furrows appeared between them. Once more, I looked at the children in the photograph. Then I looked at John. Did he expect me to be friends with them? I was the only Chinese child in the town and since coming to Canada I had only played with *to fon* children. Did these children from China know about *Howdy Doody* and *Captain Kangaroo?* What would I have to teach them besides English? I began to feel a weight on my chest.

When an arrival date for John's family was established, Sam permitted his sons to close the restaurant for a half day. Both brothers were to go to the airport to greet the family from China. The brothers recognized their father's generosity in giving them a half day off. For five years, the restaurant had never been closed. However, there was one problem. It was winter and they had only the one coat to share between them. Both John and Ken realized that a new coat was a significant purchase, one that would have to have Sam's approval. As the arrival date of John's family drew nearer, and the temperatures grew colder, the need for a second coat was becoming urgent.

John and Ken discussed the purchase of a second coat from every angle. How could they convince the old man to part with enough money for a new coat? Timing was essential. After closing, Ken and John always scurried around the restaurant. They swept and washed the floors, filled the glass sugar dispensers and the miniature china creamers, and cleaned up the dirty dishes. Meanwhile, Sam sat alone in the wooden booth at back of the restaurant. He carefully calculated the day's profits, his fingers flying over the rings of a black wooden abacus brought many years ago from China. If the earnings were good, Sam invited his sons to share a glass of whisky. But if the earnings were poor, Sam drank alone and glowered at the wooden walls of the booth while his sons continued silently working. Naturally, John and Ken decided to approach Sam on a night the whisky was shared.

The day after his discussion with Ken, John came to visit my parents. Though I heard him chuckling as he confided to my mother about the logistics of the timing, every word was coated with resentment. At first he decided that Saturday should be the asking day. But then my mother pointed out that if permission to purchase was granted on a Saturday night, Sam might change his mind by the time stores opened on Monday. She convinced John that Friday was a better day. Business was usually good. And the stores were open on Saturday.

On the chosen Friday, John visited us late in the afternoon. The wind sounded particularly shrill that day as it sprayed blasts of white powdery snow over the sidewalks. When John walked into the laundry, he looked as if someone had dusted him with icing sugar. He seemed quite agitated. I remember hearing him speak with great determination. "In a few days my family will be here. We'll all be living upstairs. I will be the one responsible for them." He glanced at my mother who nodded in agreement. "I'm going to have to stand up to that old man. I carry all this money in my pocket." He patted the front pocket of his pants emphatically before continuing. "And I have to ask permission to spend it. What right does he have to object? I work hard. This isn't China. Things are different here." Again, my parents said very little. They mostly smiled and nodded reassuringly. Then John suddenly remembered, "Today is payday at the mill!" He smiled and exclaimed, "Today business will be good. Guaranteed!"

Just before he left, John walked over to the corner where I sat pretending to read a comic book. He patted me on the shoulder and grinned. "Not too much longer now." I looked up and smiled. John looked so happy. As I nodded, I felt an ever so slight cramp in my stomach.

That Friday, after the restaurant closed, Sam counted his money, smiled, and invited his sons for a glass of whisky. This was the moment John had been waiting for. His father offered him a glass. He took a large, quick gulp. "Father, you know that my wife and family will be arriving on Wednesday. You have been generous enough to let Ken come with me to the airport to greet them." Sam nodded his head.

John continued, with Ken nervously looking on. "But, Father, we have only one coat. The weather is very cold. We need to buy another coat."

Sam carefully set down his whisky glass. His face slowly hardened at the boldness of his son's request. John was ready to panic, but then Ken blurted out, "John's son will need a coat for school. Your grandson cannot walk to school without a coat. A second one for us, one the boy can grow into."

Sam's face broke into a smile. His gold teeth gleamed. "Very good," he said and finished his whisky. The brothers breathed a sigh of relief.

The next morning, John and Ken dashed across the street to the clothing store that was owned by Paul Holmes. Paul had arrived in the small town from Europe just after the Second World War. Like Sam Sing, he saw opportunities for a new life in the New World. He had been in business for only a few years when Sam Sing, having purchased the restaurant from its previous owner, arrived with his sons. Like Sam and his sons, Paul had worked hard building his business. And like them, he owed his present financial security more to selfdenial and hard work, than to astute business sense. Over the years, Sam and his sons had bought the occasional piece of clothing from Paul, and Paul had eaten the occasional meal in the restaurant. Although everyone kept pretty much to themselves, they had a mutual respect that arose from a recognition of each other's hardships, honesty, and frugality.

John and Ken looked carefully around the store. Dark suits hung sombrely on racks, and shirts wrapped in plastic were stacked inside a case of wooden shelves. A cabinet with a glass counter and sides contained more shirts, sweaters, cuff links, and tie clips. Everything had a place. The air smelled faintly of sizing. The brothers suddenly became acutely aware of the shabbiness of their own clothing and the dim scent of cooking oil emanating from their pores. Paul smiled politely at them. And they smiled politely back. Finally John said to Paul, "My wife, my boy, and my girl come to Canada from China. We want a coat."

Paul showed John and Ken many coats—grey ones, blues ones, brown ones, double breasted, single breasted, with belts, without belts, but none would do. As John's fingers gently touched the thick pile of one coat and the borg fur collar of another, he realized without even being told that each was too expensive. Ken pointed out the price of one coat: It was twenty dollars! John sucked his breath between his teeth, making a whistling sound, to show his shock. At the restaurant a cup of coffee was ten cents, and a full meal of fish and chips with soup and dessert was fifty cents. How many would they have to sell, to pay for even the cheapest coat which was twelve dollars?

The brothers were both extremely frugal and not at all concerned with personal adornment or style.

Then Paul had an idea. He went into the storage closet at the back of the store. In contrast to the showroom where every item of clothing knew its place, the storage was crammed with outdated garments that Paul brought out twice a year to sell at reduced prices. He brought out a brown and orange plaid coat, covered in plastic. It was definitely not in style but; it was brand new. He offered it to the brothers for half the price of the cheapest coat in the store. That meant it was only six dollars. This was a bargain the brothers could not refuse. Ken tried it on. He admired himself in the fulllength mirror. The coat was slightly too large. But no matter—the price was right. John turned to Paul. "Okay. We take." John reached into his pocket and brought out a thick wad of bills. He carefully handed Paul a blue five-dollar bill, and a green one-dollar bill.

Just as they were about leave the store, Paul shouted, "Wait!" He quickly returned to his storage room and brought out another coat in dusty plastic wrap. John could tell that underneath the wrap the coat was a brownish grey tweed with large red flecks. With a twinkle in his eye, Paul cried, "One dollar." The brothers couldn't believe their luck! They didn't even bother to try on the coat.

After the purchase, John immediately hurried over to our laundry. My mother sat on a stool sorting socks for the wash, as John chuckled and bragged about their triumph. We heard every detail. Sam had apparently only grumbled a little about their over spending. But John knew that he was secretly impressed with the bargain they had struck with Paul. As John left, he reminded me, his voice nervous and happy with anticipation, "In another few days there will be Chinese children for you to play with." I nodded and smiled stiffly.

Four days later as I was walking home from school for lunch, I saw John and Ken waiting in line, outside the five-and-dime store, to board the bus to Toronto. Their coats were large and stiff, the shoulders too wide and the length too long. They reminded me of turtles with their heads poking through hard protective shells, one decorated in a brown and orange plaid, the other in dark grey with large red flecks. From the way they looked at the other passengers—the large heavy woman whose girth strained against the buttons of her faded wool jacket, and the young woman who stood slightly shivering in her thin fashionable coat and furtrimmed ankle boots—I could tell that

John and Ken were proud of their coverings, proof of the success they were experiencing in the Gold Mountain, decent shells for the old, shabby clothes hiding underneath.

I stood and waved to them. They smiled proudly back. In a few more hours there would be three more Chinese people in our small town. I would have to take the new children to school with me, introduce them to the teachers and to my friends. Translate for them, and more. I waved for a moment longer, then turned and ran all the way home.

Madeleine Thien

Bullet Train

HAROLD

When Harold was a boy, he drowned his sorrow by flying kites. In the mornings, he pedalled his bike out along the residential streets where the winter drizzle made the asphalt shine. He biked under the street lamps, through the rain puddles, all the way to the lake. On the grass, he slid off and left the bike lying on its side, the front wheel still spinning.

Harold unravelled the line. He ran and looked backwards. He was good at keeping it up, good at angling it over the lake. The kite shouldered left then straightened out. Harold put some slack on the line, then pulled it taut. And all the time he thought about the rain, or when the lake would freeze over, or how his mother kept spare change in a red metal box. He wondered how far down in the ocean he'd have to swim to see phosphorescence with his own two eyes. He could swim forever, he thought. From this side of Trout Lake to the other, and back again. His dad was a fine swimmer too; he always mentioned how he used to swim competitively, back in his university days. But that was long ago, too long to count. Donkey's years, his dad would say.

After half an hour, he let the kite down, watched it fall in slow motion to the lake. Then he reeled it in fast, just like fishing. Watched it tear across the surface of the water. Right until it bumped against Harold's shoes. He gathered it up and held it in his arms, the bright yellow fabric still damp.

On the way home, he dodged between cars, pedalling so fast little droplets of water shot off the handlebars and off the wet tires. Right up the alley to the front door, where he dropped his bike in the grass and pounded up the steps, the kite in his hands, right into the coffee-smelling kitchen and his dad's Famous Breakfast. Famous, his dad said, because it was as dull as dull could be. Two pieces of toast each, and a bowl of lumpy oatmeal.

His dad leaned down to pat his head and then they sat across the table from each other, gulping breakfast down before his dad hurried out the door and off to work.

Harold was nine years old and he felt he was living life on his tiptoes. One morning, he crept downstairs to put the coffee on. He tried to move as softly as he could past his mother's bedroom. The door was slightly ajar and he could see the narrow outline of her body beneath the blankets. In the kitchen, he stepped over his dad, who was lying on his back, head and torso under the sink, taking the pipes apart. Harold made coffee and his dad yelled out, "Don't make it so damn weak this time!"

And Harold thought of his grandmother, her soft, wrinkled arms and watery eyes. He thought of snow falling on Trout Lake, how it melted on the surface of the water. He thought of elephants in the National Geographic, their sad, baggy eyes.

"Get me a glass of water, will you?" His dad's voice echoed from underneath the sink.

Harold walked to the bathroom and turned on the tap. He thought of dream catchers, the netting and the beads woven together, holding his most secret wishes.

Sooner or later on the weekends, his father would make him climb the ladder onto the roof. It was a kind of punishment. If Harold forgot to put away the dishes in the dish rack, or if he fell asleep on the couch, as he often did in the afternoons, his dad would lose his temper. He would point his hand towards the roof, "Go think about things. Go sit where I can't see you."

This morning, a Saturday, Harold had forgotten to buy milk for the coffee. When his father asked for the money back, Harold couldn't find it. His father pulled him by the arm onto the back lawn and shoved him up the wooden ladder onto the rooftop. Harold was afraid of heights. He was too terrified to stand so he crouched on all fours. Down below, he could see the neighbourhood boys flocking to the back alley, circling the house on their bikes. They turned wheelies in the soft gravel road. "Hey, Harold! You stuck up on the roof again? Can't get down, can you?" They laughed, tilting their bikes up, hopping them gracefully on the back tires. "Hey, when can I go up on the roof? Is it my turn yet?"

Harold's father, weeding the garden, laughed out loud. "Only Harold," he told them, crouched down, his hands full of soil. "Harold's the one who doesn't want to be there."

Harold looked out over the back lawn, at the solid figure of his father pulling up the ground. Nine years old, and all his life he'd been afraid of heights. What he wanted more than anything was to ride his bike up and down the alley, to stand side-by-side in the yard with his father, their four hands full of weeds. On his stomach, he straddled the roof, cheek pressed to the shingles, and thought about the bullet train in Japan, speeding across the country. Cherry blossoms bursting on the street out front. How people described hearts lodged in their throats and he knew that feeling. He missed his mother, missed her like crazy even though she was right there, inside the house. She had a thick braid that swung when she walked. Now, she barely came out of her bedroom at all.

Last week, he had wandered through the house, from room to room, with a pain in his chest. He had gone to his dresser and taken out his clothes, three pairs of pants, a stack of T-shirts, sweaters, socks and underwear, and laid them in neat piles on the bed. One book, his well-worn encyclopedia. His father came to check on him, and when he saw the piles of clothing, he said, "What's all this for?"

Harold said, "I'm running away."

His father leaned against the door frame.

Harold sat beside his clothes. "These are for me to take. I'll leave the rest in the dresser."

"Will you be gone long?"

Harold nodded.

"I'll tell you what," his father said, clearing a space to sit. "Why don't you give it a few days? See what happens. I think, maybe, things will get better." Harold sat tight lipped. His dad turned around to look at the items of clothing. "Why don't you put these back in the drawers for now?" He looked at Harold, his expression pained.

Harold did as he was told. When all the lights went out he lay very still in bed, listening for change. Hoping that by morning, she'd be up and about again.

Now, sitting on the roof, watching the neighbourhood boys, he stared down at his father leaning forward into the vegetables. Harold thought of all the chance moments, his mother's car accident, the weakness in her chest, and how she had a cancer there. He always thought that if they let him go free, if he had all the time in the world, he would make himself into a great runner. The kind that ran long marathons, through New York or Chicago, who came to Heartbreak Hill and just kept going. All skin and bones, like his mother said. The kind of boy who, try as he might, could never eat enough to keep himself running.

When it started to rain, Harold's dad climbed up on the ladder. He leaned forward on the rooftop, chin in his hands. "I know you hate it up here," his dad said, "but it will make you stronger. No matter what happens to you from now on, you'll always have this well of strength to draw on."

Will I, Harold thought. He let his father help him down.

In silence, they made ham sandwiches for lunch. Then they carried them into the living room and ate, plates balanced on their knees. He saw the slope of his father's shoulders and the stiffness in his knees, and Harold mirrored it back, curving his spine just so, holding his feet slightly apart. If his mother came down the stairs, she would see the two of them and it would make her laugh. Trying to hide it at first, then letting it burst out. "Look at the both of you," she might say. How he missed her voice. When she walked with him at Trout Lake, when she said to him, "It's the details, you see. Once you get the details right, it will fly all on its own." She adjusted his wrist and looked up high, away to the kite he was pulling in. And she threw rocks in the water. And she said he was doing "fine, just fine." When she died, he would take her red metal box, the one that held her spare change. It was filled to the top and he would always keep it that way, he would never remove a single penny.

When he was ten, Harold experienced what he would come to think of as the turning point of his life. There he was, face-down on the roof. It was months after his mother's funeral. She had told him that nothing would ever be the same again, saying this in a voice that was like her voice if it had been left outside in the cold all night. It wavered and it was exhausted, but she still smiled at him and told him he was going to be a fine man. Harold had nodded his head, afraid to look at her. He had closed his eyes and pictured his mother walking along beside him at Trout Lake, the two of them holding hands. He looked her straight in the face and said, "I will never forget you."

Nothing was the same, except here he was again on the roof. It was summer and he could see the waves of heat. They blurred the ground. Down below, his dad sat on a lawn chair, sipping water from a plastic bottle. The shingles on the roof burned Harold's arms and legs. He felt a wave of sickness passing through his body. He turned over, gingerly, so that he was spreadeagled and facing the sky. An airplane was lowering itself through the clouds. He thought it could see him. It could drop a line and he would catch it, like James Bond. Hold on and swing low across the city. He pictured a flower of skydivers billowing from the plane, the wind pressing their faces into stunned amazement.

Harold turned over and pushed himself up on all fours. He crawled slowly down the slant of the roof. He could no longer see the ground so he kept his eyes on his hands. Nobody was watching him. He crawled backwards, each moment expecting the roof to end. When his body began to slide down, he wasn't afraid. Even when his elbows bruised off the rain gutter and his arms darted away from his body as if he was coming apart, he wasn't afraid. This was the end of it, he thought, all the weight of his body left on the roof and the lightest, strongest part of himself tumbling through the air.

Harold opened his eyes and saw the yard and the house. He heard footsteps in the grass. He sat up and saw people running towards him.

For most of his life, Harold will be shy with women. After he moves out of his father's house, he will keep to himself, making a living by doing repair work and caretaker jobs. Every night for two decades Harold will do one of three things: read, watch television, or listen to the radio. He will take pleasure in the ritual of his day-to-day tasks. Then one day he'll meet Thea and everything will change.

One day he'll wake up beside her, in their apartment on the seventeenth floor. He'll find his mouth open against her neck and he will remind himself of a small animal, dreaming, feeding. In the living room, Thea's daughter Josephine will be watching television and he'll listen to her heavy steps back and forth to the kitchen. Harold will surprise even himself. He'll think, I've woken up into a dream. I've dreamt up an entire family.

At first, when Thea and her daughter argue, as they often do, Harold will try to remain unobtrusive. He will pretend to read a book. One night, he will sneak a glance at them: Thea, tough as nails, Josephine, emotional and sarcastic. Both of them yelling to kingdom come. Slouched on the chesterfield, he'll feel a pang of regret that he hadn't met Thea fifteen years earlier. Josephine will be the closest thing to his own child he will ever have.

This fight will be worse than the others. Josephine's eyes will be red and swollen. "I hate it, I hate it here."

"What has gotten into you? You hardly know this boy."

"We want to move back east!"

"Over my dead body."

"Let me go," Josephine will say, cradling her body in her arms. "Harold, tell her. You understand. Tell her I want to move to Toronto."

"No! Not with that boy. Listen to me. I know what I'm talking about. I was just as impulsive as you once."

"We want to get married."

"It's ridiculous! The two of you are still children."

"Harold!" Thea's daughter will sink to the floor. "Talk to her. Make her see. He's moving and I have to go with him. Or else I'll die. I can't stand it."

Harold will stand up and walk towards them. He will remember a magician he saw once lying on a bed of nails, how the magician laughed the whole time. He never even shed a drop of blood. Harold will think that he could do that, if he put his mind to it. All the things that once seemed impossible. He will walk towards his wife and daughter and realize how far away he is from the boy who sat sorrowful on the roof. He'll feel a pain in his heart, reach up to touch it, and Thea will walk across the room to him. His body will be so light she'll catch him in her arms. He'll see the look on her face, terrified. Terrified. But not Harold. He will be holding on to her with all his strength.

THEA

When Thea met Harold last year, she was a decade younger than he. Thea worked as an outreach nurse. She drove around in a government van handing out clean needles and condoms and jokingly called herself the Protection Lady. In the van were racks of brochures and pamphlets. She sometimes scribbled notes to Harold on these, grocery lists in the margins of Hep B info sheets.

Thea kept her hair loose, long enough to reach the small of her back. There were fine lines webbing out from the corners of her mouth, streaks of grey in her hair. They radiated from her forehead, single strands that Harold would seek out with his fingers.

"What did you go and do that for?" she asked when Harold plucked one with his thumb and forefinger.

He had a boyish smile. She strung her arms around his waist and they sat on the couch together watching television. They watched *The Price Is Right*, Thea biting her lip nervously while a middle-aged man swung the big wheel. "Go Big Money," Thea said, squeezing Harold's hand. Parked in front of the television, she thought of all her days spent lying on the brown carpet in her parents' basement, watching Divorce Court and Donahue. When she was sixteen, she used to lie there and plan out the details of her life, what kind of marriage, what kind of children, what kind of person.

Driving with her partner Betty in the outreach van, she kept her eyes on the drug addicts and young girls. The girls seemed to turn old right in front of her. Their skin just dried right out, their hair turned limp. If she were the Pied Piper, she would lead them away from the city, over the Cascade Mountains, down into the idyllic valley. If she hadn't drowned herself in Donahue episodes when she was a teenager, would she be here now, working these streets? The very idea made Thea laugh. To think that talk shows had shaped her life. It was so ludicrous yet true.

Early in her relationship with Harold, they had driven down to the docks to watch the longshoremen, the Lego blocks of cargo being loaded deep into the freighters. It was a bright afternoon. Thea told him, "I have an excellent memory. It goes with my line of work, I guess. I remember everything someone tells me. I just pack it down. I've always been good with secrets."

"I don't have any secrets to give you," Harold said.

She nodded her head. After a moment, she asked, "Do you trust me?"

"Yes," he said. His face was tired and he had grown too skinny for his clothes. They hung in creased folds along his sides.

"Good," Thea said, grasping his hand. "Because I'll never, ever forget anything you tell me. I'll always remember. I'll always remember everything you tell me."

Thea came from a good family. Her dad was a lawyer who had a tendency to yell in conversation. "How was school?" he would shout. "Did you learn anything at all today?" Her mom, a nurse, curled her body forward as if fearing attack. She whispered to Thea, "Is that lipstick you're wearing? Who gave you lipstick?" Thea yelled at her dad and whispered at her mom. At sixteen, she diagnosed herself as schizophrenic.

"I'm hearing voices," she told her father.

"What?"

"I'm hearing voices." She danced around like a witch. "Boo! Boo! You know, voices."

"Ridiculous!"

Her mom puttered around the kitchen, lips puckered in a constant "Shhh."

Thea developed a booming voice. She had to, just to make herself heard. Dinner conversation was warfare.

"You wouldn't believe how much I paid for this asparagus—"

"Pass it over!"

"—per pound. Isn't the world crazy?"

"Here, Dad. Have them all."

"You won't believe what the supermarket girl said to me—"

"Is that the check-out girl with the lazy eye?"

"She said I should just climb down off my wallet and get in line behind everybody else. Can you believe it?"

"It just rolls out the side of her head, like she's crazy."

"Really. Why, I just stood there with my mouth hanging open."

"Can't they operate on something like that nowadays?"

When she was twelve, Thea asked her mother if she loved Thea's father absolutely. Her mom frowned. "That's a difficult question. Do you want me to answer honestly?"

Thea nodded, bracing herself.

"Feelings come and go," her mom said softly. "Some days I love him more than others. Some days I don't love him at all."

At sixteen, Thea fell in love. It was the first time and she was carried away by it. The man was thirty-one years old. He was a helicopter pilot. All year round he worked for Search and Rescue on Mount Seymour, scanning the ground for missing people. At night, she would sit with him, parked in deserted schoolyards, falling in love in the front seat of his truck, the steering wheel marking patterns on their pale winter skin. After months of this, Thea decided to bring him home. She snuck him through her window and into her bed. She pressed her index finger to his lips, daring him to have sex with her on her adolescent bed. He couldn't resist. Thea didn't know she could be this way, her face shocking into misery and happiness, her hand coming down hard on his bare back, believing that some unknown part of her was breaking off and deserting her. She glimpsed its shadow, its out-of-breath escape, and knew she'd never bring it back again.

When her helicopter pilot fell asleep beside her, Thea made the decision not to wake him. She held on to him, her fingers tracing patterns across his chest and down his leg, then over onto her own bare skin. In the morning, she heard her mother climbing out of bed. She heard the shower come on. With her heart in her throat, she listened to her mother's approaching footsteps. Thea pictured what it would look like, her sixteen-year-old body tangled up with this hairy man. She closed her eyes. The bedroom door swung open. Her mother took a half-step into the room. Thea's heart was deafening. There was a long silence. Then her mother closed the door. Thea listened to her mother's silent retreat down the hallway, and the firm click of her mother's door closing.

She was overcome by joy and disappointment. See, she wanted to cry, I love him absolutely. It is possible, and I do. I do. She didn't move. She lay in bed, already missing her mother. Her helicopter pilot, sound asleep and snoring, didn't wake for hours.

Pregnancy never frightened her, even when she packed her suitcase, the same one that had seen her through summer camp and three weeks in Germany. She left her parents' house, the sad, faded carpet and the basement television, and booked herself into a home for unwed mothers.

Her helicopter pilot carried her suitcase. He was melancholy. He talked about looking down from the helicopter into the white-out snow, looking for a glimpse, a colourful jacket, a tarp, a single thread of smoke. And when they spotted it, he zeroed in, the helicopter swaying above the ground like a damaged bird, the missing persons looking skyward, arms lifted. Thea lay in his arms and thought of all the growing she would have to do to keep him happy. She was so young, after all, and now this baby was coming. Life was running away with her. Months ago, she was fumbling through trigonometry, sines and cosines, now she was reading up on baby's first month, she was watching videos of underwater births, midwives, breathing. Some of the other girls in the home had ultrasounds of their babies. Thea held them up to the light, and studied them. This baby was just like her. Coming out of this blurriness, waiting to come out sharp and resolute.

On the day of her ultrasound, Thea waited at the clinic for him to come. He was very late. She did the ultrasound without him. Her baby wrapped its legs around the umbilical cord, and bobbed like a deep-sea diver. She sat on the steps of the clinic afterward, the photo on her knee, untouched. A strong wind might come and blow it free. When it started to rain, she walked home. There were no messages for her taped to the door. She phoned his number, fingers sliding over the rotary dial, but no one picked up. Thea scanned the papers for stories of hikers lost in the mountains. She willed one up there, waiting in silent desperation with his tarp, his fire dissipating into air. Her soon-to-be husband wavering above, tuttuttut of the choppers.

One day, she stepped out to stretch her legs. On her return she found a note from him, and a gift. A silver-plated bracelet, something that wouldn't cost more than thirty dollars, the kind of thing you rushed to the mall to get before you hurried to catch a plane on your way out of the city. She held the note to her chest and tried not to miss him. But she remembered everything he had ever said. Every word.

Years later, when Josephine is almost fully grown and Harold has moved into the apartment on the seventeenth floor, Thea will be taken aback by her life. She'll look at her daughter and Harold, her strange and wayward family, and be overcome with fear. She'll think that this is the trouble with having too much. She cannot bear the thought of losing one thing.

One day, Harold will collapse in the living room. Even as she is terrified, even as she catches him in her arms, some part of Thea will be relieved. She will think that if Harold survives this, they will have paid a debt—a debt to unhappiness, a nod to tragedy. In the hospital, she will think, Just one decade of happiness. Please, whoever you are, just one.

Standing by his hospital bed, Josie will hold Harold's hand. "You were really scared there, weren't you?" she'll ask.

Thea will nod, afraid to speak.

"You really love him, don't you?"

How Josie will remind Thea of herself – those probing questions, that youthful wisdom. She will steal a look at her daughter. "Absolutely."

"It's funny. You hardly know him."

"What do you mean?"

"It's only been a year. How did you get so attached?"

Her daughter will leave her at a loss for words. That night, Thea will drive through the dark Vancouver streets, out to Trout Lake, where Harold once rode his bike as a boy. Out to Rupert Street, and the house for unwed mothers. She will see the ski runs on Mount Seymour all lit up, and in the foreground, the rows and rows of houses. Late at night, she will park her car in front of the apartment. Fumbling for her keys she will catch a glimpse of a car she recognizes. Inside the car will be Josie. The boy will be reclined against the driver-side door. Josie, pressed up against him, her hands on his neck. Thea will feel her heart stop. She will step off the sidewalk, into the bushes. From behind the row of trees, she will stand and watch them.

Thea will remember holding Josie for the first time. Josie was red and scrawny, with a full head of thick, brown hair. One eye was open just a crack. Her hair was tousled and wet. Thea had hugged the bundle to her chest, weeping, not because she saw Josie's father in Josie's sad, scrunched-up face. But because Thea realized that in all her mistakes, in all the failures and missteps, she had finally managed to do something supremely well. Before that moment, she had never understood it was truly possible. Thea will stand on the grass, leaning against a tree. Inside the car, Josie will slip her T-shirt off. Thea will stare up at the rooftops. She will rest for a while standing there. Then she will catch her breath and head inside.

JOSEPHINE

It was a clear night. Josephine and her mother sat on the balcony drinking fruit punch, looking out over the expanse of houses and industrial docks. They could see as far as the sulphur hills and the double strand of lights along the Lions Gate Bridge. Inside the apartment, Harold watched Jeopardy!, shouting out the answers.

Josie sipped her punch. She had never been afraid of heights. Even as a child, she used to come out here and pitch forward over the railing, her legs lifting high off the ground. The sensation made her dizzy, as if her stomach were plunging straight out of the soles of her feet.

Inside, Harold called out, "What is Alsace and Lorraine?" Josie's mother got up, nudged the door open, and slipped inside.

Josie kept her back to them. There was a stiff breeze coming from the west, so she folded her legs together and hugged them to her chest. In Social Studies, she'd learned about Alsace and Lorraine, too. Those little provinces in France. But now Harold had quieted down, and Josie could picture them sitting arm-in-arm on the fold-out sofa. She knew they never got any privacy. This was a one-bedroom apartment, and her mom and Harold slept on the couch. Josie slept in the bedroom. When it was just the two of them, before Harold moved in, her mom used to knock softly on the door. She would push the door open, her face creased and pale, her dark hair swinging loose. Josie would pull aside the covers and her mom would clamber in beside her. Even though Josie was fully grown, seventeen years old, she liked sleeping beside her mom. She liked her mom's clean, antiseptic smell. Even though Josie had gotten used to Harold, and she called him "old man," and they yukked it up in front of the same tv programs, she missed the way things were before.

She'd stopped counting the times she'd lain in bed, listening through the walls while her mom had sex with him. Josie even put a pillow over her head to drown it out. She reprimanded herself for listening, called herself a freak, and a loser. Once, she even burst into tears. She flirted with the idea of running into the living room, yelling, "Cut it out!" and then slamming her bedroom door behind her. It infuriated her because she was supposed to be the one with boyfriends, the one illicitly sneaking them home. Josie had a boyfriend, but she suspected that her mom cared more about Harold than Josie cared about Bradley. It was her mom who was the girlish one, the one who daydreamed and doodled and preened in the bathroom. And Josie just sulked on the couch, flipping channels, boring herself to death with television.

She propped her legs up on the balcony railing. Still, she loved Bradley enough. She planned to run away with him. He had asked her, last week. He wanted to be an actor. There was work, he told her, in Toronto. She saw him in a new light then, as someone whose dreams could make her happy. In this apartment, Josie thought she might drown. Her mom tried so hard but it wasn't the same. Now that Harold was here, it would never be the same again.

When Josie was young, she wanted to be a diver. She loved their stretched limbs and taut bodies, their arms cutting the water. Part of her wanted to just dive off this balcony, her body in perfect position while the highrise fell away behind her. Through the backdrop of this city, on and on and on, not caring at all if the water ever came.

The worst thing her mother ever did to Josie was hold her under burning water. She didn't argue that she deserved it. In hindsight, Josie thought she was lucky her mom hadn't lost her temper and smacked her good. The thing was, Josie had only been trying to help.

She had taken the silver-plated bracelet, the one her father, the helicopter pilot, had given her mother, and tied it to the balcony. Her plan was simple. She was sending a message, the same way people used telegraphs, carrier pigeons, or prayer flags. When her father searched the mountains, he might see the chain fluttering from the post. It might catch his eye like a dry spark. At dinner time, she and her mother would see his helicopter hovering outside the patio window, his eyes searching through the glass for them.

She looped a long piece of thread though one end and knotted the thread to a post on the balcony. The bracelet lay flat, but when a gust of wind came, it shook very gently.

Josie left it there while she went to school. She was in grade four. All day she thought of it, a glinting that would stop him, out of the corner of his eye, make him stop in his tracks and look up. When she came home in the afternoon, the piece of thread had come loose from the balcony. The bracelet was gone.

That night, when her mom realized the bracelet was missing, she walked in on Josie in the bath. She held the empty box out. "Sweetheart," she said, "where is Mommy's bracelet?"

Josie dipped her hands into the bathwater. She lowered her eyes. "I lost it."

"Where?"

Josie looked up at her mother. She gave her most innocent smile. "I dropped it," she said, shrugging. "Off the balcony."

Her mom wrenched the hot-water tap on, shower spurting, steam filling the room. The water was burning. Her mom started crying. "You terrible girl!" she said. "You had no right. It was the only thing I ever had." The water burned her skin, it scalded her right to the bone. Josie screamed hysterically. Her mom wrenched the other tap and the water turned freezing cold. Then she pulled Josie out. Josie's skin was raw. "I'm sorry," her mom whispered, all her rage gone. She repeated it over and over again. "I'm sorry, I'm sorry." Josie wished she could go back, retrace her steps, have the bracelet in her hands again before all this happened. For the first time, she looked at her mother in a new light, full of love and hate and incomprehension. Her mom applied an ointment to Josie's skin and kissed the air so her lips wouldn't hurt her. They slept beside one another that night, and no matter how Josie moved, her mom kept her arms tight around her, and Josie couldn't pry herself loose.

Josie admitted to herself that she didn't really love Bradley. She liked him well enough. She liked the way they held hands and walked through the empty schoolyard. It made her chest burn with warmth, as if from exertion. He called her by her full name, Josephine. She thought it made her seem more important than she really was.

When Josie was a little girl, she had worried that her mother would abandon her. A common fear, she later learned. A sign of the child's first awareness of the encroaching world. She remembered lying on the couch, asking her mother, "Will you always take care of me?" and her mother nodding fervently, "Yes, I always will."

Now, Harold had made her mother's eyes young again. It convinced Josie of what she knew deep down, that she wasn't meant to be here any longer. She recognized a hardness in herself, razor sharp, wanting to be set loose. It wasn't Toronto so much as the fact that she needed to be gone. Whether she went with this boy or on her own, it didn't matter so long as she left here. Last night, she'd struggled with a note to her mom. She'd tried saying it in different ways, but no matter what she wrote she ended up sounding trite.

Before she left, Josie went into the cabinets and took out the plastic bottle of Aspirin. Under the cotton wadding was a roll of bills, her mom's emergency money, in case of earthquakes or disasters. Josie pocketed it, knowing her mother meant it for her. What did they call it back then? Pin money. The words made Josie smile.

She was leaving them something in return—the bedroom, the living room, the kitchen, and the balcony. Years to themselves. A missing child. She loved her mother to death, but that wasn't the kind of thing she could write in a note. They wouldn't believe her anyway. They would never understand how much thought Josie had put into this, how much she missed them already. On a scrap of paper, she wrote that she would call soon.

When Harold walked into the kitchen and saw the money in her hands and the rucksack on the floor, he guessed everything. He said, "If you do this, you're going to break your mother's heart."

"She'll recover." She and Harold stood facing each other, like cowboys in a Western, hands loose at their sides. Josie didn't know whether to fight or run. Replacing the cap on the plastic bottle, she said, "I tried to tell her. You heard me trying."

Harold stared down at the linoleum floor, down at his worn slippers. "I heard you." When he said this, he gazed at her steadily and Josie had a glimpse of Harold as a young boy. Stubborn, relentless in his own patient way. He surprised her. "Better leave now, before she gets home."

She was running late. She swung her rucksack up. The weight pulled her back and she had to grasp the walls for support. Harold opened the door for her, and Josie turned to him quickly, planting a kiss on his cheek. Then she took the elevator down seventeen floors, and walked calmly through the glass entrance. She started to run. She was holding her coat in her right hand. The grass was wet and her coat dragged along the grass. Josie imagined that the sound of her coat in the grass was her mother running behind her. She was pulling at Josie's arms and legs, and begging her not to go. And Josie didn't know what to tell her, so they just kept running like that, across parking lots and front lawns. She was sweating, and the rucksack bounced painfully against her shoulders. Her friend, the boy with the dark hair and brown eyes, was holding the passenger door open for her. Sliding in, Josie pictured herself falling out of the sky, the bag in her arms, highrise blurred in the backdrop.

In the end, Josie will not marry the boy with the dark hair and the brown eyes. She will move on from him and from a dozen other men and women. A decade later, when Thea's hair is fully white and Harold has put on too much weight, she will go home once more and sleep in her old bedroom. But it won't be for long. Soon she'll be on the move again because something in her can't rest, something inside her fights it tooth and nail. Over the years, Josie will ask herself, What are you running away from? Each time, she will answer the question differently. Because I can is the answer she likes best. Josie will tell people that she has always been a free spirit. Some men will think she is asking them, obliquely, to pin her down, to give her a reason to stay. They will ask her, "Don't you want a family?" and she'll laugh at them, say, "I already have one." She leaves these ones faster than the rest.

When standing on high landings—balconies, suspension bridges, lookouts—she still has the compulsion to jump. She believes in her own recklessness. It is the only faith she has.

When she is very old and she has set foot in most of the countries in the world, Josie will tell her friends that her father was a boy who jumped from a roof and her mother was a woman who fell from a helicopter. They will know she is lying but she will never tell them how, or which details of the story are true. Until she dies, she will wonder about her real father and the twists and turns that have marked his life. She tries to imagine his helicopter, the people he has saved, or more importantly, the ones he has lost. All her life, Josie will wonder how she bypassed love when it was the very reason for, the root, of her disappearance. When people ask, she will say that her favourite country is one that has not yet been discovered.

The Contributors

Judy Fong Bates was born in China and came to Canada as a young child. She is the author of *China Dog and Other Stories from a Chinese Laundry* (2001); *Midnight at the Dragon Café* is scheduled to appear in 2004. She lives in Toronto.

Lien Chao was born in China, came to Canada in 1984, and lives in Toronto. She is the author of *Beyond Silence: Chinese Canadian Literature in English* (1997), *Maples and the Stream: A Bilingual Long Narrative Poem* (1999), and *Tiger Girl (Hu Nü)* (A Creative Memoir; 2001). Her first book won the Gabrielle Roy Prize for Criticism (1997). (www.candesign.com/lienchao).

Grace Chin was born in Petaling Jaya, Malaysia and is a Vancouver editor and writer. Her nonfiction has appeared in publications of *The Commonwealth of Learning, Business in Vancouver,* and *Rice Paper*. "Ma's Kitchen" is her first published work of fiction.

Ritz Chow was born in Hong Kong and currently resides in Vancouver. Her work has appeared in Canadian feminist and poetry journals and in various anthologies, including, *Swallowing Clouds: An Anthology of Chinese-Canadian Poetry*, *Anti-Asian Violence in North America: Asian American and Asian Canadian Reflections on Hate, Healing, and Resistance*, and *Hot & Bothered 4: Short Short Fiction on Lesbian Desire* (forthcoming).

Wayson Choy was born in Vancouver and currently lives in Toronto. He is the author of *The Jade Peony* (1995) and *Paper Shadows: A Chinatown Childhood* (1999); *All That Matters* is scheduled to appear in 2004. His first book won the Trillium Book Award in 1996. His second book won the City of Vancouver Book Award in 1999 and the Edna Staebler Award for Creative Nonfiction in 2000.

Jessica Gin-Jade was born in Ottawa, Ontario, raised in Singapore, and resides in British Columbia. She is currently working on a master's degree in publishing and is the editor of *Rice Paper*. "Just Dandruff" is her first published work of fiction.

Kagan Goh was born in 1969 in Singapore. He is an award-winning film-maker, a spoken-word poet, romance novelist, and actor. He hosts a poetry night called "Spoken Revelations" at the Cedar Restaurant in Vancouver. He is currently working on his first book of poetry, "Surviving Samsara." A central theme running through his work is his exploration of mental illness as a vehicle for spiritual transformation. "Life after Love" is his first published work of fiction.

Goh Poh Seng was born in Kuala Lumpur and worked as a doctor in Singapore for twenty-five years. He now lives in Vancouver and Lark Harbour, Newfoundland. He is the author of four novels: *If We Dream Too Long*, *The Immolation*, *A Dance of Moths*, and *Dance With White Clouds*. He has also published five books of poetry, among them, *The Girl from Ermita & Selected Poems* and *As Though the Gods Love Us*.

David M Hsu was born and raised in Toronto and subsequently educated at Cornell University in Ithaca, New York. He is currently a medical student at Queen's University in Kingston, Ontario. "Prodigies: A History Lesson" is his first published work.

Harry J Huang, also known as Freeman J Wong, was born in China and currently lives in Toronto. He has authored 130 short short stories published in three collections entitled *Nothing Comes of Nothing*, *Morality, Eh?*, and *A Bride in Washington*. He has also published five English text-books, including *Essential College Writing Skills* and *Refining the Sentence,* as well as early childhood education how-to books.

Winston C Kam was born in Trinidad. His short stories have appeared in *Impulse Magazine, West Coast Line,* and in the anthology, *Many Mouthed Birds*. Two of his plays have been produced in Toronto and Vancouver, and he has written a radio play for the CBC. He presently resides in Toronto.

Khoo Gaik Cheng was born in Penang, Malaysia and currently resides in Singapore where she is a postdoctoral fellow researching the Malaysian independent film scene. Her short fiction and poetry have appeared in *West Coast Line*, *The Toronto Review*, *Uprooted*, *Rice Paper*, *Third Space*, *Swallowing Clouds: An Anthology of Chinese-Canadian Poetry,* and recent two Malaysian anthologies—-*Silverfish Writings I* and *Silverfish Writings III*.

Alexis Kienlen is a poet, fiction writer, and journalist originally from Saskatoon, Saskatchewan. Her work has appeared in over thirty publications including *Rice Paper*, *Broken Pencil*, *2000% Cracked Wheat* (Coteau Books), *Prairie Fire,* and *Planet S Magazine*. She is of English, French, Irish, German, Scottish, and Chinese ancestry.

Lydia Kwa was born in Singapore. She came to Canada in 1980. She now works as a writer and psychologist in Vancouver, British Columbia. She has published a collection of poems, *The Colours Of Heroines* (1994), and a novel, *This Place Called Absence* (2000) which was short-listed for the amazon.ca /Books in Canada First Novel Award.

Larissa Lai was born in La Jolla, California, grew up in St John's, Newfoundland, and has lived in Vancouver for most of her adult life. Her first novel, *When Fox Is a Thousand* (1995) was nominated for the Chapters/Books in Canada First Novel Award. Her second novel, *Salt Fish Girl* (2002), was nominated for the Sunburst Award, the Tiptree Award, and the City of Calgary W O Mitchell Award. She currently lives in Calgary, where she is working on her PhD. (www.ucalgary.ca/~lalai).

Fiona Tinwei Lam was born in Paisley, Scotland, and was raised and currently resides in Vancouver, BC. Her collection of poetry, *Intimate Distances* (2002), was short listed for the annual City of Vancouver Book Award. Her work has appeared in *The New Quarterly*, *The Malahat Review*, *Descant*, *Grain*, *The Antigonish Review*, *Event*, and other literary journals as well as in the anthologies *Swallowing Clouds: An Anthology of Chinese Canadian Poetry*, *Vintage 2000* (2000), and *A Room at the Heart of Things* (2000). (www.writersunion.ca/l/lam.htm).

Edward Y C Lee was born in Montreal, Quebec and currently lives in Toronto where he is a lawyer and writer. His writing has appeared in *The Toronto Star*, *the Globe and Mail*, *Descant Magazine*, and *Millennium Messages*. "Into a Far Country" is from a novel-in-progress. (www.edwardyclee.com).

SKY Lee is the author of *Disappearing Moon Café* (1990) and *Bellydancer Stories* (1994). Her first novel won the City of Vancouver Book Award. She now lives in Montreal.

Iris Li was born in Edmonton and raised in Calgary. She is a regular contributor to *Rice Paper* and a founder of *SLANT Magazine*.

Andy Quan was born in Vancouver, BC. He is the author of a short fiction collection, *Calendar Boy*, and a book of poetry, *Slant*. He is also a coeditor of *Swallowing Clouds: An Anthology of Chinese-Canadian Poetry*. His fiction and poetry has appeared in many other anthologies and magazines. (www.andyquan.com).

Loretta Seto was born and raised in Vancouver. Her work has been published in *Transitions* and *Rice Paper*. She has worked in book-publishing and film, and recently earned her MFA in creative writing at the University of British Columbia. Her current projects include completing a children's novel and helping to produce one of her short scripts for CityTV.

ben soo was born in Hong Kong and lives in Montreal. "Antiques" is his first published work.

Madeleine Thien was born in Vancouver. Her short stories and essays have appeared in *Best Canadian Stories*, *The Journey Prize Anthology*, *Islands West: Stories from the Coast*, and *Write Turns: New Directions in Canadian Fiction*. She has also written and recorded for CBC Radio. *Simple Recipes*, her first book of fiction, won the Ethel Wilson Fiction Prize, the City of Vancouver Book Award, the Vanity Book Prize, and the CAA Air Canada Award for most promising Canadian writer under the age of thirty. *Simple Recipes* was also a Kiriyama Pacific Rim Book Prize Notable Book and a finalist for the Commonwealth Writers Prize for Best First Book; as a manuscript it won the 1998 Asian Canadian Writers' Workshop Emerging Writer Award. Thien currently lives in Fryslan, the Netherlands, where she is at work on her first novel.

Sherwin Tjia is a poet, painter and illustrator, and author of *Pedigree Girls* (2001) and *Gentle Fictions* (2001). Born in Toronto and now residing in Montreal, his work has appeared in *Adbusters*, *Kiss Machine*, *Maisonneuve*, *dig*, *Geist*, *Trucker*, *Quarry*, *the Literary Review of Canada*, *Hive Magazine*, *Queen Street Quarterly*, *THIS Magazine*, *Crank*, and *Wegway*. He appears in the anthologies *Career Suicide*, *Geeks*, *Misfits* and *Outlaws*, *Sun Through the Blinds*, and *The I.V. Lounge Reader*.

Fred Wah was born in Swift Current, Saskatchewan, and grew up in the West Kootenay region of British Columbia; he presently lives in Vancouver. He has published seventeen books of poetry. His book of prose poems, *Waiting for Saskatchewan* (1985), received the Governor General's

Literary Award in 1986 and *So Far* was awarded the Stephanson Award for Poetry in 1992. *Diamond Grill* (1996) won the Howard O'Hagan Award for Short Fiction. His most recent book, *Faking It: Poetics and Hybridity* (2000) was awarded the Gabrielle Roy Prize for Writing on Canadian literature.

Gein Wong was born in Toronto. Her poetry has been published in *Fireweed, Rice Paper, the Coming 2 Voice Anthology, Big Boots,* and *Bamboo Girl.* She is also a member of the female asian spoken-word and music group, maewon, which spreads messages of community, antioppression, antiracism, asian empowerment, and love. (www.maewon @poetic.com).

Jim Wong-Chu was born in Hong Kong and came to Canada when he was a young child. He is a founder of the Asian Canadian Writers' Workshop, author of a poetry collection, *Chinatown Ghosts* (1986), and coeditor of three Chinese Canadian literary anthologies: *Many-Mouthed Birds: Contemporary Writing by Chinese Canadians* (1991), *Swallowing Clouds: An Anthology of Chinese-Canadian Poetry* (1999), and *Strike the Wok: An Anthology of Chinese Canadian Fiction* (2003). He lives in Vancouver.

Terry Woo was born in Hamilton, Ontario and lives in Toronto, Ontario. He's the author of *Banana Boys.* (www.banana-boys.com)

Kam-Sein Yee was born in Vancouver to Chinese immigrant parents. Her poetry has appeared in the anthology *Swallowing Clouds* and in the feminist quarterly, *Fireweed.* Her other writing has appeared in *The Province Newspaper*, as well as the magazines *Banana, Jasmine,* and *Restaurateur*. She currently lives in Vancouver.

Paul Yee was born in Spalding, Saskatchewan, and currently lives in Toronto, Ontario. He has produced two works of nonfiction on Chinese Canadians, *Saltwater City* (1988) and *Struggle and Hope* (1996), as well as nine works of fiction for children and young adults. Among the many literary awards he has received is the Governor General's prize for *Ghost Train* (1996), which was also staged as a play in Toronto. Two other stories were made into animated films by the National Film Board of Canada.

PERMISSIONS

"Gold Mountain Coat" by Judy Fong Bates from *China Dog and Other Stories from a Chinese Laundry*, copyright 2001 by Judy Fong Bates. Published in Canada by Sister Vision Press. Reprinted by permission of the author.

"Nanking" by Wayson Choy, copyright 1998 by Wayson Choy. First published in Canada by *Descant* 100, spring 1998, Vol. 29, No. 1. Reprinted by permission of the author.

"Bullet Train" from *Simple Recipes* by Madeleine Thien. Reprinted by permission of McClelland & Stewart Ltd.

"I hardly ever go into King's Family Restaurant," "I'm not aware it's called tofu until after," and "Juk is a soup we always have after" from *Diamond Grill* (1996) by Fred Wah. Reprinted by permission of NeWest Publishers Ltd.